More Critical Praise for Lucy Jane Bledsoe

FOR *A THIN BRIGHT LINE*

"It triumphs as an intimate and humane evocation of day-to-day life under inhumane circumstances."
—*New York Times Book Review*

"Empowering and bold." —*Publishers Weekly*

"A stirring and deeply felt story." —*Kirkus Reviews*

"Is it possible for a novel to both break your heart and to heal it? . . . Bledsoe is deft in the way she shows . . . various models of how to be a lesbian in the world of the '50s and early '60s."
—*Lambda Literary Review*

"Gripping historical fiction about queer life at the height of the Cold War and the Civil Rights Movement."
—Alison Bechdel, author of *Fun Home*

"Lucy Jane Bledsoe's *A Thin Bright Line* is a testament to courage and perseverance in the face of oppression. It's also a compelling, literary page-turner worthy of standing alongside the works of Pat Barker and Graham Greene. It reminds us that we are nothing, deep down, without love and dignity."
—Patrick Ryan, author of *The Dream Life of Astronauts*

FOR *THE EVOLUTION OF LOVE*

"In the context of a twisting plot, in the company of appealing characters, Bledsoe asks us to think about the resilience of love and hate; what our responsibility to each other is; and who we really are, right down to our DNA. Highly recommended."
—Karen Joy Fowler, author of *Booth*

"Lucy Jane Bledsoe's writing leaps off the page with striking clarity. Her characters take you by the hand and lead you through their freshly broken lives, and with them you'll discover shelters of friendship and loyalty."

—Shanthi Sekaran, author of *Lucky Boy*

FOR *LAVA FALLS: STORIES*

"In these twelve remarkable stories, the reader journeys from the remotest inner reaches of Alaska to deceptively calm suburban neighborhoods to a research station at the bottom of the world. Yet Lucy Jane Bledsoe's true territory is the wild, uncharted expanse of the heart . . . A wise and wonderful collection."

—Kirstin Valdez Quade, author of *The Five Wounds*

"This novella and group of stories by Lucy Jane Bledsoe will move and surprise and thrill you. Bledsoe brings us right into her characters' lives, taking us on unexpected journeys, and through it all, the empowered and vulnerable women in Bledsoe's lively fictional world continually find themselves, so as readers we learn more about survival and are reminded of hope, and find ourselves being delightfully renewed."

—Allen Gee, author of *My Chinese-America*

FOR *NO STOPPING US NOW*

"This autobiographical novel, with richly developed bold, courageous characters, and raw emotion, deftly captures the period of transition, not just for Louisa but for women's rights in the 1970s."

—*School Library Journal*

TELL

THE

REST

TELL THE REST

LUCY JANE BLEDSOE

BROOKLYN, NEW YORK

This is a work of fiction. All names, characters, places, and incidents are the product of the author's imagination. Any resemblance to real events or persons, living or dead, is entirely coincidental.

Published by Akashic Books

ISBN: 978-1-63614-079-7
Library of Congress Control Number: 2022933223
First printing

Akashic Books
Brooklyn, New York
Instagram, Twitter, Facebook: AkashicBooks
info@akashicbooks.com
www.akashicbooks.com

Where whoever had hanged the arm from its pole had made certain that it was as much a gesture of grim and humorous defiance as the old house; where whoever had taken the trouble to swing the arm out into sight of the road had also taken the trouble to tie down all the fingers but the middle finger, leaving that rigid and universal sentiment lifted with unmistakable scorn to all that came past.

—Ken Kesey, *Sometimes a Great Notion*

CHAPTER 1

The rain stopped falling just as the first light of dawn paled the bits of sky showing through the dripping forest canopy. Delia and Ernest ran awkwardly, hurdling over fallen logs, kicking through fern tangles. She refused to let go of his hand, even though that would make running easier, even though twice he'd tried to shake free of her. Both were panting. When they came to the road, they dropped to their knees and Ernest put his face to the weeds growing along the shoulder. Delia put hers on his back, absorbed the up-and-down movement of his heaving lungs, the damp of his sweaty shirt. When he raised his head, she slid off him and sat back on her heels. He looked at her, frowning slightly, sweat and rain wetting his face. She smiled, wanting to affirm their partnership. *You and me,* she thought. She barely knew him, but she loved him. He wasn't her boyfriend. He wasn't her brother. He was so much more than her friend.

"Let's go," he said, pulling her to her feet. A whisper of a mustache, soft and black, sweetened his upper lip.

"Shouldn't we stay out of sight of the road?"

He looked up the deserted highway where it narrowed to disappearance and then down in the other direction where it curved out of sight. Just kids, a sixteen-year-old Black boy and a thirteen-year-old white girl, escapees, they weren't just conspicuous, they were targets. Someone would be tracking them soon.

"It can't be far to a town," he said. "And it'll be much faster if we hoof along the road."

A few minutes later they came to a junction. Boggy wetlands

surrounded the dilapidated mini-mart and gas station, as if the entire place were about to be swallowed.

"Call your brother," Ernest said.

"I don't have any money."

"Call him collect."

Ernest stood by her side, glancing in every direction, while she made the call using the public phone sheltered by a blue plastic hood on the outside of the mini-mart. As she punched in her home phone number, she rested her eyes on Ernest. He was already six feet tall, softly muscled and hard-blinking, as if he were forever trying to bring things into focus. His ears were large and flared, giving the impression of a boy listening intently. To everything. As the phone rang and rang, she thought Ernest was watching out for dangers as he stood in front of her, surveying the gray sky, the mesh of Douglas fir across the road, the occasional traffic rumbling along the highway. In fact, she soon learned, he was looking for opportunity.

Dylan sleepily answered on the eleventh ring. He accepted the charges.

"You okay?" he asked.

"Yes. But maybe you could come get us."

"I'll get the address," Ernest whispered, gesturing at the interior of the mini-mart, then he went inside.

"Who's *us*?" Dylan asked.

"Me and Ernest."

"Who's Ernest?"

"Can you just come?"

"Should I call Pastor Quade?"

Delia almost said yes. Her brother's voice brought back the *before*. She saw Pastor Quade's slate eyes, the way they sheened in righteous joy. She heard his hot and decisive way of speaking. He wasn't only their pastor, he was their family friend. He would correct this mistake. But then she remembered.

"No. Don't."

"Okay." Dylan didn't ask for more explanation. "I'll come now."

Ernest returned to her side and told her their location, which she repeated for Dylan. Then she asked, "Where's Mom?"

"At work."

"Doesn't she have the car?"

"She keeps a spare key in her underwear drawer." He laughed. "I guess she thinks I'd never look there." It wasn't the first time Dylan had taken the car, though he was fifteen and didn't have a license.

"You'll walk to the store?" It was at least a mile to their mother's place of work.

"I'll run."

After Delia hung up, she and Ernest moved away from the front of the building and hid behind a porta-potty on the edge of the parking area. Was there a map in her mom's car? Even if there was, would Dylan be able to find the junction?

As they waited, a seafood truck pulled into the gas pumping lane. A lithe and homely white man jumped down from the driver's seat, pumped gas, and went inside to pay. When he came back out with a bag of Doritos and a can of Mountain Dew, Ernest rubbed his hands on the tops of his thighs, as if warming them. He didn't look at Delia, or say a word to her, he just glided over to the man who was climbing back into his truck. Delia hustled along behind.

"I need a ride to Portland," Ernest said. He blinked rapidly as if delivering a message in Morse code. He pointed at the big green sign across the road, white lettering announcing Portland in one direction and Tillamook in the other, his hands sensual and promising. He licked his lips and looked into the driver's eyes.

Delia was stunned. She thought Ernest was coming back to Rockside with her.

"Dylan can take you to Portland!" she shouted, even though

she stood just a few feet away, even though she didn't know if that was true.

The ferret-faced man pulled the tab off his can of Mountain Dew and took a long drink. He looked at Ernest, glanced at Delia, and then back at Ernest. "Who's she?"

Ernest read the exchange as a yes. He walked around to the passenger side, pulled open the door, and leapt up into the seafood truck. Before shutting the door behind him, he blew Delia a kiss.

She watched the truck lumber onto the highway, turning in the direction away from Portland. That was the last she saw of him.

CHAPTER 2

As Delia came into the office, the secretary's eyes grazed her bare legs. She should have worn slacks and a nice blouse. But the day would only get hotter, and she wanted to get in her workout before it became stifling. Anyway, it was summertime. It was just Ashley. So she wore her long-distance sneakers, running shorts, and a hot-pink tank top.

Delia headed straight for the dean's door, but the secretary swiveled in her chair and said, "Oh! Have a seat. Dean Pruitt will be right with you."

Why so formal? Delia and the dean sometimes ran together, and often worked out side by side at the gym. Ashley and her husband had both spoken at Morgan's and her wedding.

"No problem," Delia said and forced herself to smile. She perched on one of the built-in benches that circled the room. The same darkly polished wood trimmed the two windows. A portrait of the college founder, painted in saturated oil colors, hung behind the secretary's desk, and Delia wondered what it felt like trying to do her job with him looking perennially over her shoulder, reading her letter drafts and listening to her phone conversations. All the visuals on campus were a bit overstated, a reach for twenty-first-century royalty, even if no one outside the Ivy League acknowledged the pretense.

Delia popped back to her feet and walked to the open window. The groundskeeper rode his lawn mower lazily across the quad, the smell of freshly cut grass spicing the air. Heat already shimmered off the stone buildings. A velvety breeze coming in the window lured Delia into a tentative hopefulness. It'd been a helluva year. But she still had basketball. She had her team. Without her marriage, she could give herself, all of herself, over to winning.

"Come in, Delia." Ashley didn't look at her as she held open the door to her office, and again, Delia regretted the hot-pink tank top, wished she'd worn more clothes. The dean was dressed in a white blouse and tan linen suit, gold flats on her feet. As always, her flaxen hair was pulled back in a short, glossy ponytail. In unfortunate contrast, Delia's messy ponytail hung out the opening at the back of her baseball cap. She sat in the big padded chair facing the dean's desk, the backs of her thighs sticking to the brown leather.

"Sorry about the outfit," Delia said, taking the cap off. "I didn't mean to—" The word *disrespect* was too much. They were friends.

Ashley held up a hand, shook her head. She looked seriously upset. Had her troublesome sister been arrested? Had one of her sons gotten in an accident? Was she leaving Monroe College to take another job? Delia waited.

"One way of putting it," the dean said, "is that you did a very good job convincing the president and athletic director of the need to improve our women's basketball program by insisting on the recruits."

As a Division III school, Monroe College didn't offer athletic scholarships. The focus was squarely on academics. Admissions expected Delia to find her talent from the pool of kids who were accepted on those merits alone, and she'd had to lobby hard for the right to scout at all. She'd won that battle, arguing that the school loved wins, even fundraised on their winning teams, which Delia could also produce if only she were able to look for those girls who were both top students and excellent athletes; girls, for instance, who might be overlooked by Stanford's Tara VanDerveer, or who wanted a serious sports program without the pressure of winning the NCAA Division I title. In a meeting with Ashley, as well as the athletic director and college president, she'd finally made a convincing case for recruitment. They gave her two slots and she'd filled them for the coming season with a player from Wisconsin and one from Florida.

Delia smiled and said, "Thank you," but she didn't like Ashley's tone or the opening phrase, *One way of putting it.* She added, "With June Kirkpatrick at point, and the two new recruits, I think we have a chance at a Division III title."

Ashley's mouth opened, as if she were going to speak, but couldn't. Her shoulders wilted.

"I need a heftier budget, though," Delia said. "If I could hire a real assistant, then—"

Ashley rallied, raising her chin and passing a hand over the shiny blond hair on the crown of her head. She interrupted, "The number of wins have not been commiserate with school standards and expectations."

Delia's sense of innocence held stubbornly for another couple of beats. They would offer her a bigger budget. Or give her the green light to recruit more high-profile players. They wanted the wins. They did.

But no, obviously that was not where this was going.

Ashley—Dean Pruitt—waited.

Delia felt like she had five seconds to find the right words to change the course of this meeting. "We're not UConn," she said.

Those were the wrong words.

"It's not just the losses. I got a call from June Kirkpatrick's parents. They were both on the line. Both very upset."

"What? I started her. As a freshman. I can't imagine—" The kid was a major pain in the butt. She challenged Delia's every decision. But she was the best point guard she'd had in years and Delia spent an inordinate amount of time and energy cajoling her along.

"You threw a basketball at her."

"You can't be serious."

"They're very upset."

"That was an accident."

"Was it?"

"Oh my god, Ashley. *Yes*. June knows it was an accident."

"June said you lost your temper. Her father used the word *assault*."

"You've got to be kidding."

"I'm not." Ashley seemed to draw the words from some gravelly place at her center.

"Okay." Delia paused to breathe. She checked herself. She'd long monitored a subterranean anger that she considered native to the country of herself. But she'd kept it under wraps, on mute. Always. Almost always. She said, "Let's back up. We wouldn't even be having this conversation if I were a male coach. They lose their tempers all the time. Do much worse than throw basketballs."

"So you admit you threw a basketball at her."

"No. I do not admit that. I admit that I lost my temper. And I admit that I threw a basketball. At the other side of the court. It hit June, but I certainly did not intend to hit her. I mean, let's get real. She wasn't hurt."

"She had a bruise on her shoulder. They sent us a picture of it."

The incident occurred months ago, on February the twentieth, a Wednesday, at the very end of the season. The night before, Delia's wife Morgan had explained—yes, that's the right word, as if she were giving a lesson in relationships that Delia would only understand if told in clear, concise language—that she'd fallen in love with Mary Hunt, the vivaciously didactic chair of the Women's Studies Department. Of course they'd both known Mary for years, everyone on campus knew her, she was a star with her PhD from Yale, her seminal volumes on feminist history, her TED Talk on American women in colonial times, which had received a record number of views, and of course her tenure. She played cello in a community orchestra and loved to tell people that she read only nonfiction, as if that were a badge of seriousness. Delia and Morgan had even made fun of her, on numerous occasions, her tendency to lecture and her forced expansiveness. And yet, like spontaneous combustion, Morgan and she had fallen in love. One day Delia and Morgan were married, and then, *poof*, love instantly happened somewhere else. Morgan made no mention of an affair, of clandestine meetings, of the development of attraction. She just stated the fact that she was in love. Now. With a different person.

Morgan's announcement made Delia feel as if she were wearing an underskin of insects. A buzzing fury ran up and down her arms and legs. She knew, even then in that moment she knew, that the feeling reached all the way back to Celebration Camp, the betrayal of Pastor Quade and the cold cruelty of those weeks. She prided herself on being clear-sighted about the anger that dawdled just off the map of her life. The way she'd kept it at bay. Consciously, deliberately. She watched for, and blocked, triggers. Morgan had, earlier in their relationship, admired Delia's self-mastery. But that night when Morgan explained why she was moving on, she cited Delia's self-control, calling it a defense, an unacceptable armor. She said she had come to the conclusion that she could never reach Delia, the true Delia.

Maybe if Delia had exploded then, shouted profanities and accusations, Morgan would have been impressed, maybe even been lured back. But Delia didn't. She listened. She kept an outward calm as she mentioned the fact of their marriage, their vows, and what she'd given up for that marriage. Morgan held her gaze, a practice she'd developed from years sitting in her psychotherapist chair, and said only, "I'm sorry."

Delia put on her sneakers and ran twelve miles. When she got back home, Morgan was already asleep. Delia grabbed a comforter, took the couch, and lay awake all night humming with rage.

So, yes, the next day she got angry at how her team was

executing their offense and threw a basketball the length of the court. It hit June Kirkpatrick, who was lollygagging where she was not supposed to be, on the far side of the gym, a defiant smirk on her face.

None of which was germane to this moment in Dean Ashley Pruitt's office. Ashley did not want to hear any details about the end of her marriage. Delia needed to pivot, as she was so good at doing, to the necessary action. *Take care of the ball,* Coach had said daily. That homely sentence always steadied Delia.

"So what's the fix?" she asked. "A formal apology?" She lifted first one sticky bare thigh off the leather seat of the chair and then the other, her skin making a regrettable ripping sound.

"You didn't have a great season, Delia. You haven't had a winning season in four years."

Delia badly wanted to point out how well the team did her first five seasons, twice nearly getting to the Division III finals. Even Division I coaches were given a little slack for a few bad years. But she hated people who made excuses for themselves and she had to acknowledge that Ashley was right: she'd been underperforming.

She said, "With the new recruits, I'm looking forward to a strong year."

"I'll write you a good reference."

"Wait."

Delia knew Ashley well enough to recognize a hint of shame in her posture, though the dean leaned forward, bracing her elbows on the desk, to mask it.

"Are you firing me?"

"I'm sorry," Ashley said, speaking as plainly as Morgan had. "I can't renew your contract."

"Throwing a basketball is not a fireable offense." Delia knew that technically she was on a year-to-year contract, and that Ashley didn't need a reason.

"It's my job," Ashley said, "to protect our reputation—"

"The girls love me. Their families love me."

"—and our funding."

There it was. June Kirkpatrick was a legacy student. Her family undoubtedly had donated thousands, maybe hundreds of thousands, to the college.

Delia rose from her chair. She put her hands on Ashley's desk and leaned forward, the heat rising into her head. "That incident took place in February. It's August."

"It's been a difficult decision. I'd like you to know, Delia, that I fought for you. The president wouldn't budge."

"You've already hired someone, haven't you?" That's why they waited to let her go. They needed to make sure they could find a replacement.

Ashley didn't answer the question.

For a hot second, Delia tried to blame Mary Hunt. The woman had so much clout on campus, could she have engineered Delia's ouster? So the new couple could enjoy life in this small town without constantly running into a guilty reminder of their two-timing path to happiness? No, Mary was full of herself, but not sinister, not devious. She was, or at least thought of herself as, rigorously ethical. Delia could only imagine how she justified plundering someone else's marriage.

Delia turned her back on Ashley and walked to the window, looked out at the muggy heat and copper sunlight, the campus that had been home for a decade. Where would she go?

To her back, Ashley said, "I can offer you the option of resigning."

Delia drew down her shoulder blades. She pulled in her navel to engage her core. She lengthened her spine so she stood her full five feet eleven inches. The "option" of resigning would benefit the dean and president. They wouldn't have to explain a thing. They wouldn't have to answer to the many students and parents who loved her. She turned and said, "No, thank you. Fire me."

Ashley looked truly crushed. Delia imagined her talking to

friends about what a difficult bind she'd been put in, squeezed between her friend and the president. She might even shed a couple of tears after Delia walked out of her office.

Managing her anger in that moment was a task on par with winning a championship game. It took a herculean effort of control, discipline, focus, and strength. But she'd had a lifetime of practice. She did it. Delia nodded at Ashley and left the office.

Take care of the ball. Survive and advance.

CHAPTER 3

Crossing the country, from Massachusetts to Oregon, Delia drove too fast and stopped too often. She lingered in roadside diners, drinking lots of coffee and flirting with waitresses. Stretched out on motel beds, she watched movies late into the nights, slept in, and didn't check out the next day until the last possible minute. She stopped in small towns to shoot baskets on funky outdoor public courts and twice joined pickup games with local guys, enjoying their surprise at her skill. She detoured to state parks and ran their trails. Once, at a highway rest area, she spent thirty minutes talking NBA politics with a homeless guy.

At dawn of the last day, as she neared her hometown, Delia recognized the intersection where Ernest had left her. Where she'd waited alone for three hours after he climbed into that seafood truck and before Dylan arrived. The moss-covered roof sprouted ferns, and blackberries had grown in the surrounding bog, but otherwise the place looked unchanged, and that told her too much about the Oregon coast. Twenty-five years had passed, and even the blue-hooded pay phone still hung off the outside of the mini-mart. Delia pulled in, bought gas, and walked to the edge of the parking lot, noticing the ache behind her breastbone. A few late-fall blackberries withered on the ends of the thicket branches. The smell of Oregon, sweet and fecund and moldy, brought back so much. She would have to steady herself.

The mist became a heavy rain soon after she got back on the highway. Her windshield wipers needed replacing and they smeared rather than cleared the water. Twice she pulled over to reconsider everything. What if she made a U-turn and headed east again? But where? Where exactly would she go?

Delia arrived in Rockside a couple hours later, having driven all night to get there in time to meet with Jonas, followed by tryouts that afternoon. She drove directly to the high school, grabbed her basketball from the backseat, and slammed the car door shut behind her. As she strode through the rain to the main entrance, she tried to muster a sense of purpose.

She should have slept last night.

She should have gotten here earlier.

Delia mounted the steps and pulled open the door to Rockside High School, knowing, as she'd known on the entire drive across America, that she'd made a mistake. A three-thousand-mile mistake. A reversion-to-childhood mistake. Holding the door open, she looked behind herself, out at the coursing rain, backdropped by a patch of the Pacific Northwest forest, now just a blurry field of green. Rainwater streamed down the cement stairs she'd just climbed and sluiced across the parking lot. A few late students gunned their rusty cars through these miniature lakes, triggering arcing sprays. Seagulls screamed as they circled overhead, protesting the storm, as if they didn't experience this weather constantly.

What had she been thinking?

Delia stepped back outside. The rain pelted her head and shoulders as she took several deep breaths. The teeming adolescent mess on the other side of that door, filling the institutional hallways of Rockside High, was now her responsibility. At least a dozen of them would be. She couldn't, she just couldn't, let regret immobilize her. She had a job to do.

Morgan had hated when she used platitudes. As if the occasional cliché did anyone any harm. Delia found them comforting. Coach had used them constantly. Pat Summitt could deliver entire lectures populated by platitudes, and Delia welcomed those lectures. They were like architectural plans for behavior. The plans themselves looked bland and rigid, but the structure could lead to the complexity of surprise and beauty. Morgan did not, could not, see that. She wanted everything to have, or at least appear to have, the grandeur of the Taj Mahal. If something was easy to understand, she thought it was just stupid.

How Delia wished Coach were still alive. If she were here now, she'd metaphorically (or maybe even actually) twist Delia's arm behind her back, ask her what she wanted to accomplish, implore her to forgo the time-wasting tears and rants, the energy-sucking regrets and blame, and get to work.

Just the thought of Coach's face, those steely blue eyes, the thin tight lips, her squat heels smacking the hallways at the University of Tennessee, the fury of purpose that drove every word she uttered, every step she took, eased Delia. *Coach*. No matter how hard you fell, how far from your goals you landed, how badly you messed up, she was there for you. Once you made her team, you'd never get rid of her rooting for you, devising strategies for you, prodding you out of your personal hell. How many former players had Coach put up in her backyard cottage, for as long as they needed to stay, after they'd gotten a felony or left a husband or battled addiction? *This is for Coach*, Delia thought as she stepped inside the high school.

She walked briskly down the main hallway to the heavy metal music of slamming lockers and obscenity-shouting kids, to the wet dog stink of damp clothing and teenage sweat, heading straight for the glass cabinet where the trophies and championship-team pictures resided. She thought it might be corrective, maybe even energizing, to view herself at age eighteen.

But when she got to the display case, she couldn't look. Her gaze bounced away like reflected light. Those trophies and photographs captured an innocence so tender it hurt. How could anything from then possibly be useful now?

She should never have come. At the very least she should have arrived in town much sooner. Taken stock. Gotten her footing.

Reabsorbed the history, *her* history, deliberately, carefully. She should have made her way to this building long before today, breathed this stale air, acclimated, walked these halls late or early in the day, after or before they were infested with youth. She should have known better.

She made herself look. There it was, an enormous gold—well, gold-colored plastic—trophy topped by a basketball player. Words etched into the base plate read, *1998 Oregon State Champions, Girls Basketball.* The cabinet glass was polished to a shiny glare, and she knew that was the work of her brother Dylan, who now worked at the high school as the night custodian. She imagined him at four in the morning, alone here in the hallway, rag in one hand and Windex spray bottle in the other, lustering her childhood glory. He'd always been proud of her, often going so far as to take credit for her success. She gave him that. Basketball had been his idea, and it'd saved her life.

"Hyperbole," Morgan said when she thought Delia gave Dylan too many points for her achievements.

"Maybe."

"Dylan is a sad soul," Morgan drilled down, "who's ridden your coattails. What you're feeling is survivor's guilt."

Of course that's what she felt. Delia never denied that. Nonetheless, he still deserved her gratitude.

She turned her back to the trophy display case, as kids streamed around her, and mentally scrabbled for a way forward. If this were a basketball game . . . But that was the problem. This wasn't a basketball game and no complicated set of plays, no amount of strength training, no number of practice free throws, would change the events of the past.

She needed to proceed down the hall and face Jonas. It would be a pleasure to see him again, it would be. So just do it.

A skinny boy with thick black, bed-smashed hair whizzed by on a skateboard. He looked comical with the straps of his huge backpack, the corners and rectangles of too many books filling out the shape, tugging his slight shoulders. The locomotion, the fast-wheeled ride down the hallway, as he swiveled his hips, simultaneously pulling up his baggy jeans, to move around other kids, broke the spell holding Delia in place. She made herself smile. Forward movement by any means possible.

"Zeke!"

The voice came from an older version of the same kid who stood at an open locker a few feet down the hall. Short, unruly black hair, along with chunky black glasses, accentuated a spindly neck. *Girl? Boy?* Did they do nonbinary in small towns on the Oregon Coast? Delia smiled at the lovely idea. Skinny jeans sheathed the kid's long, coltish legs, and an untucked cobalt-blue button-down shirt hung loosely on their narrow shoulders. The look on the kid's face, as they called out to the skating boy, was part strict and part indulgent, and the apparent brother dropped a foot as a brake, expertly flipping the board up into his hands. Of course he wasn't supposed to be skating in the hall, Delia realized, wondering if she'd be expected to discipline kids who were not on her team. Zeke continued on down the hall, loping on his awkward adolescent feet, without stopping to talk to his sibling, who shouted to his back, "Come find me in the library when you get out of Chess Club!" After shoving a backpack into the bottom of their locker, the kid looked up, saw Delia standing in front of the display case, and smiled, revealing a mouth full of braces.

"You're the new coach!"

The red Adidas tracksuit and the basketball cradled on her hip gave Delia away. "Yes."

"I'll be at tryouts today!"

Okay, so could Delia assume female pronouns? Maybe she should just ask. Always a good policy. But then it'd seem like she was questioning the kid's right to try out for the girls' team.

"I'm Mickey." The shiny, braces-enhanced grin, beaming delight about the prospect of tryouts, alleviated Delia's angst.

Game on: her job was to lead a team of girls toward as many wins as possible, and in the process expand the frontiers of their capabilities. She loved teaching young women how to find their voices, work cooperatively toward a common goal, discover beautiful strong selves they didn't know existed. Challenge accepted.

And there was Morgan's smirk at the platitude, as vivid as a hallucination.

"Awesome," Delia said. "Great to meet you. I'm Delia Barnes."

"Yeah," Mickey laughed, "I know."

A stocky and pale-skinned boy slid on the hard leather soles of scuffed dress shoes, pulling to a stop right behind Mickey, as if he were a performer coming onstage. A gold cross, hanging from a thick gold chain, glinted on the white fabric of his T-shirt, right on top of his sternum. He cupped his crotch and said, "Good morning, Mick! How's it hangin'?"

Mickey kicked the locker door shut and twirled the dial to make sure it was secure, then paused before turning around, as if trying to figure out an escape route.

"Or wait," the boy said. "I guess you haven't found an organ donor yet, right?"

"Dang, man," said another boy catching up to him. "You offering yours?"

"Maybe. But not in the way she'd want it."

Delia didn't think or consider. She didn't make a decision. She just acted. It was as if her considerable will got sucked out to sea by a strong, fast undertow. Then the roller came tumbling forward, cresting, and she could no more stop herself than the waves crashing onto the beach a mile from the high school. She dropped her basketball, grabbed the boy by the neck of his T-shirt, and slammed him against a locker, thrusting her face close to his.

"If I catch you disrespecting a fellow student like this again,

I'll have you expelled." Delia pulled back on the handful of T-shirt and gave him another jangle against the locker, his skull making a satisfying clunk.

The boy's friend, standing behind Delia, chortled, "Whoa."

"Who are you?" the one against the locker asked.

"I'm the new basketball coach."

"No way. Mr. Banks coaches our team."

"The girls' coach," Delia clarified, then wished she hadn't.

The boy rolled his eyes to the left and right, noticed he had an audience now, and allowed himself a grin. The words *girls' coach* were as impotent to him as a limp dick.

Delia let go of his T-shirt and stepped back, her heart thudding, the adrenaline coursing. She was appalled by what she'd just done. Never in her life had she physically assaulted someone. Unless you counted June Kirkpatrick, which had been an accident, probably.

Still grinning, the kid rubbed the skin over a large pink birthmark covering half his neck and throat, made gagging sounds, as if she'd been strangling him. Then his grin faded.

"Delia? Adam! What's going on?" The deep voice came from several paces down the hall.

Jonas strode toward them, and for a second Delia forgot all about the altercation. She hadn't seen Jonas in twenty years, not since that late-summer night before they left for college, and here he was in a gray suit, white shirt, and striped tie, his curly red hair—which he used to wear in an adorable, longish tangle—trimmed close to his head, more rust than carrot now.

Jonas. Just Jonas. The fact of him was still beautiful.

He stared at her, and she saw the mix of bewilderment and pleasure in his expression, both feelings hooks, and their eyes caught, held. Delia gave him a close-mouthed smile. This was so not how she intended the reunion to go. He started toward her, then pulled back, seemed to remember that he was now the principal of Rockside High School. He shifted to the crisis at hand. Which she'd just instigated, or at least exacerbated.

How much had he seen?

She wanted to defend herself. This boy had crudely mocked that kid's gender expression. But even the thought sounded plaintive, almost ridiculous, especially given Delia's full-body attack on the boy. This was a high school. What did she expect? Besides, the kid was gone. Delia looked down the hall in both directions and saw no head of black hair, no skinny legs scissoring away. It was as if Delia had made up the entire scenario. Made *them* up. She doubted her reading of the incident.

That too was new. As new as the outward expressions of anger. She'd always had a sharp memory and been confident about the accuracy of her perceptions. She held facts close, even when they were painful. It was this trait—more than a trait, her character, her very essence—that Morgan first fell in love with. While as a psychotherapist Morgan applied theories and analysis, dug for hidden causation, Delia observed with eyes wide open, added up the discernible details, and nailed her interpretation of an event or a person's behavior. It used to make Morgan laugh out loud in admiration.

Delia hated this new muddiness of doubt. And the unleashed anger! It was like discovering your body had begun hosting a pair of troglodytes.

Anyway, what she'd just witnessed, or thought she'd just witnessed, was hardly anything new. She knew better than to engage. She knew the best response was to let him wither in the fever of his own idiocy.

It'd been the gold cross. Sitting on his chest like a wink. The license he thought it gave him.

Jonas rested a firm yet avuncular hand on Adam's shoulder and looked back and forth between him and Delia, waiting for an explanation. She knew she'd messed up big time, physically attacking a student, and that Jonas was already regretting hiring her. He looked almost frightened.

"It's okay," Delia said weakly. "We're going to just drop this one and start fresh. What do you say, Adam?"

She held out a hand for a shake and Adam widened his eyes at Jonas, his face asking if he had to. The boy clearly thought there was a chance the principal would side with him against her, that male bonding would work even in this weighted situation. Jonas nodded at Adam, who held out a hand without making eye contact. He squeezed hers too hard, then hitched up his pants and lunged down the hall, using an extra-wide gait. Jonas and Delia both watched him go, stalling, having no idea how to look at each other now that they were alone.

Delia's basketball had rolled a few yards down the hall, and she went to get it. When she returned, she said, "Hi."

Jonas took her in, his gaze shyly sliding down to her Nikes, and traveling back up, more slowly, skimming over her breasts but hesitating at her shoulders, since meeting Delia's eyes was going to be awkward at best.

She wanted to think that the thirty-eight-year-old woman he saw today looked pretty much exactly like the eighteen-year-old girl he remembered. She still weighed a hundred and forty-five pounds, still wore her hair parted in the middle, usually pulled back. Faint lines now framed her mouth and eyes, and her hair color had muted into a duskier brown, a shade a little darker than mouse. Her best friend Skylar once described her face as "bald," meaning straightforward, and Delia was good with that. She knew she wasn't beautiful, but she liked to think she made up for that with a hell of a good attitude. She arranged a smile to ease the whole situation.

Jonas smiled too, those crooked teeth of his still crooked, the pale early morning blue-sky eyes with white blond lashes, the acne scars, the short rust curls, all coming together in an appealing goofy kindness.

"It's good to see you, Jonas."

Despite the smile, he looked confused, and why wouldn't

he be? Within five minutes of entering the high school, she'd jumped a kid. He said, "Come on."

They walked side by side down the hall and turned into the admin offices. Delia noticed he didn't ask anyone to bring coffee, but instead fetched two cups himself, putting cream and sugar into hers, as if she still drank coffee the way she did in high school, and jerked his head toward the back corner office.

Delia went in first and he followed, closing the door. He didn't sit at the big desk. Instead, after setting the two cups down on a short round table, he used both hands to pinch a bit of pants fabric just above each knee, plucked the shiny suit material away from his skin, just like the grown man he now was, and sat on one of the green leather love seats in a corner of the office. Green had been his boyhood favorite color and now he got to furnish his big principal's office with green leather. She remained standing for another few seconds, looking out the rain-blurred plate glass window at the football field. Jonas had been the star wide receiver during their tenure as students at Rockside High and she could still picture perfectly his fluidity running down the field, reaching up and, as if his hands were magnets, catching passes no one dreamed he'd catch. Delia sat on the other love seat, placing the basketball at her feet. She took a sip of the creamy sweet coffee.

She'd better say something about what happened in the hall. Nothing ever just went away. She knew that. "So that boy. Adam. He was taunting a kid about their, uh, you know, clothes and hair and—" Why couldn't she just say what actually happened? The way he grabbed his own genitals and referenced theirs? "I mean, he was pretty aggressive."

"Must have been Michaela Vlasak-Jones."

"They said their name was Mickey."

"She recently started going by Mickey instead of Michaela."

"Mickey uses female pronouns?"

"What?"

Delia looked out the window.

Jonas sighed. "Look, don't give us the hick treatment. I know about pronouns. But Mickey is a girl."

"If she says so."

"She does."

"Okay. But you don't just let that kind of harassment happen, do you? He was pretty vulgar." In spite of the Christian announcement swinging brightly around his neck.

"No. Of course not. But I didn't see what he did and it got a little confused by what happened after. Um . . . you can't, you know, do that. Not ever." He looked shocked that he'd had to say that.

Delia set down her coffee cup, miscalculating the short distance, as if she weren't, never had been, an athlete, and the ceramic clanked against the glass tabletop. Coffee sloshed out.

"Sorry." Her voice snagged. Of course she couldn't slam a kid against a locker. She sat on her hands.

"Hey," Jonas said softly, as if he regretted having spoken too harshly to a child, as if tears brimmed her eyes. "I bet it's super weird being back. I mean . . ." He stalled out and finished with, "Everyone is super psyched to have you."

"Thanks." She'd told him in their email exchange about the breakup with Morgan, and let that stand as the reason she'd left her coaching job at Monroe College. It wasn't a lie; it was part of the truth. She took a slug of the hot coffee milkshake. Thinking she should say something more affirming, she added, "I'm super jazzed about the new challenge."

Did they both need to use the word *super* in every sentence?

Jonas noticed the repetition too and smiled. Ah, Jonas. Delia let the relief of his comfortable face ease her. He was nothing if not loyal, and the way he'd hired her, barely questioning why she wanted the job, respecting her privacy, trusting her, she needed that, his kindness.

Finding each other at the beginning of their senior year of

high school had solved so much for Delia. After Celebration Camp and before Jonas, her life had felt like a regime. Workouts and studying, aiming for every kind of excellence, satisfied her in some deep way but also left her deeply lonely. In Jonas she found a true friend, as well as an answer to the confusion of romance. They seemed destined, a perfect fit, he a football star, she a basketball star, the soothing triumph of their bodies. They believed they could conquer anything, that even greater victories hovered in their futures. Yet here he was, commander in chief of the same high school, and here she was, returned to muster one of the armies.

"I sort of expected you before today," he continued gently.

"Oh. I know. But you said . . . I mean . . ."

"Yeah, sure. I said *by* today. I guess I sort of thought that you'd, you know, get here a little earlier."

"I know. Driving cross-country took me longer than I expected." Jonas waited and Delia smiled. "Yeah," she said, "I have stories."

He raised his eyebrows.

She laughed. "Later. I got tryouts this afternoon."

"You do. I was beginning to think I'd have to run them myself."

"I'm here. And ready." She didn't need to tell him that she hadn't slept in the last twenty-four hours.

"So you have four returning starters. All seniors."

"Great."

"The team almost got to the state tournament both of the last two years. With frankly, you know, uh, shitty coaching. But with you here now, and, I mean, with that kind of maturity on the team . . ."

When they were kids, Jonas had spoken with assurance, even cockiness, though a sweetly innocent cockiness, a delight in what he perceived as their formidable prospects. That voice was all but gone. He spoke more quietly now, hesitantly, almost stuttering. So he too was experiencing the juggernaut of doubt.

"We got a shot," Delia said, injecting the confidence he'd left out. "Four returning starters in their prime. I got this."

Jonas laughed tentatively, almost defensively, like she'd spoken too cavalierly.

"You know how closely the community follows the team," he said.

"Yep."

"They expect wins." Ah, there he was: his lovely pale eyes did that thing they did in high school whenever he talked about athletic competition, crystalizing to a harder blue. It reminded Delia of the blue in Coach's eyes, and she leaned into the comfort.

"I do know that."

"This team really is special. That they got as far as they did the last couple of years is kinda miraculous. The Spanish teacher coached, and she knows nothing about the game. She pretty much sat with the girls while they scrimmaged every day. Mike Foster, one of the girls' dads, showed up when he could, helped with fundamentals. But with you, this is going to be a whole new level of experience for them. I think you're going to find you have some rare talent. With your direction, it's going to be an awesome season."

Jonas's words came quickly now, the halting gone, his red lips mobile with feeling. He and Delia understood each other perfectly when it came to the starch clarity of sport. He asked, "Do you know what it would mean to this town to win another state championship?"

"I think I do."

"In spite of the lack of coaching, several university scouts came to games last year. I won't tell you who they were looking at. You'll see that for yourself."

Jonas's challenge entered her bloodstream like a sedative, calming the shivers of anger, the confusion. Her job: hone talent and win games. Everything had gone awry at Monroe College.

She'd been knocked off her rails. It was possible that the isolation of Rockside could be restorative.

"Everyone in town is talking about your return." Jonas kicked out one leg and then the other, his own excitement ramping up. "Hometown girl who played for Pat Summitt at Tennessee. Ha. It doesn't get any better than that. I just gotta tell you, their hopes are very high." He fake-grimaced. "But no pressure."

"You know I love pressure."

Jonas gave her his big, crooked-toothed grin. "Just wanted to remind you what Rocksiders are like. In case you've forgotten."

"I've forgotten nothing."

He micro-flinched.

She laughed and raised her upturned palms. "Come on, Jonas."

He reddened.

"That was a lifetime ago," she said.

"I was talking about basketball."

"I know you were." But she laughed again at the memories, at the fact of sitting here with Jonas as two adults, the wash of their lives in the years between. The devastation of so much innocence. You had to laugh, or you'd cry.

Delia and Jonas dated for eight months before they had real sex. They waited for the end of football season because his coach had a theory that sex reduced the players' competitive drive. They'd laughed at this idea, but they'd also believed it and waited all the way through her basketball season too. Looking back, she knew that the wait for her hadn't been nearly as excruciating as it had been for him, but at the time she'd basked in the excitement of anticipation. They were such good friends, spending every free moment together, shooting hoops, tossing the football, talking on the phone, walking along the river, or diving into the icy winter waves at the beach to prove their toughness.

Delia and Jonas had believed that their waiting, that erotic potency, fueled her team's state championship. Delia soon learned, during her four promiscuous years at the University of Tennessee, that winning had nothing to do with sexual abstinence, that the wait for her had been more of a convenience than she admitted to herself at the time, but during those months of their senior year, it was the sweetest delusion.

In the second week of May, shortly before graduation, they packed a flask of whiskey, a block of chocolate, two fleece blankets, and a box of condoms, and drove to their favorite spot, the small pebbled beach on the Siletz River. It was a warm afternoon, a breeze rippling the surface of the water, a coming spring storm purpling the sky. They never would have touched the whiskey or even the chocolate during their seasons, and as it turned out, they left them untouched that afternoon.

Broad daylight splashed across their bit of public beach, and yet they were oblivious to the possibility of anyone walking in on them. The rest of the world swirled away into the black hole of insignificance. As athletes, they knew their bodies, down to each sinew and skin cell. That's where Delia went, into the depths of their biology. The kissing cascaded into such vigorous explorations of each other's bodies, they were practically wrestling. They wore tracksuit pants, so there were no zippers or buttons to get in the way, just stretchy, easily shed fabric, shoved to their ankles.

They both assumed they'd marry after college, after they fulfilled their scholarship commitments by playing ball for four years, he at Oregon State and she at the University of Tennessee. He wanted lots of kids. For Delia, Jonas was a harbor.

"I'll have the squad list by the end of the week," she told him now, breaking the eye contact.

"I don't think you'll have much trouble choosing your team."

"It's harder than you think."

He gave her a judicious nod as he rose to his feet. "Uh, in the future? Leave the student discipline to me, okay?"

"What about my team?"

"Well, sure, I mean, you're manager of your team. But—" He

rubbed the whiskers on his chin in the exact same way he had back then. It used to make her laugh, like it was a pantomime of being an adult. Now he *was* an adult, and he owned the gesture legitimately. She suppressed her smile, tried to look appropriately attentive as he warned, "A high school community can be thorny. We got parents. We got teachers. We got hormone-drunk kids. It can get messy real fast."

"I have pretty strong opinions about how to coach a basketball team."

"I don't doubt it." That same winsome smile, only now with a measure of regret aged in. He added, "I trust you."

Why did he have to say that? As if the issue of trust were even on the table.

"So where's my office?"

"Oh. Wow. Even the two guidance counselors have to share an office. There really isn't . . . I mean, why do you need office space?"

"I like to be available to the girls when they have questions, issues." Plus, at Monroe she'd spent hours every week studying plays, other teams, statistics. An office held the seriousness of her work.

Jonas shook his head. "I'm sorry. There is literally nothing. Nowhere. I mean, you'll have the entire gym for two hours every day. Alternating with the boys' team for the before-school and after-school time slots. Let me walk you down there now."

"I know where the gym is."

"Of course you do." They both smiled. "And the truth is, nothing has changed. We have a new computer lab. And we've remodeled the library. But the gym is pretty much exactly the same."

Delia wanted to see that sanctum on her own. She held up a hand as he tried to follow her out the door. "I know you're busy."

"I'm not that busy."

"I'm fine. I'll just go have a look."

Jonas still knew her, and seeing that on his face gave Delia more reassurance than was healthy. *I'm me*, she thought. *I'm still me.*

"Hey," she said, turning in the door of his office, hugging her basketball against her belly like a bumper, "I look forward to meeting Megan. And your daughters."

His face said she'd broken something. Good. She liked having the offense. But she was sorry, too, for the way his silence told her there was still something to break. She'd always regretted how much she'd hurt Jonas. He didn't even answer.

As Delia emerged from the admin offices, she found the hallway empty, the students ensconced in their first-period classes. She walked slowly through the sea of charged silence. Jonas wasn't kidding when he said little had changed. The same pale-green tiles cooled the bottom four feet of the walls, and above them, the drywall was still painted a military white, staunch and armored. Swaths of fresher paint, probably applied by Dylan, covered up sections of the wall where colorful tags ghosted through. Wads of paper and gum, a rolling pencil and loose paperclips, littered the linoleum floor.

Delia depressed the metal bar on the door to the gymnasium and it clanged softly as she pushed it open against the cold air inside. She stepped into the empty gym, letting the door hush closed behind her. The cavernous, unheated space was bracing, fresh, lovely. A deep pleasure rose up through her feet as she absorbed the silence and took in the bleachers folded against the walls, the gleaming glass backboards, the orange hoops forming perfect circles of dare. Delia longed to hear the quiet breath of a swish, the white net swaying with the passage of the basketball. Almost as good: the *ka-klunk* of a shot ricocheting off the rim before dropping through.

She closed her eyes and heard the cheers of the Rockside fans, game after game, as her senior-year team made their dogged way to the Oregon state championship. Such pure joy. Perfection.

When she opened her eyes, she saw the hoop, only the hoop. She dribbled to the free throw lie, pulled up, and dropped a jumper. Good sign, draining her first shot in the gym in twenty years. Delia kept shooting for another ten minutes and didn't miss a single shot.

CHAPTER 4

Ernest Wrangham didn't think he liked cats, but Virginia Woolf—he'd been instructed to only ever call her by her full name, never just Virginia—came with the house he'd been lent for the year he was teaching poetry at Lewis & Clark College in Portland, Oregon. He'd heard stories about dictatorial cats who peed on beds to establish dominance or express displeasure, so he girded himself for all manner of unpleasantness, including yowling, clawing, and furred clothing. But the house was rent-free, just so long as he scooped the litter box every day, changed the sand weekly, and put the plate of putrid food down for Virginia Woolf twice a day.

The big surprise was that Ernest and Virginia Woolf fell in love with each other within twenty-four hours of his arrival. How could he not love a creature named after that hella ethereal author? But it was more than that. It was the way Virginia Woolf—the cat—read him, the way she took action to protect his vulnerabilities, right from the start. Everything about her behavior gave the distinct impression that she thought it was her duty to guard him. He appreciated that. He needed that. Besides, Virginia Woolf was gorgeous, silky seal gray, short-haired with green eyes. Her devotion flattered him.

It also distracted him, along with the tasks of feeding and cleaning up after her, and he needed distraction because ever returning to Oregon had been unthinkable until now. When Lewis & Clark College offered the position, it was his boyfriend Dennis who insisted. This place that had tried to destroy Ernest as a boy now wanted to honor him as a poet. Wasn't that the best kind of redemption? That had been Dennis's argument, anyway.

Just stay within the city proper, friends who knew the place had advised. Rural Oregon was a rookery of bunker-building, gun-loving yahoos who would not appreciate either his skin color or his sexual preference. The city should be fine, they said, maybe even a fun (if kept brief) change from Brooklyn. Ernest watched all the episodes of *Portlandia* before agreeing to the position. He decided he could hang with the hipsters, if he needed to see anyone at all, other than students. Mostly he just wanted to write. Once he got here, though, and saw the house, he didn't feel particularly safe. The profusion of greenery surrounding the place created perfect hideouts for all manner of threats, including beasts he could not even name. There were no bears, Dennis assured him, within the Portland city limits, but how could Ernest know that for sure when you couldn't see past the rough-barked tree trunks?

Anyway, people were always the scariest species. There was the excessively handsome, not to mention married, man next door who actively flirted with Ernest every time they crossed paths at the garbage cans or parking strip. And also the ultra-conservative student in Ernest's poetry seminar whose work was clearly the strongest in the class, despite its subject matter. The young man seemed to relish turning in beautifully penned odes to patriotism and chaste heterosexuality, holding eye contact as he handed over his work, as if each word was meant to goad Ernest. Why had the guy even taken Ernest's class? Had he not read his work? Or did he enjoy the prospect of conflict?

On a rainy day in November, six weeks into the first semester, Ernest set about cleaning the cat box. He dumped the shit-studded sand in a paper grocery bag and carried that outside to the garbage bin, failing in his resolve to not glance through the window of his neighbor's house. The wife was there, in the kitchen, chopping carrots. Ernest waved. She wiped her hands on her apron and smiled too hard.

Returning to the house, he sprayed the bathroom floor with disinfectant and dried the area with paper towels. As he leafed through the Sunday *Oregonian* for a section he didn't care about to spread under the cleaned box, he came across the sports page. Shaking loose two sheets, he squatted to spread these out on the floor.

His gaze snagged on the picture of a woman below the headline: "Homegrown Hoops Star Returns." He looked away, set the newsprint on the floor, and then looked back again.

He recognized that grin.

Ernest sat down on the toilet seat and read the short article, no more than three inches, just a little human-interest filler. Once, twice, three times his eyes roved over the words as Virginia Woolf, who'd jumped onto the back of the toilet seat behind him, rubbed back and forth against his spine. The one quote from the homegrown hoops star personified that blend of innocent and gutsy he remembered so well: "Yeah, I'm back and here for the win."

It was her. It was definitely her.

So Delia—Delia Barnes, it said, giving her last name, which he'd never known—was alive. Not just alive, but functioning at a high enough level to take a coaching job, albeit at a high school on the Oregon coast. He could still feel the grip of her hand, the way she wouldn't let go of him. He still felt bad, too, about abandoning her at that gas station, alone, and only thirteen years old. But he'd never intended to bring her along in the first place. He'd fetched her at the last minute, unable to leave her behind with those circling wolves.

The night they ran had fueled so many poem attempts, the darkness, the sweat, the thick green undergrowth, the stars, the payment he'd made for both of their freedoms. Every draft wadded and tossed. Untangling that night, those last few days at Celebration Camp, had become both his Sisyphus and his north star, dread and guidance. As hard as he tried writing a poem that told that story, his words kept going awry, pushing those events into the peripheral vision of his work, never keeping them at the center. It was the poem he most wanted to write, though, the one that had eluded years of effort. He'd never been able to find the language.

Time and again he'd considered looking for Delia, but besides not knowing her last name, he had to admit that he really hadn't wanted to know what had become of her. In some draft attempts, he even tried to push her out of the story. She'd been so fiercely innocent, a startling combination of tough and wide-eyed, and he wanted to protect his memory of her. He needed to believe that, unlike Cal, she had found her way to safety and sanity. He couldn't afford to learn about a meth addiction. Or a bandy-legged husband and six kids, a yard full of rusted car parts. Or a staunch and boisterous churchy life, overinvolved with her congregation to compensate for the swallowed pain. Even this, the PE teacher thing, he'd imagined. The kid had loved doing push-ups, sit-ups, and running in place. She'd been dedicated to tuning her body, as if fitness could ready her for the rapture. He'd often pictured her in gray sweats, her voice echoing in a cold rank gymnasium, a silver whistle around her neck, and this too had saddened him. Coach was maybe a step above gym teacher. But still.

The worst word in the *Oregonian* headline was "Returns." He'd never imagined her escaping this place, had always assumed that for all these years Oregon had held her in its moldy, soggy, specious grip. He remembered that she'd grown up in some small coastal town. That she *had* escaped, and was coming back, made him sad.

How hard they'd run that night. For what? Both of them sucked back to the state.

Ernest left the bathroom, forgetting the hosed-down cat box drying under the eaves outside, and slid into a chair at the kitchen table. Virginia Woolf allowed nothing to get in the way of her meals being served and her box being cleaned, except when Ernest was writing. Then she shape-shifted into another being altogether, a patient and stalwart guardian of his process. She sat upright at his feet, front paws perfectly aligned, head held high, and concentrated.

When over an hour later Ernest put a period at the end of what might be the last line of a partial but decent draft, and said "Huh" with satisfaction, Virginia Woolf meowed once. The cat box! He got up, retrieved it from outside, filled it with fresh sand, and set it down on the thin slips of newsprint, right on top of Delia Barnes.

Basketball. The word gave Ernest a little shiver of distaste. According to the brief article, Delia had been a high school star, going on to play for some famous college coach, a Pat Summitt someone. Ernest couldn't care less about sports. But in these three inches of newsprint he glimpsed a world, a culture, about which he knew nothing, and it was almost enticing, the idea that there could be meaning in that world. He said "Huh" again.

As Virginia Woolf used her freshly cleaned box, gray tail lifting and green eyes glaring, Ernest returned to the kitchen table and read his draft another time, perhaps too well pleased. Tomorrow he'd see the purple bits, mucked transitions, sharp edges, and dull words. He'd read and groan and rewrite. But the poem wasn't bad. It was a good, perhaps a very good, start.

CHAPTER 5

According to Jonas, the girls turned out in record numbers, with over sixty candidates showing up for tryouts. Lots of them dropped out over the course of the first two days, and by Wednesday, thirty-six potential players remained.

At Monroe College, Delia had cut the team every single day during tryouts, a brutal process, painful for those cut early on, maybe even more so for those cut later, but college kids need to have, or at least should be able to handle, clear information about their skill levels. High school sports are a different animal, and Delia tried to bear that in mind. She made the decision to not winnow. She'd keep all the girls who wanted to stay until the last day of tryouts, and then post the team roster, so that no one had to know how soon or late she got cut. This method made Delia's job harder. Some of the girls were quite simply in the way. Their flailing obscured the talent on the court. Yet there were a few players who, over time, showed Delia sides of their skills and personalities that she might not have noticed immediately. By the end of the last day of tryouts, a Friday, she'd picked her likely squad, but gave herself the weekend to mull the final list. She was on the fence about a couple of girls and while she preferred to limit the team to twelve players, it was possible to carry up to fourteen. She told the girls to check the locker room for the team list on Monday and that practice would begin Tuesday afternoon.

Early Saturday morning she sat down at the kitchen table with her laptop, opened the spreadsheet listing her roster of contenders and detailing extensive notes about each girl's strengths and weaknesses. Skills were obviously important, but so were personalities, the ability to work on a team, to contribute to group synergy, and to not detract from that delicate chemistry. Delia highlighted the names of the girls her team couldn't live without. She counted up those names and there were twelve:

Casey Murphy
Lupé Gutierrez
Emma Williams
Isobel O'Brien
Debbie Beekhof
Sophie Murphy
Kayla Smith
Taylor Knight
Kirsten Sorenson
Isobel McPhee
Brittany Wilder
Brittany Nguyen

A tight traditional team. Only the best. She wanted everyone to have playing time. It did no one any favors to carry players who'd sit the bench all season. Still, it hurt to exclude some of those girls who'd run their hearts out, sweat rivers of effort, concentrated with every cell in their brains. Delia hadn't worried about feelings at Monroe, at least not much. She'd worried about winning games, period. But these were just kids, some as young as fourteen, their confidence as fragile as sandcastles, their aspirations as tender as jellyfish.

Delia got up from the table and poured herself another cup of coffee. Now was not the time to start being soft. Jonas had let her know, in no uncertain terms, that he was looking for a winning season. Not just a winning season, but a championship season. The girls too deserved her highest expectations. She'd fueled her way through the past five days, as she ran drills, taught plays (observing who were quick studies), and monitored attitudes, by indulging herself in memories: the sauna heat of the fan-packed gym, the clanging school band backed by ear-splitting cheering, the bouquet of adrenaline and sweat, muscles alive with the joy of perfect execution, time and again, as she'd soared toward the 1998 state championship. While she worked with the girls, she let those memories rip because she knew they were the cocktail for success. She needed to inhabit that mindset, as much as was humanly possible, aiming for it every waking minute, from now until March. It wasn't just good for the girls, and for Rockside, it would save her too. She grabbed Jonas's challenge, another state championship, and held tight.

Dylan's truck purred into the driveway. A moment later her brother came through the kitchen door, gave her that grin of complicity they'd shared their entire lives, and poured himself a glass of orange juice. She'd barely seen him all week, since he worked nights and slept days. He groaned as he sat across from her at the kitchen table. Tall and skinny with pale brown hair, still shaggy like he wore it as a teenager, he'd never had much of a beard and compensated by letting the patchy bits grow. People always said they looked alike.

"Back hurt?" she asked.

"Always."

"I wish you'd try physical therapy."

Dylan shrugged and shucked off his sneakers. "Nothing really helps."

Delia had been so relieved when Jonas hired her brother a couple years ago. Dylan had three children—twenty-two, nineteen, and seven years old—with two different women. The older two girls lived in Tillamook, and Poppy, the seven-year-old, lived in Portland with her mom, Yvette. Dylan had tried to pay some child support to both mothers, but he'd been underemployed for years, taking odd jobs wherever he could find them, chopping and stacking firewood, house-painting, and working as a security guard at Bi-Mart. When their mother decamped to Arizona with her third husband and left the house with Dylan, Delia paid off the mortgage for him.

"When will you learn that your successes have no relationship to his failures?" Morgan had asked.

"Actually," Delia said, "it feels like a direct relationship. He took care of me, and as a result, I broke free, he didn't."

"It's not the money," Morgan argued. "Dylan will never take responsibility for himself if you constantly bail him out."

Morgan refused to acknowledge, no matter how many times Delia told her the stories, that Dylan had bailed *her* out, time and again, when they were children. Even now. When Delia's life collapsed this year, Dylan had been the one who thought of the high school hiring her to coach the girls' team, presented the idea to Jonas, and then welcomed her unconditionally back home. When she arrived at the house on Parker Street Monday morning after her meeting with Jonas, he made her a big breakfast of bacon, eggs, toast, and coffee. In her childhood bedroom, she found clean sheets and a new comforter on the twin bed.

Now Dylan grunted back to his feet and padded into the bathroom. Delia hadn't seen him in a few years, and it pained her to see how old he looked, though just forty. An exceptional, even graceful athlete lurked somewhere under that skin. He'd once been a rising basketball star himself. After the toilet flush, Delia heard the rattle of pills sliding from their plastic bottle, the stream of the faucet, the clunk of the water glass being returned to the counter.

"Still," she said when he came back to the kitchen table, "you have benefits and everything now. The insurance would pay for the physical therapy."

"You're right. I'll give it a shot."

"Now you're just humoring me."

"It's hard to find time for appointments since I work nights."

"That should make it easier. You're available during business hours."

"You have no idea how hard my job is." Dylan sighed heavily. "I've been trying to find something else. Over the summer I applied for a job with the City of Rockside, maintenance supervisor for everything. Basically a desk job. It included a fair amount of driving too, which would have been hard on my back, but not nearly so hard as running the floor polisher, moving furniture, cleaning windows, all the shit I do at the high school. It would have let me get a handle on the pain. Plus make more money. The city manager gave it to some Mexican guy who's probably not even a citizen. I've lived in Rockside my entire life."

Delia hated when Dylan made excuses for himself. "Yeah, I get what you're saying, but come on, I bet the guy is qualified."

Dylan glanced up, almost accusingly, and she felt guilty for not taking his side. He shook his head. "The city manager toes every politically correct line in the book. I've heard she only buys food from a radius of a hundred miles. They have this massive garden and drink rainwater."

"You have to keep on applying," Delia said. "There're other jobs. For now, you have a pretty good one. With benefits."

He rubbed his eyes and said, "I gotta sleep." But he didn't get up.

For the next few minutes, Dylan told stories about his long hours alone in the school building at night, scrubbing away graffiti, disinfecting toilets and sinks, checking rodent traps and disposing of rats, mice, and raccoons. He told her about the nightly surprises, like finding a stash of meth in a teacher's drawer or a wadded love note from one married teacher to another in a wastepaper bin. Once Dylan found a dead newborn in the girls' bathroom. He never mentioned the meth or the love note to anyone, and no one ever learned whose baby it was.

"What were you doing in the teacher's drawer?" Delia asked.

"He'd left some money on his desktop and I thought it should be put out of sight. You have no idea. There's a lot of shit I have to deal with. It's exhausting. Emotionally and physically."

"Yeah. I hear that."

"Be careful, Dee. High schools are crazy places."

"Okay." She forced a laugh.

"I'm serious."

"Okay. Got it." She made a funny face, as if they were still kids, and it worked, he smiled.

"So. Hey. Any chemistry left with Jonas?"

"Jeez, Dylan. That ship has long sailed. You know that."

"You should have maybe stuck with him. Given how things have turned out."

"You have a point." Delia tried to laugh again. "But the man's married with kids."

"Who's not?"

This time her laugh was genuine. "I'm not. Morgan definitely wanted the full-service divorce."

"You get alimony? Shrinks make piles. I bet she's rolling in it."

"Her lawyer was a hella lot better than mine."

"You had a lawyer?"

"No. That was the problem."

"So she got the house?"

Delia nodded.

"That's fucked up." Dylan shook his head disdainfully. His loyalty felt like oxygen. "Well, welcome home. You can stay here for as long as you want. I mean, the kids used to stay in your room sometimes, but they hardly ever visit anymore. So. It's yours. You're home."

Home. For the entire three-thousand-mile drive from Massachusetts to Oregon, Delia had looked for the comfort in that word. The initial *h* like *hush*, like a soft wind, like breath. The long *o*, round and deep, like meditation, like a cave. And the *m*, forgiving like a mattress, creamy like yogurt. The *e* was a stopper, a clean boundary, a silent pause. She'd tried to let the four letters convince her that home was benign.

"Thanks. I'm going for a run." Delia rinsed her coffee cup

and went into her childhood bedroom, with the twin bed, and changed into running clothes. By the time she came back out to the kitchen, Dylan had retreated to his own bedroom. She took a long run along the Siletz River. After showering, she typed up her final roster, listing the squad alphabetically. When she finished, she found herself typing one more name at the bottom: *Mickey Vlasak-Jones.*

All week long she'd watched the girl play. Mickey wasn't bad. She wasn't good, either. But Delia had never seen a more eager player, such desire. A yearbook photographer, Mickey kept a Nikon camera on a bleacher and every chance she got, she photographed tryouts, catching funny moments and grim ones too. The girls loved how she used her big serious camera to document their efforts, to document *them,* as if she were certifying their experience. Still, these were yearbook skills, not basketball skills. There were twelve other girls who were far better ball players, and thirteen was an unlucky number.

Delia printed out the list of thirteen girls and looked it over. She wadded it up and went back to the keyboard to delete Mickey. She'd never had this problem at Monroe. Once she selected her team, it was cemented with confidence. But after printing out the new squad list, without Mickey, she once again wadded the sheet. She added her back in, this time in her alphabetical place, and printed out the list.

Early on Monday morning, Delia posted the girls' basketball team on a prominent wall in the locker room. Practice would begin the next afternoon.

CHAPTER 6

Ten minutes before the start of practice, Delia entered the gym through the school hall door rather than the locker room. It was a trick. No one expected her to come from that direction, so she had a moment to watch her team, unnoticed. Four girls lounged on the bleachers, feet crossed and elbows propped, waiting for something to happen. Isobel O'Brien and Casey Murphy sat on the bleachers too, a little apart from the others, shoulders and thighs touching, watching video on a phone. Three more girls demonstrated dance moves, shouting insults at each other, at center court. At least they were on the court and moving. Only three of her selected team members were shooting baskets: Lupé Gutierrez, Emma Williams, and Mickey Vlasak-Jones.

The lazy girls on the bleachers irked Delia. But even more disturbing were the number of adults sitting in the stands, apparently planning on spectating. Parents mucked up a coach's job, their demands and concerns, and especially opinions, often not matching reality. But in a college program, the parents were rarely on-site. They voiced their issues via phone or email, which made them easier to dispatch.

Delia decided to ignore the moms and dads and grandparents in the bleachers. For now, anyway. They had a right to check her out, and they'd soon tire of the highly repetitive practices Delia had planned for the first month.

She walked out onto the court and let the team notice her presence. Their response pleased her. They instantly quieted, stood up, put away phones, picked up basketballs, looked expectant. She didn't need to do anything as clichéd or unpleasant as blowing her whistle, although she was perfectly ready to deploy that shrill blast if necessary.

"What are you all doing?" she asked quietly in a tone of intentional disbelief.

Isobel O'Brien piped right up: "Practice doesn't start until three thirty."

Delia could never manage a glare as intense as Pat Summitt's, the famously clenched jaw and iced eyes, but she had her own—softer, briefer, probably less effective—version. The tall redhead with lots of freckles and green eyes stood with a basketball under her arm and legs spread, as if she were playing defense, and stared right back. Delia had written *excellent defense* and *rebounding potential* in her strengths column. Her offensive game was erratic, although with her height, she could be a strong asset inside the key.

"No one sits down in my gym unless they're sitting the bench." Delia turned away and didn't give anyone time for a response. "Line up on the end line."

Mickey was the first one under the basket, toeing the line, black glasses askew, arms swung back like wings, ready to give everything she had. That's why Delia put her on the team: leadership.

She ran the kids through three straight suicides, assuming she'd have at least one quitter in those first five minutes, another good reason for having kept on thirteen, but every single girl completed the lung-splitting sprints. She followed up the running with two full hours of drills, nothing but passing, footwork, and positioning. No shooting. Delia made the practice as boring as possible. Anyone not willing to do the work could retire from the team right now. They needed to learn on day one—not with a lecture but with execution and exertion—that the key to a winning basketball team is defense and rebounding. Denying shots and ball possession. As Coach used to say, "Offense sells tickets, but defense wins games."

Delia worked them a full fifteen minutes past quitting time, and not a single girl complained, and more surprising, she heard nothing from the attending parents. When Delia told the team to sit on the bleachers, everyone fell exhaustedly on the benches. They put their forearms on the tops of their thighs, dropped their heads between spread knees, heaving for air, sweat running down their necks and backs. Everyone but Mickey. She remained standing, eyebrows raised, shifting her weight from one foot to the next.

"Mickey," Delia said, "go ahead and take a seat."

"Oh! I thought you said—" She didn't want to contradict the coach, so she stopped herself but still hovered over a bench, looking up questioningly.

Delia wanted so badly to laugh. Laugh with joy at this crazy kid. Yes, she'd said they were to never ever sit except when benched. Mickey must have thought this was a test, to see if they'd listened, or maybe to see who had the most stamina.

Delia kept her face straight and said, "Except when I say to sit."

Mickey grinned, flashing the silver braces, and lowered herself onto the bench.

Delia handed a pile of team contracts to Mickey and asked her to take one and pass them along. The sheet of paper spelled out Delia's requirements. One, showing up on time, without fail, or sitting the bench for that practice or game. Two, giving 100 percent on the floor, in practices and games. Three, eating a strictly healthy diet, including plenty of protein and abstention from sodas and candy. *See me*, the contract stated, *if you need more guidance in this matter*. Delia left this one purposely open to allow for family customs, which she knew she could only nudge, not buck, but she wasn't aware of a single religious or cultural practice that required the ingestion of junk food. Four, getting a minimum of eight hours of sleep a night. Five, perfect attendance in all classes, except in the case of illness. Six, maintaining a C+ or better grade point average.

As she gave the girls time to read through the contract, she studied her team. Casey and Sophie Murphy, a senior and sophomore, quick and wiry players with sharp 360-degree court vision, were both members of the Siletz tribe. Casey would likely be her starting point guard. Tall, gawky, pale Emma Williams was definitely her center. Delia would have cut her the first day of practice, despite her height, but her learning curve, in just five days, had been nothing short of astonishing. And she was only a sophomore. Lupé Gutierrez, chunky with a mobile face, was one of the seniors and would start as shooting guard. She had a strong work ethic and a playful presence. Delia noticed that she masterminded all the team pranks during the course of the first week. The girls called her Loopy. Isobel O'Brien, the tall, loudmouthed redhead, also a senior, would likely start at forward. Debbie Beekhof, a painfully shy girl, lacked confidence, which was a difficult trait to develop. She could be the other starting forward, but only if she stopped apologizing on the court. Mickey, Taylor, Kirsten, Kayla, another Isobel, and the two Brittanys, one Vietnamese and the other white, completed her lineup.

"Any questions?" This was the time she usually got some pushback. *What if I can't help being late because I had to finish my homework? I only need five hours of sleep! Fanta Orange is my lucky beverage! Can you define 100 percent?* The contract made players nervous and most teams cracked jokes about it throughout the season, starting right now. Occasionally a player rebelled, wadded up the sheet, walked off the court. Delia hated those moments, knowing she'd stepped on a habit or problem the girl felt powerless about overcoming. But—and she knew this was harsh—quitters walked away and winners worked through their problems. All season long, the players who stayed would have their own battles with her contract, but the ones who wanted to play basketball, to win games, would talk to her about those problems, would work on solutions. She didn't mind the girls cracking jokes about her strictness, and they always did. Jokes were fine. But she needed each and every player to sign off on the commitment.

No one wadded up the paper. No one walked off the court. No one even cracked a joke. The Rockside girls ate up her team policies with a startling eagerness. Each of them appeared to study every word of the contract, their faces bright with anticipation. Delia had never worked with girls this young, and it broke her heart how badly they wanted to be taken seriously, to be asked to give everything they had to give. Coach always said, "Survive and advance," which was another way of saying play (and win) one game at a time. But right now, looking at her new team and their exceptional zeal, Delia couldn't stop her thoughts from racing forward to the possibility of a state championship, what it would mean for these fledgling souls.

What it would mean for *her*, the return to transcendence.

"Good," she said, as if she hadn't expected questions. "I want the team contract back in my hands by the end of the week. No exceptions. Discuss it with your families. Make sure you're ready to sign on. Know that I will be working you harder than you've ever worked in your lives. My phone number and email address are at the bottom. Shoot me a text or email if you have questions. If you want to talk, we can arrange a time."

Delia let a long silence go by. She made eye contact with every single player. No one blinked. Their chests still rose and fell from the workout.

"Who has a pen?" Mickey shouted. Sophie dove for her backpack on a nearby bleacher. Three of the girls signed right then, without consulting their families, and handed back the sheets.

A few parents had scooted closer so they could listen in on the team talk, and this unnerved Delia a bit. She needed to establish a bond with her players, and she didn't have much time to do it, just a few months. The coach/player relationship is a unique and potent one that exists outside the family. If done right, it respects the girl's will and talent far more than most families do, but the bond has an absolute quality. Delia couldn't afford to have it muddied by family dramas, jealous parents, or know-it-all ones getting in the way of her girls achieving the most they could achieve. So Delia stepped close to her team and crouched down in front of them, spoke quietly now, the soft voice meant to deliver the message that she was talking to her players, not to the parents straining to hear.

"What's on that sheet of paper is the easy part. The sprinting and drills are even easier. The hard part—" Here she let another long silence go by as she looked out to the other side of the gym, as if there were a looming opponent, just waiting to take them on. "The hard part can't be said in simple words. Can't be put in a contract on a piece of paper. It has to be built, day by day, and earned. It's going to make the difference between our being a winning team and a losing team."

Delia waited a few beats.

Mickey's eyes rounded big behind the glasses, her thin neck craned forward, and the words hushed involuntarily from her mouth: "What is it?"

A couple of the other girls glanced at her, and then back at Delia.

"Respect," Delia said, "for your teammates, on and off the court. For the next five months, we'll have each other's backs. Absolutely and without fail. Is that clear?"

She heard some squeaks of assent. All the girls bobbed their heads. Delia paced a couple of laps in front of them, stuffing back a smile as she witnessed their early buy-in. Managing to keep her face straight, she stopped abruptly, as if setting a pick, and faced them. So quietly they could barely hear her, she said, "I asked if that was clear."

They shouted their answers now, a few just "Yes," and a few more, "Yes, Coach," and one, Mickey, ringing out with, "Yes, Coach Barnes!"

Delia embarrassed herself sometimes with the theatrical aspects of her job, but corny as they might be, they worked well this afternoon. She dismissed the girls, and they tumbled off the bleachers, erupting into a giggling mess of euphoria. Loopy started a towel-swatting fight, and everyone joined in. When Kayla began squirting her teammates with a water bottle, Delia thought she'd better intervene—someone would have to mop up the water—but she let them play. They'd earned a bout of silliness.

She turned her attention to the parents, clapping her hands in an overly cheerful way, and told them her plan to run nothing but drills for the first two weeks, possibly four weeks, of practice. She babbled on with a lengthy platitudinous talk and watched their eyes glaze over. Good. Bore the parents out of the gym. When she asked if they had any questions, two mothers spoke up about how relieved they were that the new coach was an experienced player, one complaining that the previous coach had called the girls "ladies" and hadn't expected enough of them. Brittany Wilder's dad introduced himself, saying that he and Delia had been in the same class here at Rockside High. She had no memory of him whatsoever but pretended to remember him well. Taylor Knight's dad, who she did remember, though he'd been a sophomore to her senior, recounted, at great length and with gulping glee, several of the key plays in the 1998 championship game. Jonas was right: these parents were a bit starstruck by Delia's high school and college accomplishments. It was one thing to fantasize, in the privacy of her own thoughts, about her adolescent glory. Yet it was a bit discomforting to cash in on that timed-out reputation. But hey, she'd exploit their goodwill if that's what it took. She needed to shepherd these parents along on the ride to a winning season and that would take its own kind of finesse.

As the girls emerged from the locker room, joined their parents, and left the gym, Delia mopped up the puddles from the water fight and gathered the stray basketballs. When at last she was alone, she allowed herself a whoop of satisfaction. Day one of practice went well. Very well. She grabbed a ball off the rack and launched a forty-foot shot. It hit the front iron and ricocheted back into her hands. She was about to shoot again when she heard the clunk and clang of someone's heavy feet descending from the top of the bleachers. She turned, ball still aloft in her hands, to see a man, white, fiftyish with graying hair at his temples and a round taut belly, jump from the last bleacher onto the court.

"I hear you played for Tennessee," he said.

"I did. Few years ago, though." As if she had to explain that missed shot.

"How'd you like Summitt? Heard she was quite the taskmaster."

Delia didn't respond to the comment that didn't feel like a compliment.

"And you coached at Monroe College for the last few years."

"Yep. I'm Delia Barnes. You are?"

"Mike Foster. Alice's dad."

"I'm sorry I can't carry more girls."

Alice Foster was the fourth senior Jonas had mentioned, and it had been radical to cut her, since she'd played on the team the last two years. But it hadn't been a hard decision. She'd been so lackadaisical, pushing indolent, during all five days of tryouts, that Delia became convinced she didn't want to be on the team. She'd almost asked the kid why she'd bothered trying out, but decided the less said the better.

"So this is an affirmative action kind of thing," Mike Foster said.

Delia understood that an attack was coming. She'd fielded this one before at Monroe. There was always one parent who resented a student of color making the team instead of—or getting more play time than—their daughter.

"I'm sorry," she said, and then regretted the words because she wasn't at all sorry about her team choices, only that he was disappointed and that she couldn't help him.

"I'm not prejudiced, but the demographics of this town are white. You even managed to get a Chinese girl on your team."

"Well, obviously the demographics of this town aren't all white, as evidenced by my team. Brittany is Vietnamese, by the way."

"You have thirteen girls on the team. That's atypical. How'd you choose?" He cocked his head to the side.

She didn't like the bad-luck number either. But her team selection was none of his business.

"Look," he said, not waiting for her to answer. "You're just starting out, so maybe you don't completely understand—"

"Actually, I've coached for twelve years."

"I meant in Rockside."

Delia smiled to contain her anger. "I grew up here. I definitely understand Rockside."

"Sure. I remember you. In fact, my family's hardware store sponsored some of your team's travel. But you've been away. A lot has changed."

"No doubt."

"You got the two Indian girls. You got the Mexican. Okay, the Oriental girl. The Vlasak-Jones kid can't even play. Why is she on the team?"

"Her name is Mickey."

"She could be trouble if someone decided to challenge her gender."

"Why would they do that?"

"Fair is fair. Male hormones would give her an edge."

Delia considered her possible responses. One, pointing out that he had no idea what hormones existed in Mickey's body, nor was it any of his business. Two, pointing out that he himself had just used a female pronoun for her. Three, pointing out that if she "can't even play," then she clearly didn't have any kind of "edge" over the other players.

She simply said, "Again, I'm sorry that you're disappointed in my choices, but—"

"Her mother is the city manager. Real pushy gal. Forever telling people how to live their lives, like what to do with their trash and what language is allowed at city council meetings. The husband is a sculptor." He spoke the last word the same way you'd say *scoundrel.*

"I'm just coaching a basketball team, Mr. Foster."

"Mike."

She didn't really want to be on a first-name basis with him, but murmured, "Mike."

"I don't like it," he said. "The numbers don't work out."

"You mean carrying thirteen players." She knew that wasn't what he meant, he meant *demographics*, but maybe she could steer him onto common ground. "I hope no one quits. But it's likely. We'll have twelve players then. If not fewer. These first weeks are going to be challenging for some of the girls."

Mike Foster hadn't smiled once. But he had been listening, and it occurred to Delia that he seemed more baffled than angry. That didn't stop him from staying on the offense, however. "Why'd you leave Monroe? Seems like a step down from college to high school."

Her palms and soles started tingling, that new heat under her skin, the way it flamed without notice. Diplomacy was 50 percent of her job. She absolutely couldn't afford to blow it again.

"Uncomfortable question?" he asked.

She squeezed the basketball between the heels of her hands. What if she just answered honestly? *My wife left me for a tenured women's studies prof. The college fired me for losing my temper. Rockside, Oregon, is my last resort.*

Delia started dribbling the ball, executing a couple of between-the-legs maneuvers, and longed to make a fast break for the basket. That echoing rhythm of the leather ball striking the hardwood floor calmed her, helped steer her thoughts and the conversation back to her authority to choose the team she wanted.

"As it happens," she said, pulling off a cool, measured tone and still dribbling, "the demographics on the Oregon coast, all over the country for that matter, especially in rural areas, are changing. And changing fast. In any case, I selected my players based on their skills."

"My daughter can hit a three," Mike Foster said. "Consistently."

That was true. Alice could hit threes. Consistently.

"I need players with a range of skills. Physical and interpersonal. Hitting threes is great, but it's not enough. I'm building a winning team and that means choosing a complex mix of players." She may have made a mistake. That three-point shot would be valuable. But she'd calculated that she'd never be able to correct Alice's attitude.

Mike Foster's face flared red. "Interpersonal skills."

"Yes. Team players."

"You're saying that Alice isn't a team player."

Alice was a listless player. She as often walked down the court as she ran. She stood outside the three-point line and waited for a pass. If she got one, and she was open, she usually made the shot. In a game situation, she'd be a cinch to guard; if she had no other tricks in her repertoire, the opponent needed only deny her the long shot and she was dead in the water. When Delia had encouraged her to pass, to cut into the key, to communicate with other players, she smirked. Delia didn't think it was animosity for herself, or for the other girls. Alice was obviously hurting, and likely the source of her pain had nothing to do with basketball. But Delia wasn't the school counselor. She was the basketball coach.

"I'm sorry," Delia told Alice's dad. "She didn't make the cut."

"I think you're making a mistake. A big one."

She wanted to tell Mike Foster that he needed to find out

what was making his daughter unhappy, not threaten the basketball coach. Afraid she wouldn't be able to control her temper, Delia walked away, waving a hand over her head, a dismissive gesture rather than a goodbye.

CHAPTER 7

Ernest worked on the poem all week, each draft becoming more muddled than the one before. His hope that his first draft had finally gotten a handle on the shape of the thing, that he'd at last captured the essence of Cal's rebellion, his escape with Delia, was false. The poem was about a place, about two boys and a girl, but also about so many other boys and girls, and somehow bringing the events and histories together, culminating with a white girl and a white boy and a Black boy in an Oregon forest . . . No, he just couldn't find that convergence. He wanted to show both the pain and the beauty of those last nights, how the two extreme emotional fields were like binary stars, trapped forever in a gravitational loop, never coming together, forever polarized.

On Saturday evening around dusk he crumpled up his most recent effort and threw it across the kitchen, delighting Virginia Woolf. She played soccer with the paper ball, her claws skittering on the floor, her eagerness so intense it made him laugh. Why had he shunned cats all his life? Virginia Woolf performed a full skid, only stopping when she collided with a wall. She thudded softly against the baseboard and looked up at Ernest with dazed accusation, as if he'd caused the smash-up.

The doorbell sounded. What now? For a second he allowed himself the fantasy that Dennis had hopped on a plane and come to surprise him for the weekend. But that would never happen. Feeling bone-weary, Ernest made his way to the front door and looked through the peephole.

Standing on the porch was the handsome married neighbor.

When Ernest pulled open the door, the man held out a plastic container, a defensive look on his face, as if Ernest had been the one to come to his door. Ernest tried to sound butch as he said, "Hello?" But he missed the mark, the register of his voice coming out higher rather than lower than usual. Anyway, who says "hello" with a question mark?

"The cat," the guy said. "I thought he might like the pork scraps from our dinner."

Okay, just weird. Really a stretch for finding a reason to ring the doorbell. Or was Ernest reading way too much into the exchange?

"Thanks, but I have really strict instructions about her diet, so I better say no. No thank you."

The man marched away without another word.

Ernest was not tempted. GQ-level good-looking just read shallow to him, even if the man couldn't help his looks. Even more off-putting was the closet aspect, if in fact he was coming on to Ernest. Just no thank you. To pork scraps. And to a cowardly, skittering closet case. But Ernest *was* lonely. Dennis had gotten a small fellowship for his play-in-progress and he'd been working long hours, excited about an artistic director at Wonder Theater who'd expressed interest in a possible production of the work. When Dennis was writing, he could concentrate for up to fifteen hours at a time, taking catnaps on the floor beneath his desk, then leaping back to the keyboard with an intensity Ernest found almost frightening. And miraculous. For Ernest, two hours of writing was his max. Then again, Dennis would go for days without writing a word. He was currently in a writing mania and Ernest missed him. He hadn't picked up a call in two and a half days.

Ernest FaceTimed Dennis now, not expecting to reach him. But his laptop blinked, beeped, and there was his boyfriend's beautiful face!

"You'd love her," Ernest said, aiming his laptop camera at the gray cat who now crunched down mouthfuls of owner-approved kibble at her bowl.

"You lie. You told me you're allergic."

"I told you I *thought* I might be allergic. So no. It wasn't a lie. I did think that."

"But you're not."

"Not to her. She's my queen."

"Seriously? I've wanted a cat, cats plural to be clear, for forever. You wouldn't even talk about it. One house-sit and you're a bona fide cat lady."

"That pretty much sums it up. I'm sorry, babe. But change is good, right? Admitting being wrong, also good. Come meet her." Ernest had been trying to talk Dennis into coming to Oregon for a visit ever since he'd arrived in late August.

"Uh uh. You're pretending you love her to lure me out there."

"Not true. Check it out." Ernest regaled Dennis with cat stories for the next ten minutes and it worked. Dennis listened with total attention, laughing at Virginia Woolf's antics. He loved just about any animal that wasn't human.

As they talked, Ernest watched their side-by-side images. He himself was tall, not as thin as he used to be, with long lustrous (Dennis's word) eyelashes, and ears that stuck out to the point of seeming to Ernest, when he was feeling insecure, ridiculous. He didn't much like the way he looked, but he was proud of his flawless, smooth skin, and he indulged in an array of moisturizers to protect it, especially now that he'd tripped into the other side of forty. Dennis was only five years younger, but he lorded it over Ernest when he got the chance. He had a wide mouth— which became wider when he was talking freely and excitedly, as he was now about his play—freckled cinnamon skin, and tight well-formed ears that lay flat against the side of his head. His curly black hair was thinning on the top, a vulnerability that Ernest cherished, and also mentioned when the age discrepancy unsettled him. Dennis was basically misanthropic, but that was only because as a playwright he studied the shenanigans of his fellow humans. If you paid honest attention to people, how could you not shudder with horror? His plays were hilarious.

After listening to Dennis's lengthy ruminations about the revisions he'd made, Ernest complained about not being able to write the elusive poem.

Dennis said, "Go find the camp."

"What?"

Dennis sighed, loudly and pointedly. He hated the way Ernest used "What?" as a way to hold space, like erecting an instant miniature wall to whatever comment he was trying to block. Dennis usually countered the stupid word by simply pretending Ernest literally hadn't heard him. "I said, go find the camp. It's probably still there. Going to the actual, physical site of a memory is the best way to find its heart."

"No need," Ernest said, trying another evasion tactic. "It's come to me."

"Gavin?"

"Yeah." Ernest had told Dennis about the evangelical student in his class who wrote seriously beautiful poems about his relationship to Christ. "He came to office hours again this week."

"Probably hot for you."

"Nah. He's constantly running his mouth about some chick he's gonna marry."

"Of course he is."

"He's trying to decide whether or not to go into the seminary."

"And he wants your advice?"

"I guess."

"Suspect."

"Yeah, maybe. He doesn't seem queer, though."

"Prolonged eye contact? Accidental touching?"

Ernest laughed. "No. And no. At least he hasn't tried to proselytize."

"Yet."

"Yet."

"What does he look like?"

"I guess I'd say heartbreakingly homely."

"Heartbreakingly?"

"Dumpy body. Pasty ultra-white skin. Duck-footed." No need to mention the pretty eyes.

"Soooo . . . what? You're afraid his seriously good poems will lure you back into the fold?"

"Fuck off, man."

Dennis huffed. He disapproved of Ernest's ongoing flirtation with faith, sometimes likening it to sleeping with the devil. "You need to see the camp," he said, his tone aggressive now.

"Gotta run. I got a ton of student poems to read for tomorrow's seminar. I'll talk to you later."

"You're afraid that if you step into those woods again, you'll never come out."

"You know what, babe? I thought I missed you, but I don't anymore."

"I meant metaphorically," Dennis said. "But maybe even literally. You need to go and prove to yourself you're okay. Do it for your work."

Dennis was right, of course. A trip to the camp would surely help with the poem. But returning to those woods was the last thing Ernest wanted to do, and anyway, it surprised him to realize that he had no idea, no clue whatsoever, where the camp had been. In Oregon. He knew that much. He and his father had flown from Los Angeles to Portland, stayed overnight in a motel, and then rented a car. The drive that morning had seemed interminable. It could have been three hours from Portland, but it also could have been half an hour. Whether north or south, east or west, he didn't know. The two of them rode in silence, a silence he now realized was a torturously ambivalent one on his father's part. The camp had been his mama's idea, suggested by her friends at church, and she'd insisted on enrolling him. She claimed now that she had never felt critical of her son's "nature"—a bit of revisionist history, but Ernest loved his mama, and if that's what it took for her to forgive herself, he was fine with that. She still complained about not having grandchildren, citing that deprivation as the original source of her struggle with Ernest's queerness. She'd come a long way, though. On their last visit, she'd taken Dennis aside and told him that if the two men were going to have children, they'd better get going. Time, she said clutching his wrist, was running out. As if pregnancy, an actual biological clock, were on the table. Ernest was an only child, which meant a complex combination of adoration and pressure from his parents.

"You're right there in Oregon," Dennis prodded, the excitement about his own writing project making him impatient with Ernest's reluctance. "It's a perfect opportunity. You've been talking about this unwritten poem since I met you. Clearly this is the reason you took the job at Lewis & Clark in the first place."

Ernest grunted his nonagreement. Wrong. He came out here because the college offered him a decent salary to teach poetry for two semesters. Period.

"Celebration Camp, right?" Dennis asked.

Oh lord, he was googling it.

"Wait," Dennis said. "So I haven't found an address yet. But it says here that conversion therapy became illegal in Oregon in 2015."

"All right. Good." Sometimes Dennis could be so literal. As if Ernest were afraid, should he actually visit the camp now, of someone showing him photos of handsome men while popping an ammonia capsule under his nose.

"Hold up." Dennis was still typing.

"I gotta go," Ernest said. "I'm so not prepared for tomorrow's class."

"Yeah, okay. Bye, babe." Dennis clicked off FaceTime, leaving Ernest alone at the kitchen table.

Virginia Woolf sauntered up and rubbed against his calves.

He took a few close-ups of her and sent the best one to Dennis, hoping to distract him from his research, and then settled into reading Claudia Rankine, taking notes, writing scraps of poetry, trying to organize his knowledge into something resembling a class plan. He'd read the student assignments tonight.

A half hour later, his phone dinged with a text from Dennis. He'd found Celebration Camp. The property had changed hands a couple of times since Ernest was a boy, and now another church owned the camp and operated their own summer program on the premises. Dennis was not able to ascertain whether they targeted queer kids at the new camp, but given the 2015 law, he doubted it.

Rent a car, Dennis wrote. *It's only an hour drive from Portland.*

CHAPTER 8

Delia needed access to a big monitor and ideally something better than her phone for recording video, maybe even a student assistant to do the recording. Nothing corrected on-the-court problems faster than seeing multiple examples of the error. She could talk to the girls until she was blue in the face about, for example, hustling back on defense, but when she showed them tape of their slothful ambling, it made a much stronger impression. She found that video triggered a healthy competition among the girls too. Viewing their shortfalls in front of the group, and in comparison to other players, expedited improvement.

She loped down the hall to Jonas's office, feeling yesterday's miles in her legs. She'd been running too much, but what else was there to do here in Rockside? Her hamstrings felt like tight bungee cords and her knees ached. Good thing no one counted on *her* playing defense anymore. And yet she felt so much better than she had walking down this hall for the first time a week and a half ago. Who was she if not a woman who relished a challenge? She felt almost cocky swinging into the admin offices and stopping at the counter. Just beyond, two secretaries shuffled papers at their desks. The older one looked vaguely familiar, like maybe she'd been a friend of her mother's, and the other looked like a young, updated Dolly Parton, only with smaller hair. The latter stood up and Delia decided that the whole getup was purposely ironic, to mock herself and femininity, a kind of reverse goth. Rockside wasn't all bad.

"Hey," Delia said, stanching the urge to flirt.

"Oh, hi!" A big lopsided smile. "You're Delia Barnes."

Last time I checked almost came out of her mouth. Morgan was right: she was a walking-and-talking cliché. The long pause was its own prelude to flirtation. "Yeah."

"I'm so pleased to meet you! How can I help?" The secretary approached the counter, wobbling on tall heels. Usually women who wore heels but couldn't walk in them annoyed Delia, but this morning she found the foible endearing because it was so obviously a satirical performance. Full-figured in her royal-purple blouse and black satin skirt, she was way over-dressed for a job at the high school. She wore no wedding band, plus was definitely not Delia's type, which added up to there being no danger in indulging in a bit of recreational and imaginary philandering. No one could police her mind. Anyway, she was fully single, free as a bird. She could collect a herd of lovers, if she wanted.

"I was hoping to speak with Jonas," Delia said with her best smile.

"There are no meetings on *Mr. Kowalski's* schedule," the other secretary, who was seventy if she was a day, gruffed from her desk. She picked up her phone and buzzed Jonas. "Mr. Kowalski, Coach Barnes says she has a meeting with you."

Delia refrained from correcting her.

The secretary hung up and said, "All right. Go on in. Next time please get on his schedule."

"Thanks," Delia said to the younger one standing across the counter from her. "What's your name?"

"I'm Heather."

"Great to meet you."

"It's so exciting to meet you!"

The older secretary, who'd resumed typing, might have rolled her eyes.

Heather opened the gate between the waiting area and the inner recesses of the admin offices. Once Delia was safely inside

Jonas's space with the door closed, she said, "Okay, so who's the scary one?"

"Which one's *not* scary?"

Delia laughed. "I was asking about the older lady."

"You don't remember Mrs. Riley?"

"Oh my god, are you serious?"

"She had her fifty-year employment anniversary last year. We had a big party."

"Wow. Mrs. Riley. I don't even know what to say."

"I know. It galls her that she isn't in charge of everything."

"I can see that. I'll be extra careful from now on not to step on her toes."

"That would be helpful."

"She calls you Mr. Kowalski?"

"Only in public. Privately, she treats me like I'm still sixteen. She's quite free with advice."

"I don't think she likes me."

Jonas's silence was a confirmation.

"What? Why? Why wouldn't she?"

"She knew us both as kids. It's hard for her to accept me as a decision maker."

"And she thinks you hiring me is inappropriate. A bad decision."

"She did share that opinion with me."

"Wow."

Jonas shrugged. "It's easier to let her have her say."

"On what grounds did she think I was a bad idea?"

Jonas shrugged again. He was right. It was probably best if she didn't know.

"And the other? Heather?"

"That's just Heather. Goofy. Obviously. Fairly competent at her job. This is her second year. Anyway, I'm glad you're here. How'd you know I wanted to talk to you?"

"Telepathy?" What was wrong with her? That was one of

their romantic jokes as kids, their explanation for everything serendipitous between them. They'd loved claiming that they didn't even have to talk, so joined they were by a common way of thinking.

He looked surprised by her blurt, but then smiled.

Delia opened her mouth to correct the overfamiliarity by getting right to her ask for the monitor, video recorder, and possible student assistant, but he spoke first.

"Mike Foster called me last night."

"I'm not surprised."

"So, like, what's up with Alice not making the team?"

"Alice doesn't want to be on the team. She's apathetic, to say the least. I can't get involved in Mike Foster's parenting issues."

"But she's a senior. She's been on the team the last two years. As a starter."

"You told me that Mike was helping coach the team."

"A little. Yeah. But—"

"That might explain Alice starting," Delia said.

"No. I wouldn't say that it did. He'd be fair. But the point is, a few other players who did make the squad are less skilled than Alice."

"What's this?" Delia picked up the top book in a stack on the coffee table in front of the green love seats. *Poker Math for Geniuses*. "You spending time out at the casino?"

"That's not funny."

"Sure it is. The picture of you gambling is actually hilarious." Again, the overfamiliarity. But the idea of straight-laced Jonas hanging out at the casino owned by the Siletz tribe was pretty funny. She flipped through the other three titles in the stack: *Winning Against the Odds, Card Shark,* and *The Upper Hand: How to Win at Cards Every Time.*

"They were confiscated from a student." Jonas stood, tugged on his tie, and moved the books from the coffee table to a spot on the floor under his desk.

"Is there a rule against having books? The First Amendment protects the right to read." She was being obnoxiously challenging, but it was fun.

"I know that. Obviously."

Delia smiled. They'd sat next to each other, and passed volumes of notes, in civics class. Once Ms. Barton intercepted the notes and made them read them aloud to the class. The event was the highlight of the entire student body's week, including Delia's and Jonas's. Even Ms. Barton was able to joke about how the punishment had backfired on her. On Friday of that week, the school paper published the full text of the note exchange.

"Which student?" Delia asked.

Jonas paused but answered: "Zeke Vlasak-Jones."

"Mickey's little brother." And son of the city manager, the "pushy gal," in Mike Foster's words, who did not hire Dylan.

"Yep."

"Confiscated how?"

"This is my problem, not yours."

"So you're going to give the books back to the kid, right?" When he didn't answer, she added, "Even the word *confiscated* is wrong. It implies something illegal. Which books are not."

"He also had dice and cards in his locker."

"Wow. Sounds criminal."

Jonas shook his head at her sarcasm. "This is a high school. They're considered contraband."

"Weapons and drugs, I'd understand, but—"

"Apparently he's been running games in the bathrooms and making a lot of money off of some kids."

Delia laughed.

"It's actually not funny."

"Sorry. But it sort of is."

"In eighth grade he figured out how to build mobile phones. He was sourcing the parts from China. He sold four of them before he got caught."

"Is that illegal?"

Jonas sighed.

"He sounds like a smart kid."

"He's super smart. Aces all his tests. Even though he skips half his classes. He's a problem."

"Okay."

"But not your problem."

"Got it." She decided not to ask for the recording equipment or student assistant this morning. Jonas was all squirrely and nervous. He would say no. She headed for the door, saying, "Okay. I'm off to do some errands."

"The Foster family has been part of this school for years. Both of Alice's older brothers started on the basketball team."

So he wasn't going to drop it. "You hired me to coach. I can explain my choices to you. But bottom line here is that Alice clearly doesn't want to play this year. The reason doesn't matter. You know as well as I do that attitude is everything."

Maybe Jonas didn't know that. He'd never coached, and he hadn't played anything seriously since his freshman year at Oregon State. He'd gotten injured in the first season and never made it back out on the field.

"Would it hurt to add her to the squad?" Jonas asked.

"You can't both ask me to develop a winning team and let some blowhard tell me how to do it."

"Come on. Be reasonable. We're a community. That means a lot of different angles and perspectives need to be taken into account."

That sounded like principal-speak. "Mike Foster's comments to me weren't particularly community-oriented. They certainly weren't respectful of 'different angles and perspectives.'"

"You're putting me in a bit of a bind."

Delia shook her head. "I have to hold my ground on this one. One apathetic—or resentful or lazy—player can ruin a whole team. Her father wants her to play, and that's a problem. For her.

For their family. Maybe for you. But it's not a problem for me. I'm not carrying someone who is there by force."

"I'm asking you to do this one thing."

"You're undermining my authority."

"Jeez, Delia." He paused, rubbing his chin. "You used to have so much humility."

"Jonas!"

"I'm sorry," he said. "That was uncalled for. But . . . I don't know . . . you just seem different."

Delia let go of the doorknob and walked back into the center of the room. In that moment, she would have liked nothing more than to still be that starry-eyed teenage champion, lunging into the future with sky-high expectations. But she wasn't. Not even close. "I'm twenty years different."

Jonas nodded, looked miserable. "I'm sorry," he said again. This was exactly why he never would have made a good coach. He wanted to please everyone. He hated conflict. As a wide receiver he only had to go long, catch the ball, and run like hell. "This must be a really hard transition for you. I mean, with your, you know, relationship ending . . ."

"My marriage," she corrected.

Jonas was twenty years different too. She had no idea what his life experiences had been, other than the basics of marrying Megan, teaching in Portland for a few years, having two daughters, and returning to Rockside to be the high school principal.

"Anyway," Delia said, "you don't make winning teams with humility."

Jonas tucked his chin and looked up at her with his cornflower eyes. He made a little entreating squint, a facial *please*. Delia used to love that expression, the childishness of it, his willingness to ask for what he wanted.

She walked to the window, looked out at the drizzle. She owed him. He'd hired her, no questions asked. And yet, if she gave in to this, her hope for a redeeming year and the possibility of building a healthy team would begin to wash away. She turned, tried to hold on, but said, "How do I make the addition without losing authority with the rest of the girls?"

"You've only had one official practice. Just say it was a mistake. An accidental omission."

"You're asking me to lie to the girls."

"I'm asking you to put Alice Foster on the team."

CHAPTER 9

The hall was full of kids as she left the admin offices and weaved her way through the throng, her good mood having fizzled. That rogue anger came back and she wanted to kick a locker. The satisfaction of sneaker rubber colliding with metal, the pain radiating from toe to ankle to shinbone, she wanted all of that.

"Dude!"

She looked over her shoulder and saw Adam running toward her, pushing his way through the other kids. He waved at her. *Not now, please not now.* She picked up her pace and pretended to not realize he was calling to her.

Adam caught up and bounced alongside her for several paces before speaking. Then, "Dude, I owe you an apology."

She stopped and turned to face him. His pink cheeks matched the birthmark covering half his neck. The gold cross had caught on his collar and swayed there. She managed to speak calmly: "Apology accepted."

"I mean, besides wanting to apologize, I wanted you to understand. You're new around here. You deserve an explanation."

She should have just kept walking, but she waited for his elucidation.

"Yeah, I mean, Mickey has a really good sense of humor. You totally misread the situation. She's good at taking a joke."

"Oh, I see. It was a joke."

"Totally. She, like, went on with her day, right? You didn't see her getting her panties—or should I say boxers?—in a wad over my wisecracking."

Delia decided on silence and started to step away.

"Cow obviously got it," Adam said.

"Cow?"

"Yeah, like *mooooo*. That's what we call Mr. Kowalski."

"That's disrespectful."

"Ah, dude, you're reading everything wrong. He doesn't care that we call him that. For real."

"Thanks for the help. Appreciate it."

"Sure. You're welcome. Actually, Cow is the friendly name. When we're mad at him, we call him Heifer."

Because of course anything female is insulting.

"Anyway," Adam said, "Mickey can hold her own. Trust me. She's the photography editor on the yearbook. She wields that camera like an AK-47. She does not have a confidence problem."

Adam winked before peeling off down the south hall.

CHAPTER 10

Dylan was sleeping. The ranch house on Parker Street had three small bedrooms and a single bath, all on one floor, and there was no place where she could talk on the phone in privacy or without waking him. So when Skylar called, she grabbed her phone and stepped outside.

"There you are!" Skylar shouted into the phone. "I've been worried about you."

Delia smiled at the comfort of her best friend's voice, raspy from years of yelling at her players. Tucking in her earbuds, Delia sheltered under a pine. "Not worried enough to call."

"I just did."

"Before now."

"Beginning-of-season craziness." As a coach at a Division I school, Skylar had enormous pressure riding on her program. She had three assistant coaches and a large scholarship fund all carrying the expectation that she'd make it to the Sweet Sixteen, at the very least, and preferably to the Final Four, although she'd been thwarted in that goal the last several years, a failure she never tired of analyzing.

"I know," Delia said. "You're forgiven."

"What's up? You in Oregon?"

"I sure am." Delia pictured Skylar sitting out on the wrap-around porch of her big Southern house, her two beautifully groomed brown-and-white collies lounging at her feet. She wore her blond hair lopped off at earlobe length, with a short fringe of bangs at the top of her forehead. She'd be sipping the strong, sweet iced tea she drank from dawn to dusk. Though originally from upstate New York, she'd picked up a bit of a Southern lilt since taking the job twelve years ago. The South suited Skylar, but Delia worried about her. She hadn't had any love life for as long as Delia had known her, as in none, no partners ever, casual or otherwise. She hung out with her assistant coaches, and occasionally with the athletic director, and that was it for social activity. Then again, Skylar wasn't the one with a cheating ex-wife, banished to her rural hometown, living with her adult brother and employed by her childhood boyfriend.

"And?" Skylar said.

"I don't miss the snow" was the best Delia could do.

"Can you round out the picture a bit more?"

Skylar knew Delia better than probably Morgan ever had. They'd met when they were fifteen, at summer basketball camp, and bonded instantly, becoming a powerhouse guard/forward pair. Pat Summitt recruited them both, recognizing their symbiotic relationship on the court. In their four years at Tennessee, they developed several signature plays. In their favorite, Skylar drove for the basket, letting the trees collapse on her in the paint, then dished the perfect assist right past their knees out to Delia waiting in the corner, where she'd sink the three. She needed a bit of an assist now.

"The rough ride continues," Delia said.

"Cryptic. Let's start with your team."

Of course that's where Skylar would want to start.

"I'm cautiously optimistic." Delia wanted to say that she looked forward to enjoying less pressure than she'd had at Monroe because it was just high school, but what she actually felt was more pressure. "I don't expect you to visit."

"I didn't say I wouldn't."

"Maybe when the season ends." A few days hanging out with Skylar—fishing, drinking IPAs, basketball gossip—was exactly what she needed. Skylar always knew up-to-the-minute scuttlebutt on Tara VanDerveer, Dawn Staley, Muffet McGraw, all the big-name coaches. "Buy a ticket for May!"

Skylar made a guttural noncommittal sound. Once the season began, she could never think past March Madness.

"Listen." Delia needed to seize the moment because she wouldn't get her full attention again for at least four months. "Something strange is happening to my personality. I feel like I have a brain tumor or something. You know, exerting pressure somewhere particular and causing crazy behavior."

"Shit. What do you mean, brain tumor?"

"Not really. Not an actual brain tumor. I'm healthy. Feel great. Never felt better. Physically, I'm fine. Other than my shot knees. But I've been having these erratic episodes. Crazy mood shifts."

Skylar remained silent. She was as thoughtful a friend as she was a point guard. When Delia didn't go on, Skylar said, "You mean the anger."

"You noticed? I haven't blown up or, you know, expressed it with *you*."

"The thing with your point guard at Monroe. Throwing the basketball."

"Yeah, that. I'm just used to being in full control of my emotions. It's kinda frightening to behave in ways that are unpremeditated."

"Have there been more incidents?"

"No." Why was she lying to Skylar?

"So, cool. I mean, breaking up with your wife of eight years . . ." Skylar blew air out of her lips. "That's bad enough. But the *way* it happened. Of course you feel crazy."

"True."

"And that was only, what, nine, ten months ago?"

"I guess I feel like I should be able to move on. I *am* moving on. It's just . . ." She really should mention slamming Adam against the locker. Instead she veered and shared her impressions of Heather the secretary, trying to make Skylar laugh.

Skylar didn't laugh. "You need to be careful. Where you are. I'm talking geographically. What's the name of the place? Drip, Oregon?"

"A second ago you were being understanding."

"It's just that I know you. You're prime for a situational crush, and those never go well. Ever. Try to think this through: one, you flirt with the ironic Dolly Parton and she's homophobic as fuck and panics; or two, you flirt with her and she takes you up on your interest and then you have to get out of it but you can't because she's there every day at the high school, because you and I both know she's not really your type. Any way you spin it, you lose."

Delia loved getting a rise out of Skylar, but conceded, "You're right."

"Please just remember: you're in Bog Trap, Oregon."

"You keep reminding me of that. Granted, this isn't San Francisco, but it's changed here. I think a couple of the girls on my team are together."

"Change is relative. Be careful."

"I wouldn't mind a dalliance, but trust me, there is nothing for me in this town."

"I don't trust you, not in that regard."

In college, and in the years that followed, Delia had been as promiscuous as Skylar was celibate. It was part of their symbiosis, Skylar feeding off Delia's outrageous stories, and Delia taking refuge in Skylar's abstinence. But Delia had had no wild stories for years, no licentious entertainments for her best friend. Skylar had heard all the details of her first dates with Morgan, of course, before anyone realized they'd make a commitment, actually get married. After that, gossiping about her intimate life with Morgan seemed in poor taste. Nor did Delia want to admit, even to Skylar, that her intimate life had diminished to shared cups of herbal tea and binge TV, the latter at least in bed.

It was on her cross-country trip this fall, just west of Des

Moines, the browning cornstalks towering on either side of the highway, that Delia began to consider the upside to her current relationship status. Her divorce had been finalized and her coaching job terminated. She had no ties to the shackles of marriage, nor to an illustrious institution of higher learning requiring her to be a role model. She was in transit, on the road, driving through farms and heading toward deserts and mountains, accountable to no one, personally or professionally. Not to put too fine a point on it, but she was sexually free. Even to her own ears, that sounded a bit crude. But who wouldn't have had the same thought? Sooner or later. Anyway, she hadn't had sex in nearly five years. No joke.

So there she was, in the heart of Iowa, entertaining full-blown sexual fantasies as she drove eighty-five miles an hour down the freeway, her best playlists blasting. What a strange, wild, billowing feeling that was. After everything that had happened. Alongside her equally strong feelings of hollow despair. The intensity was nearly mystical, a brand-new kind of deliverance. She must have been sweating pheromones, which perhaps accounted for the way people responded to her on the road.

There was the park ranger in Rocky Mountain National Park whose campfire talk on the life cycle of mountain goats wooed her. She chatted with her after the talk, and the ranger invited Delia back to her cabin for a glass of wine, and she stayed the night. In Salt Lake City, Delia slept with a woman she met in the motel fitness room. The most alarming instance of her cross-country sexual abandon took place in a private campground outside of Reno. At dusk a couple invited Delia to help them eat the over-large steak they were grilling on their campfire, and against her better judgment, Delia said yes. After a couple of beers and that steak dinner, Delia asked about the gun rack in their truck, and an amicable argument about the Second Amendment ensued. The husband, who'd been sipping from a flask in concert with the beers, soon passed out sitting in his camp chair. When Delia got up to make a trip to the restroom, the wife joined her and on the way confessed, pretty much out of the blue, that she'd always been curious about what she called "girl-on-girl action." They wandered away from the campground, off into the desert, eventually stretching out on their backs in the sand to look up at the stars. The woman artlessly flung herself on Delia, who worried the whole while that the drunk husband would show up with his gun.

"I got all that out of my system on my drive across the country," Delia told Skylar. "You want details?"

There was a pause. It'd been a long time since Delia had had the opportunity to scandalize Skylar.

"No. I don't. I'm already picturing barbed wire in Wyoming."

"There were three of them."

"Three of what?"

"Women."

"You know, I have something I want to say—"

"What's happened to your sense of humor? For crying out loud, it's just biology."

"Arguable."

For years Delia had tried to convince Skylar that sharing her body didn't need to be on par with showing someone the contents of her journals. Sex could be just sex. You didn't have to tangle psyches and souls. One time she'd tried to make the argument that enjoying sex could be as simple as playing an excellent basketball game, and Skylar had called her bluff. The best basketball games were the ones where you *did* pour your psyche and soul into the mix. You gave everything—emotionally, mentally, and physically. Delia had felt as though she'd revealed a deep flaw in herself, her ability to share her body with another person while withholding her essential self, and she quickly conceded that the metaphor didn't work.

Skylar called her bluff again now. "I don't think this anger you've been experiencing is about the end of your marriage. I don't think you finding, what, three random sexual partners on the road is about freedom."

Whoa. Delia stopped breathing, noticed, and counted her next five breaths. She couldn't snap sarcastically at Skylar when she was being this sincere. Instead, to head her off, she just said, "Yeah. I know."

"I'm not saying the end of your marriage is your fault. Not for a second. You know I was never a big fan of Morgan. But the anger issue started before the marriage ended. I'm guessing it's part of why things fell apart between you. The first time I noticed it was when you told me about snapping at that colleague of Morgan's. It was so unlike you. You'd been at a faculty party and some prof was lecturing you about violence against women and how sports culture plays into that. Remember?"

Of course Delia remembered. The woman said that competitive sports celebrated combat and conflict. In a tone just one notch below shouting, Delia told the woman that she didn't have a clue what she was talking about. That might have been okay—those academic types enjoy verbal sparring, even when it gets contentious—but Delia had followed up with a bit of profanity, and then abruptly left the party, slamming the door on her way out.

"You have an opportunity now," Skylar said. "To find out what's really going on. I have an idea."

"I'm fine. This is a break from real life. A little time to reconnect with my brother. Help some girls get their game on."

"Why don't you go see that church. Where you kissed that girl. Shawna, right? You could even confront Pastor Quade."

Delia had told Skylar, and of course Morgan, even Coach, all the stories from her early relationship with the church, but she couldn't believe that Skylar remembered the names.

"You're a grown woman now," Skylar persisted. "You're an ass-kicking grown woman. You're my best friend. And you're coming apart at the seams because for way too many years you've been trying to prove that you're okay with god."

Twenty-five years, to be exact.

Delia asked, "Since when do you talk about god?"

"Since he busted my best friend's balls."

Delia laughed. "I don't believe in god."

"That doesn't mean you haven't spent all these years trying to prove something to him."

"Him?"

Ernest had written that poem about Jesus being female. She wished she could remember how it went. Those long lashes of his, that insistence on poetry. She should have stopped him from getting in that seafood truck. Why had she stood silently by while he left? He was older, bigger, stronger. She knew that. But it still felt like her fault.

"Whatever," Skylar said. "If you don't believe in god, why do you care what gender I assign him?"

"Because, real or imagined, he has a helluva lot of power in this world and giving him male privilege is just unnecessary."

"He has a helluva lot of power over *you*."

"No. I hear you about my anger maybe reaching back to childhood. Whose doesn't? But I'm good with my nonexistent god, and I definitely don't need to see Quade. I'm here to teach a team of girls to respect themselves and each other, to find strength in their bodies and hearts. I'm here to win a championship."

"I'm just saying a basketball championship is not likely to bring you peace."

"So now you're preaching?"

"I'm also saying that risky sexual behavior on the highway is you being desperate."

Wow. Just wow.

Skylar dug in: "I don't want you trying to seduce the high school secretary."

"Of course not. What's wrong with you? I was joking. How

are Sinead and Blair?" Skylar's collies were the loves of her life.

"You're changing the subject."

"Okay. You're right. My road behavior was irresponsible."

"I just don't want you getting hurt. Or worse."

"No more highway hookups."

Skylar didn't even laugh. "And no hookups in Torrents, Oregon. Why don't you take the opportunity to chill a bit. Rather than speed up, slow down."

"You're right."

"Now you're just humoring me."

"No. No, I'm not. I just . . . I just feel so tired. You're right. You are. I need to slow down. Maybe even rest a little. Somehow." Luckily, Skylar couldn't see the swell of tears.

Or maybe she heard them because she softened up with, "How could you possibly manage to have three affairs in one cross-country trip?"

"It's three thousand miles."

"Oh. Right. I forgot. And the law says a girl can't cover more than a thousand miles without a sexual act."

Delia cleared the tears with a forced cough and laughed, relieved to have the regular Skylar back. "The first one—"

"I have to go," Skylar interrupted. "Practice in an hour. But we need to address the brain tumor thing."

"I told you. Not an actual brain tumor. Look, I'm admitting that my behavior does need to be addressed. But my health is fine."

"You can't afford to behave erratically. You can't afford crazy. You're a coach. Working with girls. Toeing some lines, a lot of lines, comes with the territory."

"Message received."

"No joke."

"I asked how Sinead and Blair are."

Skylar ended the call, as she always did, without any closing remarks.

Delia yanked out her earbuds. She knew Skylar was being the best kind of friend, the one who told you the truth rather than delivering words to tranquilize or placate. Still, the effect was unsettling, as if Skylar had challenged her with an ultimatum.

CHAPTER 11

Delia needed to run. Skylar citing Pastor Quade and Celebration Camp as the source of her current temper issues—fine, call it rage if you want—was as annoyingly obvious as Morgan pointing out her survivor's guilt. Yes. She knew. She'd never forgotten or denied anything that happened that summer. She kept the memories close like a prayer, a factual prayer, an actual prayer, one that in its truth could truly, or possibly, save her. She felt the loss of Cal and Ernest, as well as the foolishness of her childish belief that they were hers to lose, every single day. So what. Did that change anything about the present?

All the shrinks could go fuck themselves. Starting with Morgan.

She'd been waiting all day long for the rain to stop. When it finally did, just after sunset, she strapped on a headlamp and took off. She ran to the high school and did a few laps around the football field, and then ran down Highway 101 to the main drag of town. The saltwater taffy shop, where she and Shawna had nicked handfuls of the licorice and bubble gum flavors, looked exactly how it had then. Don's Plumbing, Rockside Knick Knacks, and DeGiacommo's Pizza also all looked entirely unchanged. Delia turned down a side street to reach the beach and ran along the surf for a mile. The cloud cover pressed low, blotting out the stars, but the waves still splashed bright. Turning toward town again, she crossed the highway, intending to go home, but instead headed down an unpaved road, soon losing track of exactly where she was. As she plunged forward into the wet void, the mud slurped under her sneakers and she ran harder, faster.

That night, running through some other forest, Ernest had spit, over and over again, his saliva stringing down his chin. Once he stopped and sucked on a cupped leaf, rinsing his mouth with the rainwater. At the age of thirteen, you understand everything perfectly but don't quite believe your own knowledge. Life couldn't possibly be what it seemed. It just couldn't. So while she knew what he'd done to gain their freedom, she simultaneously refused to believe what she'd witnessed.

Once, long before they reached the road, he collapsed onto the forest floor. He lay on his belly, facedown on a bed of moss, and heaved long shuddering breaths. She'd tried to lie down next to him, to snuggle against his side, and he'd been kind and slow to move away, but he did move away, as if right then he couldn't bear human touch. She was flying in the sweep of her own fear, and managed it by deciding she had to protect him. She sat cross-legged and assumed watch. The skin on her arm prickled and stung where it'd brushed nettles.

"Ernest?" she said when she couldn't stand it any longer.

He didn't answer and she knew she should wait for his shuddering to stop but she couldn't.

"Are we going to find Cal?" she asked.

Ernest sat up, blinking. He rubbed his hands down the front of his wet jacket.

"*Are we?*" She couldn't keep the panic out of her voice.

"Yes," Ernest said, finally looking at her. "We are."

He meant it. She could see that. He believed so hard.

"How will we know where to look?"

Ernest shook his head. She reached up to pick the leaves out of his hair, but he reared back and wouldn't let her.

Her next question rose like bile: "So he's still alive?"

Ernest lay down again.

Delia forced herself to wait for his answer, to not ask again. She knew he'd heard her, the way his eyelashes fluttered and his lips spasmed.

Then, remarkably, right there among the ferns and mosses, Ernest fell asleep. Those minutes were the worst. Without Ernest's wakefulness in communion with hers, she was left to listen to creatures moving through nearby underbrush, drips of rain falling from branches, the quiet whistle of Ernest's sleep. She was left to think about god. Who had abandoned her. She was cold and wet.

Ernest's breathing slowed. She held her forefinger under his nose but couldn't detect even a wisp of exhalation. She screamed his name and slapped his face.

He jerked upright and clapped a hand across her mouth. "For fuck's sake," he said. "Shut *up*."

"You weren't breathing," she whispered. He was shaking hard, which she knew was a symptom of hypothermia.

"Listen to me." He sat up on his knees and took both of her wrists in his hands. "I'm fine. You're fine too. We're going to get to our feet now and keep moving. You need to be very quiet. You need to be brave."

"I *am* brave," Delia said.

"I know you are. You're the bravest."

His thumbs on her pulse, his eyes embracing hers, nothing had ever been more clear: they were together. They would always be together. It was the obvious answer. To everything. Pastor Bob had been right all along. They were a pair. He would be her person. She knew that her mom wouldn't like the part about him being Black, but they wouldn't have to stay in Rockside for long. She would protect him. He would be hers. Her person. She loved him.

She flipped his hands over so that she was the one grasping him, then held on tight as she got up and pulled him to his feet too. He smiled at her then, and she almost wanted to slap him again. He was too sweet. The abundance of kindness he'd given her and Cal. All that poetry. He didn't know how to flip off those people, like Shawna had. It was up to her to keep him safe.

"Let's go," she said. "I'll call my brother when we get to a town."

"Good." Ernest let her hold his hand the rest of the way.

Delia decided to take Skylar's advice. She picked up her pace and sprinted down the muddy road hoping that it would lead to somewhere familiar, and eventually it did, dumping her onto Highway 101. She ran along the narrow margin, the blackberry thickets scraping her legs as she tried to keep clear of the cars passing in the dark. She slowed, but only briefly, when she came to the bottom of the long driveway leading up to the church. Then she pushed hard, giving everything she had on that uphill bit, as if Coach were watching, deciding whether to start her in the next game. When she reached the top of the hill, she doubled over, her lungs on fire and her legs jellied. She must have done at least twelve miles tonight.

The exterior of New Day Church of Jesus Christ was exactly as she remembered it: two dreary prefab structures attached like an L, the entire place surrounded by an insanely huge parking lot which had never been even close to full. The big *New Day* sign, towering over the parking lot, used to be lit at night, a beacon to parishioners coming up the driveway. Tonight the sign was dark.

Delia let the waves of nausea trundle through. They would pass. She'd learned that pain, all kinds of pain, subsided over time. She pressed her palms against the building's vinyl siding, reached her legs back, and stretched out each calf muscle. Skylar had said to confront Pastor Quade, but touching the church, being here at all, seemed like doing due diligence to her friend's assignment. Overhead, the stars winked in and out of a passing fleet of clouds. Just beyond the parking lot, a forest of Douglas fir haunted the night. She slapped the vinyl siding and straightened up. How could she have let such an ugly, remote building so warp her existence? And yet, even now, she felt drawn to its volatility. Like a hardwired home.

On the backside of the church she found the exterior door to the basement, the *dungeon*, as she and Shawna used to call the windowless room. She twisted the knob and the door opened. Delia leapt back, as if ghosts would fly out, and then laughed at herself. Pastor Quade had never locked this door, so why was she surprised to find it open now? She flipped on the light switch at the top of the stairs and descended. Her visit would be like a vaccination against a stronger reaction, just a little dose of outrage to ward off a full viral assault.

At the bottom of the stairwell, her hand knew exactly where to find the second light switch, and with that simple flip of a lever, she revealed everything. The large room was just how she'd last left it, so many years ago, with the same swirly gray Marmoleum floor, the same fluorescent tube light fixtures, simultaneously too bright and too dim, the same gray folding tables and chairs. Even some of the toys scattered across the floor were the exact same ones from back then. She and Shawna once tried to straddle and ride the toy truck together, laughing as they fell off in a heap. Delia plucked the brown rabbit off a pile of dolls, the "fur" threadbare and one ear detached. It was missing an entire eye. She knew this rabbit. She'd held it as a kid. She sniffed the ragged thing, the smell of the worn fake pelt so familiar she had to sit down on the ratty maroon velour couch. The same one where she and Shawna had first kissed.

Delia lay back, keeping her feet, clad in the muddy running shoes, on the floor, and closed her eyes. Then, what the hell, she kicked off her sneakers and curled up. For a few months that spring and early summer, Shawna had been the center of Delia's life. Her new best friend had a shag haircut and a loud mouth, her right eye slightly higher on her face than her left. Everything about Shawna was catawampus. They had wild fun, tearing around town on their bikes and building driftwood forts on the beach. When one day they found the door to this basement unlocked, Shawna had shouted, "Eureka!" and stampeded down the stairs. The place felt nothing short of miraculous, a warm and dry cave away from their families and out of the weather.

When Delia told friends the story of Shawna, they never believed that Delia hadn't been the one who first suggested they take off their clothes. But she hadn't been. Shawna liked to say, "Let's pretend I'm the most beautiful girl in the world and you're powerless in the face of my beauty." Delia would say okay, and at first the most beautiful girl's requests were things like, "Go get us the Oreos," or, "Tell me Dylan's joke about the bats again." One day, down here in this basement, Shawna grabbed a yardstick and held it up like a scepter, ordering, "Take off your clothes!" Delia followed orders. Nothing happened that time. The girls convulsed in delicious laughter, one naked and the other clothed, and then Delia quickly dressed. But the next time they were kissing, their clothes slipped right off.

Pastor Quade came down the stairs so quietly they didn't hear him. Had he seen them enter the basement, that day or on other days, and purposely snuck up on them? Delia didn't know how long he stood there watching.

He cleared his throat.

The girls startled apart, sat upright and squinted at the man standing halfway down the stairs. He came the rest of the way and flipped the light switch—off, on, off, on—as if he could use the flashing light to erase what he saw. Or maybe he just wanted to heighten their confusion. He left the light on then, the fluorescent pallor yellowing the bright goodness Delia had been feeling moments earlier. The girls yanked on T-shirts and shorts.

Delia had never questioned her love for Pastor Cody Quade. He'd counseled her mother, who just called him Cody, through her first divorce, and he had taken Dylan fishing on three different Saturdays. He took a strong interest in all the church families, keeping the community at New Day close. That year she turned thirteen, Delia had begun to pay attention to his sermons. She looked forward to them. He didn't speak down to anyone,

but he also didn't make it complicated. He was very convincing. He would talk about what it meant to love your neighbor.
How to turn the other cheek. How god had made the heav-
ens and earth. Recently, in her favorite sermon yet, he'd talked
about how god's love is unconditional. That word *unconditional*
went straight to her heart. She didn't have to do or be anything
to have god's love. God just loved her, period. Pastor Quade's
ocean-gray eyes lustered like a promise as he delivered that sermon. It meant that her mom's rocky romances, Dylan's troubles
at school, none of that would prevent god from loving them too.

"Sorry," she said to him that afternoon in the church basement. "We should have asked permission to come down here."
She had no words to address, to apologize for, to even understand
her feelings about what he'd just seen.

"Who are you?" Shawna asked with savory defiance, as if
she had the right to be in this basement and he didn't. She wasn't
a member of New Day and Pastor Quade meant nothing to her.
She cracked that crooked smile of hers and gave him the finger.

The gesture exploded a bomb of silence in the room. Delia
couldn't believe Shawna had done that. She could tell that Pastor Quade couldn't believe it either. No one spoke for what felt
like a full minute. Then, she didn't mean to, but Delia laughed
out loud.

Pastor Quade was a vigorous man with extra-pale lips and
straight dark hair parted on the side. He had a big furious smile,
but he wasn't smiling now. He said her name, "Delia," weighting
it with sadness.

"Let's go," Shawna said, pushing by Pastor Quade.

Delia didn't know what to do, so she started to follow, but
he grabbed her arm. He pulled her to the couch and sat her
down. "Shall we talk?"

"Maybe later," she said. "I'm supposed to be home now."

"You're what, fifteen, sixteen?"

She was surprised he didn't know her age. Then again he'd

never counseled her, never taken her fishing, pretty much had never spoken to her directly. Anyway, it happened often enough. Delia's height made people think she was much older than she was. She nodded, wanting to be bolstered by a greater age, wishing she were fifteen, sixteen.

"I thought you were a nice girl."

"Okay," she said, "I need to go now."

"You will find a boy one day, and not too far off in the future. You're becoming a very pretty girl."

"Okay."

"Can you tell me what was going on down here?"

"Not right now."

He tucked her hair behind first one ear and then the other. His nautical-gray eyes drilled into her. She looked away. Her right hand found the stuffed bunny in the crack between the couch cushion and arm. She pulled it out and held it in her lap.

"I have an idea," he said. "You want to hear it?"

"Okay."

"Good. The last thing you want to do is spend more time with that ugly girl. I'm sorry she got you in her grip."

Delia looked up. Shawna didn't have her in any grip.

"I propose we start with four counseling sessions. Your mother doesn't have to know."

"She's not ugly," Delia said. Shawna's shaggy long hair. The uneven eyes. Her smile always a dare. The lifted middle finger. Delia accidentally laughed again.

"Delia."

The depth of disappointment in the way he said her name gave her a sick feeling. "Can I go?"

"Of course." Quade's mouth twitched hard. "I'll see you to-morrow at noon. In my office upstairs."

Delia jumped to her feet. As she took the stairs two at a time, he called to her back, "You're a good girl. Trust me, you want to nip this right now, before a little adolescent misstep becomes a lifestyle." She realized she had the bunny in her hand, and not wanting to steal, she hurled it back down the stairs.

Opening the door and stepping into the bright sunshine, Delia looked in every direction. Shawna was gone.

That night her mom's new boyfriend stayed over for the first time. Neither she nor Dylan could stand him. They sat outside under the pines, talking about everything and nothing, until well after midnight. She even told him about Pastor Quade finding her and Shawna in the church basement, although she didn't mention that they'd been kissing or had no clothes on, only that they'd been caught trespassing. She also didn't tell Dylan that she had a counseling session with Pastor Quade the next day at noon. He laughed at the part about Shawna flipping him off, but then said that she shouldn't have done that and that Pastor Quade was a good guy. Delia thought they should sleep outside, under the pines, but Dylan said, "Nah," and eventually they went inside to their rooms.

The next morning, while their mom and the new boyfriend giggled over breakfast, Dylan came into her room and said, "Get up. We're going swimming."

She pulled on her suit, then shorts and a T-shirt, grabbed a towel, and they were out the door in under ten minutes. They walked to the Siletz River and continued talking where they'd left off the night before. Dylan was more contemplative this morning and he told her how he was going to get a basketball scholarship to college. He'd be out of the house, he said, in three years. Maybe he'd play for the pros after that. Once he had that big salary, he'd buy a luxury house where she could live too and he'd put her through college. They never did swim. In the early afternoon, as they walked through the heat back to the house, Delia began to wish she'd gone to the counseling session. She and Pastor Quade could have just talked. He was so good at making things clear and easy. She was ashamed by what he'd seen, by Shawna giving him the finger, and even more by her own laughter. She was afraid that when she threw the bunny, he'd thought she was throwing it at *him*. She resolved to go see him the next day.

But Pastor Quade called her mom that evening. Delia listened to one side of the conversation from her bedroom. To her great surprise, her mom sounded pleased by whatever he was telling her. A few minutes later, she came into Delia's room announcing the good news that Delia had been chosen for a church scholarship to attend Celebration Camp. Pastor Quade had described forest hikes, rowing on a private lake, archery and woodworking, all in addition to bible study. She'd spend the month of July at the camp. The church would pay her full tuition.

Pastor Quade had said nothing to her mom about Shawna, the basement, or the missed counseling session. Dylan was right: he was a good person. Besides being pleased about her daughter being honored with this scholarship, Delia suspected that her mom was also happy about having one less person in the house this summer, while she enjoyed her new relationship. Maybe Pastor Quade saw that too, how Delia needed something special of her own for the summer. She and her mom went to Bi-Mart that very night to buy a duffel bag.

Though Delia had looked forward to a summer of exploring with Shawna—riding bikes, laughing hard at everything, a full jaunty couple of months of carousing—the camp did sound awesome. A week later, her new duffel packed with warm clothes, her mom dropped her off at the camp.

Delia woke up on the church couch in the dark basement. Thirty-eight, not thirteen, years old. She did a breathing exercise, then threw off the blanket and felt around on the floor for her running shoes.

Wait. She'd turned the lights on when she came in, both lights, the one at the top of the stairs and the one at the bottom. Someone had turned them off. And someone had covered her with a fleece blanket and pushed a pillow under her head. She dove for the light and flipped it on. She was alone. But clearly someone had been here, covering and cushioning her, darkening the room. Delia closed her eyes and opened them again, wanting to find herself in a different room, a different building, a different town. She picked up the stuffed bunny from the floor by the couch and threw it across the room.

She dug her phone out of the pocket of her running jacket to check the time. It was just after six in the morning. She'd slept the full night in the church basement. Practice started in twenty minutes.

She charged up the stairs and emerged into the dawn light. The rising sun burned through the understory of Douglas fir to the east. Not only had she slept, she'd slept soundly and long.

At least three drivers honked as Delia ran down Highway 101, friendly hellos to the new coach. *Look at that,* she imagined them thinking on their way to work, *she practices what she preaches. How wonderful for the girls.* Delia returned the waves with mustered cheeriness. Every muscle hurt, from yesterday's long run and from sleeping on a bad couch. She breathed oxygen into her bloodstream, imagined it flooding her heart, that muscle at the center of everything.

CHAPTER 12

As the rest of the girls rushed off to the showers to get to their classes on time, Isobel O'Brien kept shooting free throws. Delia needed to get home, drink coffee, or no, probably just go to bed, but she took her time packing up her shoulder bag while Isobel shot. When the gym was empty except for the two of them, Isobel tucked the ball on her hip and walked over.

"You said we could talk to you about anything."

"What's up, Isobel?" The exhaustion, probably coupled with an attack of PTSD, throbbed behind the bridge of her nose.

"Iz."

"Okay. Iz."

"Like i-s. As in, *to be*."

"Very existential." Delia meant to be funny but the girl didn't crack a smile.

"So, like, I need to get something clear."

"I'm all for clarity." Here we go. By the end of the season, every player on the team will have needed to talk about something she considered as existential as her own name. Thankfully, the Alice issue appeared to be stable. None of the players had questioned the late addition to the team, at least not to Delia's face, and Mike Foster had stayed away from practices, though Alice herself remained surly and aloof.

"What's up?" Delia asked again, using a flat and mildly impatient tone meant to convey that she could handle anything Iz had to dish, and also that she wouldn't brook any nonsense.

Iz's face flushed pink. "Myself and Casey. We're, like, together.

So I just need to know if you can deal with that. Because if you can't . . ." Iz looked like a rooster all puffed up with bravado, and yet she was unable to complete the threat.

The pressure behind the bridge of Delia's nose eased—this she could handle—but she kept her tone stern. "Actually, I *don't* have to deal with that. I'm your coach. Not your therapist."

"Therapist? Really? You're accusing me—us—of mental illness? Because the American Psychiatric Association struck that from the books of mental disorders in, like, the midseventies."

Delia looked her square in the inflamed and informed face. "I'm saying that your personal life is relevant to me only to the degree that it affects your basketball playing."

"I have a three-point-five grade point average."

"Glad to hear it." Delia smiled. The kid's passion was adorable.

Delia's smile confused Iz. She was trying for a contest of wills and Delia wasn't playing. Iz shifted her offense, a choice Delia noted with interest. Good instincts. She liked a thinking player.

"I'm your best forward."

"We'll see."

"My uncle works for the ACLU in Portland. If I don't get playing time based on my sexual preference, I could bring a case."

"Duly noted." Delia hoped the kid brought this fire to her game. She'd already guessed about Iz and Casey, and had noticed good on-the-court synergy between the two. It could go either way with couples: a competitive dissonance or a zealous harmony. "Look, Iz. Just play your best basketball when you're on my watch. Understood?"

Iz looked both disappointed and relieved that she hadn't managed to ruffle her coach's feathers. Of course Delia wasn't telling the truth when she said that all she cared about were her basketball skills. Keeping the team emotionally healthy was crucial to winning. All young people want to feel safe, and this team was younger by four years than her previous teams. They were smack in the heat of their adolescence, rather than coming out the back end. Basketball had been the key to safety for Delia as a young person, and if she could give these girls the gift of focus and hard work, the joy of teamwork, then she'd have done her job. Maintaining ironclad boundaries was a basic ingredient.

"Casey said it was okay if I told you." Iz's voice softened and Delia could tell that she was in the throes of first love, poor child.

"Good. Got it. Like I said, my concern is basketball. Period." Delia turned away, leaving Iz gaping at her show of indifference. The kid had been microtesting her authority for days now, reminding Delia of June Kirkpatrick.

CHAPTER 13

Ernest parked his rental car in the small graveled lot in front of the building where Pastor Bob and the counselors had had offices. He could picture them all perfectly. Pastor Bob, the camp director, with his bald head and barrel chest, the way he compensated for his short stature with a loud voice. Maureen, the educational director, with her blond hair hanging all the way down to her waist and her close-set eyes with the pale lashes, the long nose, and lips so thin Ernest always wondered how she could even kiss. Maybe she didn't. Then there was Wade. Just the name was sexy, hard and decisive, but his attractiveness didn't stop there. Wade was so beautiful he seemed like a prop, as if he'd been dropped into the camp as bait, to stir up a frenzied excitement among the adolescent boys so intense it'd backfire, collapse on itself, lead to salvation. Ernest wondered where Wade was today. Dead by suicide was one possibility. Holding court among aging homos in the Castro? No, unfortunately, there was nothing about the man that hinted at future atonement.

Just stop, Ernest told himself. He wasn't here to revisit memories of the staff. He was here, on Dennis's orders, to gather sensory detail about the setting. So he could write the damn poem and move on.

The same handful of jerry-built structures surrounded the big meadow, morning dew sparkling the well-kept grass. The chapel waited, inculpable and arrogant, like a child dictator, directly across the meadow. Ernest couldn't see the cabins tucked up on the forested hillside but knew they were there. He crossed the meadow, expecting someone to stop him, cite him for trespassing, or worse, him being a Black man walking uninvited in the Oregon outback, but he made it unhindered to the door of the chapel. He didn't need to go inside. He remembered every detail of that interior. Pastor Bob at the pulpit. Wade sitting nearby, in shorts, his guitar across his thighs. And of course Malcolm, usually off to the side, often in dark glasses, arms folded across his bony chest, like a bodyguard for Christ. Plus the clutch of kids, confused, sad, nonconforming children overwhelmed with longing. No, Ernest could not step foot in there. Never again. Not even if it meant he wouldn't write another poem in his life.

He tried to call Dennis but there was no signal out here. Of course there wasn't. Only the loud judgmental voice of god. *Their* god.

Ernest liked to tell friends that it was James Baldwin's fault he'd been sent to Celebration Camp. He hadn't appeared obviously queer as a boy and he liked girls just fine as friends. He could have stayed safely in the closet, quite happy just reading books, until he got out of his parents' house. By the time he was fourteen, he'd read the bible three times. His freshman-year English teacher introduced him to Toni Morrison, who split his heart open. The summer before his sophomore year, he discovered Baldwin on his own, just browsing in the public library, and once he did, he read every word the man wrote, all in one month. He passed the books along to the new friend he'd met lifeguarding at the pool, and Joe, a skinny and smart but scared white boy, had liked the books too. The literary conversations, as much as the two awkward attempts at sex, drew Ernest to Joe and led him to write all those poems. Which Joe read and collected for a couple of weeks before dumping them, the entire packet accompanied by a mean disclaiming note, in the Wranghams' mailbox, where Ernest's mother found them.

The part of this story that Dennis liked best was how well the adolescent poems, copies of which Ernest had kept in his journal and still had today, revealed Ernest. He didn't write explicitly sexual poems. He wrote gorgeous notes of longing. They were prose poems, maybe more to Baldwin than to Joe, exposing the brilliant tenderness of Ernest himself.

His mama sobbed her disappointment for three long days. His father, more puzzled than angry, couldn't even look at him for months. Their rejection hurt. It hurt a lot. But Ernest still had Jimmy, as he'd learned the author's close friends called Baldwin, and Jimmy knew all about his pain. Jimmy knew god too, his own god, a fierce and terrible god, but one of love, and Ernest had never quite been able to move away from Baldwin's complex expression of divinity.

Ernest hiked up the short trail to the campfire circle. It was still there, the rings of wooden benches, the stone firepit. The nightly campfire had scared him, especially walking up that trail in the dark with only a flashlight to ward off the nocturnal demons. Sometimes the fire blazed too big—Wade loved to pile on logs—and the boys and girls sang overloud, their full-throated voices announcing terror and innocence. There'd always be a rustling in the undergrowth at his back. He'd almost believed the rumor that the previous summer a kid had been dragged away from the fire ring by a bear.

Ernest hadn't dared bring his Jimmy with him to Celebration Camp. Not after what had happened with Joe. So instead, during those weeks at camp, he calmed himself by reciting Shakespeare. The same freshman-year teacher who gave him Toni Morrison had made him memorize whole passages from the Bard's plays and Ernest was grateful. Sometimes, sitting at the campfire, he imagined turning the drama before him into a playful, gender-bending *Midsummer's Night Dream*. In his mind, he danced Delia and Cal, even Wade, in and out of the firelight, assigned them rhyming lines and Elizabethan costumes.

Ernest sat on one of the log benches and found himself doing that now, as if he were sixteen years old again, as if a fire roared at the center of everything. Today, though, he recited *Macbeth* and out loud. He shouted it, in fact. That's right, he was a trespassing queer Black man. Deal with it.

Ernest dropped his head into his hands and wondered about his sanity. Why hadn't he waited until Dennis visited to come to this place? Why had he come all alone?

He jumped to his feet and ran back down the trail toward the meadow so quickly he tripped, fell, and muddied his hands and the knees of his jeans. He cursed and then cried. Cried hard.

Sitting back on his heels and wiping his face with his handkerchief, Ernest decided that Dennis was right about god and Jesus. The big ruse. Or, to use Dennis's words, Western civilization's mindfuck. Okay, so that's why Ernest had come here today. To see, once and for all, that nothing changes. Ernest had certainly forgiven his parents, and even his childhood church, but there was no forgiving an entire religion that let this happen. A church that didn't make reparations. He tried calling Dennis again, hoping that being partway up the hillside would put him in line with a tower and signal. It didn't.

Things couldn't get any more unpleasant, so Ernest decided he might as well go see the pond. He got to his feet and walked the rest of the way downhill and along the path. The pond, too, was exactly as he remembered it. He stood on the bank as a northerly wind rippled the water's surface. A fleet of wooden rowboats rocked against the dock at the end of the pier, the oars neatly crossed inside each one. If Ernest climbed into one and rowed out on the pond, a case for theft could be added to the one for trespassing. It would be stupid. But he did it anyway, surprised by the pleasure he felt in the weak sun on his shoulders, the long stretch in his back as he pulled the oars through the pond water.

Ernest could picture Cal perfectly with his mouth so red and voluble it was like a cut, his dove eyes and pixie smile. Cal had been the one rowing that day, which was funny because he was the littlest, least athletic of the three, and this had made them all laugh. Delia—grinning, eagle-eyed and apple-cheeked—sat next to Ernest on the facing rowboat bench. Cal was telling his friends that he was going to train to be an astronaut, detailing exactly how he'd get into NASA, and he spoke of this with complete candor, believing it, and Ernest almost believed it too, because Cal was like that, a little unrealistic, but with surprising and often hidden gifts. He was much smarter than he let on, as if his intelligence were something it was best to hide alongside his sexuality. Maybe all that earnest desire might just be enough to carry him into space.

Delia, more practical than either of the boys, laughed out loud at Cal's aspirations. It was a laugh completely devoid of rancor, more like a surprised wonder at the kid's ability to dream so absurdly. Then her face went abruptly slack and ashen.

"What?" Ernest and Cal asked simultaneously.

"Jinx," Cal said.

"That's my pastor," she said. "What's he doing here?"

"Don't look," Ernest told Cal, who'd already started to swivel in the direction of shore. Ernest's father had taught him this: Never give adversaries an ounce of your attention. Ignore them completely.

"Is he looking at us?" Cal asked, having obeyed Ernest's request.

Delia nodded and asked again, "Why is he here?"

"Checking up on you," Ernest said. "Your progress."

Ernest has never forgotten the look on her face then. That moment when you realize your trust has been misplaced. A smile overlaid with disorientation. She was only thirteen. That man standing on the shore had told her she was queer before she'd even known she was.

"To be, or not to be, that is the question," Ernest said.

Cal guffawed.

His tactic worked. Delia looked away from the pastor and at Ernest. She arched an eyebrow and almost smiled. "What?"

"You heard me." Ernest put an arm around Delia and gave her a sweet kiss on the lips, not so brief as to look sisterly but nothing that could be called too sexy, either. "Act like you loved that," he said. "Wiggle your shoulders a bit."

"Likely he's racist too," Cal said. "So."

"Oh. True," Ernest said. "Shit. Now I've probably compounded your problems."

But he'd succeeded in distracting Delia. She grabbed his cheeks, kissing him again on the lips. All three of them laughed.

"Delia! Hello!" Pastor Quade's voice skittered across the water. He gestured for them to come to shore.

"What are we supposed to do now?" Cal asked, the oars still in his hands. When neither of the other two answered right away, Cal started to go on with some nonsense about rowing to China, so Ernest stood up, rocking the boat, and gestured for Cal to switch places with him. They didn't have a choice. The sooner Delia dealt with the pastor, the sooner it'd be over. Ernest took the oars and rowed them to shore.

As they approached the dock, Cal said, "I love you. You're so much tougher than me. You'll be fine."

"No," Delia said. "I *want* to talk to him."

The look on her face now scared Ernest, as if something fearsome brewed in the pit of her. He put one foot on top of hers and the other on top of Cal's. He said, "I love both of you."

The two boys stayed in the boat as Delia climbed out. *She'll be all right*, Ernest told himself, as the girl added butch swagger to her walk down the pier. What he loved about her was that it wasn't defiance. It was authentic. She was a natural. She was just a kid, but she had a pure kind of resolve that he wanted for himself. "She'll be all right," he said out loud.

Maybe the poem was about those moments on the pond. Ernest sat in the rowboat, alone, bobbing among some reeds a hundred yards from the dock and pier, with his pencil and notebook. He wrote for over an hour.

CHAPTER 14

The girls lost their first game to a team with half their talent. Riding back to the high school on the team bus, Delia was furious. She knew the source of the problem and it was one she hadn't handled well. When she got the job at Monroe College, Coach Summitt had given her lots of advice, but the most important had been to guard against bad seeds and whispering campaigns. Demand full transparency on all grudges and complaints. Without air, they became toxic to a team.

None of the girls had complained about the late addition of Alice to the roster, and so Delia had assumed they were okay with it. After all, Alice had been their teammate the previous two years and Delia had insisted on team loyalty. But maybe she'd insisted too hard. Just because the girls were bucking up under the situation didn't mean that Alice wasn't sowing discontent. She'd been anything but cooperative when Delia, on the day following her meeting with Jonas, pulled her out of class and simply said, "I've decided to add you to the team."

They stood alone in the hallway and Alice looked off to the side with haunted pale brown eyes. Her long tangled hair was the color of graham crackers, her lips chapped, and a few pimples dotted the plane of her large white forehead.

She said, "My father made you."

"You have a deadly three-point shot. But a bad attitude."

"There are things in life more important than basketball."

Well, obviously, Delia wanted to say. What she did say was, "I actually disagree."

"You can't be serious," Alice scoffed.

"I am."

"It's just a game."

"It's a game based on cooperation and precision and good health and hard work."

Alice stared down the hall and struggled to maintain her mask of defiance. She was listening. Maybe she even thought the statement contained truth. But she relapsed into, "Whatever."

"On my team, that response is never allowed."

"My father is making you."

"It's true that your father spoke to me. He wants you on the team. His wishes aren't enough, though. *You* have to want to be on the team. Do you?"

The next long silence was uncomfortable for both of them. Alice still refused eye contact. She eventually spoke in a whisper: "Yes."

"Good," Delia said, trying to disguise her surprise. "Because I have a brilliant idea. I know you started last year, but I don't think I'll start you this year." The kid actually looked relieved. Maybe it was a severe case of performance anxiety? "I'd rather use you as the sixth player. Do you know that term?"

Alice glanced in both directions, as if looking for an escape route.

"The sixth player," Delia explained, "is the first player to come off the bench. Often she has a specific power skill. Yours is the three. Nobody's expecting a player coming off the bench to hit threes as consistently as you can. So I play my starters until the moment I need a few quick surprise points. That's when I put you in."

Now Alice looked positively terrified, so Delia figured she was right about the performance anxiety diagnosis. "Yeah, there's a lot of pressure on the sixth player. But if you trust me, I promise I can make it work."

A big ask, especially for this girl. "Whatever."

Delia let her have that last prideful word.

Since then she'd been unpleasantly indifferent during practices. The source of her attitude might have been performance anxiety, but that didn't make the girl's behavior any less lethal to team dynamics. Worse, Delia had no leverage, couldn't kick her off the team, so she'd chosen to ignore her. At Tennessee, being ignored by Coach Summitt was the worst possible fate. It meant she didn't care enough to even get mad at you. Delia didn't intend to be callous or mean toward Alice, but squaring off with her hadn't worked and Delia hadn't been able to think of another approach.

But that was her big mistake. And she knew better. The others had to resent Alice's presence, and no doubt they'd guessed, or even outright knew, the reason she'd been added to the team. Or just as damaging, Alice had started to convince them that "there are things in life more important than basketball." Delia should have sat everyone down right away, when Alice first arrived that second day of practice, and said *something* honest about why she was being included.

The bad-seed theory could explain most of the problems at today's game. Loopy didn't show up at all because she had a shift at Safeway where she worked as a bagger. Why should she show up when Alice did so only in body but never in spirit? Iz's performance was erratic, and Delia might have been imagining it, but it seemed like she was refusing to pass to Casey's new girlfriend, Kayla. Again, acting out was allowed with Alice, so why should Iz hold back? Emma came to the game but claimed to have the flu. Delia supposed she couldn't blame the flu on Alice, but she knew the team's chaotic distraction today was a result of poor morale, and *that* she did blame on Alice. No one gave 100 percent. Some didn't even give 50 percent.

Delia wanted so badly to channel Coach. There'd been that time, when Tennessee lost a game they never should have lost, when Coach shouted at them the whole way home on the bus. Then, though it was past midnight when they got back to the university, she made them put their sweaty uniforms back on and gather in the gym. She had them run suicides and drills for a full two hours before releasing them to their dorms. The university president had called her in the next day and told her she'd gone too far, and Coach had apologized to the team. "No," Delia told her at the time, "we deserved it." All the girls agreed. They would have dragged their bellies across gravel for Coach Summitt.

Morgan hated that story. Whenever she heard it, she took the opportunity to deconstruct the word *loyalty*, suggesting that Coach Summitt, if not Delia herself, was an autocrat.

"You worship that crazy dictator lady," Morgan had said shortly before their breakup. "It's like she's a religion." She paused and then added, "A substitute religion."

"Give it a rest," Delia said. "I'm not your client."

"Loyalty can be dangerous," Morgan continued, as if they were talking about fascism rather than athletics. "I mean, it's almost perverse to ask that of young women or girls. Haven't we been fighting our whole lives for independence, the right to think our own thoughts and be the agents of our own choices?"

Maybe Morgan was right. About everything. Maybe Delia had made all the wrong choices her whole life. As the team bus pulled into the high school parking lot, Delia stayed seated, stewing in the back of the bus, feeling as if her entire worldview was disintegrating.

The booster bus, full of Rockside fans who'd traveled to the away game, parked behind the team bus. The fans gathered around, solemn as a funeral, while the players unloaded themselves and their gym bags. Delia managed to keep herself in check, simply announcing, "Tomorrow at three thirty. Don't any of you dare be a second late."

Everyone looked exhausted at practice the next afternoon. Debbie Beekhof and Brittany Wilder stumbled into the gym, their untied shoelaces flying. Loopy Gutierrez hopped onto the court on one foot as she fitted her warm-up pants over the other foot. On top she wore only a sports bra, her practice jersey slung over her shoulder. As she struggled into her shirt, everyone laughed, and some of the tension broke. Of course Iz O'Brien and Mickey Vlasak-Jones, as well as Casey and Sophie Murphy, were all on time, dressed, and running the layup drill without being told.

Delia wished she could see the humor in her team's attempt to overcome their disarray. But she was still furious and hadn't slept. She ran a humorless, extra-strict practice. She noticed a few of the girls exchange looks, as in, *What's up with Coach Barnes this morning?* as if they didn't know how poorly they'd played. She finished the practice with double the usual number of suicides. Then she said, "Team meeting in the locker room."

She needed to talk to them somewhere private, away from the waiting parents, where they might actually divulge what plagued them. As she followed the girls to the locker room, the daytime custodian, who'd begun dust-mopping the perimeter of the gym, gave her a little salute. "Tough game, Coach."

She stared at him for a second, taking in his wispy ponytail, tie-dye T-shirt stretched over part of his hairy belly, and the gray drawstring sweatpants. She closed her eyes and simply shook her head. She didn't know how she was going to contain this buzzing, this sense of crazed anger at her team. At Alice.

As the girls clamored onto benches in the locker room, Delia paced. The cold grotto smelled like body lotion and disinfectant. Two nights ago, Dylan had decorated the dressing area with forest-green and white streamers and balloons in anticipation of the first game, and these were still festooned about.

Mickey climbed up on the far end of the bench, raised her big Nikon to her face, and snapped about five pictures, all probably capturing Delia's expression of incensed dismay.

"What are you doing?" Delia almost shouted.

"Yearbook," Mickey said.

"Yes, I know you're a yearbook photographer, but this is hardly how I'd like us to be remembered. Yesterday was a disgrace."

Iz huffed. "She's not just *a* yearbook photographer. She's the photography editor. And a kickass photographer. This is about representation. The boys' teams always have more pictures in both the paper and the yearbook. Besides, you can't just gloss over the bad moments."

"Thank you for your input," Delia responded, and then to Mickey, "Get down and put the camera away."

Mickey took a seat next to her teammates and cradled her camera, as if she might decide to redeploy its powers at any moment. What had happened to their attitudes since that first week during tryouts, when every single girl followed her instructions to a tee?

"In your locker." Delia pointed at the camera.

"Wow," Iz said quietly.

Mickey opened the empty locker right behind herself and put the camera on the shelf, and then left the door open.

"A couple of the girls could shoot," Delia said. "But that's about it. They had no defense. No offense, for that matter. We should have won by double digits."

Loopy blurted, "I'm sorry I missed the game. I can't tell you how hard I tried to get my supervisor to let me off. She wouldn't."

Delia had already spoken to Jonas about Loopy. She was a starter. A team leader. A good kid. But how could Delia let her break the rule of never missing practices, and now a game? How could she allow these absences for one player and not others? Jonas told her that Loopy had four younger siblings at home and her dad had recently gotten laid off. She needed the job at Safeway.

"Emma had the flu," Sophie said, and then glanced at her older sister, Casey. Delia noticed Casey's brusque headshake to silence Sophie. She also noticed that Emma's flu had been announced too many times already.

"You wouldn't even pass to me," Kayla said, leaning forward to speak directly to Iz. "Grow up."

Casey rolled her eyes. Delia didn't want to talk about Casey's breakup with Iz and new romance with Kayla, all of which had been obvious to Delia during the last couple weeks of practice. These were high school girls, and this was the Oregon coast. She was pretty sure no one considered it in her job description to discuss the trials and tribulations of young queer love with her team.

Emma sniffled back tears. Iz put an arm around her. Taylor leaned across two other girls to take her hand and hold it. If she had the flu, what was she doing here infecting everyone else? Why were all the other girls being so solicitous to her?

Mickey raised her hand.

"What?"

"I'd like to take just a couple of pictures. Iz is right. If I'm going to capture the full story of our team's season, it's important to show our low points too." She circled her palms in the air to indicate the gloomy tableau of the seated, losing team.

"No," Delia said.

Loopy bent to pick up a stray safety pin. She used the pin to pop a balloon, startling everyone. She said, "Ha!" and popped three more.

The girls laughed, encouraging Loopy. She jumped up on the bench. "Come on. Lighten up, everyone. Wait, wait. Watch. This is the Mop." From the bench top, she demonstrated the dance move. "Got it? Everyone now! Come on, Coach, it's like a group synergy exercise. Or want me to go again first?"

"Stop," Delia said.

Emma's sniffling ripened into full-on crying.

"We'll do better next game," Mickey announced, her eyes looking extra magnified behind the thick-lensed glasses.

"Why do I get the feeling what happened at the game yesterday is about something you all aren't saying?" Delia looked right at Alice. The new silence was as heavy and cold as the cement floor. "I can wait all afternoon. We're not going anywhere until someone tells me what's going on."

"Check it out!" Loopy again. "I can show you the Dougie. Start in the perfect defensive position. It's like basketball, Coach. Watch. Then bend your left knee, just a little, moving your torso to your right."

When Debbie Beekhof, of all people, and Sophie Murphy joined Loopy on the bench, doing the Dougie, Delia knew they were employing a full-court press to hide something.

Delia blew her whistle.

"Jesus!" Iz said. "Chill."

"What did you say?" Delia glared.

"I mean, they're just dancing," Iz said.

"Whoa," one Brittany said.

"Yeah, whoa," the other Brittany agreed.

Loopy, Debbie, and Sophie took seats on the bench.

"The bus leaves in fifteen minutes," Taylor pointed out.

"Then you better start talking," Delia said, glad to have a distraction from a standoff with Iz.

Debbie whined, "We're tired."

"Yeah," a few of the girls chorused.

Delia looked at her team for a very long moment and decided not to mention the energetic Mop and Dougie demonstrations. Instead she said, "Tired? How old are you, Debbie?"

"Uh, seventeen?"

"You're guessing?"

Debbie raised her hands, palms up. "What?"

"You said, *Seventeen?* with an *uh* and a question mark." Delia waited.

"I'm seventeen."

"You, Brittany?"

The two Brittanys looked at each other and then back at Delia.

"Wilder."

"Fifteen."

"Nguyen."

"Fifteen."

"Iz." Delia jabbed a finger in the direction of her starting forward.

"I'm seventeen. What's your point?"

She really could do without Iz's backtalk. "My point is that you girls are seventeen, sixteen, fifteen. And you're telling me you're tired. Worn out by one basketball game. Do I have that right?"

"You have us run, like, a hundred times more suicides than the boys run," Sophie had the nerve to say. "Every practice."

The girls were glancing at each other. There was definitely something they were not disclosing, and it wasn't about any team romances or hard workouts.

"My shift starts in ten minutes," Loopy said. "It takes me twenty minutes to walk to Safeway." She grabbed her gym bag and left the locker room.

"Ew," Casey said. "She didn't even shower."

Kayla grinned at Casey. Iz stood and kicked a wall.

Delia closed her eyes and squeezed the basketball in her hands to keep herself from hurling it. "Alice. Maybe you can tell me what's going on."

The pale girl, whose acne was especially bad this week, arranged her favorite facial expression of insolence and met Delia's gaze, held it, and didn't speak.

"Okay," Delia said quietly, "back to the gym and get on the end line."

They looked stunned. No one moved.

"Now!" Delia shouted, and they lurched off the bench and out the door to the gym.

Delia stayed behind, pacing the locker room for a couple of minutes. She tried to clear her anger, but it stayed in her chest like a tumor. It had been so kind of Dylan to decorate the locker room for their first game, and she tried to bring her emotions in line with that goodness. She couldn't. She tore everything down, every last streamer, all the balloons, and stuffed them into the big metal garbage pail.

When she got out to the gym, the girls were already running a suicide. Delia stood with her arms crossed and quietly ordered, "Again," when they finished that one. She ran them through five of the sprints. Then she had them each shoot ten free throws. Finally, she told the team to go out in the rain to the track and run a mile.

"Nope," Taylor Knight said, and headed for the locker room. Kirsten Sorenson followed. Her first insurrection. It was bad. But not that bad. She had fourteen players and neither Taylor nor Kirsten were starters.

Then Mickey shot off the court too, and Delia's heart sank. She was her most fervently diligent team member. She wasn't a great ball player, but she loved the game and consistently encouraged everyone on the team. She'd even written a team song which the girls sang in the locker room after every practice. Mickey was her best hope at salvaging morale. And now she was leaving too.

But no. Mickey grabbed Taylor's and Kirsten's wrists and pulled them away from the locker room door and back onto the court. As the rest of the girls made their reluctant way to the door leading to the outside and down to the track, Mickey pulled the two defectors along. They stumbled, pretended to resist, but allowed themselves to be drawn back into the team. Once outside, all the girls huddled around the faltering ones, and like whales propping up the weak, they trundled down to the track.

Delia followed and stood in the rain watching the girls do their mile. Alice was the surprising frontrunner, as if she was trying to prove something, like her innocence. Mickey clapped her hands and shouted, "Let's go, let's go, let's go!" Casey exuded sexuality even as she ran and Delia wondered how many girlfriends she'd go through during the course of the season, and how much havoc that would wreak on team dynamics. Iz kept herself apart from the others, bereft but proud, head held high as she ran.

On the second lap, Emma collapsed, falling onto her hands and knees, facedown on the black rubber track surface. Several girls noticed, and they turned around to collect her. With Mickey on one side of Emma and Iz on the other, holding her arms, they stumbled through the last two laps. Delia circled her hand in the air above her head to call the end of practice. She and all the girls were drenched, their hair wet ropes and their sneakers squeaking out tears of rainwater. As the girls panted up the hill to hit the hot showers, Delia walked directly to her car and drove home.

She knew she was overreacting to a game loss. She knew that Morgan would say her feelings of freefall were about her night in the church basement last week. And Morgan, of course, would be right. The fact of that night appalled Delia. The most disturbing part was how deeply and easily she'd slept, as if her body still considered that building home. But not being in denial, knowing the source of her chaotic sadness, did not change how she felt about losing this game. Winning had always been her drug of choice. This loss just felt unbearable.

Delia spent all evening researching the best high school teams and players in Oregon and watching clips of their play. She found a lot of material and delved deep into her study of how to beat these toughest competitors. It was satisfying work, and miles above her pay grade, but she didn't care. She even watched interviews with the coaches of the best girls' teams in the state and listened carefully for hints about their strategies, laughing out loud sometimes at how transparent some were. This was just high school and getting the attention of a microphone and a rolling camera meant more to some of these blowhards than winning. By ten o'clock, Delia had pages of notes.

She hadn't eaten dinner. Her hunger made the shakes, the tremor in her hands and feet, even worse. It'd migrated to her core, making her feel as if her lungs were humming. She needed some nourishing, delicious food. She needed some serious self-care. Delia drove to Safeway and sat for a minute in her car in the parking lot. Skylar was wrong: returning to the church had not been a good idea. If that was supposed to have calmed this new beast of anger, it'd done the opposite.

Food first. Then sleep. Good biology made for good mental health.

Safeway was soothingly quiet at this hour, and Delia rolled her cart into the produce section. She stopped first at the navel oranges, weighing a few in her hand to determine juiciness. She selected four. Then she gently pressed the pointed ends of a few avocados until she found two perfectly ripe ones. She added a bunch of kale and some leafy-topped organic carrots to her cart, then went back to the oranges. She should get more. Dylan loved oranges.

As she lifted one, again checking the skin for blemishes and the weight for ripeness, her phone whistled in a text message. Skylar! No one else would text her this late at night. Delia dropped the orange in her shopping cart and dredged her phone out of her shoulder bag. She wanted to hear Skylar's voice, so she ignored the text and called her best friend.

"Wassup?" Skylar slurred sleepily. "You okay?"

"Oh. No. I mean, you just texted me. I mean." Obviously she *hadn't* just texted her. It was two in the morning Skylar's time, and while her friend kept unconventional hours, even she would be asleep now. "I'm sorry. My mistake. I'll call you tomorrow."

"Unh," Skylar grunted before disconnecting.

Delia looked at the text message and didn't recognize the phone number. *Welcome back to Rockside! A couple of your*

*team members are in my congregation. Come by and say hi
sometime.*

At first she had a cold, rational reaction. Of course he'd reach
out. She'd fallen asleep in his basement. He'd have to prove, all
these years later, his goodwill. Or his righteousness. Or just his
survival. But how'd he get her phone number? Which players
were in his congregation?

Delia thought she was in control of herself. She mentally
ticked off what she needed: food, sleep, and tomorrow an apology to her team. She needed to keep her eyes on the prize. That's
what her brain did.

But her hand hoisted an orange from the display pyramid.
Her arm cocked back and fired the fruit across the produce section. It hit the side of a pile of onions, which tumbled to the
supermarket floor, making a jumble of soft thudding sounds.
She needed a splat, though, and so she took another orange, se-
lecting a molding one, and heaved it against the linoleum floor.
The rind split and the orange smashed. A nearby woman, who
looked like twigs in baggy clothes, jerked with shock and shoved
her cart around the boxed and prewashed greens to disappear
into the safety of another aisle. A muscular man wearing camo
shorts and a sleeveless T-shirt, his limbs fully tattooed, with two
toddlers seated in his shopping cart, grinned at Delia and waited
to see what she'd do next.

It took all her willpower to not sweep the apples—Red
Delicious and Granny Smith and Honey Crisps, all stacked in
color-coordinated sections—off their table. Or to not heave but-
ternut squashes at the gawking tattooed man. Or to not just
walk the few feet over to the dairy section, open a carton of
milk, because she was so hungry and so thirsty, and drink. She
felt like she might be going mad. But she reached for the tiny
voice, coming from some distant place deep in her brain, telling
her to salvage the situation. She was a basketball coach. In a
small town. In *her* small hometown. Allowing herself to deto-

nate would destroy only herself. She needed to find her way to safety. Immediately. She abandoned the oranges, avocados, kale, and carrots in her cart. She kept her head level and steadied her gait as she walked, slowly, slowly, toward the exit.

"Coach!"

Stop. Breathe. Relax facial muscles. Turn.

Loopy, wearing the green Safeway apron, waved—without her usual smile—from one of the checkout counters as she shoved a box of Cheerios into a white plastic bag. It was after eleven o'clock. Loopy must be working a full eight-hour shift tonight. Was that even legal? The kid should be home sleeping. Delia looked over her shoulder to see if the produce section was visible from here. No. But her relief was only partial. She wouldn't put it past either of her witnesses, the anorexic woman or the tattooed man with toddlers, to report her.

Delia waved back and left Safeway, conspicuously without groceries. The outside air—cold, dark, and wet—husked up around her.

"Coach!" Loopy ran across the parking lot and stopped in front of her. "You okay?"

"Sure." As if it was perfectly normal to stroll through Safeway at his hour without buying anything.

"Oh. I mean, because—"

"I realized I have to get home to make a call." Yeah, at eleven thirty at night.

"Um. Okay." Loopy squinted and then sniffed. "So, um, am I still on the team?" She glanced over her shoulder at the lit supermarket.

Delia had made her late to work today and now she was the cause of Loopy leaving her station. She was ashamed of the part of herself that wanted to enforce the rules. Even now. Especially now. As if she couldn't function without that structure.

"Yes. You're on the team."

"Oh, wow. Thanks, Coach." Loopy gulped a big breath and

pressed her lips together. "I mean, I'm sorry I had to leave. I heard about the suicides and mile. I can make them up tomorrow."

Delia shook her head. "No. You're good."

Loopy saluted, as if Delia were a general, and ran back inside the store. Delia stood in the dark and watched the girl jump back into place at the cash register and start bagging more groceries. She considered calling Skylar again, making her wake up and talk, but there was no emergency, there really wasn't, she was just mega-unhinged, and she could cope with that herself. At least until a reasonable hour to call Skylar.

Delia walked back to her car and got in. She locked the door, as if Quade were waiting somewhere in the shadows of the parking lot. She tried to calm herself with a breathing exercise, but nothing could quiet her panicked awareness that she'd moved back to Rockside, Oregon. And that it was another eight hours until the sun rose again.

CHAPTER 15

Delia drove to the high school and texted Dylan from her car. She didn't expect him to respond. He would be running the loud floor polisher or lying on his back under a bathroom sink fixing a plumbing leak. She was here for the wrong reasons, anyway. Basketball as addiction: the craving to feel in the span of her hands the precise heft of the ball, with its nubbly surface and black indented lines of longitude, all that rolling off her fingertips as she launched the ball toward the hoop. There were worse addictions, for sure. But the ache behind tonight's longing was too strong. She'd used basketball her entire life to burn off that pain and Dylan had been the one to give her the drug.

She tapped open the text from Quade and read it again. He was just a man. In a small town on the Oregon coast. Who thought he could still unnerve her. She'd long ago stared that threat in the face. And won. Won everything, including her own self-esteem, the biggest prize of all. She deleted the text and restarted the car, steering her mind toward the sanity of food—it'd have to be cereal tonight—and sleep. But she didn't start driving. She wanted to see her brother. She wanted to shoot a few. When, a couple of minutes later, Dylan pushed open the front door of the school, she clambered out of the car and up the stairs.

"What's up?" Dylan asked with a wily grin, as if they were about to commit a crime together.

"Mind if I use the gym for a while?"

"Man, Dee, it's midnight." But his whole face said, *That's my girl.*

"I know. Just a few shots."

He followed her to the gym and stepped to the free throw line, his back to the basket. "You can have firsts. Let's see what you got."

He blocked her first shot with a solid thump of his palm to the top of the ball. He chased it down and tossed it back to her. "Nope. You let me do that."

"No, I—"

"Yeah, you did. That's insulting."

He was right. She had let him block her shot. He was the only man she'd purposely let win, but she knew he didn't want to beat her. He wanted her to win. He always had.

Fifteen minutes later they were both sweating and Delia had twenty to Dylan's six. They didn't talk as they played, and it was just what Delia needed, that deep dive into the heart of her game, to feel every single muscle in her body move toward a single, simple goal: putting the ball through the basket more times than her opponent did.

"Fuck, man," Dylan said when she sunk the final shot to win the game. He dropped onto the floor, back against the wall behind the basket. "You still got it. You should be playing pro."

Her commitment to the truth had a brief wrestle with her desire to be the superstar Dylan wanted her to be, but she said, "I'm thirty-eight. Besides, I was never good enough for the pros."

"You were. You totally were when you graduated."

Delia sat next to him. It was lovely to be in the dark gym. Without the responsibility of a mess of girls. She felt so much better now with the endorphins coursing through her bloodstream.

"I've hardly seen you since I've been back," she said. It wasn't just that he worked nights. He slept at least twelve hours a day.

"Yeah. You should come by more often."

Or he could get out of the bed when she was home.

She swung out her knee to bop his and tried to sound casual.

"Hey, I was wondering, did you confiscate that stuff from Zeke Vlasak-Jones's locker?"

"The gambling stuff? You bet I did." He sounded like he'd just dunked a shot.

"Why?"

"Uh, *why*? Are you shitting me?"

"I mean, it's not exactly like you were a saint in high school yourself. The kid's not doing anything too awful, is he?"

"Running a casino out of the bathrooms?"

"Do you know that for a fact? Have you seen him doing it?"

Dylan shrugged. "Aren't the dice, cards, and books enough?"

Not really, no. "So it wasn't, like, a random locker check. I mean, you weren't looking into a lot of kids' lockers. You looked into his, only his."

Dylan stared at her with what almost looked like hostility and Delia felt sick with regret. She looked away.

"It's part of my job to do occasional locker checks." His voice had gone cold.

But now that she'd started, she needed to know. "No, I mean, it's just that you're pissed off at his mom for not hiring you." Okay, she'd said it.

Dylan scratched his head. He reached behind himself and massaged his lower back. He spoke slowly: "Dee, there's a lot you probably don't know about this town."

"That sounds very sinister."

"Shit has changed. You're basically a newcomer at this point."

He sounded a lot like Mike Foster now. She wanted to say that she knew human beings and that the variance in them from town to town isn't all that huge. Dylan's disappointment in his life—his employment, his relationships with women, his chronic back pain—had warped his essential kindness. It made her sad. She corrected her attitude. She'd had all the advantages. It was her job to give him any boost up she could.

"You're probably right," she said, wanting to acquiesce.

"That Vlasak-Jones kid lurks around the furnace room at weird hours. I've seen him down there, like at six in the morning. Doing *what*?"

Delia tried to shut up but couldn't help pointing out, "He comes to school early on the days his sister has morning practices."

"Why doesn't he go to the library then?"

"I doubt it's open yet."

Dylan huffed. "The whole family gives me the heebie-jeebies. The man-bun on the dad. The bossiness of the mom."

He better not say anything about Mickey. To ward him off, Delia said, "His mom is the city manager. It's her job to be bossy."

Dylan groaned to his feet. "Okay. And it's my job to protect this school. When I see stuff, I'm going to say something."

"That's fair." Delia was light-headed with hunger and exhaustion. She held out both hands and Dylan pulled her up. She'd do what she could to make his life more comfortable. "Hey, brother, have I ever thanked you for, you know, basically saving my life?"

"Ach," he said, waving her away.

"No, I mean it. With words. I've never just said thank you. There's a lot of history neither of us wants to talk about. Fine. But just, you know, thank you."

Delia gave him a long hug and he accepted it. The city manager should have hired him. Yvette shouldn't have left him. Dylan deserved so much more.

CHAPTER 16

Delia ran a reasonable practice the next afternoon, and then, fifteen minutes before the end, told the girls to take seats on the bleachers. A few dads, moms, grandparents, and even a handful of siblings crowded around the team, as if a show were about to begin. Surely everyone had heard about her brutal practice the day before, and even though she'd gotten no phone calls of complaint, Delia braced herself for the blowback now.

"I'm sorry," Delia said. "I wasn't sensitive to the fact that Emma had the flu. I should have ended practice in time for those of you who take the bus. And for Loopy to get to work on time. I believe in working hard, but I went too far yesterday in what I asked of you all. I'm sorry."

Most of the girls nodded solemnly.

To her surprise, the parents stayed quiet. A few of them looked almost approving, as if they supported a harsher, stricter regimen. Which should have relieved Delia but in fact felt like pressure. Their faces recalled Jonas's words: *Do you know what it would mean to this town to win another state championship?*

"You're a badass," Casey said. "We're cool with that."

"Badass isn't my job. Coaching is."

"We played like shit," Brittany Nguyen said. "We need to work harder."

"Agreed," Mickey said, shoving up her glasses with a knuckle. "I mean, I didn't get in the game—I'm not complaining about that, Coach!—and I'm not being critical of everyone else. But I know we can be much better."

"I'm sorry!" Debbie sang out. "I missed so many shots. And I only got, like, two rebounds. I'm sorry."

"All right," Delia said, circling her hand over her head. "Moving on, okay? Hit the showers."

Not a single parent approached Delia to express their disapproval. Sophie and Casey's dad shook her hand silently, winked, and walked away. The rest just chatted among themselves, waiting for their daughters to shower and dress.

As Delia started collecting the basketballs and putting them in the rack, Iz stepped close and spoke quietly: "We need to talk to you."

"Who?"

"The team. Maybe come to the locker room with us?"

"Can you tell me what this is about?"

"Just. You know. Come." Iz turned her back and walked away.

Delia felt a foreboding, but followed.

Once inside the swinging door, away from their families, Iz said, "There's a reason we played so badly."

"No, Iz," Mickey said.

"But we can't say," Iz continued, giving Mickey a quick scowl to communicate that of course she knew they weren't supposed to divulge more. "I just wanted Coach to know that we got this. We're good. It won't happen again."

"She told us we could talk to her about anything," Kayla said with a shrug.

"No!" several of the girls chorused.

Delia had the strong feeling she should trust their reticence. She gave a thumbs-up and started to walk out, but Emma burst out with, "They all came with me Tuesday evening. The whole team. I had the last appointment of the day so I could get there after practice."

Mickey put a hand on Emma's shoulder. Taylor, on the other side of Emma, put an arm around her.

"Jed wouldn't go with me!" Emma said through her tears.

"He's a complete asshole," Iz said. "He actually said to Emma—"

"Wait," Delia cut in. Emma was a gawky girl with a big nose and lank light-brown hair, awkward on and off the court, and a straight-A student. She lived with her grandparents.

"Loopy even talked her manager into giving her the evening off," Emma was sobbing out the words now, "which was why she couldn't take the next day off for the game and she was risking you kicking her off the team, but she insisted. We should have picked a day that wasn't before a game but I was panicked and it was the earliest appointment I could get and I just wanted . . . I mean, we just launched."

"Wait," Delia said again. "Please don't say another word."

"We had to take two cars to fit everyone and even then it was crazy," Loopy said, grinning. "It was like the circus."

"Yeah, and the way Iz drives. Shit." Taylor swatted Iz on the shoulder. "I could barely keep up. We got there, like, half an hour early."

"Did you get a speeding ticket?" Iz asked. "Okay. So."

"Please stop talking!" Delia shouted. "Please. Not one more word."

They all looked confused.

"You said—" Sophie started.

"I know." Delia had asked them to tell her why they'd played badly. She'd also said they could talk to her about anything. But that was wrong. They couldn't. As soon as she had this information explicitly, as soon as they spoke the actual words about where they'd been on Tuesday evening, her response might have legal ramifications. She didn't know the laws in Oregon. But she didn't want Emma in more trouble by telling someone in an official school capacity. By telling *her*.

She held her hand up in the air as she paced away from the girls, all the way to the far side of the locker room, trying to sort out what had just been revealed but not actually said. When she returned to her team on the bench, they stared at her wide-eyed. This was the hardest part of being a coach. You're not a parent. You're not a therapist. You're not a best friend. And yet, in some potent way, you stand in for all of those roles. You become the condensed version of parent, counselor, friend, all rolled together. It's not your job to love them, yet you can't help but love them. Already. Just a few weeks into the season.

Insight lit Mickey's face. She leapt up and stood in front of Delia, blocking her. "Coach has all the information she needs now."

Delia said, "Rest over the weekend, Emma. This flu going around is tenacious."

A couple of the girls looked scandalized. But Delia's choice couldn't be more stark: either she lied about her understanding of what had happened on Tuesday, and by extension asked the girls to be complicit in her lie, or she might be forced to take steps that would expose Emma.

"Iz, you need to work on your offensive boards. On Monday we'll run through some blocking drills. Casey, has anyone taught you how to deny a pass? You need to be a lot more aggressive on defense. You girls said you're tired. That's a problem. The most important games are won in the last five minutes, by the team that's the most fit. Get ready for a lot more running." Delia was babbling, trying to move herself and the team onto more firm footing.

The idea came to her right then, all at once. "Listen. I need everyone on the team to develop a three-point shot." That was unrealistic, but those were the types of goals that got results. Trying couldn't hurt. They'd all become better shooters in the effort, and it would make a strong statement about Delia's expectations and confidence in their potential. Best of all, it might help solve the problem of Alice. The girls were all listening with heartbreaking intensity, trying to follow her.

"Alice," Delia said, "you'll be assisting in the coaching on this."

Alice kept her expression blank.

"So over the weekend, Alice, I want you to write down three strategies for learning how to hit a three."

Alice tried to shrug but it looked more like a flinch.

"Everyone get a lot of rest this weekend. Next week we have morning practices, and we'll be doubling down on conditioning. I'll see you on Monday at six thirty sharp."

CHAPTER 17

As Delia stepped out of the gym and into the hallway, Zeke flew by on his skateboard, nearly knocking her over.

"Hey!" The big-bellied daytime custodian shot out of a classroom, mop in hand, and shouted, "You want to get expelled or what?"

Zeke dragged a sneaker brake and flipped up his board. "For skating? No way."

"Follow the rules, man. Follow the rules."

"The halls are empty. I'm waiting for Mickey to get out of practice. What else am I supposed to do?"

"Study?"

"I finished all my homework."

"You can skate outside."

"It's raining. Besides, the halls are slick. It's fun."

The custodian affectionately smacked the back of Zeke's head. With his long skinny arms and legs, the boy looked like a spider as he ambled on down the hall, big board clutched at his side.

"Bummer about the game, Coach," the custodian said to Delia. "Next one will be better."

"Thanks." She wanted to get home. Emma, of all the girls! Skylar was the only one she dared tell.

"I work with your brother," the custodian said. "Not literally. He does the night shift, I do the day."

"Great to meet you."

"They let me coach the Chess Club," he said, hitching up his gray sweatpants and tugging down the tie-dye T-shirt. "Hence my monitoring the behavior of Mr. Zeke Vlasak-Jones. Hormones zinging too crazily in that kid. His sister is on your team."

Delia looked toward the exit.

"Remember me?"

Delia smiled to cover her confusion.

"Sorry. Creepy question. Like there's any reason for you to remember. We went to high school together. Right here. The Rockside Wildcats, ha ha. I never was much of a wildcat. More like a meerkat." His cheerful expression collapsed. "Now I'm scaring you."

"No. No. Of course you're not."

"You were a star. Big-time athlete. Dated Jonas Kowalski. He's principal now, isn't that a riot?"

"It is sort of funny."

"It was kind of him to hire me. Jonas is very kind."

"He is."

"You too. Even though you were really popular, you were still so nice. From the very beginning. At freshman orientation I thought I would die of misery. All those cool kids. I was chubby then too, and not nearly so friendly as I am now. I could barely speak. That's hard to believe, right? I don't shut up now. You sat next to me at orientation that first day. You told me it was going to be okay. It wasn't. It wasn't okay. High school was high hell. A nightmare. But I always remembered you saying that, how kind you were to me that first day. Other days too. For four years, you said hi to me whenever we passed in the halls."

"It's good to see you." She remembered him now. Robin Hawkins. "You helped me with math sometimes."

"You remember! Just twice. That was our sophomore year."

"Yeah, we were in Mrs. Wang's algebra class together."

"I kind of fell in love with you. Wait. Sorry! That's too much. I shouldn't have said that. Anyway, not anymore. You're way too scary. Plus, I have a girlfriend. So that's just very old information."

Delia laughed. "Scary?"

"So fit. Disciplined. Severely beautiful." He popped all ten knuckles.

"I'll accept fit."

"I bet you're an endorphins addict. I mean, being an athlete and all. I don't mean anything disparaging. It's not like pills. Endorphins are natural."

Delia laughed again. "You got me pegged."

"I mention it because endorphins are the happy hormone. And you don't look very happy right now."

"Just had a difficult practice."

"Phew. Yeah. The game on Wednesday night. I was there. I go to all the games."

"You do? Thank you for your support. It was a disappointing loss."

"But I'll just say that even back in high school, when you had everything in the world going for you, I detected a big sadness at your core."

"Whoa. Okay."

"Sorry. Sorry. I shouldn't have said that."

"It's okay," Delia said and she meant it. Somehow this exchange with Robin Hawkins was easing the searing angst she'd been feeling since falling asleep in the church basement. He just seemed 100 percent genuine. "My ex-wife—I've recently gotten a divorce—used to tell me that. About my core. And she was a therapist."

A little jag of anxiety threw her for a second. But no, coming out now, here in Rockside, gently to this kind man, was exactly the best antidote to that text message from Pastor Quade. If she'd been in a lifetime war against him and his beliefs, and face it, she had been, then she'd won that war. Culturally *and* legally. Hell yeah, she could come out.

"Interesting!" Robin said. "Oh, wait. I'm sorry about your divorce. That must be traumatic. I love therapists, though. Imagine doing that, trying to make people whole. I almost have a

PhD in happiness. I know a lot about it. Not necessarily from personal experience, but from studying." He slipped off one red Croc and, balancing on the other foot, rubbed his Achilles tendon.

Delia looked over her shoulder at the small windows in the doors to the outside. They were already black with darkness. Probably still raining too. She needed a hot shower.

"I know," he carried on. "It's absurd. But that's exactly why I study happiness, for the absurdity factor, which is fascinating. Like randomness in mathematics or chaos in physics. I had such a huge happiness deficit for years, and so I figured I should apply my ample brainpower to the problem. I wanted to know if happiness was quantifiable, if it could be measured, if there were formulas that could help increase the experience."

"And?"

He tipped his head back and forth, and then went to work on his other Achilles tendon. "No to most of it. It's not quantifiable. I don't think it can be measured. I'm still working on that one, though. I mean, it seems like if you could measure, i.e. quantify, happiness, it'd be a key step in figuring out how to more easily attain it, right? The thing is, most of us try to quantify it by observing behaviors, and I just don't think behavior correlates well enough with interior feelings to ever be accurate. Look at the kids here at Rockside High. The ones that seem the most confident, who sweat glory, are often the ones I suspect are the saddest. I love the massiveness of my inquiry. It's like the greatest challenge for humanity, trying to understand happiness. In any case, I've developed a hypothesis to be tested, a happiness formula."

Zeke soared by, crouched low on his skateboard, making a high-pitched whine with his vocal cords, as if emulating a sound barrier–breaking vector. With surprising swiftness, Robin reached out and yanked him off his board, which shot down the hall without its passenger. Keeping a hand clamped on the kid's arm, Robin said, "What'd I tell you?"

"Mom texted that she's running late."

"Oh, I get it. That means you're supposed to skate in the hall. *Not*. Go on down to the boiler room. Now. Set up the game."

Zeke shrugged and ran down the hall to fetch his board.

"The one thing he can't resist: a game of chess. So far he hasn't beat me. But I don't cut him any slack, not a single faked move, and he's getting close. By his senior year, he'll have me. If not a whole lot sooner." Robin yelled down the hall after the boy, "I'll be right there!" Then to Delia, "Yes," as if she'd asked a question. "I've identified four components, ones that people can actually act on, as in, *do*. I mean, I've read that having hope helps a lot with happiness. Ditto trust. But you can't do hope or trust. You can't will yourself to possess either one, so saying they promote happiness may be true, but it's useless information. My four components all have actionable pathways. I'd like to write a book about it, but I don't have the discipline."

Delia bit: "What are the four components?"

Robin nodded vigorously. "One, biophilia. Be in beautiful places. Good thing you moved back to the Oregon coast."

"New England is beautiful too. So. What's number two?"

"Belonging to a group. That's different from having friends. It's a more formal connection, a commitment to other people. For example, people who are members of churches are happier than people who aren't."

"Sure," Delia said, and saw her sarcasm register on his face.

"*Some* churches," he said.

"Do teams work?"

"Oh, they must. I'd say absolutely. Clubs. Anything, really, that makes community."

"Three?"

"A life of service. Taking care of others rather than obsessing about yourself. And four is doing creative work. That's a tough one for me. Because of the discipline problem. I tried building birdhouses, but not many people want those."

"You have an actual PhD in happiness?"

"Technically, no. And technically, it would have been in philosophy. From Portland State. I was doing my dissertation on the Happiness Problem, but I never finished."

"You've cheered me up considerably," Delia said. "Thank you."

"You're welcome. Gotta run before Zeke starts dismantling the school furnace or something." He started to leave and then turned back around. "I hope I didn't talk too much."

"You didn't."

"Okay. Thank you for listening."

"Robin, I meant it. A lot of stuff has gone wrong for me lately. You've made me feel much lighter. Have a good chess game."

"Peace," he said, flashing a V with two fingers.

Delia watched him walk away. In fact, she felt so much better she decided to check the admin offices to see if Heather the secretary was still at work. It was Friday, after all. Maybe she'd be up for grabbing a beer somewhere.

The lights were out in the reception area where Heather and Mrs. Riley had their desks. The two women were gone. Of course they were. It was pushing six o'clock. But beyond the reception area, light eked out the open crack in the door to Jonas's office. She heard papers rustling and then a chair squeak. He groaned. What personal miseries was her ex-boyfriend nursing?

Delia shook her head. She walked out of the admin offices, down the hall, out the main high school exit, and through the rain to her car.

CHAPTER 18

Delia went straight to bed and slept hard for ten hours. In the morning she finally shopped for groceries, buying three bags full of fruits and vegetables and whole grains. She spent the day cooking two soups, corn chowder and spicy black bean, a quinoa-and-beet salad with citrus dressing, and a sweet potato casserole. She froze portions of each recipe to eat later. Then she took a long run, showered, and put on her most comfortable tracksuit.

Skylar picked up after half a ring: "Hey."

"I'm sorry I called you in the middle of the night on Thursday."

"It was already Friday."

"I know. Sorry. I thought you'd texted me."

"What are you doing home on a Saturday night?"

"Just putting the finishing touches on my makeup," Delia said.

"Then heading out to Moss Soak Tavern? I bet the other lady queer in town bartends there."

"You think you're joking. There's literally a place called Mosswood Tavern."

"I can picture her!" Skylar hollered through her laughter.

"Okay," Delia said, not in the mood for the hilarity.

"She looks a little like Frances McDormand," Skylar went on, describing her imagined lady queer bartender, "only harder, meaner, asymmetrical haircut. Equally lopsided heart."

"Funny," Delia deadpanned.

Skylar was still busting a gut. "Cocks a forefinger at you,

says, *This one's on me, sister*, then slides a Pabst Blue across the bar at you."

What had gotten into Skylar? All the gaiety.

"Actually, I might ask one of the school secretaries out," Delia said to shut her up.

It worked. Skylar sobered fast. "Heather."

"Definitely not Mrs. Riley."

"We've already talked about this, Dee. Very bad idea."

"Slim pickings around here."

"Drive over to Portland or something."

"I haven't yet resorted to picking up girls in bars."

"No, just along interstate highways."

"All right." That actually stung a bit. "So how's the team?"

"We're entering the unraveling stage of the season early." Skylar sighed.

"Affairs. Grades. Parents."

"Yep. We even have a stalker this year. Some nerdy kid is obsessed with Kianna. Sending her texts, waiting outside her classes. He was even sneaking into practices until I got him banned. But he's a student, so you can't tell him he can't go to the library or to our games, you know?"

"Jeez. Have you talked to a dean?"

"Yeah. And he talked to the boy. I'm pretty sure the kid is harmless. But the whole thing's totally unnerving Kianna."

"Understandably. Just be glad you have early stage adults. These adolescents are a hot mess. My starting forward Iz was dating my starting point guard Casey, who just dumped her for a bench-sitter, Kayla. Iz is crushed, moping big-time, while Casey is all hopped up on her new thing."

"Painful."

"A couple weeks ago Iz and Casey were practically married. Now they're publicly feuding."

Skylar laughed. "That's why I love working with high school kids at my summer camp, though. They're so bald emotionally.

You know? College kids think they're adults. Makes everything a lot more complicated."

"Trust me, there's plenty of complication with these girls too. I know Iz thinks of herself as queer, but I'm pretty sure the others wouldn't use that word. They're just friends who, you know, whatever. It's not like Rockside High has a gay/straight alliance club or anything. I've noticed a couple of kids at school who are likely trans, but they are definitely not talking about it."

"You need to be careful."

"You keep telling me that. But you know, even Rockside has evolved."

"Has it?"

"Yes and no."

"Right. You just told me all but one of the queer kids are in the closet. That speaks volumes."

"It's complicated."

"What isn't?"

"Skylar, I took your advice. Sort of." Delia told about her accidental night in the church basement, the darkened room, fleece blanket and pillow. She told about the text message, although not about throwing fruit in Safeway.

Skylar was dead silent through the whole story. Then she said, "God, I'm sorry, Dee. That sounds awful. Creepy. No, you're right. You don't have to confront him. Maybe go back on another night with a can of spray paint and tag the church. You know, like with *hypocrite* and *asshole*."

Delia loved Skylar. Had loved her for literally decades. There was no better friend. Why shouldn't *they* get together? People had suggested it over the years and she'd always laughed it off, a crazy idea with Delia's promiscuity and Skylar's celibacy, but now they were both nearly forty. Maturity outmaneuvered all that, didn't it? Skylar had sounded almost jealous when she chided Delia about her road trip dalliances and flirting with Heather.

"When are you coming to visit?" Delia asked. "You could scout Oregon State and the University of Oregon."

"Different conference."

"I mean for when you go to nationals."

"One game at a time."

"Survive and advance." Delia punched out the motto, but it made her tired this evening.

"Yep. I gotta go. Talk soon."

"Don't hang up! Where do you have to go?"

"I have a date."

"Yeah, eighteen inches tall, long hair, blond with brown patches."

"Actually, they're brown with blond patches."

Delia knew Skylar. She'd be spending her Saturday night diagramming plays and studying opponents' game videos, her two collies next to her on the couch.

"Okay, give Sinead and Blair kisses for me."

"Will do. And Dee, I'm joking about tagging the church. Stay away from that man and his church. Just don't."

Delia started to answer but the line went dead and Skylar was gone.

Delia had wanted to tell her about Emma's abortion, but maybe it was just as well she kept her mouth shut. She'd checked the Planned Parenthood website, and in Oregon girls didn't need parental consent. But that didn't mean it was safe for any of them—Delia, as well as the entire team who'd accompanied her to the clinic—to be seen as complicit.

Delia's Saturday night yawned in her face. She could check out the Mosswood Tavern, after all. No, not a good look for the girls' basketball coach. Maybe she should have caught a ride to Portland with Dylan, who'd gone earlier in the day to see Poppy and Yvette. At least she could have gotten a good dinner in a decent restaurant.

Phone still in her hand, Delia went so far as to tap the first nine digits of Morgan's phone number—she'd long since deleted her from the *Favorites* queue—but then shut down her phone altogether to resist further temptation. This very moment Morgan probably sat across from Mary Hunt in some lovely restaurant having a Saturday date-night dinner and discussing the intersection of Carl Jung and Judith Butler.

She turned her phone on again and called Skylar back, but she didn't pick up. Even her best friend had had enough of her.

CHAPTER 19

Delia woke early the next morning with the thought, *Why shouldn't I go see Quade?* Take the offensive. Show up for this morning's service, sit in the front row, and then greet him afterward, publicly, in front of his congregation. She could ask him whether he was still using the trust of children to gratify his own depraved theology. Maybe it was time for *his* deliverance.

She showered, dressed, and drove to New Day. A surprising number of cars were parked in the lot. The evidence that he commanded the attention of so many parishioners, that he still held sway in this community, instantly destroyed Delia's sense that she'd evolved, moved on. Her hot intent collapsed. Here he was. Preaching. Extoling. Pretending. Lying.

Delia got out of the car and walked, rather than to the front door of the church, into the forest of Douglas fir on the far edge of the parking lot. She kept walking, letting the evergreen scent envelop her, its musk almost too much, until she could no longer see anything but the tall, thick trunks.

She'd loved Celebration Camp at first. After her mom dropped her off, Maureen, a counselor with the longest blond hair Delia had ever seen, gave her a tour of the camp. A big grassy meadow cupped the bright sunshine, and the cabins tucked away in the woods on the adjacent hillside looked cozy. A small chapel, complete with a pointed steeple and tall narrow windows, nothing at all like the prefab buildings of New Day, graced the far side of the meadow. Delia couldn't wait to pray inside that storybook church. Maureen said they'd swim and row on the pond, have campfires at night.

Best of all, though, were the other campers. It was as if someone had gathered all the quirky, expressive kids and left behind the terrifyingly ordinary ones. One girl could name every plant she saw, including the tiny mosses and lichens. One boy did perfect imitations of celebrity dance steps, including some by a dead guy named Fred Astaire. For about a day and a half, before she caught on, Delia thought she'd landed in a magical place, and that first night, with her flashlight under the covers of her sleeping bag, she used a piece of the stationery which she'd brought to write Shawna, to instead write a note thanking Pastor Quade for giving her this chance, the scholarship.

The next day at breakfast, Delia asked Maureen to please mail the letter. The counselor told her that campers weren't allowed to send or receive mail. That struck Delia as strange. But Celebration Camp had a sealed feeling, a secret-garden kind of vibe, and so it made a funny kind of sense. Anyway, Maureen kept the letter, putting it in her back pocket; maybe she would break the rule for Delia this time. After all, the letter was to her pastor.

That morning, after chores, the campers gathered in the dining hall for dating lessons. This too surprised Delia. She'd gone to a couple of school dances and it'd been fine. She liked to dance. Dylan and his girlfriend, the one who became the mother of his two older daughters, were already dating by then. They just sort of hung out, though. Delia hadn't been aware of any protocols or rules. It was interesting, the idea that there was something she needed to learn about dating. Why not? She felt pleasantly curious as she took her seat at the class.

Pastor Bob and Maureen checked campers off a list to make sure everyone was in attendance. The scary-looking counselor, Malcolm, with his hollow cheeks and sharp, jutting jawline, stood to the side, hands clasped behind his back. Though they were indoors, he hadn't removed his sunglasses.

"Hey, Delia Barnes," Maureen called out, "come on over

here." She stood next to Pastor Bob at a distance from the campers, and Delia went, still feeling special, selected, a scholarship
recipient.

"I'm thinking we could send Delia over to crafts," Maureen
said to Pastor Bob. "Wade is there. He could do a project with
her."

Pastor Bob looked annoyed. "Why?"

"She's only thirteen." Maureen said this extra quietly, as if it
was a mistake.

Pastor Bob, who was a couple inches shorter than Delia,
looked up at her face. "Oh, I think our girl can handle a bit of
dating advice. What do you say, Delia?"

"Sure. Yeah."

"Good girl," he said, and turning to Maureen, added, "That's
why she's here."

"She's young is all."

"Young and, according to Pastor Quade, already . . . active."

Maureen nodded her acquiescence.

"Take your seat," Pastor Bob said.

Maureen gave Delia a confusing smile with her thin lips
zipped tight. She looked both vexed and sympathetic. It was
the jarring dissonance in that smile that first tipped Delia off to
something being awry at this camp.

But the dating class was kind of fun. In the first role-playing
exercise, the boy asked the girl out, and the girl needed to use
the appropriate amount of eye contact (very little, but enough)
and words to accept or reject, depending on several factors, but
mainly on whether or not he was a Christian. That made the
game easy: if he was, you said yes; if he wasn't, you said no.
You looked him in the face briefly when he began speaking to
you, but then for the sake of modesty you stared down at your
own knees for most of the encounter (boys don't like aggressive
girls). If the boy exhibited questionable behaviors (Pastor Bob's
phrase), but was a Christian, this was a great deal for the girl. It

was an opportunity. Girls, Pastor Bob explained, have a lot of responsibility to use their wiles (again, his word) to make boys and men better Christians. In the next exercise, the campers sat side by side on hard chairs, stand-ins for movie theater or car seats, to practice conversation.

Delia got paired with a tall boy named Ernest, one of only two Black kids at the camp. At the beginning of the class, Pastor Bob told the whole group that Delia's height, the way she towered over most of the boys, would only exacerbate their already triggered feelings of masculine inadequacy. His need to explain gave the impression that the match, despite the height fit, had problems, and Delia understood his discomfort had to do with their skin-color differences. She heard Ernest huff quietly.

Throughout the start of the morning, as other couples performed in front of the group, Delia snuck looks at her assigned partner. Finally he whipped his head around and widened his eyes. Keeping his hands in his lap and the gesture miniscule, he spread his fingers in a *What?* gesture. Delia smiled, raised her hand and waved, even though she was sitting right next to him.

He stared at her for a second before relaxing his shoulders and silently laughing. "You a trip," he whispered. "Where you from?"

"Rockside."

"Rockwhere?"

"On the coast."

"What coast?"

"Oregon coast."

"Poor child."

"Why? Where are you from?"

"Los fucking Angeles. Where the ground is properly covered with pavement and buildings."

Delia laughed, and forgot to do it quietly.

"Delia," Maureen scolded, "pay attention."

Ernest widened his eyes at her again and whispered, "Girl, subterfuge, please. Subterfuge."

She didn't know what that word meant but she liked her date.

Ernest's ears and feet were too big for the rest of his body, giving him a sweetly mismatched appearance. She'd already noticed his tendency to stumble. This morning he wore a T-shirt and khaki shorts, and the skin on his long arms and legs looked soft, as if he used lotion religiously. When their turn came, both kids strived to ace the exercise, using the proper body and verbal language, making sure they followed the guidelines. But then, right after they'd been dismissed and Pastor Bob called up another pair, Ernest bowed to her and said too quietly for anyone else to hear, "Enchanted, I'm sure, dahling," and Delia knew he was mocking the training. Delia held up her arm and made a muscle. "Girl!" he said, still quietly but with lots of feeling.

At the break, the kids all spilled out of the dining hall and met in clusters on the edge of the meadow. Delia followed Ernest into the cool yellow sunshine. He stopped to talk to a thin, much shorter, ultra-pale boy with red-rimmed eyes. His white-blond hair had recently been sheered into a crew cut, so that the upper part of his scrawny neck was even whiter than the rest of his skin, showing where his hair had recently hung longer and freer. He wore a red plaid flannel shirt and stiff new Levi's, both a size too big. The outfit looked like a straightjacket on the delicate kid. As she approached the two boys, a light breeze shook the alders surrounding the dining hall building, the green leaves fluttering nervously.

"Hi," the pale boy said to her.

"Meet my girlfriend," Ernest said, blinking his eyelashes in mock femininity. "Delia."

"You present so straight," the other boy said, looking Delia up and down. *He* sure didn't present straight. His prettiness burst out of the plaid shirt and rugged jeans.

"Straight?" Ernest swatted the ridiculous term away. "You gotta be kidding me. This girl's an Amazon, am I right?"

The boys waited for an answer. She looked away, pretended to be interested in what the other kids were doing. She wanted to ask what an Amazon was.

But she knew. All at once, she knew. These kids were queer. Homos.

"Sweetie," Ernest said, putting a hand on her shoulder, "you okay?"

"I'm only thirteen," Delia whispered, hoping Maureen's concern might pan out in some advantage for her.

"Wow," the blond boy said. "You're so tall."

"That's messed up," Ernest said. "Sending a kid here. That's just messed up."

"How old are you?" she asked.

"He's sixteen and I'm fifteen," the blond boy said. "I'm Cal."

"You're with us now," Ernest said to Delia. He stood straight, made two fists, and planted them on his hips.

"She doesn't know what that means," Cal said.

"She will. My girl is smart. Right? You catch on quick, don't you?"

Delia didn't know if he was making fun of how long it'd taken her to figure out where she was—and she still didn't know exactly—but she nodded.

"So *are* you?" Cal asked.

"Am I what?"

"Because not everyone here is. One wrong hairstyle. Wanting to be a firefighter instead of a nurse. All kinds of shit can land you here. Are you queer for real?"

"Leave her alone," Ernest said.

"Well, I am," Cal said. "One hundred percent." He covered his mouth and hunched his shoulders, as if he could hide his body with the gestures. "Totally guilty."

"Not guilty," Ernest said, slapping Cal's hand away from his mouth.

"I'm not going to lie," Cal said.

"You like what you like. But you're not guilty. Two different things." Ernest turned to Delia. "Cal's only been here a week and he's not having an easy time of it."

Cal flourished his hand and asked, "Who is?"

"They want you to be ashamed, baby boy," Ernest said. "Listen, this place is bullshit. You got to know that. You got to survive. Am I right, Amazon?"

"Yes," Delia said, "he's right."

The pair of counselors—Maureen and Malcolm—approached like a SWAT team, perhaps sensing Ernest's insurgency, or maybe spying Cal's effeminate hand gesture.

"What's up, kids?" Maureen asked, looking at Delia.

"We were just talking about how useful the dating class is," Ernest said.

Malcolm smirked.

"I enjoyed it," Delia said, trying to rescue her new friends. "Great tips."

"Heck yes," Cal said, using an unnaturally low voice.

"Get back inside," Malcolm said, laying a hand on the back of Cal's neck but pinning his gaze on Ernest. "It's time for the second module."

As Delia and the two boys headed back into the dining hall, Ernest looked up at the sky, raised his arms and hands like a preacher, and quietly called out, "What does it mean to love Jesus?" As if it were some kind of code. Then both boys fisted their hips.

"What's that mean?" Delia asked, tapping her own waist with her hands.

"We're not allowed to touch each other," Cal whispered. "So Ernest made it up. It's our virtual hug."

For the second module, the kids met one-on-one with counselors. Because there were more campers than staff, some kids had to wait for turns. They sprawled on the dining hall chairs, glaring into the distance, everyone seeming hostile, as if friendliness with other campers could get you in trouble.

Delia pulled a chair over next to Ernest. He was her designated date, after all, so they should be able to practice conversation. "So did you sign up to come here? I mean on your own?"

Ernest reared back like she'd said something absurd. "No one comes here by their own choice."

"Oh. I mean, I thought—"

He put a finger against his lips and nodded at the other kids waiting for their private sessions with the counselors. When Delia looked confused, he said, "Lots of spies." He pointed at a big muscled white boy who shaved a full beard, and added, "Like Angus."

"Shut up, fag," the boy said.

Ernest stood and pulled Delia to her feet. They walked to the other side of the dining hall.

"I'm reporting you," Angus called after them.

"I wrote a poem about Jesus being a girl," Ernest said quietly.

Delia laughed.

"I'm serious. I mean, really, those sad eyes and thin arms, the compassion and love. She's a she."

"That's why you're here?"

"Yep. I wasn't caught having sex with anyone," he added, as if that was an accomplishment.

"Just a poem?"

"Well, okay. I also sort of had a thing with a boy and sent him some poems. He didn't appreciate the attention." Ernest elbowed her gently. "Bad choice. I thought he was gay too. He probably is. Those closet types are the most dangerous." He stepped back and frowned, as if worried that he'd revealed too much.

Delia quickly said, "Oh, yeah, they are," to hold onto his trust, even though she didn't know what a *closet type* was.

"How'd you get here?" he asked, and she knew she had to reciprocate. But she didn't know how to talk about Shawna. She didn't want to connect her friend with all of this. She wanted to protect that feeling, that joy, that blast of freedom.

She said, "My pastor made a mistake. I don't think he actually knew what this camp was."

Ernest arched one brow, but then said, "Yeah, probably not."

"What about Cal?" she asked.

They both looked at the empty chair where, until a few moments ago when Pastor Bob called him to his private session, Cal had been sitting.

"He says he was seduced by his pastor." Ernest swallowed hard.

"But he really wasn't?"

Ernest arched a brow again and looked away. His chest caved a little. Delia didn't know why she did it, but she reached out a hand and put it right on his breastbone.

Ernest covered her hand with his, looked her in the eye, and said, "A minister and a kid? That's not seduction, that's rape. I've tried to tell him that."

The word punched Delia in the stomach, though she tried to conceal the jolt. She withdrew her hand and asked, "He doesn't believe you?"

"Baby boy is up against it. When he tried to make him stop, the minister told him nothing had ever happened, that Cal had fantasized the encounters. Cal didn't dare tell his parents. They wouldn't have believed him."

"How'd he get here?"

"The minister suggested it. Ballsy, right?"

Delia nodded.

"His parents were relieved. They were all over it. His dad said he didn't raise no sissy son."

Delia wondered if she could go home now.

"I didn't mean to scare you," Ernest said.

"It's just—" She needed to position herself on the side of safety. "I guess I'm lucky. My mom doesn't really care what I do.

She's too busy with her job and her boyfriend and everything. So, I mean, I have a lot of independence."

"It's good to feel lucky," Ernest said. "You're strong. I can see that."

She was. She was strong. In mind and body. "So, like, you didn't do anything with the boy you sent poems to?" She thought of the basement. She thought of kissing Shawna. That harsh exposure of artificial light on their skin.

Ernest laughed. "You're direct, aren't you?"

"You don't have to answer."

"Of course I messed around with him."

Delia wanted to ask exactly what they did. And where. "How could he tell on you then? He was as—" She was about to say *guilty* but Ernest had already said that was the wrong word.

"People lie. People lie all the time. And when it comes to sex with someone of the wrong gender, the liar wins."

"I don't like lying." Delia embarrassed herself with how passionately the words came out.

"I know. I can see that." He put his fists on his hips. She did hers too.

Maureen called Delia to her session, and she left Ernest by himself on the far side of the dining hall to follow the mane of blond hair into a private room. She and Maureen sat in facing folding chairs in the beige and airless space, and the counselor began by asking a lot of questions about Delia's friends. Delia knew to keep Shawna out of this. So she mentioned the group of boys on her street that she used to play with as a middle schooler, but when Maureen asked what they played, Delia didn't know how to answer. They built fires and played baseball. One boy had a rifle and sometimes they shot squirrels, even skinning and roasting one once, although Delia refused to eat any of the meat. None of these answers seemed wise.

"I've noticed you walk like a boy," Maureen said to her silence. "It's probably from hanging out with this set."

She should have mentioned her girlfriends. Last year at school she hung out with Brandi and Sasha and Lisa, with lots of girls. She was popular. Delia didn't have a problem making friends. But if she said she had lots of girlfriends, maybe Maureen would take that wrong too.

"Look," Maureen said. "You're young. That makes the fix a lot easier. Simple, practical solutions. Like your gaze. It's too direct and aggressive."

Delia looked down at her knees.

"Let's start by working on the way you walk." Maureen got up from her chair and demonstrated using a lighter footfall, how to take smaller steps and not swing her arms too freely. When she asked Delia to try it, Delia stood but got overwhelmed with giggling at the ridiculousness of the exercise. She couldn't stop laughing. It was just that Maureen looked like a reasonably intelligent woman. She couldn't possibly be serious about any of this.

But she was. She was very serious about all of it.

"I understand your nervousness," Maureen said without a smile. "It's natural. Change is hard. But you'll be so happy with the results. I promise you."

Delia couldn't help wanting Maureen to like her. She had that hurt mouth. Trouble stirred in her close-set eyes.

Delia reset her attitude, and as she did, her amusement at the walking exercise curdled into shame. How had she not known she walked wrong? Looked at people wrong. Couldn't Pastor Quade have just told her this himself? She should have gone to the counseling sessions with him. Why was she so stupidly stubborn?

She'd just begun to practice her walk, no longer laughing, when Pastor Bob entered the room without knocking. Maureen left right away. Pastor Bob sat down and pointed at the facing chair. When Delia sat, he took both of her hands in his. A reflex caused her to yank them away. He smiled and kept his arms outstretched, palms up, waiting for her to retake his hands. Again she rebuked herself. She should have done the sessions with Pastor Quade. She'd brought this on herself. She needed to correct her mistakes by doing it right, doing everything right, until she could go home, fixed. She gave him her hands. Remembering to avoid direct eye contact, she looked at the reddish top of his bald head.

"Have you ever done hypnosis?" he asked.

The urge to laugh again stitched the place under her top right rib. She and Shawna had played hypnosis. *Your eyes are getting sleepier. Your dead great-aunt has just come into the room. Do you see her? She has five warts on her nose and straggly gray hair. She wants you to greet her with a kiss.*

But real hypnosis? Of course not.

Pastor Bob instructed her to stare into his eyes and to not look away, not even one quick glance.

Maureen had just told her to not look directly into people's eyes. So confusing. But she did as she was told. Pastor Bob spoke calmly as he described a beach, soft surf, a warm breeze. Delia pretended to be hypnotized as soon as seemed reasonable so she wouldn't get into trouble. When Pastor Bob asked, "Are you there, on the beach?" she gave him a slow zombie nod. He told her that there was a boy her age on the beach with her and that they were holding hands. Soon they sat in the sand with their backs against a log, and the boy opened the bible he'd been carrying in his other hand. He read to her. The verses entered her heart directly, didn't even go through her brain—these were Pastor Bob's words—and he told her that she felt a surge of warmth for the boy.

"Do you feel it?" Pastor Bob asked. He still had her hands in his.

Delia nodded.

"Can you describe the feeling for me?"

She thought for a long time about how to answer. Finally she said, "The words of the bible are combining with my feelings for the boy. He's really cute. I want to sit closer to him." She paused and then added, unsure if it was right, "Maybe kiss him."

Pastor Bob squeezed her hands and let go. "I'm going to bring you out of hypnosis now," he said quietly, and snapped his fingers.

Delia blinked to indicate she'd awakened from her fake trance.

"Good start. Listen, Delia, you're very young and I think your case is going to be an easy one to resolve. You don't have a father at home. I understand that he was never on the scene. Is that right?"

Delia nodded.

"It's pretty straightforward. Without a father figure, how can you learn to attach to men? You naturally wouldn't trust them."

She nodded again. Agreement seemed to be the best path forward.

"You're lucky to have Pastor Quade in your life. I want you to start thinking of him as a father figure. I've spoken with him about this and he's generously agreed to take on that role for you."

"Oh, well, maybe—" she started to object, but stopped herself. Maybe she'd like having Pastor Quade as a father figure. She'd been a little jealous of Dylan's fishing trips with him.

"Tomorrow we'll do some hypnosis around that bond, shall we? In the meantime, spend some time imagining what kind of joy it could bring you to do your homework with Pastor Quade. Maybe cook some dinners together. Would you like that?"

Pastor Bob stood and left the room, shutting the door behind him. No one came to get Delia. She didn't know how long she sat there because she didn't have a watch and there was no clock in the room. She didn't dare open the door herself or even get up off the chair. Didn't they need the room for other campers' private sessions? She was thirsty and hungry, and worried that she'd miss dinner, but she sat perfectly still and waited.

When finally Maureen opened the door to the room, the counselor quietly asked, "You okay?" As if she actually cared.

Delia made herself say, "Yes."

"Chapel," Maureen said. "Then dinner."

Maureen stayed by Delia's side as they crossed the meadow to the church, glancing at her a couple of times, sisterly looks of concern. Delia thought she maybe hated Maureen. There was something cowardly in her essence, and at the same time, Delia wanted to take her hand. She had the disorienting desire to help her.

Once inside the chapel, Delia looked for Ernest and Cal, but they were seated near the front, in a row already filled with other campers. After prayers, she searched for them again in the dining hall, but Maureen nudged Delia down on a bench at a table far away from theirs. Delia barely touched her Salisbury steak, boiled peas, and mashed potatoes. She asked Maureen, who sat at the head of her table, if she could call her brother. Maureen said no.

"You can't call home," the kid sitting next to her said. "Not even your mom."

"Why not?" Delia asked.

No one at the table answered her.

By the end of dinner, Delia was desperate to talk to Ernest and Cal. But campers were sent to their cabins to grab their flashlights, and then they marched with their cabinmates to the campfire ring. Concentric circles of log benches surrounded an already roaring fire. Dusk closed like a fist around the seated campers, leaving the hot fire at the center to light the front-row faces. Wade stood next to the fire, the orange light shocking his handsome features, and strummed chords on his guitar. He might have been humming too, as his lips were pressed together and his eyes closed, but Delia couldn't hear over the crackling and popping of the burning wood. She stepped out of line, away from her cabinmates, and backed herself into the brush on the perimeter of the clearing. She had to make a move fast, before someone noticed her hanging back.

There! Ernest and Cal sat side by side in the third row, on the far side of the ring. She walked with exaggerated purpose, as if on business for god, scooted between the second and third rows, in front of a bunch of kids' knees, and tapped Cal on the shoulder. He looked up and smiled, and she squeezed in between the two boys. Ernest, who was sniffing hard, barely said hi. She thought he might be crying.

"Shut up already with the sniveling," Angus, who sat directly in front of them, turned to say.

"Mind your business," Cal told him.

"Do you have a cold?" Delia asked Ernest. It was a stupid question, but she wanted to say something to bring him closer.

Ernest shook his head. "It feels like my nose is on fire. The burning is so bad."

"Then don't have those thoughts, idiot," Angus said over his shoulder.

"I thought someone told you to mind your business," Delia said.

"He's faking," Angus said. "It's been a couple hours. It doesn't last that long."

"How would you know?" Cal asked him. "You claim to have never had *those thoughts*, and so you wouldn't have had the treatment. Or *have* you had those thoughts?"

Ernest smiled at last. He said, "Tell us about them, Angus. Your thoughts."

"You guys make me sick," Angus said.

Wade handed his guitar to a boy in the front row who took it like a gift, holding the counselor's instrument tenderly in his lap, and then Wade set two more logs on the fire, even though the flames already reached outside the ring of stones. Delia felt too hot and took off her sweatshirt. She looked up at the sky, the stars a thick wash, and wondered what Shawna was doing tonight.

"I like the vomiting better," Cal said. "You just have to be sure you've eaten enough. Otherwise you're dry-heaving and that hurts so bad."

Ernest sniffed and laughed, despite tears streaming down each cheek. "Besides, the more's in your stomach, the more you have to direct at the counselor."

Cal reached across Delia and slapped Ernest's knee. "You do have to try harder."

Ernest shook his head. "You know that's bullshit."

"You guys make me sick," Angus repeated.

"You already said that," Ernest told him. "We heard you the first time. But we're ignoring you."

"What burning?" Delia asked. "What vomiting?"

"The girls have it easy," Cal said. "No one can tell when they're turned on."

"Fags," Angus said.

"There's no such thing," the girl sitting next to him said. She wore her hair in a tight bun and sat straight-backed. "You know that. It's a behavior, not an identity."

"Aren't we a straight-A student," Ernest said to the girl.

"Cal is right," she said, looking over her shoulder. "You need to try harder, Ernest."

Ernest wiped his nose on his sleeve. He said to Delia, "You have a right to know. In our sessions they ask us to describe boys we like. If we refuse to do this, they show us pictures of men. If we get boners, the counselor pops an ammonia capsule under our nose. Or they give us a vomit-inducing drink."

"*Or*," Angus said, "you could correct your responses."

"Here's what you have to do," Ernest said, looking past Delia to Cal. "The trick is in the association. I connect the burning and the nausea to him, to Malcolm or Wade or Pastor Bob, not to my feelings about boys or the pictures. So it's the counselors making me sick."

"That works with Malcolm and Pastor Bob," Cal said. "Not so much Wade." And they both laughed.

"Don't worry," Ernest said. "You're a girl. They're easier on girls. And you're young. I don't think they'll try any of the hard stuff on you. I hope not." He gave her a hug, a real one.

"She'll have to do a deliverance, though," Cal said. "No one gets out of here without doing one."

"Yeah," Ernest said, "I guess so."

"What's a deliverance?" Delia asked.

Wade, who'd retrieved his guitar, started singing "I've Got a Friend in Jesus." The kids all began to settle.

Ernest lifted a foot and kicked Angus between the shoulder blades. He leaned forward and said, "Let me see your lap, bro."

"Ernest, stop!" Cal whisper-shrieked.

"How come you have your sweatshirt draped across your dick?"

"Ernest," straight-A bun girl said, not unkindly, "just don't."

"The closet types have the strongest sex drives," Ernest said. "My man Angus loves him some Wade on the guitar."

"Try," the girl said, speaking to Ernest but looking right at Delia, as if to remind her that it was the girls' jobs to keep boys in line. "By the way," she added, "I'm Emily."

"Don't flirt with her!" Ernest said. "Delia's *my* girlfriend."

Emily shook her head and looked straight ahead again. But she couldn't resist turning back around again and saying, "I'm not flirting."

"Oh," Ernest said. "Well, even if you were, it wouldn't do any good. All of us back here in this row are straight as arrows." He butted Angus between the shoulder blades again, this time with his knee.

Wade thrashed down on a G chord as Pastor Bob stepped up next to the fire, raised his arms in the air, and shouted, "Let us pray!"

For a full hour, as they prayed and sang, Delia snuggled

against her two new friends. Ernest stopped sniffing and Cal smiled sweetly at her every time she looked at him. The big fire, the night sky, using the fullness of her voice, even crying at two different stories the counselors told about kids finding their ways, all this pulled Delia into a state of hopeful contentment, rightness. She would try.

She did try. She shushed Ernest when he mocked the camp activities. She told Cal he looked handsome in the lumberjack getup. She loved both of her new friends so much and they were both boys. She steered clear of Emily.

Late one afternoon midway through her second week at camp, Pastor Quade came to check on her progress. She, Cal, and Ernest were in a rowboat on the pond, the honeyed sunshine making the three friends feel loose with affection. They were laughing and talking about their futures, who they were going to be when they grew up. She felt so free in the boat with Ernest and Cal, reaching into the perceived abandon of adulthood. When she spotted Pastor Quade on shore, and pointed him out, Ernest kissed her. Cal said the kiss might backfire.

Delia didn't quite understand what either of the boys meant—Ernest's kiss or Cal's comment—but she kissed Ernest again because she knew she wanted to be on their side. *At* their sides. That was as clear to her as the lake water.

"Delia! Hello!" Pastor Quade cupped his hands around his mouth and called to her. Pastor Bob stood right next to him.

Cal said, "We're in the Pacific Ocean and I'm rowing you to China." He began rowing in the opposite direction from the men on shore.

"That's my pastor," Delia said. "I have to talk to him."

"You do?" Cal asked.

"Yeah," Ernest said gently to Cal. "This isn't the Pacific Ocean, baby boy. This is a small pond."

Cal winced, as if being yanked out of his playful fantasy hurt. He said, "Duh."

"Switch with me." Ernest stood and reached for the oars. "I'll row us to shore so Delia can get it over with."

"It's okay," Delia said. "I want to talk to him."

The boys looked unconvinced.

"He's a friend of our family. I can explain."

"Explain what exactly?" Cal asked.

"That he made a mistake."

Neither Ernest nor Cal said another word as she climbed out of the boat and onto the dock. Their silence was her truth. She knew better. It hadn't been a mistake. Pastor Quade had told Pastor Bob that she was "already active."

She walked up the wooden pier, tripping twice on her way.

"Hey, Delia, good to see you," Pastor Quade said. "Let's head over to Pastor Bob's office so we can chat."

She wanted to turn around, run the length of the pier, and jump back in the boat. She wanted to forever row through the yellow sunshine and silver lake water with her two friends. She understood now, all at once and with her entire self, what Ernest's kiss meant. It meant love over hate. It meant kindness over meanness. It meant friendship over authority. She started to gesture for Cal to row the boat back to her, but that would draw the boys into her trouble. Ernest had agreed that she had to face her pastor. And yet the aversion she now felt was physical. Delia ran right past him, up the path, away from the pond, all the way to the dining hall, a place that was guaranteed to be public, at least not a trap of privacy.

No one followed Delia, but she knew she wouldn't be left alone for long. The cook, a mild-mannered man with a giant handlebar mustache, made her a peanut butter sandwich and she ate that, and drank a tall glass of milk, with a strong appetite. She didn't say a word to the cook, but he sat at the table with her while she ate. He told her to hang tight, that the love of Jesus, not the hate of men, would see her through. Other campers had told stories about the cook being kind to them and she felt glad for her instinct to come here, to the dining hall, for safety.

But she hadn't escaped. She knew that. Pastor Quade soon entered the big hall, approaching with a rigid smile and taking a seat at her table.

"I thought I'd give you a little time to cool down, young lady," he said. The mustached cook got up from the table and retreated to the kitchen, leaving her alone with Pastor Quade. "How can I help?"

"Oh. Nothing." Delia had no words but felt she had to find some fast to save herself. "I was really hungry and thirsty."

"Feel better now?"

"Yes."

When he put his hand on her wrist, she pulled her arm away.

"I understand you haven't been particularly cooperative."

That wasn't true. Sometimes she laughed inappropriately. She spent too much time with Ernest and Cal, and they were secretly insubordinate, but she thought they were pretty good at their subterfuge.

"I hadn't realized how young you are," Pastor Quade said, "but that's a good thing. You have a big head start over the other kids here at camp."

"I'm really learning a lot."

"Are you?"

"Yes." To provide evidence of her progress, she added, "I have a crush on . . ." She almost said Ernest, but he was Black, so maybe that would be wrong, and then almost said Cal, but he was so effeminate Pastor Quade wouldn't believe her. She thought she was brilliant when it occurred to her say, "Wade."

Quade chugged out a laugh.

"I know he's way too old for me! I'm just saying, he's so good-looking. And cool. He plays the guitar so well. And his singing voice, it's like, so . . ." Again, what was the right word? "Attractive."

That was not the right word. Pastor Quade knew she was lying. He nodded, though, as if he would, for now, accept her answer. Maybe *she* had to accept her answer. Maybe you had to fake it for a while, try, before the real feelings came.

"I really am trying," she said, meaning it for a quick second before the fact of Pastor Quade's betrayal shimmered back. He knew exactly where he'd sent her. Even worse, he'd tricked her. He'd made her believe she'd won a prize, a scholarship, when in fact she'd been dealt a punishment. Something at her core began to tremble.

"You're only thirteen," he said. "You have so much oppor- tunity."

"I do," she said. "Yeah. Totally."

He stood and said goodbye, using a formal, cold voice. He'd read her insincerity.

Delia looked around, over her shoulder into the kitchen, hoping to see the cook who talked about the love of Jesus, but he'd disappeared.

The next morning, when all the campers and counselors had gathered in the dining hall for breakfast, Pastor Bob clanged his spoon on his orange juice glass, as he did every morning, to start announcements. He told them that one of the toilets in the girls' restroom next to the crafts shack wasn't working, that they would have s'mores at campfire tonight, and that a Good Samaritan had dropped off a stack of Christian teen novels. The paperbacks were in Pastor Bob's office, if anyone would like to borrow one.

Then he looked right at Delia and said, "Pastor Quade, from Delia's church, visited us yesterday. He had good things to say about Delia's progress."

He did?

Pastor Bob smiled. "He thinks she's ready. Congratulations, Delia. We're going to start preparing you for your deliverance."

"Wait," Delia whispered. No one had asked her if she thought she was ready, if she wanted to do a deliverance. It felt like revenge. Because she had run. Because she had lied. Because Quade knew he hadn't broken her.

Now, twenty-five years later, Delia walked slowly out of the Douglas fir forest and stood once again in the church parking lot. The service must have ended because cars were backing up and rolling down the long driveway to the highway. Quade would be talking with the lingering congregation. Glad-handing. Performing joy.

She didn't go inside. She knew better. She had moved on. So far beyond all that. Her job now was to keep a team of girls focused on their own well-being and on winning a championship. She forced herself, all over again for the millionth time, to grow up. She drove home.

CHAPTER 20

Three weeks before Christmas, Dennis still waffled on whether he'd come to Portland to be with Ernest.

"It's not like we celebrate," Dennis said. "It's just a random week."

"But it is when I have time off. We could kick back together."

"Kick back in the rain? That town would Wicked Witch of the West me."

"Oh, and the weather in Brooklyn is delightful right now."

"Snow and ice is not rain. It's seasonal, even festive—"

"Festive?" Ernest interrupted. "Festive of what? You just said we don't celebrate."

"Festive of the winter solstice, which I do celebrate. The Northwest with its gloom, the gray, the uniformity, the endless dripping. Not festive."

"You know a lot about a place you've never been."

"I read *Sometimes a Great Notion* in high school. All I need to know."

"I know you want to meet Virginia Woolf."

Dennis paused. Ever so briefly. But in that tiny span of time Ernest had an idea.

"How's she doing?" Dennis asked. He loved every stupid little story about the cat: how she hunted and ate flies, the way she sat on Ernest's chest at dawn, her favorite pastime of hissing at birds she spied out the window.

"I think she's a genius," Ernest said, ashamed of himself for trying to seduce his boyfriend with cat stories. "She has a full command of the English language. Anything I say to her, she gets."

Dennis grunted his approval. Then Ernest listened, for what felt like a solid half hour, to stories he'd heard a million times before about Dennis's childhood cat, Bonkers, and all his antics.

"I have a surprise for you," he said when Dennis finally wound down. "One I can only give you in person, and I promise you'll be over the moon."

"Huh. What is it?"

"I'll book your flight."

"Let me think about it, babe. It's a lot of money. You'll be home in the summer."

"That's like six months away."

"Then why don't you come home for the solstice?"

"I agreed to look after the professor's house. Who would take care of Virginia Woolf?"

"You got a job teaching at Lewis & Clark College, not a prison sentence."

Both men laughed. The line between work and incarceration seemed thin at times.

"I miss you so much," Ernest said.

After hanging up, he fed Virginia Woolf, brushed her coat, had a long talk with her about his idea, and then that very afternoon drove to the Humane Society. The paperwork required to just look at the animals was a little off-putting. Would they do a background check to assess his character, maybe run his credit score? Ernest wondered if potential white adopters got this much scrutiny—the lady literally asked him if he had enough money to pay for kibble and litter sand—but decided, by her look of frightening severity, that they probably did.

Ernest admired the dogs on his way to the cats. A pit bull would do nicely for him. It'd be good protection. The beady pink eyes. The muscle-boy build. The fuck-you reputation. The uglier the better. He could love a pit bull. He pictured himself walking the bruiser in Brooklyn, a thick silver chain leash, brown leather collar. *Yeah, bro, fuck with me and you'll have Fido here to deal with. And he's* crazy.

But he was supposed to be luring Dennis with fluffiness, not looking for security, and so he forged ahead to the cats. As he walked the aisle between the rows of cages, both the smell of cat piss and the psychic trauma of all those imprisoned and silently suffering fuzzballs sucked the oxygen out of the room. Luckily, he didn't have to stay long. The perfect beast caught his eye immediately. A big blockhead of a Maine coon, long-haired gray-and-black tabby, maybe as much as twenty pounds, she was almost a dog. The sign on her cage said she was five years old, but she looked older, not quite gnarly but definitely not dewy either. Dennis would like the part about adopting an older cat who others might not want. She neither reached for Ernest through the cage slats, like some of her more desperate compatriots, waving their rounded paws in panicked appeals for love and a home, nor did she quake wide-eyed in the far reaches of her cage, as still others did. She sat front and center, pinned her gaze on Ernest's sternum, and dared him to pick her, brute of the bunch. The size of a raccoon, she had a muscular neck and shoulders, long white whiskers, and intelligent brown eyes. The cat had excellent self-esteem.

Ernest left the shelter with the big woolly girl in a cardboard carrier. The first Lyft driver wouldn't take a cat, but the second one did. They detoured into the nearest Target where he bought her a case of premium canned food—to spare Virginia Woolf's larder—as well as a new brush, her own box and litter, and a set of dishes.

Back at the house, the driver, a lovely woman from Peru named Ana, helped him carry all the new paraphernalia inside and stayed to witness the release. Ernest opened the cardboard carrier, and the cat leapt out and tore around the front room, knocking over and breaking a lamp. Virginia Woolf flew up onto the kitchen counter, where she knew she wasn't allowed, and hissed.

"Virginia Woolf!" Ernest said. "Girl, where're your manners? I told you I was bringing a sister home. This is Audre Lorde."

Ana got another call, so she wished him luck and opened the front door. Audre Lorde shot across the room. Ernest dived, managed to clamp and heft the cat, but strong as a cougar, she shoved off his stomach and made her escape. Ana and Ernest watched her vault across the front yard at full speed, her body stretched fully with each stride, round the corner of the house, and disappear.

"Oh!" Ana said.

The tears pressed so hard up his throat, Ernest didn't know if he could hold them back and he really didn't need to be comforted by his Lyft driver, as sweet as she was. He pretended that it was no big deal. "Go on. You got another job. A dish of tuna, and she'll be right back."

The second Ana's Camry turned the corner, Ernest started shouting for his new cat, the one he'd signed papers for, promising to protect and obey until the end of time, either hers or his. The name on her cage had been Sally, and so just in case she did answer to that, he shouted, "Sally! Sally!" as he chased around to the side of the house.

He hadn't yet been in the backyard. In fact, he'd kept clear of, been outright frightened by, that void behind the professor's house. Beyond the scraggly patch of weeds was a Hansel and Gretel forest he wouldn't dream of entering, a spooky dark mesh of trunks and branches and soil. He called for Audre Lorde, aka Sally, again and again, staring into the gloaming of the woods, dusk gathering, hearing the desperation in his own voice. He saw no Maine coon tabby cat anywhere about, just a gathering of ghosts wafting through the black tree trunks.

Ernest hurried back around the side of the house, and found the next door neighbor standing in his front yard.

"Hey, man, you okay? I heard shouting."

Ernest raised his hands in the air as if the guy had a gun, and then, embarrassed, dropped them quickly. "Yeah. No. I'm fine. My cat got out."

"Oh, he loves that cat."

"Oh, no, not the professor's cat. This is a different one. A new one. Not his."

The neighbor looked confused, but he took a step toward Ernest. "You seem really upset."

"I'm good. Hella long day is all."

"I have a really nice bottle of wine. A seriously good cab. Why don't I grab it and come over."

Was this white dude really doing this? This *straight and married* white dude?

Yep, he was. Neighbor man—Ernest knew his name but refused to use it, even with himself, as a tool for keeping distance—reached out a hand and placed it on Ernest's shoulder. Sure, the touch could be interpreted as simply brotherly, but it wasn't. It was more than that.

"No," Ernest said, "I have to work tonight. Big deadline. Thanks, though."

Ernest locked himself inside, dropped onto the couch in the front room, and sobbed so vociferously that even Virginia Woolf slunk under a nearby chair, frightened. She didn't leave the room, though. As distraught as he was, Ernest noticed that she stayed nearby.

CHAPTER 21

Jonas texted Delia, asking her to stop by his office after Monday morning's practice. As she left the gym and walked down the hall, she rehearsed her apology for last week's harsh treatment of the girls. He opened by asking why she thought they'd lost the game. She wanted to tell him it was because he made her put Alice on the team, but that would have been childish and, as she now knew, inaccurate. Instead she said, "Actually, the loss is typical for a really good team. Even a positive thing. The girls know they're good, really good. They got overconfident. It happens with every exceptional team. Confidence, rock-solid confidence, is absolutely necessary. But rock-solid confidence is based on fundamentals, excruciatingly hard work, no matter how much talent you have. Kids get flippant. They think they can wing it, play how they've played their wholes lives on the playground." Delia knew she was carrying on way too long in answer to his question. But besides just wearing him down, she thought she might be convincing him. "So a loss is corrective. A shock to the team's system. I'm pleased it happened so early in the season. Sometimes the surprising loss happens much later, and then it's more difficult to recover from. Not only did we lose, we lost to a team we should have shellacked. It's motivating."

Jonas smiled, apparently satisfied. He didn't say a word about her coaching excesses.

"What'd you decide to do about the gaming books?" she asked. Another tactic: change the subject, go on offense. "Did you get proof that he was actually running a casino out of the john?"

"I have another meeting," Jonas said, standing up. "But I needed to let you know, I'm sorry, I have a feeling you'll hate this, but the basketball coaches always chaperone the Christmas dance."

"Oh, wow. No. Sorry."

"You have to."

Delia laughed. "Who says?"

Jonas did his appealing wince, but this time it was less effective on Delia.

"I have nothing, literally nothing, to wear to something like that. I have a few tracksuits and some jeans." She and Morgan used to dress up to go out. Morgan loved her legs and bought her short skirts. But Delia had had to pare down her belongings to what would fit in her Subaru, so she'd dropped off all her dressier clothes at Goodwill, confident that coaching on the Oregon coast wasn't going to require a wardrobe.

"Megan can lend you something."

"Oh. No. I don't think so. I'm not the chaperone type. Plus, it's not like I'm on a salary that covers anything beyond coaching."

"Please, Delia. Don't be difficult."

She wasn't difficult. It hurt that he called her that. She prided herself on being a team player.

As the first bell of the day rang, she just shook her head and left his office. Out in the hall, kids were picking up their paces and disappearing into classrooms. She walked slowly, wondering which teacher she could convince to take her place at the Christmas—did they really call it Christmas rather than holiday?—dance. She was almost disappointed that Jonas hadn't chewed her out for being so hard on the girls in practice last week. *That* she would have deserved. He'd just jumped over that part and honed in on what he wanted: wins.

Plus her attendance at a school dance.

As the pack of students cleared, Delia saw, about twenty yards away, Mickey standing with her back against her own locker and Alice Foster pressing in close, red-faced and talking fast. Mickey's hands were up, palms out, as if in self-defense. Delia heard the words "don't ever" and "I told you once" coming from Alice, hot and furious.

Wow. Delia thought of Alice's dad's rude words about Mickey. She thought of Adam's hallway harassment that first morning. She needed to intervene.

But how?

The conflict wasn't happening during practice. They weren't in the gym. It wasn't her job to monitor personal relationships between the girls. She'd figured out to keep her mouth shut about Emma's abortion, and that was the right decision. Maybe Jonas did know a better way of defusing tension. Maybe cooling off was a new skill she had to learn. Maybe whatever was happening between Mickey and Alice was outside her jurisdiction.

Delia felt uneasy turning her back, but she did, leaving the building by a different exit.

CHAPTER 22

On the day of the Christmas dance, Delia went to the Dress Barn and found on the sale rack a plain sheath in deep-plum rayon, probably too short, but it was a dress. As much as she dreaded the event, she did look forward to at last meeting Jonas's wife Megan.

She arrived on time, well before most of the kids, and walked across the decorated cafeteria to where the Rockside High School first couple stood, Jonas in a black suit and green tie and Megan in a frothy red dress. Delia arranged her best smile and reached out a hand to Megan, about to deliver the warm but semiformal greeting she'd planned—she didn't want to seem too familiar and yet at the same time didn't want to be aloof.

"Merry Christmas!" Adam stepped over to Jonas and Megan at the same moment. He looked like a mock adult in tan slacks, a sport coat in a subtle gray plaid, and a light-blue business shirt, the top button undone. As always, he had too much product in his bushy hair, trying to flatten it to either side of a part. Delia almost felt sorry for him. In his own way, he tried so hard. He shook the principal's hand and greeted Megan with a small bow. The music started just then with the ballad "Unchained Melody." Adam turned to Delia and asked, "May I have this dance?"

"Get out of here," Jonas told him in a tone of affectionate jesting.

"I wasn't asking your wife, dude! Coach is single, am I right?"

"You're hilarious," Jonas said. "Scat."

Delia didn't think Adam was hilarious. The kid winked before sauntering off. She wanted to correct Jonas's perception of the encounter, but decided it wasn't the best way to start off her relationship with Megan.

"You got a flask in your purse?" Delia asked instead.

Megan had a lovely feminine guffaw of a laugh. "I wish!"

She was more petite than Delia would have expected, looking delicate next to Jonas. She watched Delia with pretty fawn eyes and a shy, tentative smile.

"That kid's a jerk," Delia couldn't help saying.

"He crosses the line sometimes," Jonas said.

"That's the prettiest dress," Megan said. "It must be an East Coast style."

"Actually, I got it at the mall down the highway. At the Dress Barn."

"You did?" That sweet guffaw again. "Oh my goodness, I would have just looked past it on the rack, not realizing how beautiful it is. I get distracted by gaudy and can't even see sophisticated."

How could Delia not look more closely at Megan's dress now? In deep red brocade, a full skirt fanned out below the fitted sleeveless top, separated by a crepe sash tied in a bow at the side of her waist. Delia searched for a compliment.

"I am so not sophisticated," Delia said. "If my dress works, it's pure luck. I yanked the first thing off the sale rack."

"Oh, it works." Megan took a bite of a lemon square and a bit of powdered sugar dusted the corner of her mouth. Jonas tapped his own, and she quickly brushed away the powder with the back of her hand.

Talking over the loud music was difficult, so the three of them used that excuse to regroup in silence, watching the holiday-attired kids flood into the space. Her job, Jonas had told her earlier in the week, was to weed out drunk kids and to break up disputes and any overt public sex. She'd asked him what made sex "overt," and he said she'd know it when she saw it. A giant Christmas tree, decked with multicolored lights, art class ornaments, candy canes, and lots of tinsel towered in the corner. On a far wall, a big blue Star of David hung crookedly, though Delia was sure it'd been plumb when she first arrived a few minutes ago. Some student had made a poster listing the seven core principles of Kwanzaa and this too graced the far wall. As if to say, *Jewish and Black kids* (Delia had seen maybe ten), *please gather over here in the dark.* The event was definitely Christmas heavy. Robin, the day custodian, sat in a big easy chair near the tree wearing a long white beard and a red-velvet Santa suit. In the momentary silence between two songs, Delia saw a girl try to sit in his lap and he bellowed, *"Ho, ho, ho!* Santa's got bad knees!" before shoving her off. Delia smiled, liking Robin. Kevin Banks, the boys' basketball coach, made the rounds of the cafeteria, joking with kids, completely at ease, and she wondered if she too was supposed to mingle, and if so, how did an adult, a coach, talk to kids at a high school dance?

Delia looked for her team. Loopy and Kayla had come dressed as elves, with red-and-white-striped tights, green felt hats, and long pointed shoes. They were laughing and high-fiving their friends. Alice danced with a tall boy on the basketball team. She wore a lavender dress with a couple layers of flowing chiffon. She actually looked happy, as if something weighty had been resolved for her, and that made Delia uneasy. Resolution for Alice might well mean something harmful to someone else. She hadn't been able to get the scene of that hallway dispute out of her head. Delia looked around for Mickey, but didn't see her. Emma was there, wearing an awkward green knit dress and black flats, presumably to minimize her height. She danced with a boy that Delia hoped wasn't Jed, waving her arms in the air like an upside-down jellyfish, her head lolling from side to side. Was she drunk? Straight-A, super-nerdy Emma? Who only a few weeks ago endured an abortion?

"So you've won all your games but that first one," Megan shouted to be heard over the music. "Bravo!"

"In double digits," Jonas said.

"Yeah. Thanks."

"Hon," Megan said to Jonas, "I'm going to get some punch and say hi to Jacqueline."

As she watched Megan walk away, Delia's mind zoomed out, hovered on the ceiling of the cafeteria, and she looked down at herself in this moment: thirty-eight years old and somehow at a high school dance with her high school boyfriend.

"Weird," Jonas said, apparently seeing the same picture.

"Yeah." They grinned at each other. Delia asked, "Who's Jacqueline?"

"Kevin Banks's wife." Jonas moved his mouth toward her ear so he wouldn't have to shout. "So tell me the real reason you left Monroe College."

"Seriously?" But it was impossible to feel uncomfortable with Jonas. "A little late for that question, isn't it?"

"I'm not asking as your boss. I'm asking as a friend."

"My boss," she said, and they both laughed again. "I already told you. My marriage ended."

"The college fired you because you got divorced? That doesn't make sense."

"Who said I was fired?"

"I know you. You wouldn't have quit—or come back here—over that."

"*Over that*? The end of a marriage is pretty devastating."

"I know. I'm sorry. But—"

"Okay, of course the story is much more complicated. Morgan got involved with the chair of the Women's Studies Department."

"*What?!*" Sweet Jonas, he found the idea of someone leaving her for someone else preposterous.

She told him everything, starting with her promiscuous years at Tennessee—at which he grimaced, because her wild coming out had meant leaving him—and how years later, Morgan resisted getting involved with her due to a fear that Delia couldn't ever be faithful. How Delia eventually convinced her that she could be monogamous, and how, when Morgan lost all interest in sex, just three years into their relationship, save the biannual efforts, even then she didn't stray. How Delia had convinced herself that it was just the high price you paid for a steady companion. How they married. How Delia thought they loved each other.

"Do you miss her?" Jonas asked.

Delia had to think about this. "Yes. But."

The look on Jonas's face could only be described as hopeful. Hopeful of what, Delia couldn't read.

"The thing about Morgan is that she's always right. In this case, she was right that we needed to separate. So in a painful way, I don't exactly miss her. I mean, I'm almost—and I do mean almost, not actually—grateful for the push out the door."

"Huh."

"Morgan said Mary—her new thing—was, and I quote, 'unimpeded by murky childhood memories.'"

"What?"

"Later she corrected herself and said that no, what she meant was that Mary had *dealt* with her issues, that she had 'matured elegantly.'"

"Murky? Nobody is more clear-sighted than you!"

"She said I was too angry."

She saw Jonas pause, absorb Morgan's words, and then choose his own: "You weren't angry when we were kids."

"I might have been. It just didn't show." She had never told Jonas about Celebration Camp. He'd been her life raft, her safe passage away from all that. Their story became a swift, clear river, and she wasn't about to muddy it with the past. Robin Hawkins, a mere acquaintance, had seen her sadness in high school, but Jonas had seen only her discipline, zeal, focus. He didn't understand that these traits had been the steel girders protecting her.

"I think *you've* matured elegantly," Jonas said, offering amends for sort of agreeing with Morgan on the anger issue.

Delia laughed. "You too. You look good."

"So you two stopped having sex?"

"Sure. Everyone does, don't they?"

"I don't know. Give me more details."

"More details about no sex seems like an oxymoron."

It was so easy being together, talking, even after a twenty-year hiatus. Jonas smelled like he did as a kid, but less grassy, more earthy, as if responsibility had a scent.

Jonas blurted, "I love Megan."

"I know you do."

"And I don't think it'd be possible to love anyone more than I love my girls."

Delia waited for the confession.

"But I feel trapped in Megan's family. They feel like an undertow."

"All families feel like undertows."

"I mean, you start to think like the people around you."

Delia could only imagine how Megan's family thought. "Jonas, you hate conflict. You always have. That makes it hard to disagree with people you love. But I know you. You have total integrity."

Delia was pretty sure by the slight stutter in his voice, which hadn't existed in the kid version of Jonas, that there'd been some integrity slippage over the years, but no harm in trying to shore up what was left. "You're only afraid you'll start thinking like them. This is just being an adult. The regrets. The stretching farther than you think you can stretch."

"I may not be able to stretch this far."

"Yes, you can."

"Her dad voted for Trump. He has guns. He uses foul language about people of color. I have to spend time with him. My girls spend time with him. And they love him. He's their grandpa."

"But you and Megan aren't like that."

"I think about leaving her. When the girls get older. I mean, like after they leave for college."

"Jonas."

"I've never said that out loud. But I think it sometimes."

"I don't think you should say it out loud."

"We never have sex either. Pretty much since Daphne was born."

Delia accidentally laughed. It was a release of tension more than finding anything amusing. Jonas laughed too.

"What's up with that?" she asked. "Why do people stop having sex?"

"Resentments build up. They become like scar tissue."

"It's lonely," Delia said.

"It's lonely," he agreed.

To change the subject, she said, "After that first disastrous game? I ran an unnecessarily brutal practice. You never said anything."

"I never heard about it."

"Really? I thought everything got back to you."

"The girls love you, Dee. They'd keep every one of your secrets. They'd follow you to the end of the earth. Already. After just, what, six weeks." He paused. "Be careful with that."

"I cultivate that devotion. For the purpose of winning basketball games."

"I know." He smiled his seventeen-year-old smile. "I know we both want this."

"The championship," she said, as if what he meant needed to be clarified.

"The conference *and* state titles."

Megan cradled three paper cups of red punch as she made her way back to them. Delia drank hers down fast. Jonas collected their empties and carried them to the big metal garbage pail decked with red and green balloons.

"That one's on your team, isn't she?" Megan meant Iz, who,

wearing a suit and tie, stood talking to a girl in a short green dress.

"Yes. That's Iz, Isobel O'Brien."

"It's lovely how much has changed," Megan chirped, her voice pitching to a higher register. "Even here."

"Yeah, it's almost an epidemic with their generation."

Megan thought that was too funny.

But Delia knew what it took for Iz to show up at the school dance in her suit and tie, to hold herself casually, as if it was no big deal. It wasn't funny. It was brave.

"You must hate being back here," Megan said.

Okay, so maybe she was more perceptive than she at first seemed. Jonas was an ass for talking about leaving her. "I can't say it's easy. But the team's great. And change is good."

"I'm sorry about your marriage."

"Thank you. Me too. Do you think Emma is drunk?" Her starting center lurched across the floor toward the refreshments table. She no longer moved like an upside-down jellyfish. Now it was more like a newborn moose learning to walk.

"Looks like it."

"Maybe I could just drive her home."

"Don't tell Jonas."

"Seriously?"

"He'd have to suspend her and then she couldn't play on the team. Trust me, he doesn't want to know. Go. Go now. I'll say you went to the ladies' room." Megan actually gave her a little shove.

"Really?"

"Yes!"

Delia intercepted Emma at the refreshments table, took her elbow, and steered her toward the door. "I'm taking you home. We'll talk later. Did you come with anyone?"

"Jed," she said, and then laughed.

"You're kidding me."

She shook her head.

"That short kid you were dancing with is Jed?"

Emma bit her lip and looked away.

"When I come back I'll tell him you left."

"I better tell him myself." She stumbled and turned an ankle.

"Nope. You have a choice and I'm going to make it for you. The choice is to stay and face the consequences of being found drunk at the holiday dance, or let me take you home right now. Let's go."

As they stepped out of the cafeteria and into the hallway, Emma peeled off her flats and tossed them to the side. She staggered on toward the exit. Delia sighed, collected the shoes, and followed.

"Hey," a voice called after them. "Need some help?"

Adam trotted toward them.

"Nope."

"She okay?"

"She's great. Turned her ankle. We're going to ice it."

"Nice legs, Coach. Who knew."

She had no idea how to counter a sixteen-year-old sexually harassing her. Before she could formulate a response, he added, "Ah, come on, Coach. You couldn't possibly think . . . Hey, I'm referring to your athleticism. Impressive."

Delia stopped, turned, and faced him. "I don't like you."

Emma honked out a big open-mouthed drunken laugh of admiration.

"That's clear," Adam said. "Kinda unprofessional, though, no? I mean, you're, like, an adult who works at a high school. I'm a kid. A student." He cocked his head. "Maybe we could sit down and talk this through?"

"Fuck you," Emma said. "Fuck you to hell and back."

The birthmark on Adam's neck deepened to cabernet in the lackluster hallway light. He said, "She doesn't have a twisted ankle. She's bombed out of her mind."

Delia took a firm hold of Emma's elbow and shepherded her down the hall toward the exit.

"Merry Christmas!" Adam sang out to their backs.

Delia had neglected to grab her jacket and the cold air seized her bare arms and legs. Emma burst into tears and Delia wanted to join her, but of course she didn't. She fitted the tall girl into the passenger seat and let her cry for the entire ride. There was so much she didn't know how to say to Emma and the nonstop crying was probably a saving grace. Pulling up in front of her house, Delia simply said, "Tell your grandparents the truth. You were drinking. I drove you home."

"But—"

"Emma. You're a smart, beautiful, talented girl. Make decisions that match who you are."

Emma stared at Delia's face as the words made their way, in drunken slow motion, through her brain. The kid never did acknowledge having heard. She got out of the car, leaving the door open, and weaved down the walkway to her front porch. Delia leaned all the way across the front seat to grab the handle and pull the car door shut. Then she watched as Emma rang the doorbell and a thin man with white hair let her in. She hoped he was kind.

CHAPTER 23

Delia wished she and Jonas hadn't confessed their mutual loneliness. She felt desolate the rest of the evening, as she drove back to the high school and finished out the dance making banal conversation with Jonas and Megan, and later with Kevin and Jacqueline Banks. Finally released at midnight, Delia drove straight to the Safeway. Loneliness can be met with food. Ice cream is no substitute for touch, for intimacy, but it's not a bad second. She wore her puffy black parka over the plum dress, but her legs were bare and she was freezing as she walked from the near-empty parking lot to the store entrance.

The bright colors, the multitude of culinary possibilities, just taking part in the human task of foraging for food, comforted Delia. She chose leeks, a knob of ginger, a big bag of spinach, and a tub of miso. She'd make soup. She grabbed some Granny Smiths for a cobbler too.

On her way to the freezer cases for the ice cream—should she get vanilla for the cobbler, just go for dark chocolate fudge chip, or both?—she wheeled down the paper products aisle and stopped in front of the massive toilet paper display. So many decisions. Quilted or not? Double- or single-ply? Five thousand squares per roll or three thousand? Name brands or knockoffs? This was what her life had become: indecision about toilet paper.

"It's impossible, isn't it?" A woman with light-brown hair, fluffy clean but messy, and saggy-tired eyes, maybe ten years older than Delia, pushed one of the giant Safeway carts down the aisle toward her.

"Yeah," Delia said. "I always try to do the math, you know, number of squares and length of rolls, but then there's the thickness factor."

The woman unleashed a big loose grin. She looked exhausted by life, a sort of happy/sad abandon in her comfortable body. She crossed her arms on the grocery cart handle and leaned forward on them. Delia felt the surprise of attraction.

"I usually just get the cheapest one," the woman said, "but that's probably stupid. If it's super thin and you need twenty-five squares per use, maybe it's not the most economical."

Delia could have done without the reference to wiping.

"Tonight," the woman continued, grabbing a big package of Charmin "squeezably soft" two-ply, "I'm going for the expensive, luxurious one." Then she laughed, maybe at the expression on Delia's face.

Too corny, Delia decided. Too whimsical. An obvious lack of discipline.

Then again, she was always falling for reserved women, falsely believing that the reserve stood for reservoir, that behind the strict sexy exterior was a lovely pool of tenderness, too sensitive to expose to the world. She ought to know by now that reserved just meant tight, stingy with feelings, or at best, just scared. It was a façade with no magical hidden pool.

Delia reached for the cheap store brand. "We could compare notes." Flirting over an extended toilet paper metaphor. After midnight on a Saturday night. In a Safeway. To make herself feel better, she began framing the story for Skylar.

"I'm Carolyn."

"Delia."

"Yes. I know. You're Delia Barnes."

"Oh. Well, hi." The woman looked smart, despite her willingness to talk for far too long about toilet paper, and Delia wished she had something half-interesting to say.

"I know a couple of the girls on your team," Carolyn said.

"The Murphy sisters, Sophie and Casey? I'm relatively new around here, but I understand you're quite the local star."

"My alleged stardom took place twenty years ago."

"The girls alarmed me the other day when they were talking about 'doing suicides,' how the new coach was making them do an 'insane' number of them. As a counselor, I can't say I've ever used either of those words lightly. But then the kids tease me about being overly literal."

"So you work with Josh?"

"Josh?"

"He's the only counselor I've met at the high school."

"Oh, no, I'm the pastor at New Day, the church on the highway just outside of town."

The din of supermarket noise—a humming fan, a rumbling shopping cart, piped music—swirled down the drain of Delia's consciousness. Everything went silent. She managed to ask, "Assistant pastor?"

"Nope. The one and only. I wish we did have the budget for an assistant."

It hadn't been Quade who found her in the church basement, covered her with a blanket, put a pillow under her head, shut out the lights. It was this woman. This goofy, spilling-outside-the-lines person. Pastor Carolyn.

She ought to have been relieved. But she wasn't. This felt like a fresh betrayal. A whole new and unpleasant situation. She hated the idea of him doing that, touching her, hovering over her, while she slept. And yet, it had felt so familiar. It had snapped right into place, fit the story she'd been bucking her whole life. Now that familiarity seemed strangely preferable to the ministrations of a stranger. As if she had a whole new enemy she hadn't even known existed.

The sensory tidings in the Safeway came clanging back. Footsteps coming down the aisle sounded like an approaching army. The ceiling lights glared prison harsh. Though she was two aisles away from the produce, the smell of rotting pineapple wafted.

Carolyn was chattering away: "We moved in almost eighteen months ago. I tell you, it's been quite a challenge—"

"You sent me a text message."

"I did!"

"How'd you get my phone number?"

"Sophie and Casey showed me the team rules. It's right on the sheet of paper."

"And you took it?"

"I did. I'm sorry. I guess I . . . I just . . . thought maybe . . ."

"The phone number was meant for my players and their families."

"I'm sorry."

"Don't contact me again."

Carolyn looked as if she'd been slapped.

Delia didn't trust what might come out of her mouth next. Her arms wanted to use the shopping cart as a weapon. She mustered self-control and, gripping the handle, steered it around the pastor. "Sorry. I don't do religion."

"I understand," Carolyn said to her back. "A lot of people have had bad experiences."

Delia commanded her feet to keep walking, her arms to keep pushing, but that surge, the same one that hurled a basketball at June Kirkpatrick, pushed Adam against the locker, heaved oranges across the supermarket, rushed on her like a tsunami. She turned around. "No, you understand nothing. You don't know anything about me or my experiences. It's sanctimonious of you to think you do."

"I'm sorry. I just—"

"No. Just no. Why do you people think you have the right to comment, unasked, on other people's lives?"

"I didn't say anything about your life, other than you being a local hero. And it's true that a lot of folks have had bad experiences with the church and I like to acknowledge—"

"Oh please. You people all talk in circles."

"Well. Now *I'm* offended."

"You're offended? You've got to be kidding. Everything you are offends me. Everything."

A surprising steeliness hardened Carolyn's gaze.

Delia made a 180-degree turn and shoved her shopping cart down the aisle, away from the pastor of New Day Church of Jesus Christ.

The two words made a soft landing between Delia's shoulder blades. She didn't believe she'd actually heard them. She turned to look, and saw the pastor standing beside her own shopping cart, one hand white-knuckling the handle, the other still clutching the eight-pack of toilet paper. A deep furrow divided her brow.

"Seriously," Carolyn repeated quietly. "Fuck you."

Delia proceeded unsteadily to checkout where she unloaded her vegetables and fruit and toilet paper onto the conveyer belt. Thankfully someone other than Loopy bagged her groceries. It wasn't until she started her car that she realized she hadn't gotten any ice cream, the whole reason she'd stopped at the store in the first place.

His surprise was somewhere in the woods behind the house, presumably playing bobcat, traversing mossy logs and hunting voles and other rodents, enjoying her unhindered independence. But Ernest didn't need to tell him that right away. Virginia Woolf might be enough for the time being.

"Patience," Ernest said, trying to sound seductive.

"How's the cat?" Ana asked.

"She knows you have a cat?" Dennis asked. He turned to her. "You know about Virginia Woolf?"

"Have fun, boys," Ana said, and zoomed off in her Camry as the guys dragged the luggage inside.

For the rest of the day, they made love and ate scrambled eggs and buttered toast in bed and retold each other all the stories they'd already covered in video calls, and then fell asleep early. Virginia Woolf spent the entire time in bed with the two men, snugged against Dennis's side, purring in mad love.

The next morning, on the twenty-sixth of December, Ernest's phone dinged in a text message while they were still in bed.

"Who's that?" Dennis asked, rolling over to face Ernest.

Ernest was afraid it would be the neighbor. Why couldn't he just stay on his side of the fence?

But it was his student. The one who wrote gorgeous poems about his love of god and country. The boy also wrote poems about his hometown, Scappoose, a bit north of Portland, depicting the place as if it were under siege, staving off the encroaching liberal hell of Portland.

Can we talk? Wesley texted. *Maybe meet for coffee? I'm in Scappoose but I could borrow my parents' car.*

No. Ernest was on winter break and Dennis had flown out to surprise him. The answer was a flat no. They could not talk. But saying that sounded harsh, so he just didn't answer. He put his phone facedown on the nightstand, and rolled over on top of Dennis.

"I think time apart is good for our relationship," Dennis said a few minutes later as he stroked Ernest's back. "I ever tell you how fine you are?"

"No, it's not. Good for our relationship, I mean. I can't wait to get home again."

"I want to write today." Dennis sat up and stretched. "Is there a room I could use?"

"There are about five rooms you could use."

"One where I won't be bothered for a few hours."

"You just got here."

"Don't be clingy."

Ernest tugged Dennis back down and licked his ear. "Stay in bed awhile."

"I love you," Dennis said. "And, I want to write today."

"You'd probably like the basement best. There's a desk down there and a bathroom and it's nice and dark and cave-like. You'll be in heaven."

After breakfast, Dennis took his laptop down to the basement and Ernest made himself sit at his usual writing place at the kitchen table. He could work on the Celebration Camp poem. Or he could start something new. He cradled his favorite mechanical pencil in his right hand and squared the notebook with his chest, trying to decide.

His phone dinged in another text from Wesley. *Please. It's important.*

Is it about your work? Ernest texted back. He meant to clarify the boundaries of their relationship but realized after he hit *Send* that the question only opened a door.

Half an hour is all I need. I'll come to your office.

Ernest left Dennis a note explaining that a student was having an emergency, and walked slowly over to campus, wondering why he always said yes. This time to a pasty white boy who cavorted with, actually celebrated and wrote poetry about, mean-spirited people.

Wesley waited for him in front of the locked Language Arts building.

"Thank you," Wesley said instead of hello.

Ernest used his key to let them in and they walked in silence to his office. He took the seat behind his desk, leaving Wesley to perch alone on the couch. Ernest cocked his head.

"I appreciate you taking the time," Wesley said. "You will probably find this hard to believe, but I've read every word you've published."

"I'm flattered."

"My fiancée broke up with me yesterday. On Christmas Day."

"I'm sorry."

Wesley folded over onto his cupped hands, his pudgy stomach puddling in his lap, and held his face. Ernest waited. He wouldn't say the words for him.

"She knows," he said. "That's why. She knows."

Still Ernest kept quiet.

"Can't you say something?" Wesley started to cry.

"No." Ernest shook his head. He thought of Angus at Celebration Camp. He thought of sweet Cal. He thought of brave Delia.

"My pastor told her," Wesley said. "In front of me. During our premarital counseling. He broke the trust."

Ernest snorted. He didn't mean his response to be unkind, but it was so typical. "How'd he know?"

"I'd had counseling with him about it. But years ago! When I was fifteen. I've recovered. He knows that. He knows I've recovered. This engagement, my girlfriend, it's all part of my recovery. I can't believe he'd do that. I mean, I know he's testing me. But it felt like he was warning her. And she panicked. Why wouldn't she? I guess he expects me to prove who I really am by convincing her I'm in love. *Again.*"

Ernest almost laughed at the way he made being in love sound like a chore, like cleaning the bathroom.

"I guess," Wesley spoke through his tears, "he's challenging me to man up."

"Look," Ernest said. As much as he needed to stay away from this hot mess, he couldn't hold his tongue any longer. "He betrayed your trust. That's wrong. Dead wrong."

Wesley looked up through wet eyes.

They should give counseling training to all poetry teachers. The students are asked to go deep into their hearts as they write, and inevitably they hit the most painful spots. How many girls had come to tell Ernest about rapes they'd survived, trusting him because he's gay? He'd listened to stories of every kind of abuse, and how could he turn away? But it wasn't his job.

"You write beautiful poetry," Ernest said. "But poetry is first and foremost about truth. The only limit you have on being a great poet is staying with the hypocrisy of your community."

"What?"

"You know exactly what I'm talking about. Don't pretend you don't." Ernest had so little patience for cowardice. And yet, his heart still ached for the young man. When someone you trust tells you that the essence of you is wrong, it takes so much strength to decide otherwise. Ernest had had that strength early. His mother's love was stalwart, even if she had moments of blindness. His dad had openly apologized, eventually, for taking him to Celebration Camp. He knew others were not so lucky. He said, "Your faith espouses a theology of love. How do they justify all the hate they spew into the world, especially at queer folks like you and me?"

"I'm not . . ." Wesley couldn't finish the sentence.

"You grew up in the belly of the beast," Ernest said softly. "Your family sounds, frankly, awful. I'm sorry. I know you've used poetry to reconcile yourself with them, and it's almost like you've revealed a shortcoming in poetry that I've never seen before—its ability to make the very ugly beautiful."

The silence then was long and painful, but Ernest succeeded in not breaking it.

"I don't know what to do," Wesley finally whispered.

"Do you love your fiancée?"

"Ex-fiancée," Wesley clarified, and did Ernest detect a whiff of relief?

"Do you love her?"

He nodded.

"Are you *in love* with her?"

He shook his head.

"Leave Scappoose. Today. Just pack your bags and go somewhere else. Come out. Save yourself and all of those around you from more grief."

"My church is counting on me. So is my pastor."

"No they're not. They're abusing you and, by the way, trying to glorify and justify themselves, by not accepting who you are."

Plain talk, but again, this wasn't his job.

Wesley stood up and managed to look almost indignant.

Ernest stood too. "Your choice. Speaking of love, I left my extraordinarily talented and gorgeous boyfriend back at the house. He came all the way from Brooklyn to spend a precious few days with me. I'm going back to him now. I've given you my advice. I can send you a list of books to read."

Ernest walked to the door and held it open for Wesley to leave, and then locked it behind them. Neither said another word as they walked out and went in separate directions outside the building.

That night he got a text from Wesley: *Thank you. I'm at my friend Sue's house in Portland.*

Ernest didn't answer the text. He was in the middle of cooking an elaborate posole for dinner. It was going to be delicious. He finished crumbling the cojita and chopping cilantro for garnish as Dennis came up the stairs looking tired but happy.

"Man," Dennis said, "this place is *quiet*. At first I couldn't work. The silence felt like an actual pressure against my ears. But then I did work. Really well."

"So you like it here."

"I'm not willing to admit anything like that yet, but what are you making? *Mmm*. It smells good."

Ernest blew on a spoonful of the stew and held it out for Dennis to taste. They set the table, lit a candle, and ate dinner. Dennis told Ernest about his idea for a new play, and Ernest told Dennis about the blank page, his inability to write a single word today. He didn't want to tell Dennis about his meeting with Wesley, because Dennis would, at best, roll his eyes, and might, at worst, get angry about Ernest cavorting with the devil. But he did tell him, and Dennis was surprisingly understanding, perhaps because he'd had such a good day of work. Ernest showed him Wesley's final text about decamping to his friend Sue's in Portland.

"You have a big heart, babe," Dennis said, coming around to Ernest's side of the table to kiss him. "How about on the kitchen table?"

Ernest laughed, but in fact they didn't make it out of the kitchen. As they lay on the floor, which he was glad he'd mopped recently, Dennis said, "So my surprise. Where is it?"

Ernest had to tell him about Audre Lorde's escape.

CHAPTER 26

By the end of January, the team had won every game except for that first unfortunate loss, but they wouldn't be able to keep it up without Loopy. She'd missed three games already. Delia decided to make the request herself, in person. She entered Safeway through the door behind the check stands, so Loopy wouldn't see her if she was working this morning. She headed straight for the stockroom in the back, pushing through the swinging doors.

"Need the ladies', Coach?" asked a middle-aged man with dry hair dyed bright red and burst blood vessels all over his face. He carried a box of turnips.

"I'm looking for Lupé Rodriguez's boss."

"I think she's up in the office. Let me get her." He set down the box.

"Mind if I wait here?" Delia stepped behind stacked pallets of olive oil, hoping to have the conversation in private.

She knew what she was doing was an overstep. She knew she should talk to Loopy first. But the conference tournament was fast approaching and she needed Loopy on the court, every single practice and every single game from now to the end of the season. If Delia made the ask herself, in person, surely the supervisor would agree to make some scheduling adjustments. They were only talking about a few weeks of shifts. Delia had hardly spoken to anyone in town who wasn't a fan of the team, who didn't want the conference and state championships.

A heavy woman wearing a green Safeway vest and tan capri pants that revealed a tattoo of a cougar on one of her swollen ankles limped toward her. She wore her thin hair combed straight back and held in place with a plastic headband. The pencil wedged on top of her ear looked more decorative, placed for effect, than utilitarian. She cradled a clipboard. Delia's heart sank. This woman looked like she loved rules.

"Nice tat," Delia said, nodding at the cougar, clinging to the only visual that gave her hope.

"I heard you came back," the woman said with a half smile. "Seen you in here a couple times. I have an office upstairs with a window down into the store. I can see all the shoplifters."

The comment startled Delia. Had she seen her throwing oranges? Or arguing with Pastor Carolyn? She flushed with embarrassment. But then she realized the woman only meant to brag about her position of power.

Delia reached for a joking tone: "Well, I've never shoplifted. Yet."

"If you do, I'll see it." The half smile again.

Delia held out her hand. "Delia Barnes."

The manager barked a laugh. "Yeah. I know."

Delia had grown tired of pretending to know people but needed to finesse this exchange. She feigned recognition. "How're you doing?"

"Married twenty-one years to the same man. Can't be all bad." She laughed again, a forced sound, as if she was mocking laughter itself. "Remember Justin?"

Delia canted against the tower of shrink-wrapped olive oil pallets. She should have felt sadness, or some permutation of compassion. But what wilted her legs was indignation. *Why?* she wanted to ask. She now saw the girl inside the grayish flesh, the prematurely lined face and thinning hair. She even heard her former booming full-throated laugh stuck inside that choked one. The cougar tattoo was the only exterior hint that this was the same person who'd cycled exuberantly at Delia's side, who'd sung dirty songs at the top of her lungs, who'd given Pastor Quade the finger.

"Sure," Delia said. "Of course I remember him."

Shawna had hooked up with Justin while Delia was at Celebration Camp. It hurt coming home to that. And confused her. Delia didn't understand what Shawna saw in Justin. Or how it could have happened so fast. But she'd forced herself to accept the shift. She never would have been able to tell Shawna about what happened at camp, or what happened with the pills and ambulance, and so it was just as well. At school in the fall, the two girls acted as if they didn't even know each other and soon they didn't. Delia made the basketball team, and the following summer she got into Pat Summitt's elite basketball camp, where she met her new best friend Skylar. When just a few years later Delia led the Rockside Wildcats to win the state championship, she took it as validation of her new and hard-won worldview. As proof that everything had been fixed and healed. Anyway, by then Jonas loved her. And Pat Summitt had recruited her.

"That's a long time to be married," Delia said. "Wow, twenty-one years. Congratulations."

"Well, you're not here to hear about my life. Bet you're here about Lupé."

For a second, Delia had forgotten why she was here. What she wanted. But she managed to claw her way back to say, "Yeah. I am."

"Sorry I haven't made any games. I got bad sugar. Plus grandbabies to watch."

Grandbabies! She was only thirty-eight years old. "That's okay. I was just hoping that maybe we could talk about Lupé's schedule."

"Can't do nothing about her schedule. She wants a job, she's got to do the hours."

Shawna had been so wildly open as a girl, her eyes nearly spinning in imagination, her voice loud with joy, her hunger for jokes and stories propelling her forward like a force of nature.

"I wouldn't want to interfere in any way with her job. I just thought maybe you could juggle her hours with some of the other baggers, so she could make the practices and games between now and the end of the season. Just for a month or so. She's crucial to the team and we're trying to win a state title."

Shawna took the pencil from behind her ear and hovered it over the clipboard, as if making calculations. But no, she was just using the props to cover her discomfort. Her left eye, the one that was slightly lower on her face, twitched. She said, "Her dad lost his job. She needs all of the shifts she's working."

"Oh, for sure. Yeah, I know that. And she doesn't know I'm talking to you. I just—"

"We got rules. Can't break them for her."

"I totally get that. It's not so much for her as for the team. For Rockside."

"I'd do something if I could. But one employee's got childcare issues. Another's got community college classes. I got two developmentally disabled baggers, and they get really upset with schedule changes."

"Okay. Yeah." Delia would try one more tactic: "The thing is, we're going to be having scouts show up during the tournaments. It could mean a college scholarship for Lupé."

Shawna shrugged. "Then she has a choice to make. Her. Not me."

"Okay. Thanks. Never hurts to ask."

"You got children?"

Delia shook her head.

"Husband, though?"

She was pretty sure Shawna knew she didn't have a husband. She shook her head again and said, "What would I do with a husband?"

Shawna laughed, finally a hearty and genuine laugh of pleasure, and for a brief moment the thirteen-year-old Shawna burned through. She shifted her stance, as if to accommodate the rare luxury of joy. She looked almost brazen. "Good for you. I got three daughters."

"How old are they?"

"Grown. Twenty, nineteen, and sixteen."

Since when was sixteen grown? Or nineteen or twenty, for that matter?

"Chrissie, my oldest, she's got drug problems. I have her babies for now. Just trying to keep the other two out of all that mess. Nicole, my youngest, wants to be a surveyor."

"I hope she gets the opportunity," Delia said. "She's at the high school?"

"Yeah. She misses a lot, though. I need her for childcare with the grandbabies. Middle girl, Trish, is over at Seaside living with her boyfriend. I got her a job at the Safeway there."

"Cool. Well, thanks for talking."

Shawna didn't leave, looked like she wanted something. Delia wished she knew what. Was there a trade they could make? Flexibility on Loopy's schedule for . . . ?

"Hey, you'll have to come over to the house sometime," Shawna said, shyly glancing off to the side and then back at Delia. "We can knock back a few cold ones."

"That'd be great." Delia pictured a yard full of rusted car parts, Justin slouched on the couch in a ribbed tank top, TV droning. "I love beer." Delia immediately regretted the inanity of that last sentence. Shawna was there somewhere, inside that shell of a woman, and would know it was a bullshit attempt at saying they were still alike, had something in common. *Yeah, beer, we both like beer.*

Delia held eye contact for another beat. Then the words just came out of her mouth: "I see you."

A glimmer of awareness lit Shawna's eyes, but she said, "You don't see nothing."

Leaving Safeway and getting back into her car, Delia felt as if there were a sandbag on her shoulders. She dropped her forehead onto the steering wheel, wondering if Shawna's view from the high window reached all the way out into the parking lot.

CHAPTER 27

Delia stepped out of the high school and stopped to admire the hard black sky, clear for once and pricked by stars. She felt happy. They'd be playing for the conference title in two weeks. That hot and addictive flight of competitiveness shot through her like an arrow. She loved winning. Plus, the day before she'd had a coffee date with a woman who owned the local bookstore. It felt good to make a friend, to step beyond the ghosts in this town, even though she needed to start thinking about how she would leave in the spring. Maybe she could leverage a championship into another college job.

Her team came out of the building in pairs and triads, talking and laughing, swinging their gym bags, hair still wet from the shower. Delia stood on the wide porch, bid everyone good evening, and watched them zoom off in their rides. She was just starting down the steps when Mickey came out of the building alone and called to her brother who was kick-propelling his skateboard back and forth across the parking lot. Despite signs posted at both entrances saying *No skateboarding,* he rode freely through the starry night. He looked like a big bat, sailing around the edges.

Mickey shouted his name again but he had his earbuds in and either didn't hear or chose to ignore her. Vaulting over a speed bump, his entire body left the board for a moment, his backpack flying away from his spine, so effortlessly airborne.

"Where's your mom?" Delia asked Mickey.

"We're walking home."

"That's a long way!" The Vlasak-Jones family lived on the outskirts of the far side of town.

Mickey shrugged and kept walking.

"Wait," Delia called to her. "Did someone tow the car again?"

Mickey and Zeke's mom always parked her all-electric Fiat next to the stairway leading to the front entrance, despite there being plenty of open legitimate spots in the parking lot. She liked to use the outlet under the stairs to recharge the car's battery. A couple of weeks ago, the car disappeared while she was inside getting the kids. The next morning the police found it in the Siletz River Regional Park lot. The second time the car disappeared, it was found in a beach parking lot, and marks on the car indicated it'd been towed. Now it seemed to have happened a third time.

Delia shouted to Mickey's back, "I asked you a question!"

Mickey turned, squinted in embarrassment, and said, "Yeah. Mom called a friend and they're driving around looking for the car. She told us to walk home."

"I can give you a ride."

"No thank you," she said, and took off.

Delia sat down on the steps in the cold wintry dark. She forced herself to consider the unpleasant possibility that it was her brother who was towing the Vlasak-Jones's car.

She called him. He wasn't due at work for another couple of hours and was likely still asleep. When he didn't answer, she hung up and then immediately called him again. She did this three times, until he finally answered.

"What the fuck, Dee," he slurred.

"Sorry. I know you need your sleep." Already her boldness in dialing his number multiple times curdled into a reluctance to confront him.

"You okay?" he asked.

"I'm fine. Need anything at the grocery store?"

"Ramen."

"Okay. I'll pick some up."

"Maybe some of those frozen pancakes. I don't know the brand. The ones that come in the white box."

"Okay."

"Why'd you call?"

The desire to protect him washed over her. If she asked, she'd have to act. Delia took a breath and said, "Someone's been towing the Vlasak-Jones's car."

"Good."

"Why would they do that?"

"She parks illegally all over town. It'd be one thing if she were a first responder. But she's just using the privilege she thinks being city manager gives her. She thinks that electric car gives her moral high ground."

"But it's not hurting anything. I mean parking here at the school in the evenings. No one is even around."

"She plugs into the outlet under the stairs. That electricity comes from taxpayers' money."

"So who's doing it? The towing."

"There are a lot of people in this town who can't stand her."

"It just seems kind of . . ." She couldn't bring herself to use the word *petty*.

"Dee, I gotta get a couple more hours rest. Jonas asked me to move a bunch of desks tonight from the basement up to the ground floor. It's going to be a bitch of a night."

"I'll pick up some ramen and those pancakes."

"You're the best. See you later."

Delia stayed seated on the school steps in the dark for a long time. She was glad she hadn't accused him directly. The truth was, she couldn't quite picture her brother pulling off such an elaborate scheme. Rifling through Zeke's locker was easy for Dylan. Towing the car would take considerable effort. Besides, he was always asleep at this time of day.

It had to be a team parent. No one else would even have seen the Fiat "illegally" parked at the school.

Mike Foster. Of course. His crude comments about Mickey's gender. Alice's aggression toward Mickey that day in the hall.

Delia drove directly to the Mosswood Tavern. Dylan was friendly with Mike Foster—had worked as a clerk in his family's hardware store years ago—and had told her that he stopped in at the tavern every evening for a cup of coffee before he went home for the day. She pulled open the tavern door and paused to get her bearings. The place was surprisingly cheery with a varnished myrtlewood bar top and a colorful array of backlit liquor bottles on the shelves behind the bar. The bartender did indeed look a bit like Frances McDormand, as Skylar had predicted. She was polishing pint glasses, holding each one up to the light to check for water spots. She winked at Delia.

Mike sat with a crony at a table in the center of the tavern, his forefinger hooked through the handle of a white ceramic coffee mug. Delia pulled out a chair at his table and sat down.

"Have a seat, Coach," he said.

"Are you the one towing the Vlasak-Jones's car?"

Mike crossed his arms and leaned back, rocking the wooden chair onto its rear legs. His friend laughed.

"She deserves it," Mike said. "Far as I can tell, she's not disabled. She can walk like the rest of us. You'd think as city manager she'd want to set an example."

"Have you seen the husband?" his tablemate snorted. "He wears his hair in a bun."

"I won't stand for harassment of my team families," Delia said. "First you tried challenging Mickey's right to be on the team—"

"One that looks like a boy?" the tablemate asked.

Neither Mike nor Delia looked his way.

"I don't know what your deal is," she continued, trying to keep her voice calm, "but if you have a problem with my choices, my team, my coaching, then I expect you to come to me, not bully the entire family."

Mike fixed his face into an expression of patronizing patience. His posture said, *Let me know when you're finished.*

The bartender set a beer, a local IPA rather than Skylar's predicted Pabst Blue, in front of Delia. "On the house," she said with another wink.

"On the house?" Mike's friend repeated, looking from the bartender to Delia and back again. "I've never gotten a damn thing on the house."

"Actually, I don't have any problem," Mike finally said. "Other than you sitting here yelling at me like you're in charge of the whole damn town."

"No, I'm not in charge of the whole damn town, but I *am* coach of the Rockside High School basketball team, and part of my job—"

"*Girls'* coach."

"Part of my job is working with the families of my players to make sure everyone stays healthy and enjoys full participation. That means making sure no one demoralizes a player with juvenile pranks, like towing their family's car. Three times. Look, I put your daughter on the team, like you asked. They're doing great. We haven't lost a game—"

"You did lose a game. You lost that first one."

Delia looked away, accidentally meeting eyes with the bartender, who smiled. She turned back to Mike and said, "We're playing for the conference title in two weeks. My team is outstanding. Each and every one of my players. And I don't need anyone poisoning our good karma."

"Karma," Mike laughed. "Good one."

His friend snorted again, and slapped Mike on the shoulder, as if anyone needed a reminder of where his loyalty lay.

"I do have my opinions about some of your choices," Mike said. "You might not know that I helped coach last year."

"Jonas told me."

He held up his hands, palms out. "I saw right away that you're prickly. Touchy. You were not going to want any help. Especially not from a *man*." He came down hard on the last word, giving it a bogeyman palpitation, and then laughed again. "So you might have noticed that I've stayed away. Kept my mouth shut."

"That's hard for him," the friend said, chuckling, enjoying being a part of this.

Delia had noticed, and been surprised, that Mike Foster had stayed away.

"Truth be told," he said, "I have a few good suggestions for your offense. But I cut a deal with your old boyfriend. You put Alice on the team and I stay away."

It took a long moment for Delia to process what he'd just said, and when she did, she felt the abrupt landslip of betrayal. Jonas hadn't told her that. He'd negotiated with someone who was challenging her authority. Behind her back.

"You were a fool to not put Alice on the team from the beginning." Mike slurped the last of his coffee. He set down the cup and pulled out his wallet. After putting two ones on the table, he looked Delia in the eye and said, "But I'll concede you've done a good job with the bunch you have."

She could tell that his compliment was sincere. More, it didn't even seem to cost him anything to deliver it. For a quick moment, he almost looked friendly.

"Alice is doing great," Delia said. She knew to meet a concession from an adversary with her own concession. Try to build trust. Even when the odds of success were slim. "I'm pleased with how much she's improved. She's playing with a lot more confidence."

"Do you know why?" Mike rocked back on the legs of his chair again, cocked his head to the side. He let about ten beats go by.

Delia gulped down some beer.

"I asked did you know why?"

"Well, I mean, we've been working on her—"

"Nope, it's not you, Coach."

"All right." She drained the rest of her beer.

"Barney," Mike said, "can I have a few moments in private with Coach?"

"What's the big secret?" Barney looked offended as he shoved himself up from the table. Mike waited until his pal had hobbled all the way over to the bar.

"You listening?" He spoke slowly and enunciated clearly as if he were speaking to a little sister. He waited until she nodded. "Alice's got a learning disability. She was failing her classes."

Delia knew her grades weren't great.

"You can't play on the team if you drop below a C+ average."

Delia nodded.

"Turns out that was why Alice didn't want to play. She was afraid she wouldn't be able to keep her grades up. What with the hard senior-year classes. You were obviously going to be much stricter than the previous coach, and she didn't want the humiliation of being kicked off the team."

"How'd you figure this out?"

"I didn't. That butch kid did."

"What do you mean?"

"I knew about the learning disability. But I didn't know that was why she was reluctant to be on the team. She did want to be on the team. But she was afraid. Mickey noticed her struggling in a couple of classes they have together. Offered to tutor her. I guess Alice didn't react so well at first. You know, she's embarrassed. But Mickey's a tough cookie, if you know what I mean."

"Hardly. Mickey is a big softie who works harder than anyone else."

Mike made his face of patience again and let a long silence go by before continuing. "So she confronted Alice about the tutoring thing a couple times. Told her she was needed on the team. Alice is stubborn as hell. I have four kids and she's by far the most intractable. Proud. Piece of work. But I guess she met her match in Mickey. The kid somehow talked Alice into being tutored and they've been working together since Thanksgiving."

Delia was stunned. She'd had no idea. In that teary encounter in the hallway, maybe Alice hadn't been attacking Mickey. Maybe she'd been resisting her offer.

"She got two B's on her December report card," Mike added proudly. He rocked forward in his chair, the two front legs making a loud *plunk* as they landed back on the floor, and put his elbows on the table. He leaned so close to Delia she could smell the coffee on his breath. "I'm not towing her parents' car."

Delia stood up on shaky legs and walked her empty beer bottle to the bar. The bartender let their fingers touch as she took the bottle, said she'd been wanting to meet her ever since she arrived in town, that she hadn't missed a game yet. Delia thanked her for the beer and her game attendance, left a five on the myrtlewood bar top, and headed for the door.

"I told you it was on the house," the bartender said.

"You should be starting Alice," Mike called to her back. "She hits threes. You'll need that in tournament play."

CHAPTER 28

After practice the next day, Delia descended to the basement, hoping Robin hadn't yet left. She found him tinkering in the boiler room. An ancient industrial furnace sat in the middle of the cement floor, surrounded by an array of lawn mowers, trolleys, shop vacs, floor polishers, and steam cleaners. There was a small refrigerator with a lock on the door and a pegboard holding rakes, shovels, and other hand tools. On the far side of the furnace, a truck-sized roll-up warehouse door opened onto a view of the damp tennis court.

"You're still here," she said. Her brother had complained that Robin often stayed well past the end of his shift, and sometimes was even still there when Dylan arrived later in the evening.

"Yeah. My girlfriend has her scrapbooking club tonight, so I figured I'd finish up a couple projects." He made a face of apology. "I'm comfortable here."

Delia looked around, wondering how anyone could like this cluttered dank space.

"Kind of steampunk, isn't it?" Robin said, sweeping a hand toward the monster furnace. He popped each of his ten knuckles in rapid succession, then kicked a foot at the locked fridge. "Can I offer you a yogurt? Apple or orange? I can make tea."

"Thanks, I'm good. I think this is the same furnace that heated the school in our day."

"It is. I enjoy the challenge of keeping it running. When it busts, which it does at least once a year, always in the coldest week of winter, I feel like a hero when I figure out the problem. There was that high school boiler that exploded in Indiana a few years ago, and Jonas threatens to find funds to replace ours, but I keep telling him, no, use the money for books and teachers. I have the furnace's back. I know, kind of crazy to anthropomorphize a furnace, but I feel that intimate with her." He popped his knuckles again.

"So, I kind of wanted to talk to you."

"Sure you don't want a cup of tea?" He took his scraggly ponytail out of its rubber band, pulled the hair back tightly, and snapped the rubber band back on.

"Okay. That'd be nice."

Robin plugged in his electric kettle and fumbled four boxes of tea bags in his forearms. "Caffeine or no?"

"Caffeine please."

"That brings your choice down to English Breakfast or Earl Grey."

"English Breakfast. With a splash of milk, if you have it."

"I have soy milk."

"Fine. Thanks."

"Okay, so tell me," Robin said, as the kettle hissed to life. "I swear on my beloved old-world furnace, I won't breathe a word to anyone. What's your offensive plan for the big game?"

"Which big game?"

"State championship."

"Come on," Delia said. "We have to get through the conference title before we can even think about the state tournament."

"I don't believe you. I know you're plotting every game weeks in advance."

Delia laughed. "You're right. I am. But I'm not going to share."

"I knew you wouldn't." He looked proud of her.

Robin poured boiling water into two chipped mugs and dunked in the tea bags. Using a key from the ring on his hip to unlock the fridge, he withdrew a carton of soy milk. He squeezed the pour opening and sniffed the contents, then splashed some into her teacup. "Sure you don't want a snack of some kind? I have half a leftover cheese sandwich. Wait. No one wants someone else's leftover sandwich. Sorry."

"I'm good. Thanks, though."

Robin moved the chessboard off the upended garbage pail serving as a table and set down the mugs. They sat facing each other in the two folding chairs. "It's a tea party," he said.

"Robin, I need you to tell me the truth."

He sighed. "Unfortunately, I'm incapable of not telling the truth. I wish I could learn to tell at least little fibs now and then. It would be helpful. And spare people's feelings. My girlfriend is always telling me to edit myself. Words just come out of my mouth, especially if someone asks what I think, which it seems like you're about to do."

"I think it's cool how you've been mentoring Zeke, playing chess with him."

"I love chess."

"Was it really necessary for Dylan to confiscate that stuff from his locker?"

Robin shifted uncomfortably on the folding chair. "I wasn't involved in that."

"I've heard the girls talk about locker raids."

"This is a high school."

"Do you do them?"

"Me personally? No. I work the day shift. They're easier to do at night."

"Dylan complains about Zeke," Delia said. "He says he lurks down here in the furnace room, like at odd hours. I told him that he comes to school early on the days his sister has morning practices."

Robin looked out the open warehouse door at the rain. He tugged his T-shirt down. "Dylan isn't the happiest guy on the planet."

"You said the same about me."

"Oh, it's a whole different kind of unhappiness. You have a grip."

"I'm glad you think so. That means a lot coming from the guy with a PhD in happiness."

"No actual degree. I never finished my dissertation."

She didn't want him to think she was making fun of him. "But you do have expertise in happiness."

"A half-assed academic expertise. My practical knowledge is very weak. But okay, I'll admit, I'm a good observer of happiness and unhappiness in other people."

Delia's tears welled up so fast they surprised her. "Oh! Sorry. It's just that Dylan launched me into my own happiness. He rescued me when I was a kid. In a big, big way. And now he—"

"Wait. There's an essential fallacy in what you're saying." Robin lifted his ample back end off the folding chair so he could shove his hand into the front pocket of his sweatpants. He fished out some wadded napkins and handed them to her. "He didn't launch your happiness. No one can do that for someone else. Which means you can't do anything about his, either."

Delia blew her nose in one of Robin's napkins. For years, whenever Dylan talked about slights—jobs he didn't get, women who rejected him, doctors who didn't understand his back pain—Delia felt her loyalty rise like mercury in a thermometer. But she'd always been at a remove, hearing his stories on the phone or in texts. It'd been easy to feel indignation for him, to love him, to pay her debt with listening and support. But now that she was here in his ecosystem, inside the community he often resented, she couldn't ignore the missing pieces, she couldn't *not* see what he was leaving out.

She wanted to believe that the seizure of gambling paraphernalia from Zeke's locker was an honest carrying out of his job, but she couldn't help seeing it as a targeted move.

Robin set down his mug, got up, and straightened some tools on the wall.

"Your girlfriend should be proud of you," Delia said. "You're editing yourself very well right now." What she wanted to know, and he knew it, was whether Dylan was maliciously messing with the kid.

Robin returned to the garbage-pail table and slurped his tea.

"Is Zeke really running card games in the bathrooms?"

"It wouldn't surprise me."

"But he's not a bad kid." Delia didn't know why she thought she could state that so matter-of-factly.

"No."

"It's just that I'm wondering if my brother's the one who's towing the Vlasak-Jones's car too."

"I don't know anything about that."

"He harbors a lot of resentments."

"Everyone does."

"You think?"

"Sure. Then they spend 90 percent of their mental energy justifying those resentments."

She laughed. "I guess you're right."

"It's not a very pleasant view of humanity."

"It's honest."

"Look," Robin said, "your job is to win basketball games."

That sentence made her feel unaccountably relieved. "That's it?"

"That's it." Robin smiled. "Delivering a championship will make so many people happy."

CHAPTER 29

On Saturday afternoon, Sarah the bookstore owner called and suggested a movie, one that very evening. It was dollar night at the movie theater and they were showing *Desk Set* with Spencer Tracy and Katharine Hepburn. As Sarah spelled out the details of her invitation, which took awhile because she was chatty, Delia decided to say no. She needed to apply brakes, even though they'd only had a coffee date so far. The woman's lively spontaneity—A movie *tonight?*—needed to be checked. Delia was leaving town soon. For the duration of her stay, she needed discipline and focus. Not spirited and impromptu dates.

She said yes. The movie, with popcorn and Red Vines, was so fun. Afterward, they went to the Mosswood Tavern for a beer. The Frances McDormand bartender was there, keeping an eye on them the whole time. She did not send Delia another local IPA on the house. In fact, she seemed a little miffed, although Delia was probably making that part up to keep herself distracted from liking Sarah too much.

The bookstore owner had dimples and curly hair and one of the most athletic minds Delia had ever encountered. She didn't just tell you about the books she'd read, which when done in a plotty way could be boring, she talked about how the stories intersected with her own life, which was alarmingly compelling. Sarah did most of the talking until the end of the evening and then she asked why Delia had said so little.

"Because I couldn't get a word in edgewise," she answered, and the poor woman, rather than laughing, blushed hard, the color rising from her throat up to her forehead. She apologized profusely for talking so much, which left Delia no choice but to apologize back for her comment. Her flirt attempt—which it had in fact been because she found Sarah's conversation utterly engaging—had misfired.

When Delia got home that night and crawled under the covers of her twin bed, alone and cold, she decided that the misunderstanding was the best possible outcome of the date. Sarah was the furthest thing from reserved, and therefore the furthest thing from Delia's type. Nipping it in the bud would be best for everyone involved. Delia would be free of Rockside by the end of March and could relocate anywhere in the country she wanted. Maybe she'd go stay with Skylar for a while and enjoy the sultry warmth of a Southern late spring and early summer.

In the morning, Delia called Skylar to suggest the plan, but her best friend did not pick up. Again.

"Where are you?" Delia asked Skylar's phone. "You never answer anymore. Call me."

Skylar finally called back that afternoon. Delia took her phone outside, because Dylan was still sleeping, and stood on the driveway under the basketball hoop, the same one he'd put up all those years ago. Pale green lichen crusted the backboard. The net dangled rotten and frayed. The hoop itself hung by one screw, now lopsided. She leaned against the garage door and had the upsetting realization that she was still the same girl who believed putting a ball through that circle meant redemption.

"Hey," Skylar said. "Sorry I've been sort of out of touch."

"It's okay. I know you've been having a tough season." Skylar's team had endured far more losses than wins this year.

Skylar laughed gaily, as if she didn't have a care in the world, and again said, "Sorry. What's going on with you?"

Delia figured Skylar was faking the good mood, and so to cheer her up, she described in detail her encounters with the

Mosswood Tavern bartender. Skylar laughed heartily. Uncharacteristically heartily. She sounded downright effervescent. Which made no sense at all in the midst of a losing season.

"Date her!" Skylar sang out.

That too was unlike Skylar. Just recently she'd warned against any kind of romantic entanglement in Rockside, which was why Delia hadn't told her about Sarah the bookstore owner. Well, for that reason, and also because Delia liked Sarah, kind of a lot, and even speaking her name out loud would bring an impossible intimacy closer.

"Hey," Delia said, "what if I came out there in the spring to stay awhile? It's been way too long."

Skylar didn't say anything. Not a word.

"I mean when the season is completely over. Obviously, I wouldn't come while you were still in the throes."

"Let's talk about it," Skylar said. "But listen, I gotta run. I just wanted to let you know I'm alive. We'll talk later, okay?"

"Where're you going?" It was Sunday afternoon. Skylar never went anywhere except for staff meetings, team practices, and games.

"Bird-watching."

Delia laughed.

"No, I'm not joking. I really am going bird-watching."

"Where? With who?"

"Apparently there's a nature preserve nearby."

"Do you even have binoculars?"

"Barb has two pair."

"Who's Barb?"

"A bird-watcher."

"Is this some new stress-reduction technique you're trying out?" It would be like Skylar to do something quirky like join a bird-watching club, but totally unlike her to do so in the heat of the season.

Skylar said, "Yes."

"Do you have one of those tan vests with all the pockets?"

"Hey, good luck at the conference tournament. You'll win."

Skylar hung up.

CHAPTER 30

Ernest felt a little bit like a stalker. He tried to tell himself that his plans were all in the service of poetry, like going out to the camp, but the truth was, seeing Delia now might kill the poem for good. He knew that. He ought to stay away. Keep her mythological. She and Cal had both seemed so innocent, in completely different ways, he with his fairy spriteness and she with the brave clarity. He needed to still believe. In her goodness. That by grabbing her at the last minute, taking her with him when he ran, he'd kept her from more trauma. How likely was that? Not very. Seeing what she'd become would shrivel all possibility of finding the poem.

He might as well go have a look, though. Hadn't he told Wesley that poetry was about the truth? Besides, it was already too late to protect his memory of her. The kid was almost famous here in Oregon. He'd found himself reading the sports pages, looking for bits about her, and there had been a few short articles this winter, since her team was winning.

Plus, he was lonely. He had to do something dramatic to ward off the temptation to have that bottle of wine with the handsome straight married next door neighbor. Or to accept the invitation to take a walk in nearby Tryon Creek Park with the pudgy fundamentalist Christian with the gorgeous eyes and a wicked command of language.

The conference championship game was being played at Portland State University and he took a Lyft over there early to have dinner in a Thai restaurant that had great Yelp reviews. The game had already started when Ernest stepped into the gym;

the place was packed. For a silly high school game. So curious, these pockets of humanity, places where people gathered in communities of passion and intense activity. A friend who played bridge often regaled him with stories from that unique and odd culture. *Only connect.* Who's to say with whom and how? Ernest climbed the bleachers to find a place squished between two family groups, wiggly with loud children. It was all very unpleasant. The crowd was mostly white and the mother of the family on his left leaned over and asked him which girl was his daughter. He pointed at a Black girl on the court, afraid that if he admitted he wasn't related to anyone, she'd think he was here for some nefarious purpose. He told himself he could just leave. The Thai dinner had been excellent, so the evening wouldn't be a total loss. Virginia Woolf awaited him at home. Not to mention Audre Lorde, who lurked somewhere in the back forty. Over the past weeks, Ernest had left out bowls of water and high-end kibble, and then watched raccoons and skunks dine on the delicacies. No, Audre Lorde was too proud for handouts, insisting on hunting her own meals. She didn't need his help. Likely she could single-handedly take down a fox. He stopped leaving out the food, but she continued to deliver rodent snacks for *him*, as if to clarify who was the dependent.

What was he doing in this loud gymnasium? He very much wanted to get back to his notebook and kitchen table. First he could call Dennis. They could have phone sex, although they'd tried a couple of times and he didn't see the appeal. It was just masturbation with distraction. And heartbreak, since your beloved wasn't actually there. Of course sex was all in the brain, he knew that, but he liked a bit of skin and muscle and bone with his.

Ernest steered his mind away from cats and sex, which he was using as a way to remove himself from the discomfort of the sports arena and the emotional upheaval brought on by being in the presence of Delia Barnes. He'd gotten himself here. He should at least try to watch, and understand, the game. Ten girls sprinted up and down the varnished wood floor, trying to heave an orange ball through an orange hoop. Ridiculous, really. But their faces were fresh, eager, desperate even, as if winning a basketball game were survival. As a child he'd been terrified of the boys who talked smack about playing pro ball—football, baseball, basketball—some were gunning for any of the three. It'd been a long time since he thought about those brawny and cocksure boys who felt that sweating up gymnasiums and athletic fields, grunting through made-up games, made them kings.

Ernest forced himself to be present. Couldn't he try looking at the world through someone else's eyes? As an exercise? He checked the scoreboard: the Wildcats, Delia's team, were winning by ten points. Good for her.

But where was she?

The white woman sitting to his left reached over her two little kids and tapped his knee, made an exaggerated face of glee, and clapped her fingertips.

"Don't tell me you missed it!" she cried.

He shook his head.

"Your daughter just blocked a shot!"

"I lied," he told her. "She's not my daughter. I don't even know that girl. I'm here to see the Wildcats coach. We were at the same Christian conversion therapy camp. Years ago."

The woman stretched her lips in what he supposed was an appalled smile and her eyes shifted away from him. *Oh shit.* He'd just outed Delia Barnes. Maybe she'd lose her job because of him. Now what was he supposed to do? Tell the woman how grateful he was that the camp had worked, that he and Delia had gone straight, blessed be Jesus Christ our savior? He was about to get up and just leave, when the woman's head snapped back around. She nearly shouted, "Our oldest son is gay."

"Oh."

"It was hard at first. But we love him. We would never send him—" She stopped herself. "I'm sorry."

Ernest tried to smile. "It's okay. My parents are great now. It just took a little time."

She grabbed his hand. Her fingers were bony and cold, and he didn't want her touch. He waited a second and then pulled away, just as a deafening cheer filled the gym. The girls on the Wildcats bench jumped into the air and waved their arms, hooting about whatever had happened on the court. Ernest still hadn't seen Delia, and he realized he'd been looking for her on the floor, as if she'd be playing ball with the kids. He'd been looking for a teenager, for the girl who stood by the side of the road in some remote corner of Oregon, waiting.

Shortly after he got into the truck with that man, Ernest regretted leaving Delia. What had he been thinking? That she would be safer without him? Or just that he needed to save himself? He'd justified abandoning her by telling himself that he would go find Cal. But that was a lie. He knew that Cal was gone.

Dead was what happened to rebellious queer boys.

Not five miles down the highway, the driver turned off onto a dirt road, into a forest, and they bumped along for a couple of miles. Ernest knew exactly what he was in for. He had invited it, but not because he wanted it. He tried to leave his body. He tried to shut off his mind. The man pulled the truck over and killed the engine. He looked straight ahead, through the windshield, for several long seconds before turning to Ernest. Then he quickly undid his belt buckle and unzipped his jeans.

The ache in Ernest's throat choked him. The pressure behind the bridge of his nose threatened to break his face. Despite his attempts to leave himself somewhere safe, he was still very much in his body. His mind was on fire.

The man pulled out his cock. He gripped the steering wheel with his left hand and reached his right hand behind Ernest's neck.

Ernest had spent all his resistance on the nightlong run. He had nothing left, despite the ache and burn, nothing but compliance. He let his head be drawn forward and down. He placed his hands on either side of the man's hips. The man groaned.

But Ernest did have something else left, after all. He had Delia standing beside the road. He had Cal walking out of the chapel. He had Jimmy Baldwin's torched words. He had poems he still wanted to write.

He had the fire *this* time. He had the possibility of survival.

That last was a bad word to think. Or maybe a good word. He didn't know the difference anymore. A roar of rage filled his chest. He reached for the man's belt buckle. He yanked, pulling hard and fast. As the leather belt slipped all the way out from around the man's hips, it whipped against the steering wheel and hit the man in the face. The man reared back, yelped. Ernest could sling the belt around his neck and cinch it tight. The back of the truck was a refrigeration unit, to keep the seafood fresh. He could put the body in there and it would look like a suicide by hypothermia.

This is the moment Ernest thinks of when Dennis scoffs at his possible belief in god. This moment when he felt pure hatred. This moment when he considered, in remarkable detail, murder. No faith, no deity, no whiff of salvation of any kind haunted the forest. God didn't speak to him. No light filled his body or mind. No voices drifted through the trees. But *something* saved Ernest that morning. He did not choke the man. He let go of the belt and slid across the truck seat, opened the passenger door, and jumped out. Rather than walking down the road, where he could be apprehended by the truck driver or worse, the police, he dove into the forest, again running as he had the night before, but this time without Delia. He sweat and ran and cried. For hours. He knew he was getting more and more lost. He'd never felt so afraid in his life. Mostly of himself. For those few moments he'd imagined killing a man.

He'd told Dennis some of this, but not all of it. He couldn't tell him how, though Ernest felt as alone as he'd ever felt then or since, he now wondered if someone had watched over him after all. If an invisible someone guided him to another road, which led him to the ranger station. The man taking down the American flag wore a uniform, a green one, but a uniform just the same, and that badge terrified Ernest. But he couldn't run anymore. He was too weak and thirsty and heartbroken.

"Do you have a phone I could use to call my dad? Please."

The ranger, a fiftyish white man with silver hair and round clean-shaven cheeks, looked at him for a long time. Ernest knew no amount of politeness could change what he saw: a tall Black boy on the run.

"You okay, son?" the ranger finally asked.

"No." Ernest had nothing left in him but the truth. "I ran away."

"From home?"

"No. From a camp."

"Where's your dad?"

"LA."

"That's a long way from here."

"Yes sir."

"What's the name of the camp?"

"Celebration Camp."

"Wait here." The ranger went inside the station, locking the door behind himself. He'd left the American flag dangling at the bottom of the flagpole, a corner sweeping the pavement. He'd be calling the police now. His father had had "the talk" with Ernest, of course he had, many times, but the scenarios never included his son's homosexuality as a factor. Ernest knew he ought to run, but he didn't have any running left in him. He sat down on the grass in front of the ranger station and watched the building's shadow move across the green.

His sweat dried and the shade cooled. Ernest wrapped his arms around his legs and pulled his knees close. Hugging himself, he dropped his face to the tops of his thighs. After a while, he heard a screen door bang. A dog barking, approaching. Footsteps crunching across the gravel parking area. When the footsteps stopped a few feet away, Ernest lifted his head.

"Honey," the woman said, "I'm Cora, the ranger's wife. We live right over yonder. I fixed you a plate. Are you hungry?"

The ranger's wife had tight curls and wore pale lavender stretch pants, a sleeveless flowered blouse. A German shepherd stood at her side, pink tongue lolling to one side of its mouth. Cora put the plate and a tall glass of iced lemonade on the grass, a few feet in front of Ernest, and the dog lunged.

"No, King!" she shouted and the dog stopped, sat, and looked at the food longingly. "Go on," she said to Ernest. "Take the plate. My husband called the camp. They'd already called your parents early this morning. Your father flew up and is there at the camp. He's on his way now. He'll be here in a few minutes."

Ernest drank the lemonade. He ate the turkey sandwich and pool of applesauce. Then he prayed harder than he'd ever prayed in his life.

For days and weeks after his father came to get him, Ernest waited for the police. For that knock on the door. The handcuffs and trial in court. He imagined the prison cell in vivid detail. He knew he hadn't actually strangled a white man. And yet that moment of wanting to felt more real to him than the truth. As the months passed, and no cops showed up, as he read and re-read James Baldwin and Toni Morrison and Octavia Butler and Zora Neale Hurston, looking for solace, even freedom, in their stories, he came to realize he was safe. And that safety, Ernest decided, required humility. Who was he to say whether or not god existed? Whether or not god had lent a hand? He'd happily embrace the unknown over certainty.

A referee blew her whistle and now the basketball audience roared in protest.

There she was. Delia Barnes. Gesticulating, shouting, jumping to her feet to holler at the ref. The sight of that tall, pale girl with her fiery aura nearly knocked him off the wooden plank upon which he sat. She looked beautiful, actually, with her embodied wildness. Of course she'd rocketed through her own life since that night they ran. She'd become someone new, different, and yet, probably, like him, also exactly the same.

Ernest didn't stay. He couldn't. He scuttled back down the bleachers, having to slide on his butt to manage the descent because there were so many people and he didn't want to bump anyone and didn't trust his long legs, his long and not particularly graceful legs, as he made his way to the floor. He was forced to wait in the corner of the gym because the play had surged down to his end, and he felt painfully exposed standing there. He just hoped that Delia didn't see him.

A needless worry, he realized as he finally was able to exit the gym. She would not recognize him all these years later. He'd come looking for her, knew she'd be here in her capacity as coach, but she had no idea where on this planet he now hung out. For all he knew, she remembered him as the devil. He needed to leave well enough alone.

Home again at last, standing before the front door in the dark because he'd forgotten to turn on the porch light, he fumbled in his shoulder bag looking for his house key. He couldn't find it. He glanced next door where the warm square of light exposed the neighbor's kitchen. Ernest saw someone moving around the far side of the room, but turned away before he could determine if it was him or her. Why didn't they ever shut that shade? The professor had mentioned the neighbor had a spare key, and Ernest hoped he didn't have to go over there and ask for it.

He found his phone in the outside pocket of his bag and sat down on the front porch. First he deleted the two texts, which both apologized for writing him too often, from his student.

Then he used the phone light to search through his shoulder bag. He found the house key, stood, and jabbed it in the lock. As he let himself in the front door, he felt a sharp pang of missing Audre Lorde. Who'd been his cat for all of about one hour. The little fucker. He'd freed her from the pound. He didn't even like cats. But he'd done it, from the goodness of his heart, and also because he wanted to give Dennis a gift that meant something, so yes, some self-interest was involved, but nevertheless, he'd certainly improved Audre Lorde's life by bailing her out of prison. What had he asked for in return? Just a little companionship. But no. His little wildcat did not need him, that much had been made abundantly clear.

Ernest locked the door behind himself and found Virginia Woolf waiting for him just inside. He scooped her up and sat on the couch, holding and petting her for a long, long time. She belonged to someone else, but tonight she was all his.

CHAPTER 31

A week before the state tournament, Delia made a pilgrimage to the trophy display case. Back at the start of the season, on that excruciating first march down this hall, she'd felt ashamed to be returning to her eighteen-year-old self, as if her very body were imprisoned in a high school display case, surrounded by plastic trophies, hers placed by her own brother in the very center. Today she felt cautiously proud, anticipatory, an open brightness.

The Rockside Wildcats won the conference title easily, by twenty-four points. More, they were the top pick for the state title. Her team was injury-free, a near miracle at this point in the season. Every one of them, including the bench-sitters, had learned the offensive plays to the point of rote perfection. Delia favored a player-to-player defense, but they had a strong zone defense in their back pocket for a surprise switch. Under Alice's coaching, both Casey and Loopy had started hitting threes. Now that Delia understood the reason behind her reluctance to be on the team, she felt a bit more compassion for the kid. As a big bonus surprise, Shawna had quietly arranged Loopy's schedule so that she'd been able to attend every practice and game through the tournaments. Shawna didn't say a word to anyone, not to Loopy and certainly not Delia, about the concession; she just made the arrangements. Delia wanted to send her flowers or maybe a case of beer, but decided that playing dumb was the best response.

What Delia saw now, standing in front of this old trophy of hers, was that she didn't have to be stuck in this display case. She could move the story along. To free herself, she just needed to link then to now. She had to break the glass.

The next day, on Saturday afternoon, Delia drove to the church. Her Subaru was the only car in the expansive lot and she straddled two parking spaces, a tiny act of rebellion. She walked past the basement door and around to the front door, two tall panels with stained glass and long wooden handles, a bizarre opulence on the otherwise plain-as-a-paper-bag building. She hefted the door open and entered the church, expecting a dramatic physical reaction, like her knees buckling or involuntary gasping, but instead felt a small trickle of relief. It was just a building. Twenty-five years, hundreds of basketball games, lots of girlfriends, and one marriage had trekked through her life since the time these walls meant something to her. She stepped into the sanctuary. Just a room. Albeit a room that held people's crazy hopes and unbearable grief.

Delia walked up the center aisle letting her fingertips slide across the tops of the pews on either side. She and Morgan had not married in a church of course; they'd taken their vows on a grassy hillside overlooking the campus, an early June heat wave ruining everyone's outfits. Would Morgan and Mary Hunt marry? She remembered a party at which the professor grandstanded about the patriarchal roots of marriage, the *institution* of marriage she'd called it, and how she would never allow the state or the church to validate her relationships. So, no, they probably would not marry. On the other hand, Morgan could be quite persuasive, using—let's just say exploiting—other people's weaknesses to achieve her own ends. The fact of the matter was, Delia pretty much agreed with Mary Hunt about the church, state, and marriage. But if Morgan wanted marriage, Delia bet she'd get marriage.

She shoved aside these thoughts as she made her way to the altar. There she stood behind the pulpit and surveyed the scenery.

Pastor Carolyn had hung quilted banners with social justice messages—*Be the Change* and *Love Is Love* and *Black Lives Matter*—on the walls, making the place cozier, so much more welcoming than it had been when Delia was a girl. Still and yet, it was a church.

She guessed that a Saturday afternoon would be a good time to find the pastor in her office. Carolyn had looked like a person who wrote her sermons at the last minute. Delia found the office door open, but no one inside. To ward off the PTSD beginning, at last, to zing through her bloodstream, Delia needed a heretical act, at least a small one, so she picked up the pile of papers on the pastor's desk and started to read the first page. The top sheet was indeed a handwritten draft of a sermon. God, in Carolyn's lexicon, was a *they.*

"Shit!" a voice at Delia's back barked. She swung around, the sermon draft still in her hand.

"You scared the living daylights out of me," Carolyn said. "I didn't know anyone else was in the building."

Delia needed to keep her thoughts crisp. Her purpose was a short apology and then she'd leave. "You must have congregants who come to see you," she said.

"Yes. But I usually hear them coming."

"Well, I didn't tiptoe or anything. I opened the front door and walked in." Already she felt defensive, attacked.

Carolyn softened. "You're welcome, of course. Have a seat. What do you think of the sermon?"

"I only read the first couple of paragraphs."

"And then I lost you?"

"And then you walked in and interrupted me."

They both smiled.

"Sorry," Delia said, dropping the sermon on the desktop. "For snooping."

Carolyn waved a hand at the air as she circled her desk and took a seat. "I'm flattered you were interested."

Delia glanced around, expecting familiar cues—the same mauve linoleum and aluminum-framed windows, the odd shape of the room, part square with one rounded side, like a mini altar—to trigger a bad reaction. But she felt okay, more evidence that the story, her story, had evolved. She would not tell Carolyn that she was here to metaphorically break the glass on the trophy display case. To open the flow of air between then and now. To make space for a new championship. She tried to formulate words for the real apology she owed Carolyn.

"Sit," the pastor said.

Delia remained standing, finally noticing the ways Carolyn had changed the space. She'd hung black-and-white wood-prints of shorebirds on the walls. Books packed a floor-to-ceiling bookshelf, arranged pell-mell, some stacked on their sides, others with their spines facing the wrong way. Curtains, rather than a shade, dressed the window, which was cracked open, despite the chill. Delia wondered if Carolyn had a spouse.

"I came to apologize for being so rude in the grocery store," Delia said.

"No need. It was the middle of the night, after all. The witching hour. No one can be expected to behave in a Safeway after midnight. But while we're at it, I apologize for being sanctimonious."

"Well."

"And for my outburst at the end."

"You mean the *fuck you*."

"Yes, I mean the *fuck you*."

Both women tried to hold their ground, but ended up smiling at each other again.

"I deserved it," Delia said.

"Of course you didn't. I shouldn't have lost my temper. But I just get so tired of people misrepresenting the church and making assumptions."

"Well," Delia said again.

"Which is perfectly understandable. No one misrepresents

Christians more than some of the people who claim the faith, the so-called Christians who act anything but."

"That's the truth."

"So what happened to you in this church?"

Delia raised her hands as if Carolyn had pulled a gun on her. "Look. I just wanted to say I'm sorry. For the grocery store thing. I gotta run now."

She'd made amends. She'd faced the church and pastor. She'd dredged the channel. Check, check, and check. Back to work.

"You fell asleep in my basement," Carolyn said. "Your feet were muddy and wet. You were shivering in your sleep."

"I wasn't shivering."

"No? In any case, I get to ask, you know, since you were trespassing. Also, if there are ghosts haunting the place, I want to know."

Delia dropped into the armchair across from the pastor's desk. "Do you?"

"I do." She took a breath. "Cody Quade?"

Delia flinched. Visibly. "You've heard from others?"

Carolyn stared back, mute. Of course she couldn't break confidences.

"I'm not looking for counseling or help," Delia said.

"Nor am I offering counseling or help."

"Okay." Delia used a reporter's voice as she said, "Quade caught me kissing a girl in that basement. He sent me to Celebration Camp. Ever hear of the place?"

Carolyn shook her head.

"Use your imagination."

"I'm sorry."

"Actually, in the end it was a life-defining experience. It was a painful but effective way out of the hypocrisy of the church." Carolyn cocked her head in that annoying therapist way, but Delia couldn't stop talking now that she'd started. Sitting here, in this office, in this church, she felt not just compelled, but moved by a force stronger than her own substantial will, to make a few things very clear.

She told Carolyn how she'd made a clean transfer from god to basketball, from Jesus to Pat Summitt. Her own body became the temple. She said that she loved sex. That she deplored injustice, sloppiness, and stupidity, in that order. She said she had a no-ghosts policy, believed in full transparency, and that she wasn't afraid. She said that she was here now because her team was about to win a state championship and she wasn't going to let any lurking demons from the past get in the way. She wanted full bright light.

Carolyn listened with so much obvious interest that Delia needed to finish by saying, "And please do not invite me to come to church. I won't."

"I won't invite you. Ever."

Delia was taken aback by Carolyn's response, but then detected some amusement in the woman's eyes, and so she added, "I'm not joking."

"I see that. Nor am I. I promise I'll never invite you to church. Even though you just told me that basketball and religion are sort of interchangeable, and I've been to every single one of your games."

"You have?"

"I wouldn't miss them."

"Well." Delia felt cornered, which made her dig in. "I'd say that basketball is probably holier than religion because it doesn't include hypocrisy."

Carolyn just raised her eyebrows.

"So why Jesus?" Delia asked. "You seem like such a normal person and everything. Why would you commit your life to an institution that celebrates a male god and some random dude from ancient history?"

Carolyn looked down at her folded hands.

"It's a real question," Delia said, drilling down.

"I know it is. I ask it of myself every single day."

"You do?"

"Yes. That's what faith is, being not sure."

"I thought faith was the opposite: being sure no matter what."

"The whole concept of faith is that no one can ever be sure. All those philosophers who looked for proof of god—Aristotle, St. Thomas Aquinas, etcetera—their arguments just sound silly and desperate to me. The most exciting part of faith is believing in spite of being unsure. Deciding to believe anyway."

"Believe in *what?*"

Ha. She'd stumped the woman of god.

Gathering a head of steam, Delia answered for her: "In some white guy who lived two thousand years ago."

"You sound more sure of him than I am."

There was that whiff of sanctimoniousness again and it pissed Delia off. "I'm sure of what Christians preach. I've heard plenty of it."

"You don't know me, Delia. And neither of us truly knows who Jesus was. I don't know if he was white. Maybe not even a guy. That person had a message and that message is like the rules of basketball, or the rules of writing a sonnet. They aren't the only rules for life, or necessarily even the best ones, but without some set of rules, we're all flailing through space."

"But we *are* all flailing through space. Literally. On planet earth. I believe in facts and evidence." Delia sounded recalcitrant, even to herself. Still, she punctuated her point with, "Science."

"And yet you act on faith all the time. For example, you moved back here to your hometown on the Pacific coast. Rockside, Oregon." Carolyn named the place with what almost sounded like mockery, like Skylar's Drip, Bog Trap, and Torrents. "There must have been an enormous amount of uncertainty in that decision. Yet you did it."

"Desperation, not faith. I basically had no other choices." Whoops, too big a reveal.

"Sometimes I think desperation is synonymous with faith."

"Word games."

"Yeah, you're probably right. All I'm saying is that I feel despair all the time. The church is the best answer I could come up with. Maybe a sign of too little imagination. God knows it's an imperfect solution to despair."

"Okay. Well. Glad we talked," Delia said. "Glad you've replaced Quade."

"I heard he died."

"Oh."

Carolyn laughed. "You can be glad. I wouldn't judge."

Delia was unsure what she felt about his death. Maybe nothing. Maybe she just didn't care what had happened to him. She wanted to leave now and didn't know how to say goodbye to the pastor, and so she rose and turned toward the door.

"See you at the tournament next week," Carolyn said.

"Thanks for your support. Of the team, I mean."

"I know what you meant. Hey, do you know the poet Ernest Wrangham? I thought of him because of what you said a minute ago about Jesus. Wrangham has a couple of poems questioning Jesus's gender and skin color."

Delia sat back down in the chair. The blood seemed to empty out of the crown of her head and face, wash down through her chest and stomach, and then surge back up again. She mustered her considerable discipline and said, "Oh, really? Huh."

Carolyn moved around from behind her desk and began searching the bookshelf, touching the volumes tenderly, as if she were reading Braille. Delia waited, counting her own heartbeats.

"Here it is. Keep it. I can get another copy. I think you'd really like these poems."

Delia didn't remember, or maybe had never known, his last name and surely there were thousands of poets named Ernest. Hundreds, anyway. Or dozens. She opened the back flap and looked at the author photo. Those ears, the way he listened to everything so intently.

"I mean, if you want to," Carolyn prattled on. "Oh. Is this the same as asking you to come to church? It's not, really. I mean, Wrangham does write about Jesus, but just a little bit, in a couple of the poems, and trust me—okay, those are the wrong words, you don't ever have to consider trusting me—but he questions faith in this deep and, maybe I shouldn't say this word either, but holy way. I do think I can promise that you won't be offended by a single one of his poems. Most of them are positively profane."

When Delia didn't speak, didn't respond in any way at all, Carolyn reached to take the book back. "Okay, sorry," she said. "I didn't meant to force them on you."

"No," Delia said, gripping hard. "I mean, thank you. I'd like to see the poems."

She exited Carolyn's office holding the book, without finding the inner resources to say even goodbye.

"Delia?" The pastor's voice trailed after her.

She didn't turn around. She continued out the front door of New Day Church of Jesus Christ and tipped her face up to the beginning-of-spring sky, pale as a bird's egg. She breathed in the evergreen air. Of course she was happy the story hadn't ended with a seafood truck at a homely intersection in the middle of a coastal forest. But this sudden expansion of knowledge might burst her.

CHAPTER 32

Delia read the whole book that night, the lyrical narratives both history and prophecy, lightning bolts of joy and dead bodies of grief. The poems were pages long and every one told a story, the words like ocean currents carrying her forward. She read for content. She wanted to know where he had been, how he had interpreted their shared past, but Ernest hadn't written about Celebration Camp, the before or the after. The closest he came to Delia was with the poem called "What Does It Mean to Love Jesus?" He'd started that poem when he was sixteen, at camp, and had recited it to her that day they escaped, his early version just a handful of lines. This published rendering went on for six pages, exploring Jesus's identity, his skin color and gender, his sexual orientation, and reinterpreting his words in the bible. Delia saw that the poem was lovely, fragile as a shell, and a revelation. But of what? In fact, she wasn't quite sure what he was writing about in any of the poems, though a few were more transparent, easier to understand, and, in a couple of cases, funny expressions of life. Most of the poems, though, were heady and potent, both too much and too little. She found, reading through again and again, that the less she thought as she read the poems, the more she understood their meanings. But then, upon yet another go through, the meanings shifted, became something altogether different. She studied them for story. Most of all, she swam in the new knowledge that Ernest was not only alive, but flourishing. According to the book jacket copy, he'd won awards and lived with a playwright named Dennis.

CHAPTER 33

At dusk, after an afternoon of writing, Ernest closed his notebook and got up from the kitchen table. Virginia Woolf had a snack and retreated to the bedroom to rest. Ernest went out to get the mail, and also fetched that morning's paper. Coming back in the house, he got distracted by a front-page article about the Oregon girls' basketball championship game, to be played the next day, with Delia Barnes's team favored to win. It was astonishing, really, to read quotes by her as a woman, an apparently confident leader, and it jarred him out of his writing reverie. He poured himself a glass of wine, sat down on the couch, and read the article all the way through to the end.

As he set the paper down, he noticed that he'd left the front door ajar. He panicked, worried that Virginia Woolf had gotten out, but then heard her back at her bowls crunching food. He quickly shut the front door and went to check on her in the kitchen.

There he found Audre Lorde crouched at the kibble bowl, helping herself to supper. The enormous Maine coon glanced up at him, nonchalant, entitled, fully in command of the situation, then resumed chowing down. After she'd sated herself, she sauntered into the living room, jumped onto the couch, and made herself comfortable on a pillow.

Ernest checked the bedroom where Virginia Woolf slept soundly on the bed. He decided to leave them each to their stations. They could manage their own greeting. Which they did, around eight o'clock that evening, when Virginia Woolf found

Audre Lorde in the front room and went ballistic, hissing and arching her back, the hairs standing straight. Audre Lorde jumped off the couch, lazily, as if she couldn't care less but wouldn't waste any time on this priss, and walked to the front door where she waited to be let out.

Ernest sighed. Rule number one about relationships: you can't control other beings. Rule number two about relationships: without trust you have nothing. So, despite all his angst about her escape and truancy the past weeks, he opened the door and Audre Lorde stepped out into the night. A moment later, her eyes shone from under the bushes.

"Have a great night partying," Ernest called to her. "But I want you back by daybreak."

At dawn, Ernest found Audre Lorde waiting at the front door. She came right in for her breakfast. Virginia Woolf hissed, but with resignation, and maybe even a little curiosity, before going to hide in the bedroom.

CHAPTER 34

The night before the championship game, Skylar called to wish Delia good luck.

"Thanks. I'm feeling good about it. The girls are ready."

"Can I offer a little advice?"

"Sure." Delia's voice wavered. They were less than twenty-four hours away from the big game. Skylar knew the psychology of that of stretch of time. You don't entertain a sliver of doubt. You're in forward-velocity mode. Advice is a kind of brakes, a second look, a reconsidering. It was entirely inappropriate right now.

"They're high school kids," Skylar said.

"And?"

"That's all. They're kids."

"I can't even believe you're saying this. They're only a couple of years younger than your players. You'd never downplay the importance of *their* games. *Your* games. This is the state championship."

"Yeah. I know. I can't believe I'm saying it either. Never mind."

"No," Delia said, "I want to know what you mean."

"You've just been so jacked up."

"Yeah, I'm jacked up. Of course I'm jacked up. If I weren't, I wouldn't be doing my job. Again, it's a state championship."

"I know. A lot is on the line."

"Yes. Exactly. So what's your point?"

"It's so strangely similar to where you were back then. A kid wanting a championship to redeem everything. In some small town in Oregon. The *same* small town. I mean, the cast of characters hasn't even changed. Jonas. Dylan."

Delia didn't understand. Skylar didn't have a mean bone in her body. Nor a passive-aggressive bone. She'd never downplay the stakes for high school kids. She wasn't saying, *It's just a game,* an expression Delia hated.

"I have no idea what you're trying to say."

"I'm worried about you."

"Skylar. What's wrong with you? My team is playing for the state championship tomorrow. This is my happy place. There is nowhere else I'd rather be."

Skylar was silent.

"I can't believe you're interjecting a what-if-you-lose scenario. That is so not how a coach thinks. You know that. What the fuck?"

"You never use profanity. That's what I mean."

"I do now."

"That's what I mean. You seem pretty unhinged. You've said so yourself."

Delia sighed as audibly as she could. There was no one in the world she trusted more than Skylar, and while she was mega-annoyed by this conversation, she did want to know what she was getting at. So she waited.

"I've been thinking about Tara VanDerveer a lot," Skylar said.

"You always do."

"If I could emulate anyone's game psychology, it'd be hers."

"Okay." They'd talked about this a million times. Skylar admired Coach VanDerveer because she managed to hold herself and her team to the highest possible competitive standards, she wanted to win as badly, maybe more badly, than any other Division I coach, and yet at the same time she played classical piano, she meditated, she accepted losses with extraordinary grace, pivoting almost instantaneously to thinking about what she and her players could learn from the losses. But—Delia now realized—Skylar wasn't predicting a loss. She was warning that win *or* lose,

Delia was standing on a dangerous precipice. She was staring into an abyss. Rockside, Oregon. Jonas Kowalski. The trap of her brother.

"You're looking for redemption in the wrong place," Skylar said.

Delia hung up on her.

She pulled on her running clothes and set out in the dark to run off Skylar's "advice." She needed to center herself on tomorrow's game. Which shouldn't be difficult. Her team had roared through the early rounds of the state tournament, easily winning their berth in the big game. They'd be playing Wilson High School, a Portland team, and being from a small town on the coast made them the team to watch, the best story. They'd had lots of media support, fuel for the win.

What was Skylar's problem? Jealousy? Possibly. She'd had a couple of difficult seasons in a row. But jealousy would be so unlike her. Not to mention she was still coaching a Division I school while Delia had been fired from her Division III coaching job and was heading up a high school team in rural Oregon. Of course jealousy was never rational. Still, Skylar had far more goodwill than that. She would not stoop that low. Not now. Or ever. She'd never undermine Delia.

When she reached the pebbled beach on the Siletz River, she dropped to her knees at the water's edge and listened to the river slurp along its route to the sea, just a short distance to the west. She grabbed two handfuls of stones, opened her fingers, and let them sift through. This spot beside the sluicing river, in the misting rain, her knees and palms sunk in the beach muck, was not home. Maybe that's what Skylar was trying to say? *Be careful with this mirage of home, this false home, this memory of home.* Yet tomorrow's challenge, this verge of championship, this gathering of every mental and physical resource, every brain cell and muscle fiber, preparing for the best possible performance—*that* was home for Delia. She loved being here.

Back at the house she took a long hot shower and went to bed early, only to wake at three in the morning, unable to remember the startling dream that broke her sleep. She swung her legs out of bed. It was hours before dawn, yet she knew she wouldn't go back to sleep and she needed to sweat off the gauzy nightmare.

Delia ran all the way to the high school, circled the campus, and then headed to New Day Church of Jesus Christ. She circled that ugly building too. When she came around to the far side, she was startled to see a light on in the pastor's office. The curtains were drawn, so it was possible, given Carolyn's general disarray, that she'd just left the light on accidentally. But Delia bet she was in there, maybe writing Sunday's sermon since she'd be at the game most of Saturday.

Delia wanted to thank her for the poems, and she almost knocked on the window, but that would be creepy. Anyway, her gratitude felt unwieldy and confusing, and she needed to stay focused. She couldn't afford to talk about Ernest and his poems now. She could sort all that out later.

By the time Delia got back to the house on Parker Street, her knees ached from running too many miles in a twenty-four-hour period.

CHAPTER 35

Delia ate a big breakfast of eggs, bacon, and oatmeal. It would be a long time before their postgame dinner at the steakhouse in Dundee, a town on the route between Portland and Rockside. Jonas booked the entire restaurant so that the team and their families, and any fans who wanted to join them, could all celebrate together. He and Megan had left their daughters with her parents and went ahead to Portland last night. They were staying in the Benson Hotel and had reservations for the hotel's fancy brunch this morning. Jonas told Delia that Megan was planning on shopping at Nordstrom between brunch and the game. Delia had mocked him a little, saying, "So you're giving the little lady the credit card?" He just shook his head, like she was incorrigibly obnoxious, which she supposed she was. Dylan also went ahead to Portland last night, to spend time with Poppy and Yvette, both of whom, to his great delight, had agreed to accompany him to the game. Before he left, he bought the groceries for Delia's pregame breakfast, arranging the food in the fridge with a card propped up against the egg carton. Inside the card he wrote, *Superstar Coach Delia Barnes. State Champ X 2.*

She tucked the card in the game-day briefcase she'd packed the night before. Next week she'd sit Dylan down to talk about the locker raid and car towing, his misplaced anger at the Vlasak-Jones family, but she couldn't deal with that now. She needed to hold onto the brother who'd given her the life raft of basketball, who'd found her the scholarship to Pat Summitt's basketball camp, who'd always been her biggest fan.

After showering, Delia laid out her new electric-blue suit and lime-green blouse. Morgan would love the colors, the quality of the fabric, the fit of the suit. She'd wholeheartedly approve of spending that much money on a single outfit for an important occasion. Delia had tried finding something at the Dress Barn, on the same sale rack where she'd found the plum holiday dance dress, but there was nothing, and on a whim she drove to Portland and shopped at Nordstrom, draining her meager savings on the outfit. Plus a new belt and shoes. It didn't hurt that the salesperson helping her was an exceedingly attractive person of a splendidly ambiguous gender.

Still in just her underwear, she rechecked her game-day briefcase, making sure she had all her notes, which she wouldn't need or have time to consult during the game, but having them stewing in her bag would help. She was due at the high school at noon and had decided to be just a tad late, even though she'd never tolerate that from her team. She wanted to make an entrance, a noticeable one. Having the coach sitting on the bus, waiting, was not the look she wanted. Sweeping up the bus steps and commanding her team, that was the plan. Teenagers took to drama like a tide pool to incoming seawater. She wanted them full and teeming with life. She planned to use every drop of their humanity today. She buttoned the lime-green blouse and pulled on the electric-blue trousers.

Delia stepped out onto the porch and popped open her umbrella. The mist of the last couple of days had developed into a tender, teary rain. Unaccountably, the sound of it tapping her umbrella triggered her own tears. She wanted this win. Skylar was right that she cared too much. But why live if you didn't care too much? Caring too much is the fundamental definition of an athlete. It's the heart of the game.

Delia's phone trilled in a text message from Skylar: *You got this*. No smiley face, no muscle arm, no clapping-hands emojis. Just three words. Her timing was impeccable. She must have felt remorse for yesterday's comments. Delia smiled and drove to the high school.

The girls were already on the bus as their families sheltered under the building's entrance overhang, waiting for the booster buses to open their doors. Sarah the bookstore owner, getting out of her car not far from Delia's parking spot, waved exuberantly, her arm like a windshield wiper through the now sheeting rain. Delia smiled but turned away, waving instead at the gathered fans on the porch, and made her way to the team bus. From fifty yards out she could hear her team braying and see them carousing. She had to harness these wild creatures, and fast, so they didn't discharge all their energy before they even got to Portland. She took a deep breath and climbed on board.

The girls whistled at her bright suit. Loopy started a low-throated hooting that they all joined, hopping out of their seats. A flash of doubt twisted her gut: what was she doing here, working with girls so young and raw?

Maybe that's why Skylar had said what she said. To inject doubt like a vaccine. So she could see it, address it, and knock it out cold. Skylar realized there was a lurking enemy, the possibility of a failure, not of basketball but of confidence, at this crucial moment. That was something Skylar would do, notice a slippage and find the fix. Selflessly offer the assist. Even if she never got credit.

Delia kicked the weakness to the floor. She brought herself into her body, onto the bus, before these girls who were depending on her belief in them. She straightened her spine and waited for the team to sober. They did, quickly.

"What's the plan?" Delia asked in a low and deadly voice.

"Pressure defense!"

"Why?"

"Offense sells tickets, defense wins games!"

"Casey, what's your job?"

"Deny their point guard the three. Force her to go left."

"Emma?"

"Dominate the boards!"

"Iz?"

"Passing precision!"

"Loopy?"

"Get good looks!"

"What single shot wins and loses games?"

"Free throws!"

Their eyes were dark and clear, their feet planted on the rubber mats of the bus, squared and ready. She didn't congratulate them on their perfect answers. She resisted smiling. For some of these girls, winning today could mean the difference between a college education or not. For all of them, it would be a significant cog in the development of their self-esteem. Joy. It'd be plain and simple joy.

Delia made eye contact with her players, one by one. So quietly half the girls probably didn't even hear her, she said, "Win this game."

Taking a seat at the front of the bus, she checked her briefcase one more time. Her notes. Dylan's card. A bag of almonds. Another bag of gold star glitter which she'd toss at her players after the win. It'd lodge in their hair, on their shoulders, catch the lights. Also, Ernest's book. Stupid to have brought that. The sight of it was destabilizing, tugging like an undertow. His virtual hugs, fists planted on hips. The way he recited Shakespeare by heart, singing out the funny parts and getting wet-eyed at the declarations of love. Most of all, how he hadn't been ashamed. How he'd made fun of the hypocrisy. The way he tried to keep Cal safe during his deliverance. The way his calloused hand had felt in hers that night they ran.

Thinking about Ernest made Delia dangerously soft. She removed the book from her briefcase and slid it under the bus seat. She felt bad leaving it on the grit and hardened wads of gum, but it couldn't be helped.

She stood up and twirled her hand at the bus driver. "Let's get rolling."

"Wait!" Casey shouted. "Where's Mickey?"

Delia counted the girls. Casey was right. Mickey was missing.

Iz said, "She was here earlier. I saw her in the gym practicing free throws."

Delia checked the time. It would be like Mickey to relentlessly practice her free throw, right up to the last minute, even though she was unlikely to see any play in this game, but it was not like her to be late. "Kayla," Delia called to the back of the bus, "be quick. Check the gym and locker room."

As she turned her back on the team and retook her seat at the front of the bus, her phone buzzed in a text from Jonas: *Are you on the road?* She decided to ignore him. He was probably texting from their brunch table while Megan was in the bathroom. Or maybe he was back in their room and Megan already at Nordstrom. It bugged her the way he administrated from a distance, like her progress getting to the game needed to be supervised. Instead of answering Jonas, Delia responded to Skylar's earlier text with a slam dunk meme. Then she reread Sarah's email from yesterday (the woman didn't text and surely that said something unsettling about her), wishing her good luck and saying she'd be at the game.

Delia leaned down, looking between her legs at the book of poems on the bus floor under her seat. Maybe it was unfair to accuse the poems of being the destabilizing factor in her day. There seemed to be a handful of forces rocking her balance. But she left the poems where they were.

"She's not there," Kayla cried as she burst back onto the bus.

"Did you check both the gym and the locker room?" Delia asked.

"Yes."

"Maybe she got sick?" Taylor said. "Nerves?"

"Nerves? Mickey? No way," Iz said.

"She's always on time," Kirsten said. "Always early."

"I tried calling Zeke," Sophie said. "He's not answering."

"Wait," Loopy said. "You called Zeke?"

"Yeah." Sophie smiled shyly.

"You have his number?" Loopy shouted. "He's like a freshman!"

Sophie full-on grinned.

"No way." Loopy jumped to her feet. "She's dating him. She is. Look at her face."

"I cannot believe you didn't tell us!" Emma hooted.

"Not *dating* dating," Sophie said. "I mean, you know. Not yet. He's cute though. Hella cute."

"Seriously?" both Brittanys said at the same time.

"Jinx," Brittany Nguyen said, and the two girls high-fived.

Delia thought of Cal saying *jinx* on the pond that day Quade came to camp. Cal's sweet pink smile. She shouldn't have brought Ernest's poems. Not today.

"Smart," Emma said. "He's a total brain."

"Besides, Sophie's only a sophomore. It's not that weird of an age difference. I mean, one year is all."

"You'd have cute kids."

"You've gone from an unanswered phone call to procreation," Sophie's older sister, Casey, said. "Stop already."

As Delia checked the time again—they needed to get going—Jonas called. Was he going to monitor her all day long? She silenced her phone. She'd call him once they were on the road.

"Eyes to the front of the bus!" she shouted, waving her arms over her head to get their attention. If Mickey were here, she'd be the one to notice. She'd be the one to curb the frazzled energy and bring the team to center. But Mickey wasn't here, and Delia couldn't process that now. She needed to get this team to Portland.

"Hey!" She didn't like the shrill in her voice, but the girls did finally quiet and look up. Everyone except for Alice who continued texting furiously. Which annoyed Delia. So much of Alice's behavior annoyed Delia.

"We have to go," Delia said, tamping her tone, keeping it simple. She turned to the driver and mimed turning a key in the ignition. He started the engine with a big growling roar, meant to be celebratory, and the crowd of parents, grandparents, brothers, and sisters waiting under the overhang sent up a cheer and swarmed down to the booster buses as those doors flapped open. The plan was for the three buses to caravan to the game.

"Hold on," Casey called out.

"We have to wait for Mickey," Iz said.

"We can't wait any longer," Delia told them. "If we don't check in an hour before tip-off, we forfeit. There could be traffic."

Delia's phone buzzed in yet another call from Jonas.

"Yep," she told him before he asked, "we're just about to leave."

"You haven't left already?"

"Chill. We'll be there."

"You were supposed to leave fourteen minutes ago." His voice sounded tinny, a little strangled, like something had scared him. She almost laughed. Skylar was right, of course. It was crazy the way Delia was all tangled up with her high school boyfriend as she approached a state championship. Again. Twenty years later. It was actually funny. She and Skylar were going to have some good laughs over good beer about it this summer, when finally they could sit on Skylar's porch and rehash everything.

"Jonas," she said in probably too familiar a voice, "if you wanted to micromanage the day, you should have stayed in Rockside."

"I'd like you to leave now."

"Uh. Sure. We are. But is everything okay?"

"Yep!" he proclaimed too heartily. "Call me when you're out of the parking lot."

She considered mentioning Mickey's absence.

"I'm just excited," he added, almost sounding like his kid self again, his seventeen-year-old awakening self. "This is a big moment for Rockside. It's going to be awesome."

"We're rolling as I speak," Delia said.

The driver laid on the horn and made a full U-turn to get to the parking lot exit. The drivers of the two booster buses did the same, leading the way, as if the ancient yellow school buses were a cavalcade.

With all the racket, Delia couldn't hear Jonas's closing words. "I'll see you in a couple of hours," she told him, and clicked out of the call, dropping the phone in her briefcase.

As the first two buses slid from the parking lot onto the highway, Alice stood up and bellowed, "They're arresting Zeke!"

The bus driver looked in the rearview mirror and then at Delia, who rotated in her seat to see if she'd heard what she thought she heard. All the girls sat forward with their hands on the backs of the seats in front of them, mouths hanging open, looking from side to side.

"Mickey's with him," Alice reported without looking up from her phone. "They're at his locker."

"Okay," Delia said, "I'm sure their parents have been called." Turning to the driver, she said, "Please. The highway. Now." It dawned on her that Jonas was fully aware of whatever was going on inside the high school at Zeke's locker, causing his frantic text and calls.

"*What?*" Iz roared.

"Arresting him?" Loopy shouted, her eyes and mouth wide.

Every single girl was on her feet now, all talking at once, calling out questions.

"Let's get going," Delia told the driver, again twirling her hand in the air in front of her chest. The booster buses had already disappeared out of sight.

"Can't go with the girls standing up," the driver said.

"Sit down!" Delia shouted.

"Mickey is really scared," Alice said, still looking at her phone. "Someone posted on Instagram that Zeke has a bomb in his locker."

"*What?*" Iz roared again.

"Damn," Casey said.

"That's fucked up."

"Hell yes it is."

Alice shoved her phone in her pocket and started up the bus aisle.

Delia said, "Sit down, Alice."

"No." She looked Delia in the face, her acne flared and her red lips darkened. She pushed past Delia and waited in front of the closed bus doors.

"Just go," Delia told the driver. "Please drive."

He shrugged and swung the lever that opened the bus door. Alice leapt, skipping all the steps and landing on the pavement. She ran for the school entrance. Sophie also pushed past Delia, following Alice.

"Sit down," Delia ordered.

The rest of the girls froze in a diorama of indecision. Then Iz inched forward, passing by Delia as if she were a sleeping cobra.

"Iz. Sit. Now."

The tall girl's freckles seemed to be popping off her face. Her mouth twisted with emotion. "Coach, there is no *i* in the word *team*." And she jumped off the bus.

At any other time, Delia would have laughed. So Iz had read Pat Summitt's books. Even Delia, lover of platitudes according to Morgan, hadn't brought out that one.

"We'll be right back. We can't play without Mickey," Emma explained to Delia, using that voice young people employ with adults when they don't expect them to understand.

"Her parents will drive her to Portland as soon as they straighten out the situation with Zeke," Delia said, but no one was listening. Short of physically trying to wrestle the girls back into their seats, she couldn't stop them. They charged off the bus. Loopy gently touched Delia's forearm as she went by, as if she were the consoling adult and Delia the child. Debbie stopped to apologize, too profusely, saying "I'm sorry" at least three times. Kayla promised to round them all up and bring them back shortly. The herd of girls sprinted across the parking lot, up the front entrance stairs, and into the building.

Delia glared at the driver. "I can't believe you opened the door."

He shrugged. "You can't lock kids in a vehicle."

"Yes, as a matter of fact, you can." She pounded the plexiglass barrier in front of the first seat before jumping off the bus herself. Walking up the hill through the rain, she tried to shove her anger aside and think of a strategy for corralling the girls. They'd built in a bit of wiggle time, but even so, her plan needed to be executed with haste. As she entered the building, she saw a gathering at the far end of the hall and forced herself to walk, not run, toward it.

Zeke sat on his skateboard, back against a locker, elbows on his spread knees, forearms shooting toward the ceiling, and both middle fingers extended. It looked as though he'd held this gesture for some time. Robin sat on the floor a few feet away, legs crossed, his big stomach resting on his thighs, talking quietly to Zeke.

Did he have a bomb in his locker?

The accusation was absurd.

Wasn't it?

Her team huddled against the bank of lockers opposite Zeke's standoff, with Mickey in front, hands on her hips. It might be the first time Delia had ever seen her scowl.

A uniformed security guard from the agency Jonas always used for school events was speaking forcefully to the girls, telling them that they had to leave now. As Delia walked onto the scene, the guard pivoted, stepped in her path, and asked Delia who she was. The woman had a point guard's build, lithe and agile, and wore her hair in short locs. She wasn't armed—Delia checked. There were in fact no police on the scene who'd have the power to arrest Zeke. Delia swerved around the security guard without answering her question.

"Girls," Delia said with every ounce of grave and quiet authority she could muster. "On the bus. Now. This is not our business."

Mickey, whose trademark was cheerful enthusiasm, glared at her brother sitting on his skateboard in front of the locker. She said, "Ezekiel, please," the words coming out in a passionate whisper.

"Someone is accusing him of plotting to bomb the school." Iz spoke directly to Delia, holding up her phone, screen out, but was too far away for Delia to see the Instagram post.

Sophie and Alice panned their phones in slow motion, filming Zeke, Robin, the security guard, and Delia. Mickey had her Nikon around her neck but she wasn't taking any photos.

"It's complete bullshit," Sophie said, without lowering her phone arm.

Zeke's eyes flicked over to Sophie. His mouth tightened. Sophie smiled at him. He might have smiled back.

Great, Delia thought, *bomb scare as eroticism.* Not just Sophie, her whole team seemed excited, locked in a stance of sizzling solidarity.

She walked over to Robin and squatted next to him. "Please tell me what's going on."

"Someone posted a photo on Instagram of Zeke at his open locker with the words, *First illegal phones, then a casino, now a bomb.*"

"When?"

"This morning."

"Who posted it?"

"I don't recognize the account. But it's been shared a ton already. Jonas is getting calls from parents." Robin hesitated, looked at his hands folded in his lap. "He didn't want you to know. Because of the game and everything. He told me to handle it."

"Let me see."

Robin found the post and passed his phone to Delia. The photo showed Zeke at his open locker. His wiry form filled half the picture. The other half showed the jumbled locker interior. She tapped the photo and zoomed in for a detailed look. "All I see is a messy locker," she said, handing the phone back.

Robin shrugged. "Doesn't really matter. Jonas can't ignore a bomb threat."

"So he called you?"

"Yes. And I called Zeke and told him to meet me here at school. Which is going to piss off Jonas and maybe even trigger my termination. In any case, Zeke had already seen the post and was here when I arrived."

Delia didn't know what she'd seen in the photo. But how could she not imagine a ticking clock set to go off . . . when? The metal locker exploding. Homemade shrapnel flying into the legs, chests, faces of Robin, her team, the security guard, herself. She looked at the expression on Zeke's face: controlled fury.

"Okay." Delia walked over to her team. "I need you on the bus." The words sounded flimsy up against the standoff. But what she felt was enormous, as if she were holding up a levee that was about to break.

"Go," Mickey said to her teammates. "It's okay. Seriously. Just go."

"We're not going without you," Iz said. Every single member of the team echoed her words. Casey slung an arm around Mickey's shoulders. Sophie and Alice kept filming. Mickey narrowed her eyes and nodded her consent, accepting the support.

Delia stepped away to get control of herself, failed, and shot back, "We will forfeit the game if we're not there on time. We will lose the state championship."

It was Loopy—prankster Loopy—who came forward, now as serious as an ambassador. She reached out and then withdrew a hand, as if Delia were too hot to touch, and spoke softly. "Maybe you don't understand. This is Mickey's family. Her brother. Zeke does not have a bomb, or the makings for a bomb, in his locker. You know that, right?"

"We're not going without Mickey," Alice called out. "Even if it means forfeiting the game."

"Mickey," Delia tried, "help me out here."

"Ma'am?" The security guard waved a hand in the air.

"Please just give me a second," Delia snapped.

"It's my brother they're accusing," Mickey said. "It's wrong."

"I get that," Delia said. "Zeke doesn't have a bomb in his locker. We all know that." She glanced at Robin to see if he concurred. She didn't like the glisten of fear in his eyes. She turned back and addressed the whole the team: "So you can let the accusers steal the day or you can get on the bus and win a state championship."

"False choice," Emma said. "We can stand with our friend or we can go to a high school basketball game."

The anger Delia felt at Emma's assessment, the value the girl placed on a state championship game, surged with such power she thought she might explode herself.

Emma. Drunk-at-the-holiday-dance, desperate Emma. Who lived with her grandparents and couldn't figure out, or insist upon, birth control. She had apparently found her voice.

"Why aren't his parents here?" Delia said to no one in particular. She opened *Contacts* on her phone and started typing *Vlasak-Jones* in the search field.

"No," Mickey said. "Don't call them."

"We have to—"

"They're in New York. Mom has a conference. I'm supposed to be in charge."

Delia's heart twisted at the idea of this lanky girl with short spiked hair trying to look after her brother. "But—"

"I said no." If the state championship game weren't riding in the balance, Delia would have been impressed by Mickey's guttural command.

"Ma'am," the guard said again.

Delia swung around to face her.

"This is above my pay grade. I'm calling the police."

"No!" Mickey shouted.

Where was Jonas? They were all locked in a stasis of inaction because no authority figure was here.

"If he has nothing to hide," the security guard said to Delia, "why won't he let the custodian open the locker?"

"Because the accusation is bullshit," Iz announced in her my-uncle-works-for-the-ACLU voice. "It's an invasion of privacy."

"It's legal," the guard told her.

"Son, just open the locker," Robin said, struggling to his feet and putting a hand on the boy's head. Zeke shook the hand away and kept his middle fingers flying.

Delia walked down the hall, away from the gathering, opened *Favorites* on her phone, and stared at the short list. *Skylar, Dylan . . .* and *Coach* was still there, though she'd been dead almost two years by now. She knew what Pat Summitt would say: *Get those girls to Portland at any cost. Threaten whatever you need to threaten. Clean it up later, if you have to.*

But Coach would never have let herself get in this situation in the first place. She would have cut out the rot when it started. She would have deployed her starch integrity, even if it meant confronting, turning in, her own family. That was Delia's failing. She'd taken the goods Dylan gave her—the protection, the safety, the survivorship—and she'd let herself sail away on wins and happiness. But maybe they were false wins, false happiness, because they were predicated on other people losing. On Dylan losing. On Dylan's losses making him the man he had become.

She'd always known that eventually she'd have to pay for her own survival.

As Delia walked back to Zeke, Robin, and her team, the security guard withdrew her phone from her pocket and started tapping in a number.

Delia lunged and grabbed the phone away from the woman, surprising herself maybe even more than she surprised the security guard. "No police!" she shouted. "Please."

The two women looked at each other for a long time. Delia tried to breathe calm into her body. Tried to communicate competence. Tried to look as though she were in full control of the situation. She considered telling the security guard that she was the vice principal, that she could make all the decisions here, but she couldn't bring herself to lie in front of the girls.

"I'm sorry," Delia said, handing the phone back. "But please, can we just do this among ourselves?"

"Who are you?"

"Their basketball coach." Delia tossed a hand in the direction of her team.

The woman leveled an assessing look at the girls clad in high-top sneakers and tracksuits, now all holding hands like a union on strike. "What're they doing here?"

Unaccountably, Delia smiled. "We're on our way to the state championship game. Zeke's sister is on the team."

The security guard listened.

"It may not look like it," Delia said, "but he's a good kid."

Was that true? Delia had no idea.

The security guard eyed Zeke. "It feels pretty risky, just taking your word for it. I mean, I mess this up and it's my job. I gotta say, the kid's reluctance to let the custodian open his locker is not inspiring my sympathy or confidence."

"Yes," Delia said, "I get that."

"So," the security guard said, "I need someone to open that locker."

Zeke made two fists, pumped his arms, and then unfurled the middle fingers again. The security guard shook her head, but she didn't seem all that fazed by him.

"Come on, Zeke," Sophie called over to the boy she was maybe starting to date. She stepped out of the picket line and pulled Mickey by the hand along with her. They stood in front of him. "Just let them in your locker. It'll be much better without police."

Zeke looked at Sophie. His posture gave a little. He licked his lips. He used one middle finger to scratch his head.

"Please," Sophie said gently.

Delia felt the lull of that lake water under the rowboat that held three friends. She saw Ernest giving Cal the eye blinks that meant love. She saw Cal walking out of his deliverance. An intense sadness pressed so hard on her chest she thought she couldn't breathe. She sat down on the hallway floor.

Next thing Delia knew, the security guard had stepped briskly over to Zeke, placed a foot on one end of his skateboard, and shoved hard. He rolled ten feet before stopping himself with the heels of his sneakers. The security guard told Robin, "Open the damn locker."

Robin hesitated, but then pulled a small, dog-eared spiral-bound notebook from his back pocket and flipped through the pages until he found the code for locker number 142. He twirled the black dial and the door swung open. Turning and looking at his young friend, he said, "I'm sorry."

Delia expected Zeke to lunge back to his locker, but he didn't. He stayed seated ten feet away on his skateboard. Sophie sat down on one side of him and Mickey sat down on the other.

"You want to unload it?" the security guard asked Robin.

"I will," he said, his voice rough with reluctance.

Item by item, Robin took things from Zeke's overstuffed locker. Lots of library books and magazines, a pile of comics. A fat coil of copper wire. A box of rat poison. Wedged in the bottom, under the remains of old sack lunches and more books, were three green panels, crusted with batteries, mounting points, connectors, and slots.

"What're those?" the security guard asked.

"Ancient motherboards, like late eighties," Robin said. "He builds computers."

The security guard nodded and asked Zeke directly, "What are you doing with rat poison?"

Zeke pressed his lips together and refused to answer.

"I'm afraid of rodents," Mickey cried out, her voice soggy with tears. "Dad has a chicken coop and . . . he won't let us."

"She's *deathly* afraid of them," Sophie said. "I mean, everyone hates them. But Mickey has, like, a phobia. Her parents are all organic, though, and against poison, even for rats. So Zeke bought the poison. They were going to put it out around the chicken coop this weekend while their parents are in New York."

"Thank you," Mickey whispered, the tears now flowing for real.

Sophie reached across Zeke and squeezed Mickey's hand.

"The copper wire?" the security guard asked Zeke.

Still seated atop his skateboard, Zeke relaunched his middle fingers.

"Stop it, Zeke!" Mickey reached up and yanked down one of his arms.

"What's this book?" the security guard asked, lifting a thick technical manual off the floor.

"Please just answer her," Sophie said.

"Fine," Zeke said. "Directions for building bombs."

"Ham radio construction," Robin said, now red-faced and sweating. "*Ham radio.*"

"I have a direct dialogue with Putin going on," Zeke said, and then he added, "I hate this town."

The security guard dropped the book back on the floor.

"There's nothing here," Robin said. "Nothing at all."

"I see that," the security guard said, then turned to Delia. "I am definitely not trained for bomb squad duty." She paused and actually smiled. "But I do know a little bit about teenage boys."

Mickey threw her arms around her brother, toppling him off the skateboard. He didn't shove her away. He let her hug him. Sophie walked back to the team.

"Thank you," Delia said to the guard. "For your kindness. For not calling the police. For seeing the truth through the craziness."

"I have a boy the same age," the woman responded quietly. She had amazing bone structure in her face, lovely lines defining her jaw and runway cheeks leading up to warm eyes. Delia's enormous relief triggered her old coping mechanism of flirting and she held eye contact for too long, damn near asked the woman for her phone number. Instead she said, "So are we good here?"

"We're good here," the security guard answered, with a faint smile that let Delia know she noticed the attention.

"I'll call Jonas," Robin said.

"Mickey," Delia said, "please get your team on the bus."

Mickey got to her feet, eyes blazing behind her glasses, and cut a deal: "Promise you won't tell our parents."

Delia knew full well that someone would tell them, if they hadn't already, but she could guarantee that it wouldn't be her, so she did: "I promise."

The girls indulged in a much-too-long group hug, most of them dissolving in tears. They walked, too slowly, holding hands, to the bus.

For the entire two-hour ride to Portland, Delia sat alone on the seat catty-corner to the driver and stared out the window, trying to calm the anarchy of feeling, trying to stop the train of betrayal barreling down on her. Dylan. Her own brother. She could not afford to entertain even a hint of speculation about what just took place. Not now. She needed to find her game-day mindset. She needed to empty her brain of all thought save footwork and floor diagrams, so she could capitalize on her team's strengths and exploit her opponent's weaknesses. She needed to bring her entire heart to the game.

The man at the big wheel drove like the yellow school bus was a race car. He got pulled over for speeding in the town of Dundee, but when the cop realized it was the Rockside team going to the championship game, he waved them on without writing a ticket. They were forty-five minutes late for check-in, but the other team, the tournament officials, and the referees all agreed to play anyway.

The Rockside Wildcats lost the game by fifteen points.

CHAPTER 36

The team muddled through dinner at the Dundee steakhouse, not seeming as disappointed in the loss as Delia thought they ought to be. They chatted with everyone, subdued but not exactly bereft. She caught a couple of them even joking around about the food and waitstaff, as if this were any day of the week, as if they'd lost a pickup game on the playground. Only Mickey seemed despondent. Delia noticed the girls checking in with her from time to time, and once she saw Iz hold an imaginary camera to her face. Mickey shook her head in response. She hadn't taken any pictures of the game or the bus rides or the dinner, as if what happened in the school hallway canceled out her ability to see anything else. Fine, there would be no pictures in the yearbook of their humiliating loss. Mike Foster slapped Delia on the back after dessert and said, "Let's see a smile, Coach. It's just a game."

Delia and Jonas didn't share a single word, barely even looked at each other, for the entire hour and forty minutes they were in the restaurant together. She felt his ire, despite his smiles and light conversation with parents and fans. She overheard at least two people ask him about the "bomb scare" and his skillful dismissal of it as "nothing, nothing at all, just kids being stupid." He shook his head, said, "Social media, what a pain in the butt," moved on to ask someone about her new granddaughter.

Finally back on the bus after dinner, Delia lay down on her front seat. She didn't care if she looked pathetic to the girls. The season was over. Everything was over. Let them marinate in their loss. Their pointless, avoidable loss.

As the bus humped back over the coast range, Delia made herself take responsibility. She couldn't blame anyone but herself. She failed to corral the team when she needed to, and even worse, she let herself be emotionally toppled by Dylan's unforgivable treachery. She, and no one else, lost them the game. Delia could not wait to get home where she could scream.

About ten miles out from Rockside, as she considered sitting up, knowing she needed to say something to the girls, at least a few words of closure, she remembered Ernest's poems under the seat and reached for them. Holding the book with both hands, she tried to figure out how to rise above her feelings of devastation. Instead they swamped her.

CHAPTER 37

One morning during Delia's third week at Celebration Camp, two boys named Jacob and Christopher went missing. The boys had been at breakfast and then didn't show up for lunch. They were missing at dinner too, and then again the next day at breakfast. They were just gone.

"I really liked Jacob," Cal told Delia and Ernest that morning as they left the dining hall.

"Hush," Ernest said. "Keep that to yourself."

You could never admit to caring too much about another camper, not one who appeared to be the same gender as yourself. You couldn't afford to draw that kind of attention.

"Be strong," Delia said, wondering where those words came from, how she found them in herself.

Cal stared wide-eyed at her face, as if he didn't understand what either *be* or *strong* meant. "His shiny hair," he persisted. "He reminded me of a raven. I saw him the day he first arrived, before they buzzed it off. He was so—"

"What'd I just tell you?" Ernest said.

With her eyes on Cal, Delia planted her fists on her hips.

A few brave kids dared to ask where the boys had gone, but the staff refused to acknowledge that Jacob and Christopher had ever existed, answering with blank faces and dull headshakes, taking away the possibility of a comforting explanation. Like a sister's wedding requiring their attendance. Or a simple arm break that needed a real doctor. Or best of all, a mom or dad, or both, who changed their minds, decided they loved their child just as they were.

Apparently other kids had disappeared, before Delia's arrival. It wasn't that uncommon, according to Ernest. But these two were Delia's first and she speculated along with the rest of the campers: murder, abduction, and escape were all on the table. One puzzling problem was that the campers had left at the same time. Were their fates entwined?

"Maybe," Cal whispered to her and Ernest that night at the campfire, "it's like a Romeo and Romeo thing. A suicide pact. A love so unbreakable they'd rather die together than be separated." Cal held a hand at his throat as he spun out this scenario, fire-light shining in his eyes.

"You don't know anything about what happened, baby boy," Ernest said. "For all we know, their grandmas talked, made a pact of their own, and came to rescue them. Leave it."

"But you like Shakespeare." Cal sounded disappointed that he hadn't wooed his friend's attention with the literary interpretation.

"I do," Ernest said. "But I don't like suicide pacts."

Delia shifted her butt on the hard log and checked to see if any counselors saw them whispering. Maureen was busy lifting a sobbing boy from his seat and leading him away from the camp-fire. Wade played his guitar and sang with his eyes shut in what was supposed to be, maybe truly was, spiritual bliss. Thankfully, Malcolm seemed to be off for the night. But Pastor Bob looked right at her. She couldn't read his expression, yet knew from their sessions—they'd been working together all week planning for her deliverance, scheduled for this coming Saturday night—that he didn't like her attitude. He accused her of smirking. Of dodging questions. Of harboring sinful thoughts.

"You don't know my thoughts!" she'd cried out at that last accusation.

"Oh, young lady, I do. I do know your thoughts. I know them all."

She believed him.

"We're being watched," she now whispered to the boys.

"Sing," Cal said.

"I don't feel like it." Ernest folded his arms.

So Delia didn't sing either.

When the song ended, Wade opened his eyes and lowered his guitar. Pastor Bob walked around the fire ring, heading straight for Delia, Ernest, and Cal. He handed a bible to a kid in the front row and asked her to pass it back to Delia.

"Since you have so much to say this evening, why don't you read to us."

"Which part?"

"Your choice."

Delia didn't have a favorite bible verse, and she had no idea how to choose one. The most she knew was that, roughly speaking, the Old Testament was about god and the New Testament was about Jesus. Ernest tried to be discreet when he reached a hand over to open the book to a verse for her, but Pastor Bob stopped him.

"No. Delia chooses."

"It's too dark," she said, pushing her flashlight under her thigh. "I can't see the page."

She could feel Cal holding his breath.

"Okay, Ernest," Pastor Bob relented, smiling, faking kindness, "go ahead. Read us something."

Ernest took the bible from Delia but he didn't click on his flashlight. He looked over the camper heads in the two rows in front of them, straight into the firelight, and recited by heart, "First Corinthians 13:13. *And now these three remain: faith, hope, and love. But the greatest of these is love.*"

Delia had never heard anyone say the word *love* with so much feeling. As if he knew exactly what love was. As soon as Pastor Bob turned away, she pressed her face against Ernest's shoulder. She wanted that big-boy muscle, the one at the top of his arm, for herself.

Later, as the kids filed out of the campfire clearing, traipsing down the path toward the turnoff for the cabins, Cal said to Delia, "You need to be more careful."

She shrugged. The bobbing beams from all the flashlights disoriented her. The air smelled metallic, green. She didn't want to head over to the girls' cabins. She wanted to stay with Cal and Ernest.

"Your deliverance is going to be a doozy as it is," Cal persisted, the worry in his voice ratcheting.

"Maybe they'll delay it, I mean if I convince them I'm not ready," she said.

"The opposite," Ernest said. "They like to squeeze you. The deliverance isn't your grand finale, it's part of the therapy. You better start cooperating in your sessions or it's not going to go well for you."

"I do cooperate!" Pastor Bob and Maureen just didn't like the truth. She laughed to disperse the tension.

"It's not funny," Cal said.

"It'll be okay. I'll do fine. It's no big deal. Words, that's all he has, right? Words."

"*The* word," Cal shrilled.

"Don't worry so much." Delia thought of Shawna giving Pastor Quade the finger, flipping it up as easily as pulling the tab off a can of soda. "I'm strong."

She believed that.

As she left the boys, forking off to the girls' cabins, a light rain began to fall. Changing into her pajamas and crawling into her sleeping bag, she wished she felt sleepy. Time passed so slowly here, especially the nights.

The rain intensified, and soon a storm tore through the camp, lightning zapping the treetops, flashing the interior of the rustic cabin. Delia lay in her bunk listening to Angie, the girl above her, turning over every ten seconds, the bunk squeaking, and to the muffled crying of Becky, the girl in the far corner. Besides Angie and Becky, there were Elena and Sonia, and one bunk slumped empty, waiting for a victim, the off-white and institution-blue striped mattress stained with urine and tears. The cabin counselor, Mrs. Bradshaw, who only came to sleep, arriving after dinner and leaving before breakfast, had her own single bed, not a bunk, as well as a bedside table, on which she kept an alarm clock, a flashlight, and a book. Delia had snuck a look at the book cover, puzzling over the picture of a cowboy, guns in holsters on each hip and a ten-gallon hat on his head. The book seemed like a prop. She'd never once seen the woman open it. Mrs. Bradshaw was a middle-aged, prematurely gray pastor's wife who said she donated her time at the camp. Every night at bedtime, she popped a pill in her mouth, and no whimpering, whispering, weeping, or even laughing ever woke her up.

Delia had never read a Western, and didn't think she'd enjoy reading one, but she was tempted that night as the wind blew through the trees, shaking the wooden cabin, to borrow the book. She wanted distraction so badly. The missing boys. Why wouldn't someone just say where they'd gone? She did believe she was strong, especially compared to Cal, but tonight each bolt of lightning, each shudder of thunder, jacked up her jittered dread.

To calm herself, she counted breaths. She counted days too, trying to figure out how many she had left at Celebration Camp. She reminded herself that the thunder and lightning were just weather. She'd studied clouds, rain, hail, and wind in science class. Atmospheric disturbances.

Even if god were throwing the lightning bolts, orchestrating the rumbles, humans couldn't possibly know what he meant by any of it. Right? To think that she, a thirteen-year-old girl, could know the mind of god would be arrogant. Anyway, god loved everyone unconditionally. That meant no matter what. He wouldn't hurl a storm at the bad kids. He just wouldn't.

So the storm was just a storm. Delia listened to the wind howling and tree branches creaking and rain splashing. She listened hard to what was going on outside and tried to block the sounds inside the cabin. Eventually, Angie stopped tossing and turning, and Becky stopped crying. Even the thunder and lightning passed, leaving a gentle patter of raindrops on the cabin roof and an occasional whoosh of wind through the trees. Delia was glad there was no glass in the windows. She liked smelling the piney wetness, breathing the fresh air. She pulled the sleeping bag up around her neck and finally dozed off, entering into a soft and gauzy sleep.

A scream tore the fabric of night. She lay perfectly still, clutching the metal edges of her bunk, holding her breath. Silence. A long drizzling silence. It must have been a dream.

Then another scream, one that didn't stop, sliding into a wail. She recognized the voice, even in its keening mode. It was Cal.

Delia sat up, searching for a response, what she should do. Why weren't the other girls getting up?

Because it wasn't a fire alarm. It wasn't the morning bugle. It was a terrified kid and that was none of their business. To respond meant you'd enter the terror yourself.

But this was Cal.

Delia slipped out of her sleeping bag and shoved her feet into her sneakers. Mrs. Bradshaw appeared to be out cold, her back turned to the bunks, so Delia grabbed her flashlight and crept out of the cabin. She was sure Angie, Becky, Sonia, and Elena all heard her go, but no one uttered a word.

A man's shouts joined Cal's screaming. The deeper, older voice called out, "Hey! Hey!" sounding almost as frightened as Cal. Delia moved carefully, quietly, toward Cal's cries. She heard other feet pounding squishy soil. A second man's voice swept into the swirling dark trees. She switched off her flashlight.

When the boys' restroom came into view, Delia stopped. The wooden structure housed three stalls and two washbasins, just like the girls' restroom. The entrance was wide and doorless, which meant, according to Cal, bears or coyotes could enter and shelter there. He hated the restrooms.

Ernest had told her there were no open urinals because then the boys could look at each other's penises. Stupid, he'd said, because the doors on the stalls provided cover. Cal had screeched at that remark, objecting that two pairs of feet under one stall door would get you the severest correctional therapies.

A toilet stall rendezvous might be worth the temporary nostril torture, Ernest had joked, causing Cal to choke on the soda he was drinking. Ernest had had to calm him, say that he was only joking, of course no one would be fool enough to have sex in a restroom stall.

But then Ernest added, "At least not here."

"Just don't," Cal had said. "Please."

At night the restrooms were lit with one dim bulb hanging from the ceiling over the washbasins. A bit of murky light slopped out the wide entrance and onto the pine needle–covered ground. Cal knelt in that splotch of dirty light, sobbing, gasping for breath. He wore flannel pajamas with buttons and a collar, like a little boy, and was barefoot. Delia wanted to grab him, hoist him up, and carry him away. She knew she could shoulder his pain. She could carry him. But to where?

She stayed back in the darkness of the trees and watched Wade and Malcolm approach. At first the two men stood staring at the crying boy, and then they looked at each other, as if they didn't have a clue how to handle the raw pain. As if they'd never seen it before. Or maybe as if they'd seen it often before and were still lost in the face of it. Wade surprised Delia by kneeling in the mud next to Cal. He put a hand between the boy's shoulder blades and spoke softly. Malcolm remained standing with his hands on his hips, spine erect, peering down at the man and boy. Wade's pleas got louder.

"Come on, Cal. Calm down. You have to be quiet."

Cal did not quiet. His sobs came from the pit of his stomach, rasping up through his esophagus, howling out his mouth. Delia knew that every single kid and counselor in the camp would be awake by now. Listening. Acutely wondering. Most of them were probably praying, and Delia decided that she should be praying too, so she did.

She prayed for god to keep Cal safe.

She prayed for god to keep loving her unconditionally. To keep loving all the kids here unconditionally.

Wade wrapped his arms around Cal's rib cage and held him. It didn't look quite like a hug, it wasn't exactly tender, maybe more like the starting position in a wrestling match, but it wasn't unkind, either.

Love thy enemies, Delia remembered. She tried to pray for the two counselors too. Those words of prayer were difficult to form in her mind. The stain of hate spread up her legs and down her arms. She fought it. Ernest said the greatest of these is love. She wished she could again press her face against his shoulder that smelled like laundry detergent and woodsmoke.

Wade's gentler approach didn't help to calm Cal. His sobs didn't stop.

Malcolm reached down, yanked the boy away from Wade, wrapped an arm around Cal's neck, holding him from behind, and put his other hand over Cal's mouth. He began dragging him away from the restroom. When Cal thrashed, Malcolm removed his hand from over the boy's mouth and punched him in the side of the head. Cal stilled and Wade picked up his legs. The two men carried him away, down the hill toward the dining hall.

Delia had seen the chasm behind the dining hall, even though it was strictly off-limits. When one of the kids—a boy who was rumored to have female genitalia and therefore forced into flowered blouses with puffed sleeves and strappy sandals, but who nonetheless insisted he was a boy—told her that that's where they'd tossed Jacob and Christopher's bodies, she'd gone to see for herself. To get there, you had to walk around to the back of the dining hall and across a small unkempt meadow, pushing through the tall grasses. Beer and soda cans littered the sides of the deep weedy ravine, and a dirty stream meandered through its low point. She knew that no one had tossed kids' bodies in a ravine on the camp property. That was preposterous. But it had made her curious about the spot, and it always helped to reconcile what she knew to be true with actual research. Now, though, with her own friend being carried away, and having seen the ravine—the dirty, ugly, boggy gutter—she couldn't help picturing him being taken there.

But they wouldn't, she told herself. They wouldn't. They'd carry him to the infirmary. They'd put him in a bed and give him a mug of hot milk. Maybe Wade would sit in a chair beside Cal's infirmary bed until he went to sleep.

She could sneak there very early in the morning, before dawn, and see if he was okay. He'd like to see her, she knew that.

For now she ought to return to her own cabin, but there was no reason to hurry. Even the drugged Mrs. Bradshaw would have been awakened by this time. She would have found the empty bunk. Delia was busted, whether she ran back or walked slowly. Another ten seconds wouldn't change anything.

Delia approached the restroom. She was surprised the men hadn't checked the interior before taking Cal away. Maybe they didn't want to find another boy in there, standing on top of a toilet seat, hiding his feet from view. Maybe one victim satisfied them, was as much as they could handle in a night.

Both silver faucets mounted on the white porcelain washbasins dripped. The cement floor below the basins was wet from plumbing leaks, darkening the gray slab. At first she thought the other dark liquid, toward the back of the restroom, was also a plumbing leak. More water.

But a plumbing leak didn't explain the boy lying in the puddle. The liquid was viscous, blood not water. It was Angus. Whose bass voice dominated the dining hall just a few hours ago. Angus, who told anyone who'd listen that he was straight, that a mistake had been made. He'd publicly begged to do his deliverance, saying he'd welcome the opportunity to prove how much he loved Jesus and god. The counselors hadn't bought it. They said he wasn't ready yet. A lot of the campers agreed, taking the staff's side on this, complaining that Angus just wanted to fake his way through a deliverance to shore up his lies. He'd even come on to Maureen, blatantly, to prove his heterosexuality. No one believed him, least of all Pastor Bob. The halved soda can he'd used to tear open his wrists lay on the floor next to his right hand.

Delia vomited.

She backed up until she bumped into the doorjamb.

Fleeing the restroom, she sank herself deep into the forest, where she fell to the ground. She counted. She breathed. She didn't cry.

When she could stand, she began walking back to her cabin. By now the rain had stopped and the clouds had opened. A half-moon lit her way and she didn't bother turning on the flashlight. Mrs. Bradshaw was gone from the cabin and the girls lay motionless in their bunks, as if dead themselves.

"It's okay," Delia said to her cabinmates, "just some kid freaking out."

"Who?" Becky asked.

"Some boy."

"Some sinner," Angie whispered.

Delia sat on top of her sleeping bag and waited. For the night to end. For the day she could go home.

When Mrs. Bradshaw returned a few minutes later, she asked Delia where she'd been and Delia said she'd gone to the girls' restroom.

"You're not allowed to go alone." The woman did not address the screaming they'd all heard.

"I tried to wake you," Delia lied. "I couldn't."

Maybe Mrs. Bradshaw felt guilty about the pills because she accepted this answer. "Go to sleep," she said. "I'll go tell Pastor Bob you're found."

"Thank you," Delia whispered. She did want to be found, not lost.

A few minutes later Mrs. Bradshaw returned and sighed heavily as she slid back under her sheet and blankets.

In the morning as Delia walked, after the camp-wide sleepless night, to the dining hall for breakfast, she saw, to her enormous relief, Cal among the rest of the kids. Ernest reached him at the same time she did.

"I had to pee so badly," Cal said, as if nothing more than a slight wrong turn had occurred in the night. He built on his opener, reminding them that Ernest was always advising hydration to stay as emotionally healthy as possible. Which meant Cal always had to pee at night. Kids were strongly discouraged from using the toilets after lights out. If they did need to, it was an absolute rule that a counselor accompany them. None of the cabin counselors took kindly to being woken up, so most kids held it. Cal had been drinking extra water because of the disappearance of Jacob and Christopher and the need to bolster his emotional health, and he had to go so badly. When the storm finally calmed, he figured he'd just sneak to the john and back. It was only ten yards away from his cabin, and the light coming from the place, weak and grayish as it was, could guide him. He just needed to take the steps, one after another, and go. His cabin counselor was literally snoring.

By the time he was out of the cabin and on the trail, he regretted his decision. He'd left his flip-flops next to his bed as a decoy. A quick surveillance of the cabin would reveal footwear in front of every bunk, evidence of no defections. That was his first mistake. The rocks and sticks on the trail dug into the soles of his feet. Every step hurt.

But then there was the restroom, Cal carried on, talking longer than Delia had ever heard him talk, manically, his eyes glistening as if he were telling a fairy tale rather than describing his own experience. The restroom, he said, was scary any time of day with its cold cement floor and daddy longlegs crawling up the unfinished lumber walls. Standing outside the structure, he balked, figured he could just pee in the bushes. No one was there to see him. But the thought of being caught with his dick in his hand, out in the forest at night, and having that be misunderstood, scared him even more.

"So what I did," he said, "is pretend you both were with me." He took their hands and squeezed so tight it hurt. They'd stopped outside the entrance to the dining hall, the other kids making wide berths around them—around Cal—as they entered the building, as if his terror was contagious. They didn't have much time, thirty seconds at best, until an adult shooed them inside. Delia wanted to tell Cal that she knew what he'd found. The smell of the dead boy's blood and urine stayed in her nose. The image of him on the cement was imprinted on the insides of her eyelids. She wanted to spare him having to say it.

"I love you," Cal said. "I love you both so much. You talk like starlight," he said to Ernest, and to Delia, "You walk like a river."

"Hey, baby boy, we love you too. But what happened?" Ernest didn't say, *Everyone heard you screaming in the night.*

"Meeting you two was worth coming to Celebration Camp," Cal said.

Those words sounded like a goodbye. Delia wanted, again, to hoist him on her shoulders, carry him to safety.

"Breakfast," Maureen announced, coming up the graveled path to the dining hall. She looked weirdly listless, her eyelids heavy. In some lapse of kindness, she walked right by the trio, letting them stay outside to talk. All three watched the dining hall door close behind her.

"I'm doing my deliverance," Cal said.

Delia laughed. Too hard. She started to joke that they could do a doubleheader on Saturday night.

"Nah," Ernest said to Cal, "you aren't doing that. You're way too pretty to let them touch you."

"You have to do it eventually." Tears wetted his gray eyes, and Delia was embarrassed about her laughter. "That's the fastest way out of here."

"Fool," Ernest said. "They don't let you go after you do it."

"They might. At least they'll think I'm cured. So when I do get out, they'll leave me alone."

"Look at me . . . No, look in my eyes." Ernest tapped his own cheekbones with the splayed pointer and middle fingers of his right hand. "You can refuse to do it. They can't make you. Just get through the month. Then you can go home."

This was news to Delia. No one had told her she had a choice.

Tears slid down the planes of Cal's smooth white cheeks and eddied into the pink corners of his mouth. "It's worse at home."

"Baby boy," Ernest said softly. He leaned forward and kissed Cal's cheek. "Listen to me. You aren't ever going to be left alone. Fact. Best you can do is keep them from getting inside you."

"Tell you what," Delia said, making a decision right there on the spot. She'd cooperate. Fully. For Cal's sake. She'd lead the way. "Let's talk about this after mine on Saturday." She'd go first, model toughness, tire out the staff. She could show him how to survive.

"I'm doing it tonight," Cal said. "Pastor Bob already agreed. He says it's a good idea. That I'm ready."

No one even noticed that Delia missed breakfast that morning. As the boys went into the dining hall, Ernest with angry resignation and Cal with fragile resolve, Delia ran up the hill to the boys' restroom. She went inside and saw nothing but a very wet floor. Someone must have scrubbed that cement half the night, sloshing buckets of water to wash away the blood.

CHAPTER 38

Delia found no words for the team. They had lost.
She walked her phone to the back of the bus, ignoring
the girls trying to get her attention, took a seat in the last
dark row, and punched Jonas's phone number. She knew he'd
answer.

"You authorized the raid on Zeke's locker," she said in a
low voice to keep from being overheard, although that was
hardly necessary given the volume of the ancient school bus
motor.

"*Raid* is a bit of an overstatement."

"Zeke was singled out by someone with a vendetta against
his family. His locker was opened. His possessions were combed
through. It was a raid."

"Can we talk later?"

She pictured him in the car on the highway, pressing the
phone to his ear while he drove, Megan sitting worriedly in the
passenger seat. They were probably nearby, a few miles ahead or
behind the team bus.

"No. I need to know now. I need to know why you allowed
that to happen."

"Why are *you* mad?" he asked.

"You—"

"I handled it. I called Robin. I chose not to call the police."

"Oh, that's big of you. You chose not to call the police on a
kid you knew was innocent."

"You can't just ignore those kinds of threats," Jonas said.
"I couldn't say for sure what he had in his locker. Don't forget

the gambling books. I took a big risk not calling the police."

Blaming Jonas wasn't entirely fair, yet she couldn't pull herself back.

"You have no idea what it's like being in charge of an entire community of kids and parents," he said.

"In charge? You were missing in action, Jonas. You let this happen and you didn't even show up to take responsibility."

"You've got to be kidding. The entire responsibility is on me. If there's a school shooting, if someone decides to detonate a bomb, that's on me."

"So why weren't you there?"

"Sometimes," Jonas said, using his calm, explanatory principal's voice, "you have to keep your eyes on the prize. I was expecting a championship. Do you know what that would have meant to the girls?"

How dare he.

"Yes. I do know what it would have meant for the girls. I also know that they wouldn't desert their teammate, ever. That they stood by Mickey and her brother. That they would give up, that they did give up, a championship title to stand by a threatened friend."

"That's not what happened."

"It *is* what happened."

"You lost the game. Talk about not taking responsibility. You're the coach."

She wanted to hang up on him. But she didn't. She let the silence between them muffle everything: the sound of the bus engine, the chatter of her team, the siren on a passing ambulance. "All right," she finally said, "I take responsibility for the loss. I got completely derailed by what happened at Zeke's locker. I should have been able to rise above all that."

The note coming from Jonas sounded like a whimper. He hated winning arguments, admissions of guilt, being the one who'd inflicted the most pain. "Okay," he said quietly.

"Not okay. We're not done. Who posted that picture of Zeke's locker?"

She heard him swallow. She wondered what Megan was doing. Had she laid a pale hand on his forearm? Was she signaling for him to get off the phone? Telling him to let that crazy ex-girlfriend coach lady go steam in her own heat?

"It was Dylan," Delia said.

"Dylan?" Would he actually try to protect him?

"My brother." As if there were three Dylans.

"No."

"Jonas. Come on."

"Look," Jonas said, "Zeke is fine. That incident is closed."

Delia pictured Jonas with a football tucked in the crook of his arm, running for the end zone. A tight end. A keeper of locker room secrets. The dark side of being a team player. He knew who'd made the post.

"Tell me," she said. "I have a right to know."

"I need to get off the phone. I'm driving."

"Why are you protecting him?" She kept the decibels down but her tone shouted.

Delia heard Megan's voice, softly advising, maybe even reaching for the phone. She pictured Jonas twisting away from her hand. To Delia he said, "You know what? I don't think I like the person you've become." He spoke in an astonished hush, as if just now realizing this. And it hurt.

"I'm the same person," Delia said. "Both of us are. Just more so. That's what maturity is. Becoming a concentrated version of yourself. If you're a coward, you become more of one."

His silence let her know she'd hurt him back.

"Who're you protecting?" she asked. "Him or yourself?"

"That's my job. To protect my students."

"Zeke is one of your students. Doesn't he deserve protection?"

"Of course he does. No one was hurt. It all ended fine."

Debatable. But she'd let that part go. For now. "Who was it, Jonas?"

How many other acts of revenge was Dylan exacting on the people who didn't give him what he wanted? He probably didn't even realize that by triggering that hallway chaos, he'd killed her win.

Jonas sighed heavily. Said something indecipherable, but clearly argumentative, to Megan, who Delia guessed was trying to stop this conversation. "Come on. Is it that hard to guess? The kid has an exaggerated sense of responsibility. He's been to my office a couple of times to tattle on other students. I don't like it. But I can't *not* follow up when the accusation is a bomb. You have to understand that, Dee."

The boy's image lit up like a hallucination: the ruddy cheeks, brushy hair, birthmark on his neck, gold cross nestled in the V of his shirt.

"Wait," Delia said. She depressed the metal bar that lowered the bus window. It dropped with a thunk. She sailed her arm out the window, let the rain pelt her skin. Not Dylan. The revelation was as relieving as the rain. It was not Dylan.

The team bus turned into the high school parking lot. The girls began gathering their gym bags from the racks above the seats, and the driver shouted for them to stay seated. Loopy started singing the team song Mickey had composed earlier in the season, and all the girls joined in. The song was goofy, but tonight they sang it solemnly, leaning across the seats to hold each other's hands. They were so very young. Delia put her face out the open bus window. She thought she could smell the Pacific Ocean washing to shore a short distance away.

Neither she nor Jonas had left the phone call. She knew he couldn't hang up on her. "Say his name."

"No." Jonas lowered his voice in an attempt to sound authoritative. "Do *your* job. I'll do mine."

"You're shielding the arrogant little prick."

"Come on, Dee—"

"No. I won't keep this a secret. I will tell the Vlasak-Jones's. I will tell the girls. I will tell the entire community."

"You're not principal of Rockside High School."

"No, but I have more balls than he has." And she clicked off her phone.

Delia was nearly hyperventilating, a heady combination of rage and relief spinning her thoughts. The bus had stopped rolling. The driver shut off the engine. The girls murmured quietly as they hefted their gym bags off the racks.

"Coach?" a couple of them called gently to the back of the bus.

Delia got up and sloughed down the aisle, not wanting to speak, or even look at her team right now. But they didn't run off to their families who waited for them in nearby parked cars. They waited for her at the bottom of the bus steps.

"Coach?" Loopy said. "We're sorry."

Delia looked out over their heads into the drizzly darkness. She made herself say, "We played our best."

"No, we didn't," Casey said.

"Not even close," Iz said.

"It was impossible to shake off what happened at Zeke's locker," Emma said.

"But," Iz spoke forcefully, "we don't regret waiting for Mickey. We had to."

"We want you to understand that," Loopy said, touching Delia's shoulder.

Every one of the girls had big round eyes, bright in the dark parking lot. Their smooth skin shone with hope. For them, this was a moment, maybe an important moment, but not a paramount one. They had lots of other moments ahead, millions and millions of them.

"I know," Delia said. It was far too late at night for scolding, for any kind of correctional speech. Her voice quavered though, and the girls waited in an awkward and protracted silence, as if it were their job to find comforting words for her.

Then, suddenly, Loopy hollered, "Alice! Show her the video!"

Alice tapped her phone a couple of times and held up the screen. The girls crowded behind Delia so they could all watch together. In the three-second video, Delia yanks the phone out of the security officer's hand, shouting, "No police!"

Had she actually shouted that?

Alice played the clip again. And then again. While the girls cheered.

"Coach is dope," Casey said.

"This'll go viral," Iz predicted.

"Probably already has," Alice said.

Wait, Delia thought, *wait.*

She wasn't dope. She wasn't a hero. She'd just wanted to get the girls to the game. She'd wanted a win. A state championship win. Their willingness to read her actions as a show of principled integrity, as an example of taking a righteous stand, just about broke her heart. She wasn't anywhere near that good.

"Get some rest," she told her team, and one by one they all hugged her.

As Delia walked to her car, she remembered that she'd left Ernest's poems on the bus. She sprinted after the empty bus, which was already rolling slowly toward the highway, and caught up with it. She ran alongside, pounding the door, until the driver noticed her, stopped, and opened up. She didn't say a word to him—what was there to say?—just boarded, retrieved the book, and got off again. The girls and their families had surely witnessed the whole thing.

CHAPTER 39

Delia drove to the church. She got out of her car and stood in the rain, letting it soak her and the book of poems in her hand. She couldn't go home to that bedroom with the twin bed. The same twin bed.

Walking around to the back of the building, Delia found the door to the basement still unlocked, as if the cavern waited for her always, and she entered. Rather than turning on the lights to descend the stairs, she used the light on her phone. She lay down on the couch and closed her eyes.

"You won," she said out loud to the dark.

Cody Quade was dead, but Adam was the new messenger. He'd menaced Zeke, a fellow student, who he probably hated for his brainy daring. But Zeke hadn't been his primary target. He'd timed his caper to sabotage her team's moment of triumph. He'd done this to *her*. To Delia. And it had worked.

CHAPTER 40

Many of the campers shunned Cal that day. The delicate boy with white-blond hair and blue rivers of blood at his temples, who'd freaked out so extravagantly in the middle of the night, became their focus. His fagginess, his failure of courage, his obvious distance from god and Jesus, all this had caused him to panic at the storm, the darkness of night. His full bladder triggered hysteria, some kids joked.

As she walked across the meadow to the chapel after supper, the slanted evening light spiced by the smell of the storm-soaked grasses reminded Delia of what she'd usually be doing after dinner in July. Riding bikes fast. Prowling through town on foot, kicking curbs and making fun of adults. Laughing so hard. Swimming in the river. This summer, all of it would have been with Shawna.

Delia lagged behind the group, wanting to be alone, but Emily, the perfect girl who wore her hair in a tight bun, stayed back too, and walked beside her. Lately she seemed to always be nearby. Delia bent to pick a dandelion blossom, crushed the yellow petals between her thumb and forefinger, and smelled the acrid oils.

"Smell nice?" Emily asked with a tentative smile.

"No," Delia said. Not wanting to be entirely unpleasant, she stooped to pick another dandelion and held it out to the girl, who looked over her shoulder, as if accepting the gift of a flower could be punished. She took it and sniffed.

"I see what you mean," she said. Delia waited, figuring the girl would add something about the stinky flower being, nonetheless, a gift of god, but she didn't.

When Delia entered the chapel, she saw Cal, already at the front, seated in a straight-back chair next to the altar. With the giant wooden cross looming on the wall behind him, Delia thought he looked a little like Jesus.

None of the other campers were laughing at him now. Seeing Cal in the hot seat reminded them of their turns. Their inevitable turns. Delia needed to make a plan for how to navigate hers, in just two days.

Someone grabbed her elbow. "Let's sit up front," Ernest said.

"Really?"

"We have to." Ernest led her to the front pew.

All the counselors were on-site, busying themselves with preparations. Malcolm checked the slots behind the pews, straightening bibles and hymnals, his movements jerky and awkward. Wade sat up on the chancel tuning his guitar. He kept glancing at Cal and twice went to him, once to stop him from biting his nails by pulling his hand away from his mouth and another time to whisper something in his ear. Maureen set out plates of cookies, bowls of chips, and big plastic bottles of soda, all in full view of the kids, like bait. When Wade announced the first hymn, the campers started singing.

Delia didn't like the slump of Cal's shoulders or the blank of his eyes. His pale lips were slack, as if he were about to drool. She wished that she and Ernest were sitting in the back. Up here she felt on display, in plain sight of all the counselors and other campers.

Ernest kept his eyes on Cal, willing his friend to look back at him, but Cal wouldn't. In the middle of the second hymn, Ernest snapped his fingers in Cal's direction, obviously trying to get his attention, but then kept snapping, as if he were keeping time with the music. It definitely was not that kind of music, and Delia watched the counselors scowl at Ernest, who made his face worshipful, god-loving, and kept snapping. Malcolm stepped to the end of their pew and shook his head at Ernest, who made his face even more innocent and whispered, "Oh! Gosh! It's a Black thing, sorry. We clap and snap in church. I'm just bringing god into the room."

Delia laughed out loud, too nervous to hold it in.

"Don't be rude," Ernest said to her, loud enough for the counselor to hear. "It's my culture you're laughing at," even as he pressed his thigh against hers.

When Malcolm walked away, uncomfortable with any comment about skin color and culture, Ernest's face immediately reverted to his true expression and he blinked his long lashes at Cal, who now did look back. Neither Ernest nor Delia did the virtual hug. The last thing they wanted was for the counselors to figure that out. But Ernest put his hand over his heart, pretending to be scratching himself, and held eye contact, blinking slowly, saying I love you with his lashes.

Cal sat up a little straighter and pressed his lips tight. That afternoon he'd sworn, "I'm not going to cry," as if that was his only goal for the entire proceeding.

Deliverances could last thirty minutes or they could last for several hours. Delia hoped Cal would find a way to move his along, although the context for this one—the way Pastor Bob and the counselors were using it as a portal out of the grief and fear that had gripped the camp since the disappearance of Jacob and Christopher, followed by last night's soda-can suicide—made brevity unlikely.

Pastor Bob climbed up onto the apse and stared at the seated sinners. He raised a hand toward Wade who set down his guitar. Delia knew the routine by now: Pastor Bob and the counselors would transport everyone from their sorrow and sinfulness to a fever of joy and redemption. Often a successful deliverance gave birth to a couple more that week. Everyone wanted the release.

Emily, who sat with perfect posture in the pew right behind Delia, reached forward and whispered, "You're Saturday night!" as if offering congratulations on having a prom date.

Delia turned and tried to smile.

After Pastor Bob's welcome, Wade led the group in singing "Turn Your Eyes Upon Jesus." Then Maureen, who had a beautiful singing voice, soloed "Amazing Grace." Delia closed her eyes to listen because it was her favorite hymn. As Maureen held the last note, Pastor Bob stepped to Cal's side and put a hand on his shoulder.

The music stopped and the pastor stared at Cal for an uncomfortably long time, burrowing all the way into his soul. Softly he said, "I was blind, and now I see."

"Amen," Ernest said.

Pastor Bob looked up, surprised.

Ernest smiled, shrugged.

Delia knew he was mocking the event. Maybe the counselors and Pastor Bob thought so too, but she saw the confusion on their faces, because who could scold anyone for an *amen?*

Pastor Bob launched into a marathon prayer that lasted for at least half an hour. He prayed for god's presence and love, for a righteous life path for everyone in the room, for the ability to follow Jesus's example, every moment of every day. When he finally finished, assorted counselors—the sleepover cabin counselors usually attended deliverances—stepped up with long requests for god to rescue Cal's soul. Wade played background music while they prayed, using silence in key places for emphasis.

These early entreaties were loving: they cited Cal's sweetness, his wide-eyed innocence, his willingness to work hard at his faith. Their voices were soft, even kind, and Delia let herself be soothed into the drone.

Cal visibly relaxed too. Delia could tell that he'd begun believing that this wasn't going to be so bad. The intensity of being on display, of having the eyes and expectations of so many people focused on you for so long, drained you, siphoned off your will. They used this. They took their time wearing you down. You knew this. Yet even as a spectator, like Delia and Ernest were now, you needed to tell yourself that maybe this time it would be okay. That you could survive this. Delia watched this happen to Cal, knew it was happening to him, and yet simultaneously joined him in the hope.

Her mind wandered to that day in June when she and Shawna walked to the beach and built a bonfire, in the middle of the afternoon, throwing on driftwood and talking about their families. It was the only time in their short friendship that they'd talked so seriously, and Delia said things—about her mom and brother—that she didn't even know she thought. The words just came out of her. Shawna told about her dad's drinking and her mom's unwillingness to confront him, how she felt responsible for her younger siblings. They'd kissed, in the daylight of midafternoon, and held each other, using the toes of their sneakers to push the unburned ends of driftwood into the fire. They became a little embarrassed after a while for having revealed so much, and they returned to their rowdy selves as they kicked sand over the fire. Delia thought they'd walk back to town together, but Shawna ran ahead of her down the beach, calling back, "Gotta go. Bye!" Delia started to run after her, and could have caught up, but realized that Shawna wasn't waiting, didn't want to be caught.

The next day they pretended nothing out of the ordinary had happened, though they kept their distance from one another, riding bikes up and down Highway 101 at top speed, then getting burgers and fries at the Dairy Queen.

Delia couldn't wait to get back home to Rockside. They'd still have the end of August, a couple of good summery weeks. They'd start the school year together in the fall too. Delia imagined meeting Shawna at her locker in between classes, their alliance, the safety and fun in that.

She'd lulled herself into a place of anticipatory contentment thinking about the happy times ahead when Pastor Bob grabbed a chair and set it down next to Cal. She tried to keep refuge in her own mind. She tried to keep herself out of the chapel. She imagined that she'd done it differently that day on the beach, that she had run after Shawna and caught her arm. Maybe they could have walked the rest of the way down the beach holding hands. They'd have had to let go when they walked up the lane toward town, but no one had been on the beach that day, and anyway, they could have been seen as sisters.

Pastor Bob put his face close to Cal's and screamed, "Who are you?"

Delia flinched. Ernest squeezed her hand gently and let go.

Cal recoiled so violently he nearly fell off his chair. Pastor Bob grabbed his arm. Delia knew the dig of his fingers was deep and painful. "Son, I'm asking you to confront the demon of perversion. I'm asking you to do it *now*."

Cal tried to speak but only whimpered.

Pastor Bob lowered his voice and asked again, "Who are you?"

This time Cal managed to answer correctly: "I'm a perverted soul."

Delia's mouth vibrated. Her hands clenched. Her ears buzzed. She felt herself leave the chapel, again, and knew that meant that she too was perverted. If she were good, her soul would stay here. She wouldn't lose herself in memories about Shawna or stop listening to Pastor Bob. But she did. She left her body sitting there and traveled elsewhere while Pastor Bob asked questions, gave clues, and Cal responded. The responses weren't good enough. Delia knew that, even though she didn't listen to the words, because Cal's voice was chalky with insincerity and Pastor Bob didn't let up. She knew he would push and push, and he did, until all at once, Cal yelled at the top of his lungs, "I will never again allow the demons of disgust to enter my body!"

Pastor Bob smiled at the release. He turned to the campers sitting in the pews and raised his palms, inviting participation. He nodded at Ernest, his gesture masquerading as encouragement though it was a chide too, as in *now* it's appropriate to speak up. Ernest did not offer an *amen*. Delia heard the exhalation of revulsion coming from his nose. That sound, his presence, brought her back into her body. She scooted a little closer to him.

Other kids began praising god in quiet voices, as they were meant to do. Pastor Bob asked the campers to make specific requests to Cal, and a butch girl called, "Let the devil go!" Then she guffawed, as if choking on her own sanctity or hypocrisy, one or the other. The bookish kid who knew dozens of bible verses by heart called, "Empty out the poisons!" Delia heard Emily, behind her, whispering a long prayer to herself, but she did not call anything out. Pastor Bob raised his arms in encouragement and more campers made spiritual requests, soon competing for who could come up with the most creative declarations, shouting to be heard over each other. Cal, in all his femininity, was a particularly sticky target.

Pastor Bob improvised, thrilling on his own performance, hollering and whispering, yanking Cal to his feet and tossing him back in the chair, addressing his seated flock, god, Jesus, and even himself, in turns. Wade played the guitar; Maureen shook the tambourine. Though it was late, far past the usual lights out, Delia was wide awake. She felt like an electric current was being shot through the bottoms of her feet. She was lit. Glowing. She felt like everyone could see her insides.

Her empty, abandoned insides.

God was supposed to be love. Unconditional love. But he wasn't in this room. And that was their fault. The campers' fault. They'd driven god out from even the chapel. Watching Cal absorb the barrage of words, the jangle of the tambourine, the judgment of Pastor Bob and his team, Delia felt a complete absence of god.

And yet, she knew more. She knew better. The dissonance in her knowledge, the dueling truths, confused her to the core. These contradictions sang together loudly and off-key. She was only thirteen years old, and apparently a sinner, and yet she knew. With all her heart. She knew that Cal was good.

When at last Pastor Bob thought he had the deliverance wrapped, he eased back to a voice of kindness. He squatted next to Cal—who looked limp in the chair, as if at any moment he'd slide out of it and onto the floor—and tipped his head to the side.

"How do you feel about yourself now, Cal?" he asked.

"I hate myself."

"Tell god that your desires are ugly."

"My desires are ugly."

"Good boy. You're almost cleansed."

In her peripheral vision, Delia saw Ernest shake his head, ever so slightly. She turned and saw that his eyes were pinned on Cal. She saw the fire, rage, and love, all mixed up together. She scooted so that her entire side rested against his. Ernest kept shaking his head at Cal: *No, no, no.* Delia butted him with her thigh. She didn't want him to get caught communicating the wrong message to Cal. She didn't want him dragged out of the chapel, away from her.

"Tell Jesus," Pastor Bob was saying. "Tell god. That you are not a homosexual."

"I'm not—"

Delia saw everything on Cal's face. He did hate himself. He did hate perversion. He did believe that his desires were ugly. But he wasn't a liar. He was a homosexual. He'd told Delia and Ernest that he'd known he was gay since he was three years old.

"We're waiting, Cal."

"Stay with me, baby boy!" Ernest shouted. "Come on now, you got this!"

Cal shook his head, his sheered blond head, and looked right at his two friends. Delia risked being seen and understood by the wrong people: she placed her fists firmly on her hips. She held Cal's gaze.

Ernest's outburst distracted Pastor Bob, interrupted his

rhythm. He paused, appeared to have a moment of indecision, and then smiled at Ernest, chose to take his interjection as support, not insubordination.

Cal stood up. Tears streamed down his face.

"That's right," Ernest said. "Come to Jesus."

Like a bride leaving her wedding midvows, Cal descended the steps of the apse and walked up the aisle, shocking all the counselors into complete silence. Every single kid turned to watch him make that long walk. He was so skinny, so pale, and yet his walk was nearly resolute, only a couple of wobbles. Anyone watching him knew he'd made a choice.

"Cal!" Pastor Bob shouted.

Cal kept walking.

"Get back here!"

Cal's back lengthened. His chin lifted. He walked right out the door of the chapel.

"You just chose hell!" Pastor Bob yelled. He turned two complete circles, looking to Delia like the wildebeest trapped by a pack of hyenas she'd once seen on a nature show, before dispatching Wade and Malcolm to apprehend Cal.

Delia laughed out loud at the sight of the unraveling.

"Shh," Ernest told her, but he was grinning.

Maureen led the campers in another fifteen minutes of prayer, her voice shaky, uncertain, as if her own memories had also hijacked the deliverance. They never got to eat the cookies and chips, or drink the soda, and Delia felt very hungry and thirsty when at last she crawled into her bunk.

In the morning, Cal was gone.

CHAPTER 41

"Wait," Delia said aloud, sitting up on the couch in the dark. She had the ragged bunny in one hand and Ernest's soggy book of poems in the other. She set them down by her side. "Wait."

She got up, walked to the light switch at the bottom of the stairs, and flipped the lever. As the fluorescent tubes fluttered on, she realized how hungry she was. How exhausted she was. How lonely she was. She also realized how innocent this room was, and probably always had been. She toggled the light on, off, on, as Quade had done all those years ago. She quietly hooted at her sudden realization.

"Cal walked," she said.

That sweet, effeminate child did not succumb. All these years, for decades, she'd been mourning her friend. He might be gone, but they didn't get him, not that night. Though only fifteen years old, he'd held fast to the heart of his truth.

The girls held fast too: they might have lost the game this afternoon, but they'd bested Adam.

What they wanted most of all, the hypocrites, the Adams, the Pastor Quades and Pastor Bobs, was to separate you from your truth, from your community, from love. They failed with Cal—why had she never before seen this?—and they failed with every single one of the girls on the Rockside High School Wildcats basketball team.

CHAPTER 42

Delia kicked off her sheets and checked the time. She'd slept late. Dylan had stayed in Portland—perhaps Yvette had permitted him an overnight—and the house was hers for the morning. Thank god she'd managed to get her backside off the church basement couch and back to Parker Street. This entire town was as good as haunted, but she'd be leaving very soon.

She was drinking her third cup of coffee when someone knocked on the front door. She hadn't showered or brushed her teeth, wore only a big T-shirt and flannel pajama bottoms. She'd been considering what she did not have to do today: go to the high school, coach anyone, take a run, talk to anyone at all, get dressed. When the intruder knocked again, Delia tried to keep herself from wondering who it might be, because it didn't matter, she didn't want to see anyone, but couldn't stop the names from lighting her thoughts: Jonas, Robin, Sarah the bookstore owner. She didn't have to answer the door. Her job was done here and the persistent knocking only highlighted that fact. Any one of those people would want to ferry her along into the next phase of their own stories. She did not need to talk to any of them. She allowed the rhythmic pounding to drive her thoughts from what she didn't have to do today to the possibilities of what she might do. She could throw her belongings in the car, leave a goodbye note for Dylan, and just drive. She could eat potato chips and watch movies all day. She could call Morgan and ask how it was working out with Mary Hunt. She could definitely ignore the irritant at the front door.

They'd lost the game last night. She was no champion. She didn't have to behave like one anymore.

"Hellooo?"

As Delia stood with her coffee cup in the doorjamb separating the kitchen from the living room, the front door wedged open. A head of messy light-brown hair poked inside.

"It's unlocked," said the attendant voice.

"Who tests front doors to see if they're unlocked?" Delia didn't even try to edit the annoyance out of her voice.

"Mostly burglars, I guess," Pastor Carolyn said, stepping inside, leaving the door wide open behind her. "Your car is in the driveway. So I knew you were home."

"Yes, my car is in the driveway. And I didn't answer the door. Which means—" Delia flung her arms wide.

"I'm sorry about the game. And what happened with Zeke Vlasak-Jones's locker."

"How'd you hear about that?"

"I was at the game, so that part I witnessed. Robin told me about the locker."

"You're letting in the damp."

Carolyn gave the door a little shove. "Whoops. Didn't mean for that to slam. I came by to see if you wanted to drive to Portland with me. My congregation sponsored a food and clothing drive for the homeless. We did so well that we have more of everything than the folks in Rockside can use. I have a friend who runs a shelter in Portland, so I'm delivering the rest to her. Come with me."

"I just got back from Portland late last night."

"I know. Me too. But it's not like you have anything else to do today."

"How would you know that?" Delia said.

"There was going to be a victory rally. Which has been canceled. I thought a distraction might be helpful."

"Yeah, I'm sort of having to figure out my next move here. So."

"Me too. I could use your help." The circles under Carolyn's eyes were bigger and a darker shade of purple than usual.

"Are you okay?" Delia asked.

"Not really."

It was true that Delia had nothing else to do. And yet she'd almost begun to enjoy wallowing in her lonely disappointment. To have that interrupted was itself a disappointment. She sighed and walked to the bathroom, brushed her teeth and showered. She dressed in a green plaid shirt, jeans, and some high-tops. When she emerged from the bedroom, Carolyn still inhabited her living room, now seated on the couch, paging through an old book of Delia's mother's called *The Faces of God*.

Carolyn held up the book and raised an eyebrow.

"My mom's."

"Nice pictures, anyway."

"Her Christianity isn't as intellectual as yours."

"I wouldn't call my faith intellectual."

Delia smiled in spite of herself. "Ready to go?"

Carolyn drove an elderly pea-green Honda. The interior smelled sour and the backseat was loaded with plastic baskets filled with clean, folded used clothing. The food, she said, was in the trunk. Delia cracked her window, in spite of the cold, and for many miles tried to let the fresh air and silent ride soothe her.

They were long out of Rockside, now in the coastal range, barreling through a corridor of sky-high evergreens, when her mood caved. She didn't like being in the passenger seat, in the dark about where exactly they were going, and the trees were too close, the woody green smell overpowering. She heard a scream ripping through the forest. She glanced at Carolyn who appeared to have heard nothing. Delia both believed with all her heart that she had heard an actual scream, and also knew with equal conviction that she had not.

She wanted to tell Carolyn to pull over and let her out of the car. But then she'd be in this forest, and that was as unacceptable as being in this car. Delia knew Carolyn was benign. She did. But when she again glanced at the woman, she saw the bloodshot eyes, disheveled hair, chapped hands gripping the steering wheel too hard, and feared this was some kind of new age deliverance. She was in this stinky car against her will. Being driven to some off-site location. By a pastor, to trick her. Over and over again she tried to swallow back her panic because she knew it was false.

When they emerged from the coastal forest and began whizzing through farmland and vineyards, Delia said, "Excuse me. Please stop the car."

Carolyn looked over at her.

"I mean it. I'd like to get out."

"We're in the middle of nowhere. At least let me get you to Dundee."

"Here is fine. I can call a Lyft or something."

Carolyn pulled to the side of the road and put the car in park. "I just thought—"

"You thought what? Why do you people always think you know what's best for everyone else?"

Carolyn burst into tears. She dropped her forehead onto the steering wheel and cried. A minute later, she lifted her head again, shook it hard once, and said, "Okay! I'm turning around. I'll take you back to Rockside."

"Wait. You're kind of not safe right now. I mean as a driver." Delia meant it in so much broader of a sense, but she needed to rein herself in, at least sound sensible. If she could just get out of this ride, this car, this accompaniment, back to the house on Parker Street to start the day over, she'd be okay. Delia knew she was acting a little deranged, maybe a lot deranged, but so what. They'd lost the championship game. She got to be crazy.

Carolyn had resumed weeping.

"Why . . . why are you crying?"

Carolyn reached around to the floor of the backseat, found

a box of tissues, as if driving cries happened frequently for her, and blew her nose. "I'm sorry. I should never have subjected someone to me today."

Delia put a hand on the door handle. What if she just jumped out? She could hitchhike. Or walk. Running would feel so good. Her legs ached to sprint, now that she thought of it. Her lungs needed real oxygen, big volumes of sky-rich air. She would run toward the snow-dusted mountains in the distance. Nothing between her and freedom.

"I like you because you're not a member of my church," Carolyn said in a husky, tearful voice. "I even like that you distrust pastors so much. I don't have to be anyone for you. I can just be me. I get so tired of trying to be some kind of example. Of not showing that my life is falling apart."

"It is?"

"Yes, as a matter of fact. It is." She punched out the last two words with so much feeling she made herself cough.

Delia looked out at the rippling spring-green alfalfa.

"My husband left me last night," Carolyn said.

"Last night?"

"I got home from the game and he was waiting on the couch. He made me a cup of tea and then said he was leaving."

"I don't know what to say." The revelation broadsided Delia. The idea that Carolyn could have a crisis of her own. She'd only ever known pastors who kindled crises.

"I was hoping you'd tell me to walk it off." Carolyn smiled past her running nose and red-rimmed eyes. "Or maybe to do ten suicides."

"I was just jonesing for a run, actually. We could do that together."

"Yeah. Thanks. Maybe in a while."

"Why is he leaving?"

"Ostensibly because he never wanted to move to Oregon."

"Ostensibly?"

TELL THE REST   309

"He still has his job in Chicago. He mostly works from here, but he has to go back a lot. Or says he does. I think he's fallen in love with a coworker. Greg is too principled to have acted on it. I'm pretty sure of that." Delia kept herself from commenting that no one is that principled. "But I can tell in the way he talks about her. The amount he talks about her. She's everything I'm not. All her behaviors are super prescribed. What she eats. How much she exercises. The precise way she speaks. Apparently she's very intentional. That's the word Greg uses to describe her, *intentional*, and he says it like it's a highly superior moral position."

"I'm sorry."

"How do I counsel people about their marriages when I haven't been able to hold mine together?"

"That seems like a good question."

Carolyn laughed. "I like your honesty."

"Maybe you can counsel them better if you yourself have experienced marriage failure?"

"Theoretically. But I don't think my church community will see it that way. They'll just see a failure. And who would want to be counseled by a failure?"

Delia's hand slipped off the door handle. "Is your husband offering you a choice to leave Oregon to save the marriage?"

"He knows I wouldn't do that."

"So . . . you're kind of choosing Oregon over him."

"I got a job here. I'd like to think he could support my career. But you're not wrong. I love it here. It's so beautiful. Restorative."

"Robin says biophilia is a crucial ingredient in happiness."

Carolyn nodded.

"How do you know Robin?" Delia asked.

"He's in my congregation."

"He also says doing good works is an ingredient in happiness. Maybe we should go deliver this stuff." Delia waved a hand at the backseat.

"Really? I can take you back to Rockside if you want."

"Let's go to Portland."

The contradictions of the past twenty-four hours dizzied Delia. Dylan hadn't made the bomb accusation, and yet he wasn't exactly innocent. The girls lost the championship game, and yet she was so proud of who they were, as individuals and a team. Carolyn was a pastor who she actually sort of liked.

Carolyn turned the key in the ignition and started the car, but she didn't pull back onto the highway yet. She said, "I admire what you're doing with the girls. Helping them know their strength, believe in themselves, and support one another. I sit in my office and listen to people drone on about alienation, dysfunction, all the big disconnects in their lives. It's so easy to say what's broken. It's so easy to talk, talk, talk. But what you do with those girls is about giving them a full-body place for connection, grace, even forgiveness." She paused and then added, "Greg is a whiner."

Delia heard the crunch of gravel and saw, in her sideview mirror, a patrol car gliding onto the highway verge behind the parked Honda.

"Perfect," Carolyn said. "This tops my lovely weekend."

Both women rolled down their windows, and a sheriff appeared on Delia's side of the car. He bent at the waist and removed his clichéd mirrored aviator glasses. He peered into both of their eyes, as if checking for drug use.

"Afternoon, ladies. Is there a problem?"

Carolyn leaned across Delia to say, "No, officer. We're just chatting."

"Most people do that in cafés or living rooms."

"I know. It got kind of intense, and I thought I should pull over while we finished."

"Finished?"

"Talking."

"You're not allowed to randomly stop on the shoulder."

"Okay. Thanks for letting us know." Carolyn placed her hands at two and ten o'clock on the steering wheel. "We're off, then."

"Driver's license and registration, please."

He carried the documents back to his patrol car and the two women waited in silence, as if their voices could disturb the possibility of clemency.

"Reverend," he said when he returned, pausing to take off his hat, "with all due respect, you have two outstanding speeding tickets."

"I intend to pay those," Carolyn said. Then she launched into a long explanation of how she'd recently moved from Chicago to the Oregon coast, taken on the new church, and how overwhelming the entire experience had been. She did not mention the pending desertion of her husband. The sheriff listened to every word.

"Next time you need to pull off the highway," he said, "find a side road or a town."

"I will, and god bless."

They waited for the sheriff to walk back to his patrol car, get in, and take off. As Carolyn pulled onto the highway behind him, Delia said, "God bless?"

"Yeah, well, it worked, didn't it?"

"Your whole spiel was effective."

Carolyn shrugged. "There've gotta be some perks. The job sucks a lot."

Delia fully surrendered to liking Carolyn. "Greg is a fool."

"Thank you. I tend to agree."

In Portland, Carolyn found a parking space on Burnside, a couple of blocks away from the shelter. A cadre of homeless folks helped them unload the food and clothing, and when the car was empty, Carolyn's friend who ran the shelter hugged and kissed her, said she was too busy for a visit right then, but that they should get together soon. She left Delia and Carolyn with the emptied car.

"This is a good parking space," Carolyn said. "I'd hate to give it up so fast."

Delia realized she hadn't eaten since midday yesterday. "I'm hungry. Let's get a sandwich."

Carolyn checked the time. "Okay, a quick one."

Why the hurry? Hadn't Carolyn just said that they ought to keep the parking space for a while? Delia pointed at the diner down the block. The food was bound to be bad but it'd be fast. They took stools at the counter. Delia ordered a tuna sandwich and Carolyn asked for a burger and fries. Two more times while they ate Carolyn checked the time.

"Do you have to be somewhere?"

"Well. Maybe."

"You're being cagey and I'm getting anxious all over again. Are you going to drag me into some skid row evangelical compound?"

"That's not funny."

Delia had said it as a joke, but Carolyn was right: it was stupid and juvenile. How easily she tumbled into the theological maze of her youth. As if just outside the door of her meticulously trained consciousness waited an alternate consciousness which churned with chaos. As if that door could fly open and suck her into its parallel universe. Where she'd be lost forever.

"But," Carolyn said, "you're sort of right. I do have a little bit of an ulterior motive."

"Why am I not surprised?" Delia aimed at sounding light but was still trying to rein in her rogue fear.

"I mean, we're in Portland, so why not?" Carolyn said.

"Why not *what*?"

"We could turn around and go home. But it'd be a waste of such a long drive."

"Or we could . . . ?"

"Just up the block is Powell's Books."

The bookstore! Delia laughed in relief. "Sure. Let's go. I could use a good novel."

"My ulterior motive is a little more specific."

Delia reached for her phone. Dylan might still be in Portland. She could get a ride back to Rockside. They needed to talk, anyway.

"Don't be mad," Carolyn said. "I should have mentioned it at the outset."

"Let me know when you're ready to divulge."

"There's a reading at four o'clock. By that poet whose book I gave you."

A glob of overly mayonnaised tuna dropped out of Delia's sandwich and she set the sloppy bread back on the plate. She took a bite of acidic dill pickle.

"I just think you'd really like him. The event will take all of an hour. Then we can drive back to Rockside."

Delia drank her glass of water. She engaged her abs, as if she were about to lift something heavy. She said, "Okay."

Even after reading his book of poems, it was hard for Delia to believe that a real person named Ernest still inhabited the same earthly plane of existence as she did. He had left her twenty-five years ago. Alone at some intersection with a mini-mart and road sign. Alone with an entire theology of hate to decode on her own. In those few moments, after he'd come out of the mini-mart and before the seafood truck pulled up to the pumping station, she'd meant to hold him: *Tell me your poem again.*

Ernest had smiled his toothy sixteen-year-old smile, graced by the soft new mustache, and right there in the morning light, at the intersection of two highways, of home and away, of heaven and hell, he said, "It keeps changing. I'll never get it right. But here's how it goes today."

How could he have, just moments after saying his poem, climbed into a truck full of slimy fish with a beady-eyed man who looked nothing like Jesus?

CHAPTER 43

The bookstore was packed, the rows of metal folding chairs already full, though the event didn't start for another ten minutes. Carolyn went straight for the table of new nonfiction, where she quickly collected an armful to buy. Delia felt silly trailing her, and so she followed the hissing sounds of an espresso machine and found the café. She got a large tea, adding the juice from two squeezed lemon wedges and a dollop of honey, as if she were nursing an oncoming illness. She once again entertained the possibility of there being more than one poet named Ernest, but of course that was ridiculous. She'd seen the picture on the jacket cover. She'd read the poems. None of them mentioned the sliver of life she'd shared with him, those few weeks at a summer camp, but it was him, it was definitely him.

When she heard the bookstore events coordinator speaking into the microphone, she looked for Carolyn and spotted her in the back of the crowd standing behind the full seating area. The pastor grinned with anticipation. She couldn't be grieving the departure of her husband that much, Delia thought, if the prospect of listening to a poet transported her so much. Delia found a place to stand on the other side of the crowd, also in the back.

As the events coordinator gave a laudatory introduction, listing the poet's achievements, the audience murmured its admiration. They clapped when the events coordinator said the title of Ernest's collection. Then he rose from a chair in the front row and stepped to the podium.

Ernest was beautiful. Gray tinged the hair just above his ears. Sadness saturated his eyes, though maybe she was just projecting that. His smile looked weathered, as if he'd had to use it more often than he wanted. He looked completely different and just the same.

He said he'd read some poems from his book, but wanted to start with a new one he'd written this winter in Portland. It was a funny poem about a giant Maine coon cat he'd adopted. The ingrate whom he'd sprung from cat prison had no problem wolfing down the gourmet salmon and turkey meals he provided, yet she wouldn't make eye contact with him and certainly wouldn't purr or sit on his lap. Her trust issues were so intense, she slept with her eyes open. The only time he'd tried to pick her up, she first went rigor mortis, her huge log of a body stiffening and elongating, before unfurling herself in a chaos of flailing and hissing, shredding Ernest's hands and forearms. The second half of the poem switched gears, became serious as Ernest said he identified so closely with the cat that she broke his heart. He planned on taking her home with him to New York and had already bought the airline-approved travel carrier and secured a letter from a doctor friend stating his need for a companion animal. He did, he said, need a companion animal.

The audience loved Ernest Wrangham. They laughed and gasped and cooed at his lines. A couple of times Delia was sure he looked right at her, but that couldn't be possible; she was at least ten people deep, and anyway, she was a thirty-eight-year-old woman now, not a thirteen-year-old girl. There was nothing to recognize.

Then, after reading the third poem from his collection and looking out into the audience during the applause, he did. He saw and recognized her. She was sure of it. Their eyes met. His slid away and then riveted back. His mouth went slack. With the microphone amplifying any sounds he made, she—and everyone else—heard his sharp inhalation. He set the book down on the podium and put both palms against his cheeks and shook his head, softly, slowly. Then he closed his eyes and licked his lips.

When he opened his eyes again, he said, "There's a poem I've been working on the whole time I've spent in Portland this year." He laughed. "No, for much longer than that." He laughed again. "I guess it's fair to say I've been working on this poem for a couple of decades. It's not finished. I certainly wasn't going to read from the working draft tonight. But I've changed my mind." Ernest rummaged in the shoulder bag sitting at his feet and pulled out a notebook.

He huffed once, and then again, as if protesting his own actions. He opened the notebook and turned the pages, looking carefully, as if the place where the poem began was a matter of interpretation. Then he nodded at a page, passed a hand down the paper, smoothing the words, and said, "Here. No title."

"*A pale ghost boy ran beside us all night.*" Ernest stopped reading and looked up, his gaze sailing over the heads of his audience, avoiding Delia. He went back to the page. "*Our lungs exploding, our faces soaked with tears and rain and sweat— our beauty, our salvation, our sobs mingling with the hooting owls, our feet tangling, our bodies falling, the forest-floor roots and stones bloodying our faces. Both of us silently screaming Cal's name as we ran. Our muscles burning, our sweaty hands gripped, our hard breathing.*"

This time when Ernest lifted his gaze, he directed it right at Delia and said, "It's not really a poem yet. They're just rough words looking for meaning."

He turned back to his pages, flipped through, his hands trembling and his eyelashes fluttering. He was nervous, unhinged. She saw his hard-earned composure, and she saw it coming undone. He had all those awards. She knew they didn't mean that much, just as her championships meant so little. He looked, as he tried to go on, exactly sixteen years old, exactly like the boy she knew. Then he shook his head, dropped a finger on the page, and began reading again.

CHAPTER 44

Ernest looked out at his audience. He should stop. He'd been carrying on for way too long. He was doing that embarrassing author thing of publicly flipping through his manuscript, choosing bits to read, a behavior he knew many considered affected. A behavior he himself had ridiculed in other writers. He'd stopped reading his own manuscript altogether a few times and just told the story. He told about the dating lessons, about the sounds of boys crying in their bunks at night, about Cal's deliverance. He told so much.

He told right up to the day of Delia's deliverance. He should stop there. That was *her* story. Or her story too. Did he have the right to tell it in public, in her presence?

He shut his notebook. He thanked the audience for listening, the bookstore for housing and protecting and disseminating our stories. He heard himself thanking his parents and Dennis too. He thanked Virginia Woolf and Audre Lorde, the cats and the writers both, and then started naming more poets he loved. He thought he might never stop thanking.

She said his name. He thought he heard Delia say his name. He could swear she did. *Ernest,* she said, *tell the rest.*

CHAPTER 45

On Friday night, less than twenty-four hours before her deliverance, Delia lay in her sleeping bag on her bunk, wide awake. Whole weeks, months, years seemed to pass as she lay there. Or maybe time had ground to a stop altogether. Maybe she would remain here in this cabin for the rest of her life. She wished she'd memorized some bible verses which she could recite tomorrow night in answer to Pastor Bob's questions. Who could fault someone for reeling off words from the bible? Even if they didn't appropriately answer his questions, they wouldn't be wrong words. She'd meant to be an example for Cal, show him how to survive. Instead, he'd gone first, told the truth, and now he was gone.

She couldn't think of a single path forward.

He entered the cabin so quietly, Delia didn't hear him at all, didn't know he was there until he knelt by her bunk and held a hand over her mouth. Delia opened her eyes and looked into his. Ernest jerked his head toward the door. She eased out of her sleeping bag, tied on her sneakers, and followed him from the cabin. If any of the other girls heard them, they kept quiet.

The moon was a little bigger tonight, though it loomed behind a cloud cover. A fresh bout of rain drizzled through the trees. He took her hand and led her to the camp's locked front gate where a small kiosk sheltered the sleeping counselor.

So it was true. Delia had heard that Malcolm manned the gate at night, but she hadn't believed it. The story was too ghoulish even for Celebration Camp. Yet seeing him now, slouched on the stool in the kiosk, mouth open, hands folded on his crotch, eyes closed as he dozed, she realized that this was his habitat. The self-appointed night guard, encased in a tiny shell, the kiosk. She almost felt sorry for Malcolm sometimes. He had a habit of folding his arms and rubbing his own triceps, as if trying to hug himself.

He leapt awake.

"We're leaving," Ernest said.

"The hell you are. What are you doing out of your cabins?" Malcolm glanced at Delia as if she, not Ernest, was the problem. "It's two in the morning."

"Open the gate."

Malcolm reached back into the kiosk for the handset on the phone.

"Oh good," Ernest said. "Good idea. Let's call Pastor Bob. We can tell him everything."

The place between Malcolm's left eye and left cheekbone twitched. "Tell them what exactly? Go back to your cabins. Now."

"There's only one thing keeping anyone here," Ernest said quietly. "It's the thing keeping you here. Fear. Me and Delia, we don't have that. We're not afraid. Open the gate."

Delia almost spoke up. She had fear. She had lots of fear. At that moment, she was terrified. If Malcolm opened the gate, where would they go? They were in the middle of the woods somewhere. The faces of the kids who'd disappeared floated in the dark recesses between the trees beyond the gate. She pictured Cal somewhere in those woods, lying in the dirt in his little-boy pajamas, eternally screaming.

"Right," Malcolm said. "Get out of my sight. I'll give you ten seconds to fly back to your cabins. After that, I'm calling Pastor Bob."

"No need to wait ten seconds. Call him now. Here, let me have the phone. I'll call him for you." Ernest stepped toward Malcolm and the phone, half entering the kiosk.

"Come on now, Ernie. Let's just chill." The man put a hand on the boy's shoulder.

"One, my name is Ernest, not Ernie. Two, I don't feel chill. I feel kinda treacherous."

Malcolm cleared his throat.

"Open the gate."

"I can't do that."

"Let me be specific then. I've given you three blowjobs. Documented each time in a little notebook." Delia knew the notebook part was a lie because of how often Ernest had lamented not being allowed to have paper and pencil for his poetry. "Precisely for this moment, fool. You think I wanted that? Gag. I did it for the option of future blackmail. That future has arrived. Open the gate or I'm talking."

Delia watched realization dawn on Malcolm's face. Ernest would follow through. Malcolm said, "Just you. Not her."

"How stupid is that? She knows everything now."

"But she won't talk. I can make sure of that."

"Seriously? You think I'd leave my friend behind with that threat?"

"Take it or leave it."

"I'm leaving it. We can stand here talking for as long as you like. You're the one at risk here, not us."

"You believe that?" Malcolm said.

"I do. Short term, sure, we could get some nasty punishment tossed our way. But you, man, I could make life hell for you."

Delia didn't understand the ensuing marathon pause, but Ernest did.

"Hey, listen," Ernest said to her. "Walk about twenty yards away. Stand behind a tree trunk."

"No," she said.

"Just for a minute. Be quick. I'll call you when it's time to come back."

"No."

"I'm not playing," Ernest said. "Hurry up. You have to trust me."

He'd never spoken roughly to her before and it scared Delia. She both understood, shallowly, and didn't understand, profoundly, what was about to happen. But she did trust Ernest. She walked slowly to the stand of tall thick Douglas fir, stepped behind a big trunk, and leaned against its bark. She considered running back to her cabin. To Maureen and Pastor Bob. To her impending deliverance. But that was now impossible. They'd already come too far. She wanted to be with Ernest, no matter where it took them. She waited until she heard him call her name. When she returned to his side, Ernest wouldn't look at her, but he took her elbow, as if afraid she might bolt.

Malcolm's hands shook as he used the key to unlock the gate. When it swung open, Ernest grabbed the flashlight from the man, and the two kids walked through. Ernest turned, shined the beam of light in Malcolm's face, and said, "Jesus said the truth will set you free, and I believe that."

"You're not free. They'll find you."

"You breathe a word, send anyone after us, and I'll tell. See if I don't. Why you think I just did that? You're culpable now. You're in on this."

Delia and Ernest both watched Malcolm screw up his mouth, stupid with guilt.

"Here's what you do," Ernest said. "You want to cover your tracks, walk a hundred yards down the fence. Dig a hole under it. Make scuff marks, like we scuttled under. Easy. You got a few hours before daylight." Ernest started walking, but then turned to add, "Oh, and I happen to know I'm not the only one who's sucked you off, neither. That's why you sit here in this kiosk at night, bro. Good deal for you. But you know what I call you? I call you a pervert. A molester. A child molester. Oh, hell, a predator. Serious prison time for that. Oh, and maybe you've heard how other prisoners treat child molesters?" He pointed a finger at the man. "I call you a sinner too. You think prison is bad. Just wait until you get to hell."

Ernest took Delia's hand and they ran, crashing down the unpaved road lined with forest, rocks crunching under their sneakers, sticks snapping. Every time she tried to talk, to ask questions, to understand what they were doing, he shushed her. When he tripped on a downed branch and fell on his face, Delia dropped to the muddy road and laid her body alongside his. He cried then. He cried hard. She petted his back, told him she loved him. She had never said those words, *I love you*, to anyone before. But they were true.

"Should we go back?" she asked when he quieted. It was a stupid question. She knew that.

"No."

"I have my deliverance tonight." She wanted to hear him say the words.

"You're not doing a deliverance." Ernest got to his feet. He spit, three times. He used the bottom of his T-shirt to wipe out his mouth.

They covered so many miles that night. They walked and ran for hours, only coming into the intersection with the mini-mart gas station at dawn. They stopped on the far side of the highway and looked at the homely building. Neither spoke for a long time. They just stood there, watching the morning sunlight hush in the day. Delia felt blank with exhaustion. She waited for Ernest to say what was next.

He kissed her on the cheek. "You gonna be okay?"

"Sure!" she answered too shrilly, the word spiking the morning air.

"That's my girl."

The expression on his face softened. He blinked his long lashes. He licked his lips. He stared down the road, not at her, as he said, "Remember me, okay? We'll hold this memory together."

She let the twinge of confusion pass. She didn't need to remember anything. They would never separate. As they started to cross the highway, she repeated the only word of his that made sense: "Together."

CHAPTER 46

Delia did not need to tell anyone that Adam had been the one to make the Instagram post about Zeke's nonexistent bomb. Adam proudly announced it himself. At the school board meeting called to discuss the locker event, Adam was not chastised for his unsubstantiated accusation. In fact, at least two members of the school board lauded his service to the community. They asked, what if it *had* been a bomb? One school board member called for the resignation of Zeke and Mickey's mom from her position as city manager, at which Delia stood and asked why someone should resign because of something that hadn't happened. Her team, all of whom attended the meeting, applauded. When pressed to make a public statement, Jonas thanked Adam for speaking up about his suspicions and also apologized to the Vlasak-Joneses for what he called a false alarm. Delia never did learn who'd done the car towing.

Skylar finally admitted that she was dating the bird-watcher. They had almost nothing in common. The bird-watcher, whose name was Hannah, did not like to exercise, literally didn't know the difference between a home run and a touchdown, and felt claustrophobic in crowded, closed spaces, like gymnasiums. For her part, Skylar was afraid of insects and had zero patience, the trait most needed for birding. None of that mattered, Skylar reported. They shared a deep love of charts and graphs—Hannah's about birds and Skylar's about basketball, of course. These visual aids to their respective passions were bridges they used to communicate with each other. They also shared basic values, like how to vote, spend money, treat people, and, most important of all, a sense of humor. They killed each other with jokes. Skylar was extraordinarily happy. Delia was extraordinarily jealous, but she managed to keep that to herself.

Delia spent hours making a tape of Loopy's best moments on the court and sent this to Skylar, begging her friend to offer a scholarship. Skylar said she just couldn't do it, but if Loopy improved her defense over the summer, there was a decent chance she could make the team as a walk-on. Delia and Loopy committed to a weekly practice schedule to accomplish this, which brought all kinds of anxiety to Delia because she didn't intend to stay in Rockside for the summer. Meanwhile, Skylar convinced a dean to give Loopy an academic full ride.

Casey signed with Stanford. Her exuberant parents threw a huge party on the beach, including a bonfire, to celebrate.

Alice enrolled at Portland State where Delia hoped she could make the team. Mike Foster shook Delia's hand the last time she ran into him in town. He didn't say thank you or congratulate her on a good season, but nor did he mention the defeat in the championship game or give his explanation for the loss.

Iz got accepted to UC Santa Cruz, her first choice. She planned on doing a double major in women's studies and social justice. When Delia asked her if there even was a major in social justice, Iz gave her a look of pity about Delia's ignorance and said, "Of course."

At the end-of-year assembly, the Rockside High School yearbook advisor named Mickey Vlasak-Jones as the next editor in chief. Mickey unexpectedly jumped up on the stage and asked for a moment on the mic. Speaking to the entire assembled student body, Mickey said they'd like to use gender-neutral pronouns going forward. Delia, who was in attendance at the assembly, groaned when Adam, sitting a few rows behind her, stood and shouted, "Excuse me? May I have a word?" Mickey smiled, leaned into the mic, and said, "No." But he continued anyway: "I just want to offer my hearty congratulations. And I have one question. What do we call you? It?"

"You," Mickey said, still speaking clearly into the mic, shoving up their black glasses with a knuckle as they looked out at the sea of students seated before them, "can just call me Editor in Chief Vlasak-Jones," which brought down the house in a roar of laughter. "The rest of you," Mickey added, "can call me Mickey."

The members of the team who were not graduating held a meeting in which they told Delia they were going to work like dawgs, for twelve straight months, to take the championship next year. Sophie led the discussion on what specific skills they needed to improve, and Brittany Nguyen took notes on how they were going to accomplish these improvements. It didn't occur to any of the girls that Delia wouldn't be with them on this journey.

She didn't know what she was going to do. Intimacy with Sarah developed at an alarming pace and, put frankly, the sex was unprecedented. Delia didn't like the idea of her libido pinning her to this small wet coastal hometown. But not only did she have nowhere else to go, Dylan moved to Portland, abandoning both his job and the house on Parker Street. Yes, it was a place to stay, and she did clean the gutters and get the dishwasher fixed, as if she were staying, but she knew that staying meant, would inevitably mean, dealing with the mess of her now unemployed brother. She was pretty sure he'd be back. Then again, even if she moved to the other side of the planet, she'd still be her brother's keeper.

In June, Delia picked up Ernest in Portland and they drove out to the camp. As they passed through the open gate, Delia noted that the kiosk was gone. A sign now claimed the camp for the First United Methodist Church. They parked in Pastor Bob's old spot and, after getting out of the car, waited for someone to apprehend them. No one came. The place looked deserted, yet they heard construction sounds up on the hill. Cautiously, they began to explore, poking their heads in the dining hall, walking down to the pond, sitting on the flattened logs at the campfire circle, and finally climbing the hillside to the cabins. Two men hammered loose nails into one of the rustic structures. Another two worked at chainsawing limbs from a dead tree. The men smiled and called out greetings, as if Delia and Ernest were camp administrators inspecting their work.

"This was your bunk," Ernest said, stepping inside a cabin and crossing the floor to sit on her palette.

Delia sat next to him, running a hand along the thin blue-and-white-striped mattress, maybe the same one. She heard Angie's churning body overhead and Becky's tears across the cabin. She heard Cal's screams.

"Let's not look in the restrooms," Delia said.

Emerging at the bottom of the wooded hillside, they started for the chapel on the far side of the meadow. Big white cumulous clouds drifted across an intensely blue sky, and sunlight quivered the cool air. Ernest stopped in the middle of the meadow, the grasses tall and laced with wildflowers. He sat and then stretched out on his back. Delia lay down beside him. Over by the administration building, someone started the engine on a tractor mower.

"Still trying to mow us down," Ernest said, and Delia laughed.

All morning they'd been sharing their life stories, where each had gone, physically and emotionally, since the night they escaped this place together. They didn't touch and they didn't cry. They talked and they listened. Now, lying on their backs in the meadow, they started in on shared memories, the events of those summer weeks, funny and bitter and heartbreaking, and the fellow campers they remembered, speculating on what had become of them. The boy who knew the bible by heart was surely a preacher. The girl with the tight bun, Emily, probably sat on the board of the National Center for Lesbian Rights. All the while the man on the lawn mower cut the grass in smaller and smaller concentric circles with them at the center. When he got within about twenty yards of them, he turned the tractor away, drove to the edge of the meadow, and shut off the motor, leaving them in their bed of tall grasses.

"Hmm," Ernest said.

"I wish Cal were with us," Delia said.

"Hmm," Ernest said again.

"Do you think he's alive?"

Ernest didn't answer.

"I feel like he freed us. The way he walked out of his deliverance. He showed us the way."

"Yeah."

"Maybe now you can finish the poem."

"Nah," Ernest said, "I doubt it."

CHAPTER 47

Cal celebrated his fortieth birthday in the dive bar directly below his apartment in the Tenderloin district of San Francisco. He'd been clean and sober for eleven years now, and he was proud of the fact that he'd managed, miraculously according to his AA sponsor, to do this without deserting his friends. He'd invited everyone to the party and the place burst with tattooed, scarred, snaggletoothed, stuttering, mute, brilliant, ravishing, ugly, loud, gender-bending queer folks, plus a few straight alcoholics and addicts, and even a couple of social workers. Of course he'd invited his newer friends from the sober community, not expecting them to show up in this raunchy bar, but even some of them had come. Tonight, to celebrate making it through four decades on this wretched planet, he needed to embrace his whole, all his friends and all his years. His only regret was that he didn't have the funds to buy rounds for everyone who wanted them. He did buy a big coconut sheet cake from Safeway and the baker had given him a discount, and she'd also thrown in fabulous decorations—frosting flowers and balloons and a rainbow, plus edible confetti—gratis. The cake graced the bar top surrounded by dozens of mismatched lit candles. He wouldn't let anyone cut into the work of art until a few minutes before midnight, so he could enjoy the gorgeousness.

Cal sat at his usual table in the back, nursed a Diet Coke, received greetings from well-wishers, and watched his friends party. Most of them still needed smack and booze and pot to get through their hours and manage their pain. He wouldn't mind another go at any of those delightful enhancers, but his drug of choice these days was survival.

He'd spent the early hours of his birthday at one of his favorite pastimes: stalking his two friends from Celebration Camp. He'd been doing it for years. Learning their last names hadn't been that difficult, it just took a little time on the Internet, searching their first names and key words. It helped that both had become a little bit famous. Using an alias, he'd friended them on Instagram and Facebook. They should be more careful. He'd never accept a friend request from someone he didn't know, but they both made plenty of public posts, and that alone made him proud of them, their open fearlessness. When the anxiety threatened to put him back on the street, Cal immersed himself in their lives. Ernest had a goofy-looking boyfriend named Dennis, a playwright, and Delia had married a therapist. She'd hit some bumps in the road lately, big ones it seemed, and he'd been a little worried about her. She'd moved back to Oregon.

Cal often fantasized about visiting them. He longed to tell them his story: How within a week of being hauled home by his parents after his failed deliverance, he ran away to San Francisco where for many years he tricked for a living. How sick he'd gotten. How well he'd become. Paradoxically, though, the two people who might best understand his choices, his mistakes and maybe even his small triumphs, were also the two people he most wanted to hide from. He didn't want them to see that he was no longer beautiful or smart or innocent. He was afraid they'd scorn his dyed hair and fake cheerfulness. He did and didn't want to explain the scar above his left eyebrow where a john had split his head open. Sometimes he imagined them wondering what had become of him. He liked to think of them believing he'd made it into the space program. Though sometimes, when he was down, he groaned at this fantasy, as if he could have ever attained anything close to that grand. Still, when a happy calm claimed him, which it did more and more often, he indulged in wanting Ernest and Delia to picture him floating, gravity-free, surrounded by stars, marbled planets spinning in the distance.

Acknowledgments

Writing novels means being a part of a big-hearted and creative community of readers, writers, editors, publishers, and agents. This book in particular has been the recipient of a tremendous amount of help with funding, research, fact-checking, editing, and ballyhooing. I cannot say enough about how much my agent Reiko Davis enhances every aspect of doing my work, day after day, year after year. Thank you, Reiko.

I've long admired the books that Akashic Books publishes and I am honored to be on their list and working with Johnny Temple and Johanna Ingalls. For being so generous with time and knowledge on wide-ranging topics, everything from Christian ministry to broken arms to high school locker raids, I am grateful to Reverend Jim Mitulski, Jamie Morantz, Dr. Robin Ellett, Dr. Laura Bledsoe, and Allen Gee. For astute reads of early drafts, thank you to Roya Arasteh, Laurie Frankel, Molly Gloss, Jewelle Gomez, Dorothy Hearst, Laleh Khadivi, Gar McVey-Russell, Maya Samuels, Elizabeth Stark, Jerry Thompson, and Meg Clayton Waite. Mary Volmer and CQ Quintana have offered and delivered support in so many specific and invaluable ways. A generous Civic Arts Grant from the City of Berkeley contributed to much-needed research and writing time.

Always, most of all, for listening to every boring and exciting detail, for riding the roller coaster with me, thank you to Pat Mullan.